IMAGO SERIES
COLLECTION

N.R. WALKER

COPYRIGHT

SERIES BLURBS

IMAGO - BOOK ONE

Nerdy, introverted genius lepidopterist, Lawson Gale, is an expert on butterflies. He finds himself in a small town in Tasmania on a quest from an old professor to find an elusive species that may or may not even exist.

Local Parks and Wildlife officer, Jack Brighton, is an ordinary guy who loves his life in the sleepy town of Scottsdale. Along with his Border collie dog, Rosemary, his job, and good friends, he has enough to keep from being lonely. But then he meets Lawson, and he knows he's met someone special.

There's more to catching butterflies, Jack realises. Sometimes the most elusive creatures wear bow ties, and sometimes they can't be caught at all. Lawson soon learns there are butterflies he can't learn about it in books. They exist only in a touch, in a kiss, in a smile. He just has to let go first, so these butterflies can fly.

Imago is the story of finding love, bow ties, and butterflies.

IMAGINES - BOOK TWO

Jack Brighton and Lawson Gale have been together for six months and are very much in love.

Lawson's work ensuring the survival of the Tillman Copper is as demanding as ever, and Jack's work with the regeneration of the bushfire-ravaged national park is just as hectic. When Jack suggests they take a short trip, Lawson agrees. But then he is offered a two-week research position in tropical Queensland to help determine why the Ulysses butterfly is on the decline. Figuring they could combine work and pleasure, Jack and Lawson go on their first vacation together.

Working alongside renowned professor Piers Bonfils isn't easy. But personal and professional differences aside, Lawson is offered a more permanent role in Queensland. Torn between his new life in Tasmania with Jack and a dying species of butterfly he feels compelled to save, Lawson has to decide where his fate lies. But fate changes the rules.

On a research expedition into the depths of the rainforest, suddenly it's not only the butterflies' existence that hangs in the balance. A butterfly's life cycle never changes. From larvae to imago, their course is plotted by design. Jack and Lawson need to determine where they stand, if they live through it. Because the only thing more incredible than one imago is two.

RED DIRT HEART IMAGO

A Red Dirt Heart and Imago crossover ~ The story of when red dirt and butterflies collide

Lawson Brighton-Gale receives an email request to identify a butterfly in the Outback, only to discover it's not an

Australian butterfly at all. But that's not all he discovers. The name on the request is familiar to Jack. An old friend from his university days, who also happened to be his old friend with benefits, Charlie Sutton.

Years ago, two out-of-towners met at the University of Sydney. Both studying environmental sciences, both hundreds of miles from home, and both finding their worlds open to new experiences, they fell into bed together. Meeting again after all this time, in front of Lawson and Travis, won't be awkward at all, right?

Lawson and Jack's trip to Sutton Station certainly doesn't go to plan, and what they take back to Tasmania isn't just butterflies, but a cocoon of possibilities.

IMAGOES - SHORT STORY

When Jack receives a phone call from a colleague in the southeast of Tasmania with news of a newfound butterfly habitat, he and Lawson head off on another adventure. It's not an easy trek to the location. The Franklin-Gordon National Park is famous for wild rivers, rainforests, and rocky cliff faces, and they'll need to hike and abseil in the dead of winter—to get to the site.

It's no ordinary expedition because this is no ordinary butterfly, and Jack and Lawson aren't an ordinary couple. Join Jack and Lawson on another quest in this short story of extraordinary butterflies and extraordinary love.

DEDICATION

To the folks who watch butterflies, and wonder...

IMAGO SERIES

IMAGO

CHAPTER ONE
JACK BRIGHTON

THE FLIGHT FROM MELBOURNE TO LAUNCESTON WAS USUALLY uneventful. A quick hour across the Tasman Sea, away from the rat race of city life, back to my home state of Tasmania where the air was clean and the people still said hello.

I'd attended a week-long national meeting for regional managers of the Parks and Wildlife Services. I had the best job in the world, and meetings like that—while good to keep up to date on news and trends—reminded me that my place was in wide open spaces and the great outdoors.

I didn't go much on Melbourne. The nightlife was better for a man such as myself than it was in my hometown, though this trip had been uneventful on that front too. I had to say, being a twenty-eight-year-old gay man in a small country town in the northeast corner of Tasmania, my options were limited. And when I said limited, I meant zero.

I went out every night I was visiting Melbourne, and there were guys interested in one-nighters, but I was done with that. The instant gratification was all good and well, but I would leave with a hollow, detached feeling that never quite went away. I'd hoped to find someone I could connect with, hook up with when we could, talk on the phone, video chat during the week type of thing. But there was not one guy who sparked my interest. I wasn't too happy to have come up empty handed either.

Empty handed was the only thing my sex life wasn't.

I snorted at my lame joke, and only then I realised the guy taking his seat across the aisle from me thought I was snorting at him. He gave me a rather dirty look and quickly turned his head and sniffed. I contemplated telling him I wasn't laughing at him, but then he was busy telling the flight attendant to be careful with his carry-on. He was late boarding the plane and he looked flustered enough without me adding to his troubles.

I was soon enjoying the feeling of taking off and heading home, and the guy across from me quickly had his laptop out and was typing away furiously, so I let my head fall back against the headrest and closed my eyes.

After we'd landed in Launceston, I stood up and went to collect my bag from the overhead cabin and accidentally backed into the person behind me. I'm six foot two and kinda broad shouldered, not exactly built for confined spaces.

"Oh, sorry," I quickly apologised, and upon turning around, saw it was the flustered guy from before who thought I'd laughed at him. I offered him a smile. "Not much room for guys my size."

He looked up at me like a rabbit in a spotlight, blinked several times, blushed a deep scarlet from his cheeks right down his neck, and desperately set about shoving his laptop away, all while muttering what sounded like an apology with his head down.

Well, that was an interesting reaction. One that had my attention, that's for sure.

I took a moment to look him over. He was maybe five ten, thin build, with short brown hair parted on the side and combed to perfection. He had pale skin, the pinkest lips I'd ever seen on a guy, without lip gloss anyway. Which I wasn't exactly opposed to, just so you know. But this guy was wearing a chambray business-style shirt with a navy bow tie.

A goddamn bow tie.

If I were to look up Hottest Fucking Nerd On The Planet, this guy's photo would be it.

Like seriously. He made my insides do stupid things.

He looked back up at me, and I couldn't even be embarrassed that he'd caught me ogling. He didn't seem too happy about it, frowning as he slid his blue blazer on. He put his head back down, trying to make himself smaller, tucked his laptop bag under his arm, and bustled past the people trying to disembark.

And I stood there with my mouth hanging open like a Neanderthal.

With a shake of my head, I got my gear together and waited my turn to deplane.

Man, why couldn't I have met a guy like that in Melbourne?

Putting it down to shitty luck, I got off the plane and collected my suitcase from the Arrivals carousel. But as I was walking toward the exit, I saw bow tie guy at the car rental kiosk and he seemed to be flustered. Again. Maybe flustered was how he got through his day, but he really didn't seem to be having a good one at all.

"I'm sorry, Mr Gale," I heard the car rental lady say.

"There seems to be some mistake. We don't have a booking and all vehicles are taken."

Bow tie guy, whose name appeared to be Mr Gale, had both elbows on the counter and let his head fall forward. With a deep breath, he looked up. "Well, what am I supposed to do? I have an appointment at the museum in forty minutes. I need the vehicle because I can't very well take my suitcase to an appointment with a professor, can I? And I'm supposed to be staying out of town, which I obviously will need to drive to. Surely there has to be another vehicle?"

She made a face. "Sorry. But we don't have a booking. Can I suggest a taxi?"

I almost laughed, because good luck getting a cab from the airport to a hotel to the museum in forty minutes. The poor guy looked defeated and on the verge of tears.

"It's a very important meeting," he said weakly.

Before I knew what I was doing, I stopped beside him. "Sorry for intruding. I couldn't help but overhear. I'm headed your way if you need a lift?"

CHAPTER TWO
LAWSON GALE

"I BEG YOUR PARDON?" TO SAY I WAS SURPRISED BY THE interruption was an understatement. Not so much the offer, but who it was from.

It was the man from the plane. The one who'd laughed at me when I was taking my seat, the same man who'd almost knocked me over when the giant decided to stand in the aisle at the same time as me. It wasn't my fault he was absurdly tall and built like a mountain. And of course he had to be gorgeously handsome with his perfect scruffy brown hair and perfect twinkling brown eyes. And a dimple. Of course he had a dimple. It completed his perfect face.

He was wearing a shirt with a Parks and Wildlife emblem over the right breast, dark jeans, and work boots. The outdoor type that worked with his hands was not a look that would normally catch my attention, but it somehow made him even more... perfect. One side of his mouth cranked upwards. "I couldn't help but overhear you, and I'm going your way if you need a lift."

I stared up at him and his stupidly perfect face.

His brow furrowed. "To the museum?"

"Oh." Right. He'd asked me a question. Or offered me a lift, more to the point. "Well…" I composed myself. "I'm not in the habit of taking rides from strangers."

He found something about this funny because he fought a slow grin and lost. He stuck out his hand. "The name's Jack Brighton. Now I'm not a stranger."

I swallowed hard and looked around nervously. No one seemed to be paying attention. The car rental lady was on the phone to what sounded like another disgruntled customer. Probably the person she gave my car to. I quickly shook the offered hand in front of me. I aimed for a firm grip because I loathed limp-fish handshakes, but I needn't have worried. His hand was warm, hard, calloused… perfect.

"Lawson Gale," I declared. "And thank you for the offer, though it would hardly be wise for me to accept. I've spent a lot of money on education; I'd hate for my epitaph to read that I was indeed an idiot, who rather stupidly got into the car with a man I just met. Who turned out to be a serial killer."

Jack stared at me for a second before he laughed. "Right. Well, I've been assumed to be a lot of things. A serial killer has never been one of them."

I scraped my fingertips through my hair, fixing it into place. A nervous habit I was trying to quell. "I meant no offence."

His smile was warm and wide. "None taken. I'll just be on my way then. Good luck getting to the museum in"—he looked at his watch—"thirty minutes."

I watched him turn and leave, wheeling his suitcase behind him.

Bother.

I was out of time. And out of options. I quickly scanned the taxi rank through the large glass doors to find it empty. *Double bother.*

I started after the man I'd just called a serial killer. To his face. His ludicrously perfect face. "Mr Brighton!"

He stopped and turned back to me.

"Mr Brighton, please wait," I said, hurrying to catch up to him while struggling to pull my suitcase and keep my laptop satchel strap over my shoulder. "I apologise for my rudeness, and I would graciously accept a ride. If you're still offering, that is. I'd most appreciate it."

He smiled. "Sure thing. Truck's this way."

I followed him out to the car park where he stopped at a large four-wheel-drive utility with a Tasmanian Parks and Wildlife logo emblazoned on the side. He unlocked it, then threw his suitcase into the back tray like it weighed nothing.

I looked at my suitcase, which was half my size, and wondered how I could lift it in. Maybe if he put the back tailgate down, I could slide it up...

Without me asking, he effortlessly hoisted my suitcase into the back with his. The muscles in his arms expanded and bulged. He waved at the passenger door. "Well, get in or you'll miss your appointment."

Right, yes. Of course. Clutching my laptop satchel, I climbed in. "Thank you again," I said, clicking my seatbelt in. "I really am very thankful."

"No worries," he said, starting the engine. He shifted the gearstick into reverse, looked over his shoulder closest to me, and backed out of the parking spot. He spun the wheel, slid the gearstick into place, and the four wheel drive lurched forward. It was bumpier than I expected, and louder, but it seemed the outdoor nature of the vehicle suited him.

"You work for Parks and Wildlife," I stated the obvious. I didn't need to be a detective: he wore their shirt and drove their car.

"I do." He smiled brightly as we sped down the highway toward Launceston.

"An interesting occupation," I noted. "Do you favour the flora or fauna?"

"Love it all." Then he chuckled. "You know most people would just say plants or animals."

And there it was. The ever-forthcoming dig at my vocabulary. "I'm not most people."

He just seemed to smile wider. "You certainly aren't."

I feigned interest at the passing scenery instead of trying to pretend I wasn't offended.

"That wasn't an insult," he went on to say. "Just the opposite, actually. I like the way you speak. You're obviously pretty smart."

"Above average IQ, one could say," I offered modestly.

Mr Brighton scoffed at me. "Right. And where exactly do you fit on the cognitive designation bell curve?"

I shot him a look. He knew what the measure of IQ was? Normally I would rebuff his question, uncomfortable discussing such matters, particularly with someone I just met. But I found myself wanting to be honest with him. "Genius."

The dimple in his cheek appeared when he smiled out the windscreen. "Thought so."

"Does that bother you?"

"Hell no. Why would it? Believe me, the last thing I am when it comes to a man's intelligence is threatened." He gave me a strange look with a questioning eyebrow as though he was implying something else.

Intelligence was not an issue for me either. I was, however, reminded constantly by those I worked with that I lacked social cues. And heaven knows small talk was not my forte.

"So," he started again. I must have let my side of the conversation lapse too long. "Important meeting at the museum, huh? Is it for a job?"

"Not really. Well, in part, yes." I cleared my throat. "I'm meeting a retired professor from my field. I have a two-week case study as part of my doctoral degree."

"Doctoral degree? As in medicine?"

"Oh no. Not a medical doctor, heavens no. I don't have the stomach for blood." Even the thought of it made me uncomfortable. "I'm a lepidopterist."

He nodded slowly. "And that is...?"

"I study butterflies and moths. Predominantly butterflies."

"Wow. Interesting," he said, seemingly genuine. Most people thought it was cute that I chased butterflies like a child. "They're complex little things, I bet. You know, my favourite animal is a dragonfly. Don't tell my dog that, she'll never forgive me. And I know butterflies and dragonflies are different, but dragonflies are... well, I dunno, they just defy logic."

I stared across the cabin at him. "Dragonflies are an incredible insect. I'm not sure what you mean by defy logic, though. Logic for which purpose? For whose purpose? Because logic is a human reasoning and hardly quantifiable in the *Animalia* kingdom."

He smiled broadly. "I just meant they look like they shouldn't be able to fly, but they can. And they look kinda alien. Not that I've seen any aliens to quantify this generalisation."

I sighed. "I apologise. I don't mean to offend…" I picked at the cuticle on my thumb. "My boss, leading Professor Michael Asterly, keeps reminding me of my inability to hold a conversation. Of course dragonflies can defy logic, and I apologise if I implied it was a foolish thing to say."

Now he laughed. Though it sounded loud in the confined space of the utility cabin, it was a warm sound, and his eyes crinkled at the corners. "I thought we were holding down a conversation just fine. And it sounds like your leading Professor Asterly might not know how to have interesting conversations with intelligent people."

I found myself smiling. "The professor is a smart man."

"But not as smart as you."

I shook my head, unable to draw my eyes away from this confounding mountain of a man who liked dragonflies. "No, he's not."

Mr Brighton stared right back at me and licked his bottom lip. "Um." He cleared his throat. "Well, the museum awaits."

I looked outside, only to find us parked out the front of the Queen Victoria Museum. I hadn't even been aware we'd stopped moving, let alone arrived at my destination. "Oh, right." I grabbed my satchel and quickly checked my watch. It was 11:55 a.m. I had five minutes to get inside. I quickly opened the door, then stopped. "You do know Da Vinci drew the very first design of a helicopter, hundreds of years before the Wright brothers designed the aeroplane, based on a dragonfly?"

The corner of his mouth drew up. "I knew that, yes."

"So maybe the design was not so illogical after all."

"Or maybe Da Vinci thought it was so illogical he just had to see how it worked."

I went to rebut his argument, but the more I thought about his reasoning, the less I could argue. "Possibly."

He grinned like he'd won first prize. Then he said, "You should get going."

Oh, yes. Right. I got out of the vehicle, and before I shut the door, I said, "Thank you, Mr Brighton. I truly do appreciate the lift."

"Anytime," he answered. "And please, call me Jack."

CHAPTER THREE
JACK

I sat there and watched as Lawson raced into the museum. He appeared to be the picture of perfection, impeccably dressed and not one hair out of place. But I got the feeling he ran late to every appointment he ever made.

He was like no man I'd ever met. Crazy smart—genius, apparently—and absolutely clueless about how gorgeous he was. He dressed like it was the 1920s and he spoke the Queen's English like he'd just swallowed the Oxford Dictionary.

Jesus. He made my chest feel too small for my heart.

I wanted to spend more time with him. I wanted to discuss the illogical reasoning of humans and dragonflies, and why butterflies? I wanted to taste those pink lips and see how far that blush ran down his neck...

By the way he'd checked me out when I bumped into him on the plane and then again standing at the car rental desk, I was pretty sure he was gay. Or interested. Or curious. Or something.

I just had to figure out a way of seeing him again... Then I remembered he'd left his suitcase in the back of my ute. I grinned victoriously, and without knowing how long his appointment at the museum was to go for, I had a reason to sit and wait.

And wait, I did.

Two hours later, he scurried out of the front doors, and he tripped over his feet when he saw me leaning against my ute, waiting for him. He looked around and behind himself to see if I was smiling at someone else, which only made him more endearing.

"You forgot your suitcase," I called out.

"Oh!" He looked horrified. And cute. He hurried toward me. "I made you wait all this time. I do apologise."

"Well, I could lie and tell you it was a terrible inconvenience, but I didn't mind. It gave me a pretty good opportunity to ask you out for dinner."

He stared at me like my words made no sense, then a shade of pink bloomed across his cheeks. "Oh."

"If you want to, that is," I clarified. God, I didn't even know if he was seeing someone... Or even if he was inclined to want to have dinner with a man. "If you're interested."

He stammered, his mouth opened and shut a few times, and his blush deepened.

So I softened the question for him. "I don't get to have dinner with guys who can hold an interesting conversation very often. And that's all it has to be, if you want. Just dinner and conversation. My treat."

He blinked and swallowed thickly. "I... well, I... yes. Yes, I think I'd like that. Though I must warn you, as I said before, my conversation skills are not my strongest quality."

I was grinning. I couldn't help it. "I think we'll manage just fine."

He huffed out a breath, then patted down his already perfect hair, looked around nervously, and smiled.

"Right then," I said. "Which hotel are you staying at? Did I hear you say it was out of town?"

"Oh!" He looked horrified again. "When you said dinner…"

I burst out laughing when I realised what he thought I was implying. "No, no, that's not what I meant. I'll drop you off at your hotel and, like a gentleman, pick you up again for dinner. If that's okay? I mean, I'm not opposed to seeing the inside of your hotel room, but I was actually looking forward to dinner and a conversation too."

Now he blushed a deep burgundy. Damn, and if it didn't disappear down underneath his collar. He looked down the street, anywhere it seemed but at me. "Well, I'm supposed to be staying in a place called Scottsdale—"

"Scottsdale?"

"Yes. Professor Tillman suggested it would be a good deal closer to where I needed to go. But my rental car wasn't available. If we could find another rental place, I'd really appreciate that."

"I can do you one better than that," I said. "I can drive you to Scottsdale."

His gaze shot to mine. "No, I couldn't ask that of you. You've already been terribly inconvenienced."

"I live in Scottsdale, so it's not an inconvenience at all."

He didn't miss a beat. His eyes narrowed. "You told me the museum was on your way when you offered me a lift here. I only accepted the ride because it wasn't out of your way. Now you're saying you live sixty kilometres away? Downtown Launceston is hardly on your way. And what of dinner? You would drive all the way back just for dinner?"

"Yes I would," I said honestly. "It's only a forty-five-minute drive. I make this trip all the time. And the museum kind of is on my way, if I choose to drive through the city, which in this case I did. And who's to say I didn't have something to do here anyway? Maybe my reason wasn't all about you."

This shut him up. "Oh. Well, of course it wasn't."

I tried not to smile but couldn't help it. "But it kinda really was. I only offered the lift to the museum because you were stuck. And because you're very cute, I won't lie. That was also a deciding factor."

He blinked.

I laughed. "You don't get compliments very often, do you?"

I didn't wait for him to answer; I just opened the passenger door of the ute. "Hop in."

I walked around the car and got in behind the wheel while he still stood at the door. He frowned seriously at me. "Are you making excuses about driving to Scottsdale? Is that some ploy also?"

"Nope. No ploy. I really do live there. And my dog is probably wondering where I am. I told her I'd be home today at lunch time." I started the truck. "And what ploy would I have? You've already agreed to have dinner with me."

"I could take that back," he said defiantly as he climbed into his seat. "Rescinding a dinner invitation would be well within my personal boundaries."

I barked out a laugh. "Well, we can discuss your *personal boundaries* over a drink if you don't want to eat." I could tell by the look on his face and the colour he went what he thought I meant by that, which wasn't what I meant at all. It only made me laugh more. "Not *those* kind of personal boundaries. That's not where my mind went, but clearly yours did."

He spluttered. "It did not."

"It totally did. And I'm okay with that. But please, let me buy you dinner first. I'm a gentleman, after all."

He tried to speak but couldn't seem to find the words. So instead, he looked out the window at the passing city. I could see the tips of his ears were pink and he was still clutching his laptop satchel on his lap. I felt bad for taking advantage of his embarrassment, but before I could apologise, he turned to me abruptly. "So we are clear, my personal boundaries are mine to divulge when and where *I* choose fit. Not you. Whilst I do appreciate the taxiing me across Tasmania, which you have graciously afforded me—and I am most grateful—I don't divulge such personal information on a first date. Because I am a gentleman also, after all."

Nerdy, gorgeous, intelligent, and sassy. God, he just keeps getting better.

"And you can stop smiling like that," he continued.

"No, I'm good, thanks," I said, grinning at him. "You just called dinner a date. I'm well within *my* personal boundaries to smile."

He sniffed indignantly, but now he was trying not to smile. "I think you missed the point."

I was pretty sure I didn't. I was so intrigued by this man, I was excited to know more about him. "So, I take it your meeting with the professor at the museum went well?"

"Very well. He's a very generous man. He's donated a reasonable find of specimen to the museum. He's been a lepidopterist for the better part of sixty years, and his collection is quite remarkable."

"He works there?"

"Not at all. He's into his eighties now. He has simply given his entire collection to the museum and wished for me to see it. For some reason, he seems to have taken a liking to me," he said. "He has asked me to do a field study. Chosen me, I should say. He claims to be too old to be trekking into the field these days, and he trusts me."

"Have you met him before?"

"Not before today. I've studied his works and read his many journals. I attended a lecture of his at Melbourne University."

"How can he trust you if you've only just met today?"

"Because he's studied my work and read my journal entries. My thesis, he said, was brilliant."

He spoke of his own merits without ego. I guess he didn't need to. If he was as brilliant as he claimed to be, it spoke for itself.

"I think he likes the fact I'm not... *cohesive* with my peers," he went on to say. "I tend to speak my mind, which annoys my superiors to no end. I also refuse to blindly agree with their decisions only to further my career."

"What's the field study he trusts you with?"

"Ah..."

"You'd rather not say," I concluded. "He trusts you with it, I get that."

"Thank you." Lawson sighed and studied the passing scenery again for a short while. "It's very dry here. I was expecting Tasmania to be greener."

"The drought has hit hard," I explained. "This is the third year with rainfall well below average for these parts. The west and south coasts haven't experienced any drought at all, but the north and east have struggled. Farmers are doing it tough. Towns have been on level three water restrictions for going on two years now."

"I assume water conservation is a substantial part of your job."

"Yep. You assume correctly. Land, water, ecosystems, flora, fauna. It has to be about conservation."

He smiled at me like something clicked into place inside him. "I wholeheartedly agree."

And driving down the highway at a hundred k's an hour, our gazes locked for just a moment, and something clicked into place inside me.

CHAPTER FOUR
LAWSON

Scottsdale was a small agricultural town. With a population of two and a half thousand people, there was a primary school, a high school, a small supermarket, a pub, post office, a bakery, and not a great deal more. It was very scenic, though. The main street had kept its heritage look with old-fashioned bull-nosed verandas, window shutters, and antiquated signs. It was charming.

"Where am I taking you to?" Jack asked as we drove down the main street.

I took out my phone and read the email confirmation. "Bloom's Bed and Breakfast. It was either that or the pub. I don't fancy the noise of a pub, so I opted for the quieter option."

He smiled knowingly. "The B&B is lovely. Well, I've never stayed there, but it looks real nice and the owners are good people. The pub's not bad, though. No real late nights out here, and never any trouble, if that was what you were worried about."

I ignored his implied question. "Do you know everyone in this town?"

"Pretty much."

"How long have you lived here?"

"Three years. And I love it. It was a helluva lot greener when I moved here. A lot prettier, but I do love it here regardless."

"Where are you from?"

"Hobart. And you?"

"Melbourne."

Jack nodded and pulled the ute to a stop out the front of a quaint looking cottage with a Bloom's Bed and Breakfast sign swinging from a post in the front yard. "Well, this is you."

"It is."

"So, about dinner," he started. "I had every intention of taking you somewhere nice in Launceston because I thought that was where you were staying. But now you're staying here. I mean, we can still go back to the city if you'd prefer because our dining options are limited. We have the pub or the corner takeaway shop. Their fish and chips are good, and the bowlo has pretty good Chinese food, but if I were wanting to impress, I'd rather eat somewhere a little fancier."

"Are you?" I asked. "Wanting to impress?"

Jack looked right at me. "Yes."

My stomach twisted in a strange but pleasant way. "Then I shall leave it to you to surprise me."

"Oh good," he said with a laugh. "No pressure then."

I smiled, feeling victorious. Over what, I had no clue. "And so you're aware, my expectations are not directly related to the food we eat, but rather the company. And I'm already impressed."

His smile was immediate and heart stopping. Before I

could do something stupid, I unbuckled my seatbelt, pushed on the door handle, and climbed out of the ute. Jack scrambled to do the same, and he met me around my side. He lifted my suitcase out and put it between us, his hands still around the handle. "So, is six o'clock okay? It's three hours away. Is that enough time?"

"Six o'clock would be perfect."

He grinned and stared at me.

"Uh, can I have my suitcase?"

"Oh. Sure." He took his hands off it and wiped his palms on his thighs. "Six o'clock, then. I'll just park right here." He took a step backwards, his smile still in place. He took another step backwards as if he didn't want to turn away from me, and even when he walked around his ute, he still smiled at me. He really was ridiculously endearing. The fact he was as sweet as he was tall was purely a bonus.

I found myself smiling as I dragged my suitcase to the cottage front door. I was greeted by a small, grey-haired woman with rosy cheeks who introduced herself as Nola. After I confirmed my booking and handed over my credit card, she kept eyeing my bow tie. "We don't get many folks during the week. Here on business?"

"Yes." I smiled pleasantly, and she was a friendly woman, but I wasn't one to blurt all my personal details to a stranger. A handsome, mountain-sized stranger with a delightful smile, maybe. But I got the feeling this lady was partial to gossip.

"Did I see Jack Brighton drop you off?"

Yes, gossiper for sure. "Ah, yes."

"Such a nice fellow. Moved here about three years ago. Works in the Rangers offices, lives out on Stanning Road. We didn't give his city-self long to stay before he got bored with it all, but he fit right in from day one. They say it takes twenty years to become a local, but I'd reckon he's as good as one already." She looked around the room conspiringly, like someone might overhear her. "They say he's not inclined to date women, if you know what I mean. Not that that's any of my business…"

It was clear she made everything her business, and it was also clear by the way she was looking at me, she was suggesting he may be interested in men and in particular, me. I'm surprised she didn't wink at me.

"No, not that it's any of your business," I said with a smile that belied my tone. "If you could show me to my room, I'd be most appreciative."

"Oh yes." She didn't miss a beat. She just prattled on about the goings on of Scottsdale as she showed me to my room. "It's a private room. You're the only guest here tonight, and Bill and I are at the other end of the house. You won't hear a peep from us."

"Thank you," I said, opening the door and wheeling my suitcase in. I could see all my personal effects had been delivered, as organised.

"Oh, they arrived yesterday," Nola said, nodding toward the plastic storage tubs. "We stacked them in here for you, but of course we didn't look in them. I didn't want to pry."

That told me she'd looked inside every one. She was still talking, but I needed some time. "Thank you. I do need to rest. It's been a long day."

"Oh, of course. Don't mind me. I've been known to chatter," she said with a grandmotherly smile. "What time would you like dinner served?"

"Oh, I won't be requiring dinner this evening. But thank you."

"Oh."

She waited for me to explain, which I had no intention of doing.

"Well, then. What time would you like breakfast?"

"Seven, if that's suitable."

"Yes, yes. Very suitable." She sighed dreamily. "I must say, it's such a pleasant change to have someone your age who speaks properly. Most kids these days—"

"Thank you, Nola. If you'll excuse me. I need to use the bathroom."

"Oh!" she said and stepped quickly out of my room. "Gracious. And here I am keeping you."

As I closed the door behind her, I could still hear her talking as she walked down the hall. I fell back on the bed, which was surprisingly soft and comfortable. I sighed loudly, taking in the blessed silence. I was lying about needing to use the bathroom, but I wasn't lying when I said it had been quite a day. Not only had I met Professor Tillman and had yet to truly absorb all he'd told me, but I'd also met one Jack Brighton.

And I somehow had a date with him.

Me, Lawson Gale. Nerd and brains extraordinaire. The guy who never gets asked out, who never dates. I wasn't a eunuch, by any means, but I wasn't... promiscuous either. I never caught the eye of handsome strangers. Hell, I never caught the eye of any strangers. Yet, despite all odds and reason, he'd seemed quite interested in me.

I wished we'd exchanged phone numbers. I'd call him and advise him not to pick me up for our date. Surely I could walk down to the main street and meet him, away from the prying eyes of Nola Bloom. I'd also be able to ask about what my expected dinner attire should be. I had no idea where he was taking me, if it were back into Launceston for five-star dining or to the park for a picnic.

I really should have asked. And I really shouldn't have been so brazen as to suggest a surprise.

Regardless, by the time six o'clock came around, I was showered and dressed in what I hoped were appropriate clothes. Jack was pulling up just as I walked out. "Perfect timing," he said as I climbed into his ute. The first thing I noticed was his smile. The second thing I noticed was the warm spice of aftershave: subtle but stirring.

"I was hoping to avoid Mrs Bloom," I explained. "I don't assume to know your personal business in this town, but she sure does. She told me she'd heard you don't date women. I'm sorry if you thought your private business was private, but it seems Mrs Bloom has made it... not private."

He stared at me for two long beats of my heart, then he burst out laughing. "Nola Bloom is the town gossip. And I don't hide the fact I'm gay. I never have. As far as I know, the whole town knows I am and Nola would be very upset to find out she'd been the last to hear it officially."

"Oh."

His smile morphed into a frown. "Is that okay with you? That people know? If you're not comfortable with people thinking we're on a date..."

"But we are on a date, aren't we?"

"I'd hoped so, yes."

"Then I don't care. If you're concerned if I'm out, so to speak, then yes. Since I was thirteen. It's never been anything I've had to 'come out' about because everyone who meets me assumes..."

He gave me a tentative smile. "Assumes you're kinda amazing?"

I could feel myself blush. "Ah, no."

Jack settled back in his seat. "Okay, so this surprise

date," he said. "I had to pull some strings. But I think you'll like it. At least, I hope you will."

"Am I dressed appropriately?" I'd chosen navy trousers, and a white shirt with a navy and maroon chequered pattern.

He looked at my bow tie, then back to my eyes. "Perfect."

He was wearing tan coloured pants and a black, long-sleeve shirt with the sleeves rolled to his elbows. It matched his dark eyes. "You look nice."

"Thank you." He cleared his throat and started the ute, taking us down the main street. "I had to request a favour or two, like I said. But I didn't want to take you to just any old place." He brought the car to a stop not far from the pub, which I truly hoped he wasn't taking me to.

Jack hopped out of the ute and waited for me to join him on the footpath. He walked in the direction of the pub, where I could hear music and loud voices inside, and my stomach curled. "Are we going to the pub?"

"No," he said. "We're going here."

He was standing in front of the bakery, next door to the post office, which was next door to the pub. There was only one problem... "Uh, Jack. It's closed." The lights were off and the sign across the door very clearly spelled *Closed*.

Jack grinned. "Surprise!"

He pushed on the door, and to my surprise, it opened. He stepped inside and waited for me to follow him. There was a blonde woman behind the counter, whose face split into a massive grin. Jack took a deep breath. "Remmy, this is Lawson. Lawson, this is my dear friend and owner of Scottsdale's finest bakery, Remmy."

"Hello," Remmy said to me. Her whole face smiled, if that were possible. Then she quickly looked at Jack. Something silent very briefly passed between them. "Right. I'll be off. Don't forget to lock the door when you leave." She grabbed her bag and was gone with the jingle of the bell on the door. Jack locked the door behind her, and it was then I noticed the room. There was a small table set for two with a covered basket of baked goods in the centre, some bottles of some kind of drink, and a small white vase with a single flower.

He must have caught me looking at it. "It's a native daisy," Jack said quietly. "The botanical name is *Helichrysum milliganii* or Milligan's everlasting daisy. It's found here in Scottsdale. I thought it would be a nice touch."

I was utterly speechless.

Jack swallowed hard. "I'm not strictly a fancy guy. I could take you to the best restaurants and order the most expensive wines, but you wanted a surprise. And I wanted to do something that shows you who I am. I'm just an ordinary guy, and this is my friend's bakery. Remmy's French, her husband, Nico, is Portuguese. Between them they make the best pies and pastries anywhere. And I thought this would be private."

"This is perfect." I looked at him and had to swallow past the lump in my throat. "And you're not just an ordinary guy."

His smile was pure relief. "You sure this is okay?"

I nodded. "Quite."

He pulled out my seat and I was gifted with a waft of his aftershave as I sat down. "I will admit to being nervous when you pulled up in the street. I thought we might be going to the pub."

Jack took his seat and gave me a soft smile. "Why were you nervous?"

I smoothed out the fabric on my thighs. "I'm not exactly the type of guy welcome at most small town pubs."

"The guys here aren't too bad. Like I said, I've never hidden the fact I'm gay, and no one's ever said a thing to me."

"Because you're over six feet tall and built like a mountain. I, on the other hand, am not. And my fashion sense tends to offend the masculinity of some men." I shrugged. "I also don't find conversation about sport or lewd jokes about women terribly appealing."

Jack fought a smile. "I do like football, though I prefer union, which isn't too popular here. And I'm happy to say I've never heard lewd jokes from the guys here. Not that I frequent the pub too much." He looked at my shirt and tie, then back to my eyes. "I happen to love your fashion sense. I never realised that I would find bow ties so appealing."

I could feel my face heat at his words and was grateful he didn't push it. He simply uncovered the basket between us to reveal a selection of what looked like pies and a folded note on top. "Dinner," Jack said. "I asked Remmy what she'd serve to someone she was trying to impress. She said to leave it to her." He took the folded note and opened it, smiling when he read it. He then handed it to me. It was a handwritten menu.

Lamb, mint, and honey pastry parcels made with fresh and local ingredients, served with baked vegetable cups. Suggest the local brewed apple cider to accompany. Desserts in the fridge. Enjoy!

"Wow." It was so personal and so intimate, but relaxed. It couldn't have been more perfect for me. "I didn't know what to expect, but it certainly wasn't this. If you wanted to impress, you've succeeded."

Jack slid some portions of pastries onto my plate.

"Remmy deserves the credit. I just had the idea and set up the table, she did the rest." He poured me a glass of apple cider, then himself, and held his glass up. "Cheers."

I clinked my glass to his. "To the most unique first date I've ever had."

Jack grinned. "I'm glad."

I sipped the cider and hummed my appreciation. "This is good."

"It's locally produced, not too far from here, actually."

"You're very proud of where you live, aren't you?"

He nodded. "I love it here. Small towns aren't for everyone, I get that. But I feel a part of the community here. I contribute and am rewarded with friends who make the most unique ever first dates happen." He smiled. "I like the quiet life."

"I can appreciate that. City living has its perks, but it is draining."

"You're from Melbourne?" he asked. I nodded. "So, tell me about you. What's the Lawson Gale story?"

"There's not much to tell," I started.

"You're a lepidopterist with an IQ to rival Einstein. Believe me, there's a lot to tell."

I took a forkful of pastry and meat and savoured the taste before talking again. "Wow, that is exceptionally good." Then I answered his question. "I grew up in Melbourne, lived there all my life. Studied at Melbourne University. My parents weren't too happy about my chosen career but accepted it as my decision." I ate some more, this time of the vegetable cup. It was filled with sweet potato, eggplant, and artichoke, drizzled with feta and balsamic glaze. It was incredible. I got so side tracked eating, I forgot to keep talking.

Though Jack seemed happy to watch me eat. His eyes

were trained on my mouth, his lips parted lasciviously. The look of desire on his face sent a bloom of heat through my chest. I wondered if he'd think it unbecoming of me if I stood up, stepped around the table, took his face in my hands, and kissed him.

CHAPTER FIVE
JACK

I put my fork down and took a mouthful of cider to douse the desire flaming in my belly. If Lawson moaned one more time when he ate or let the fork slide between his lips seductively like that again, I wasn't sure my promise of being a gentleman would be upheld.

Jesus. He was so sexy, and what made him even hotter was that he seriously had no clue how sensual he was.

"I'm sorry," he said, sipping his cider. "This is so good I keep forgetting to continue talking. Please tell Remmy I am duly impressed with her culinary skills."

"I will." I ate another mouthful and swallowed, trying to get my thoughts back on track. "Tell me about your family."

I learned he had a brother and sister, both older than him. He was named after Henry Lawson; his brother, Paterson, and his sister, Mackellar, were also named after famous Australian poets. All three were gifted children. "Needless to say, our time at school wasn't easy. Being the children with unusual names who preferred reading didn't make for cohesive schooling. I'm very close with my brother and sister; we all speak often. Paterson studied nuclear medicine. Mackellar, interventional epidemiological research."

"Wow."

He almost smiled. "My parents had hoped I would study medicine. Anaesthesia and perioperative medicine, to be exact." He made a face. "Though it was not for me."

"Why butterflies?"

Lawson smiled genuinely. "My grandfather started me on it, but I've always been fascinated. As a small boy, I would catch them and watch them for hours before letting them go. They are incredibly complex, yet simple creatures. Brittle to the touch, but can withstand the fury of nature."

He seemed embarrassed by what he'd just said, which saddened me. "Your passion for what you do is a beautiful thing. I'm very intrigued. I'd love to learn more."

He tilted his head. "You would?"

"Yes, of course. Why, is that strange?"

"Well, most men I've dated think it's childish, for one. They don't take my work seriously."

"Well, you've clearly dated the wrong guys. Talking about the study and conservation of an entire species is remarkable."

Lawson looked at me like a fire lit inside him. "Thank you for saying that. For understanding." He swallowed hard and his gaze seemed to intensify. "Tell me about you. Your family, what you do for Parks and Wildlife?"

"I grew up in Hobart. I have two sisters, Poppy and April, a mum and a step-dad, had a very normal childhood. Never liked school much; always preferred to be outside. Somehow got the grades, so I studied Environmental Science at Sydney Uni. Volunteered for the Rural Fire Service, which I still do. I scored an outreach program through Parks and Wildlife, landed a foot in the door, so to speak. Now I have the best job in the world."

"What were you doing in Melbourne?" he asked, finishing his dinner. "For you to be on the plane this morning."

God, was that just this morning? "A week-long national meeting for regional managers. They have them every six months or so." I sipped my cider. "I don't mind going, actually. A change of scene is always good, and a taste of nightlife one or two weekends a year might scratch an itch or two but reminds me how much I love quiet nights at home."

He paused for a moment, licked his pink lips, and his eyes never left mine. "So, did you have your itch scratched?"

Fucking hell. When he said his conversation and social skills weren't his strong point, he wasn't joking. He certainly knew how to ask upfront, personal questions without flinching. My stomach somersaulted under his scrutiny. "Uh, no. Not this time. I wasn't interested in anything on offer. But then someone on the plane caught my eye. A handsome guy wearing a bow tie."

"And how's that working out for you?"

I smiled at him. "I'm hopeful that things are going okay."

"I would think they're going better than okay."

I chuckled. "I'm glad I offered him a lift, then."

"I'm glad I accepted. My initial concern that he may have been a serial killer seems to be unfounded."

"I'm glad."

He smiled as he sipped his cider. "Well, someone who knows the local state forests terrain *could* easily hide many bodies."

Now I laughed. "Thanks."

Lawson shifted in his seat. "Tell me about your work. What is it that you do exactly?"

So, over the mini Portuguese tarts I got from the fridge and another bottle of cider, I told him about data collection and collation, water testing, soil testing, animal tagging, writing reports, reading reports, and more data collection. How we implemented action plans and the importance of public information and awareness, and how we correlated the impact humans have on the environment to changes we've seen.

Lawson listened intently, then launched into his own interpretation of ecological system conservation, and how the study of butterflies has shown decreases in habitat and reproduction, how the different species adapted, and how some were disappearing altogether.

I could listen to him speak forever. He spoke with such eloquence and intelligence, it was refreshing. When he was making general conversation, his hands rested in his lap. But when he spoke about butterflies, his face lit up and he used his hands animatedly and lost that inhibition and self-consciousness that seemed to weigh him down.

A knock at the door scared the crap out of us. I checked my watch as I stood up. Jesus. It was almost midnight. *Had we really been talking for that long?*

I peeked through the curtain to find Steve, the local police sergeant. He was maybe fifty years old, fit as a bull, and liked by everyone who met him. I opened the door and offered him a smile. "Steve."

"Oh, hey, Jack. I was passing by and saw the lights on. Thought it was too late for Remmy or Nico to still be here and too early for them to start."

"No, they're not here," I said. "Remmy graciously let me

use the shop." I stepped back, allowing Steve to poke his head in.

He saw Lawson sitting at the small table. "Oh. *Oh.*"

I almost laughed at his expression as it dawned on him that we, two guys, were on a date. "Remmy made us some of Nico's Portuguese tarts, and we'll never eat them all," I said, taking the plate with a few remaining sweets. "Please take one."

Steve acted like he wasn't going to take one, but he was totally always going to. "Oh well, okay. If you insist." He shoved one in his mouth. "Mmm, good." He swallowed that down and took a second one. "You guys have a good night."

He waved me off, and I shut the door behind him. Lawson looked a little uncomfortable. "Are we in trouble?"

"No," I said with a chuckle. "Though it's almost midnight."

"Oh, I hadn't realised it was so late," he said, standing up. He started to clear up. "What do we do with our plates?"

"Here, let me," I said, piling the plates into the basket on the table. "I'll take it all home and wash it." I packed it all away, empty bottles, vase and all, and when the small bakery was back to normal, I opened the door and waited for Lawson to walk out before pulling the door locked shut behind me. He stopped at my ute, and when I put the basket in the back, he lifted the single daisy from the vase. He didn't say a word, just gave me a shy smile, then climbed into the passenger seat holding the flower between his long, thin fingers.

I jumped in behind the wheel and started the ute. It was only a short drive to where he was staying, so I didn't have time to waste. "So, what are you actually doing in Scottsdale? I know you don't want to talk about what the professor told you, but am I allowed to know at least how long you'll be in town for?"

He bit his bottom lip. "I'll be here for a week."

"Seven days, huh?" I couldn't help but smile. "Then there's a good chance I'll see you again?"

"I should expect so," he said simply. "I'll be at the Parks and Wildlife office in the morning to collect my visitor permits. After I sort out the rental car fiasco, that is."

A slow smile spread across my face. "Visitor permits?"

"Yes. Professor Tillman organised it during the week. When you were in Melbourne, I suspect. I'll be surveying *Lepidoptera* in Mount Stronach Forest Reserve for the week. I would think there's a good chance you'll be seeing quite a bit of me in the next seven days."

I pulled up out the front of the B&B and killed the engine. I had to bite my bottom lip to stop from grinning. This was possibly the best news I'd ever heard. "Mount Stronach?"

"Yes. Have you heard of it?"

"Heard of it? That's my jurisdiction. I mean, it's one of the national parks I look after. I know it well."

"I assumed it might be," he said. "Well, I hoped. It would mean a greater chance of seeing you again." He looked at the flower he was holding and chewed on his bottom lip. "If you don't mind me saying that."

"I don't mind at all."

In the low light of the night, he looked even more pale, more beautiful. He held up the flower and stared right at me. "Thank you for the daisy. And thank you for such a lovely evening."

The air between us was suddenly electric. God, I wanted so bad to kiss him, not sure how I should proceed. There was the console of the ute between us, and if I leaned in and he didn't, I'd die of embarrassment...

He licked his lips. "I believe it's customary for a gentleman to offer a kiss on a first date."

I barked out a laugh, thankful, relieved. "I believe it is too," I murmured. I leaned across and slid my hand along his cheek, gently bringing his lips to mine. Soft, warm, sweet, and with the barest hint of parted lips and the promise to deepen but not yet...

Perfect.

Lawson's eyelids fluttered when I pulled back, and he blushed with a smile that stole my breath. "Tomorrow," he whispered.

I nodded, not trusting my voice.

He got out and disappeared into the darkness, and I drove home in a daze. I was grinning like crazy and unable to stop it. I slid the basket of dirty plates on the sink to leave until morning, gave Rosemary a pat and apologised for waking her, and for leaving her all week with Remmy, and then again leaving her tonight. She looked up at me with her big brown Border collie eyes, probably wondering what on earth made me so damn happy at half-past twelve in the morning.

"I met someone special today," I told her. "His name is Lawson Gale." She wagged her tail at me. "I dunno, Rosie, but if there's any such thing as perfect for me, he just might be it."

AT TEN O'CLOCK, AFTER I'D BEEN AT WORK FOR THREE HOURS watching the door in case he turned up, Perfect walked in. Well, not so much as *walked in* as kind of *tripped through* the doors, trying to hold a folder in one hand, hold a phone to his ear with his other hand, while opening the door with his elbow. He almost dropped the folder, managed to catch it, but caught his foot on the threshold.

He stumbled a little but thankfully didn't fall over. He collected himself and raised his chin defiantly. "I'll be in touch," he said into the phone. He disconnected the call and, looking around the office, found me smiling at him.

God, he was just even better looking today than he was yesterday. He was wearing navy chinos and a white button-down shirt. His sleeves were rolled halfway up his forearms and his top button was undone. The hollow of his throat looked inviting and I wanted to lick it. "Good morning."

His cheeks tinted a faint pink. "Well, yes. It is now. I suppose. The car rental company finally found my paper-work. It only took them two hours this morning, and I only had to yell a few times." He slid his folder onto the recep-tion counter and took a deep breath. "Sorry. It's been quite a morning."

"Did you get a car sorted out, though?"

"Yes, thank you. A rather big one. I'm not entirely sure what exactly the design team was overcompensating for when they came up with it."

I looked out the window and saw the latest model white Land Rover Defender parked out the front. I smiled at his overcompensating comment. "You'll need the torque if you're going off-road, particularly in the mountains around here."

"Yes, well, true. Not that I'll be going anywhere too dangerous." He looked horrified at the thought. "Well, I don't think I am. Topographical maps can be deceiving."

"Have you got a map of where you're required to go specifically?" I asked. I'd gone through the application this morning, so I knew where he was going. I wanted to know if he did.

"Yes." He pulled out a paper map, then a tablet, and showed me the areas on both. He was familiar with where he had to go, hypothetically anyway. In a physical sense, I wasn't so sure. Yes, he was smart, but wandering off into the Tasmanian wilds on your own was nothing to be blasé about.

"Do you need someone to go with you?"

"I'm not stupid."

I smiled at his indignant rebuff. Always on the defensive. "I never said you were. In fact, we both know you're the opposite of stupid. This area through here"—I pointed to the part of the map he was wanting to go—"isn't easy to access. There's a gorge that runs right along here. But there's a fire trail that runs across the bluff. I can get you access to it if you want."

"Oh." He blinked a few times, and I could almost hear the cogs turning behind his eyes. "Would the person who comes with me require payment? Are they talkers? Because if they don't shut up, I'd rather get lost in the forest by myself." I chuckled at that, which he ignored. "I'm not saying I can't make my own way, but I would not be opposed to guided help, even if just for the first day."

He was so adorable. I could see why his co-workers probably didn't exactly like his brashness, but I found it endearing. He didn't mean any harm by what he said or how he said it. He simply said what he thought because it made sense to him, and it was very clear he compartmentalised; emotions and ego were not mutually exclusive with his work.

"I don't doubt your competence or ability," I said with a

smile. "I was referring to a personal guide, a Parks and Wildlife Officer, to be exact."

He stared at me blankly. Okay, so genius, maybe. Clueless, definitely. "That would be me."

"*Oh*." He looked around the office again. "Are you not busy? Is the office always empty? I would have assumed for a government agency you'd put our taxes to better use."

I scoffed and put my hand to my heart. "You wound me! Robert is at a careers day at the high school, which I cheerfully let him do—"

"Let him or made him?"

"*Made* is a strong word. It was more a case of rock, paper, scissors."

"Who is Robert?"

"He's my 2IC." I waved at the desk on the right. "That's his desk and that one's mine." I pointed to the other desk. "And this one here"—I waved to the front desk—"belongs to Karen, our wonderful office manager who keeps us all organised. She has just ducked down to the coffee shop to get us both a brew. I need some extra help staying awake because someone kept me up talking half the night, and I was here early because I had no clue what time he'd drop by and I didn't want to miss him. I really should have grabbed his phone number."

He chuckled. "Well, if you're offering to be my guide and you can spare the hours, I would happily agree."

"Ah, but it's a no to a phone number."

Lawson fished his mobile out of his pocket and handed it to me. "If you would be so kind as to add your number as a contact." I did as he asked and handed it straight back to him. He held it up and hit Call, making my mobile ring on my desk. "You now have my number."

Just then, the door opened and Karen walked in

carrying a takeaway tray with two coffees. "Oh, hello there," she said cheerfully, as always. She handed me a cup. "For you."

"Karen, this is Lawson Gale. The Mount Stronach permit is for him. In fact, I'll be showing him the area today. I'll be back by five."

"Okay," Karen said, sipping her coffee. She looked at Lawson. "Nice to meet you."

He smiled politely. "Nice to meet you too."

I grabbed my phone, keys, and a handful of files, and Lawson collected his folder. I stopped at my ute. "Have you got a medical kit?" I asked him.

"Yes, of course." Lawson opened the rear door in his rented Defender. Inside were eight plastic tubs, some empty, some filled with papers and jars, and a white box with a very discernible medical cross.

I was surprised, to say the least. "Did you have these packed in your suitcase?"

"No. I had them sent ahead."

"What exactly are you doing out in Stronach? I assume it has something to do with whatever your professor asked to see you about?"

"You would assume correctly." Lawson held out the car keys. "Are you driving?"

"No. Guide only. That way you'll be familiar when you drive out by yourself."

We headed down the Tasman Highway for a while, and at my instruction, we turned off at the rifle range road. After about ten kilometres, the road thinned out and became more of a track. It was bumpy and jarring, but at least the scenery was lovely. Lawson knocked the gears back to second to navigate a steep incline. "Does this billygoat track actually lead anywhere? Or are you taking me to your favourite serial killer spot?"

I laughed at him. "You know, you actually handle a four-wheel drive vehicle pretty good. I'm impressed."

"No. You're surprised. Why would you assume I can't drive?"

"I don't really know."

"You thought I was just a lab rat who never takes off his white coat."

"Do you wear a white coat?" I asked, waggling my eyebrows.

He laughed at that. "Wouldn't you like to know?"

"Yes, I would. That's why I asked. I also asked what you were doing out here in the middle of the forest at the instruction of a retired professor, but you didn't answer that either." I pointed up ahead to a turn-off, which was more of a track than the track we were on. "The clearing you're after will be up ahead, about two hundred metres."

Lawson navigated the Defender easily and pulled up in the clearing. "What Professor Tillman asked me to look for is a specimen of *Copper Lycaenidae*."

"I'm going to assume that's a type of butterfly."

He cut the engine. "Yes, it is."

"He called you to come here, all the way from Melbourne, to look for a butterfly?"

"Yes, he did."

"What's so special about it?"

Lawson hopped out of the Defender, turned back, and grinned at me. "It doesn't exist."

CHAPTER SIX
LAWSON

THE TASMANIAN SUMMER WAS HOT AND DRY. NOT AS HOT AS Melbourne, but still, I hadn't expected it to be this warm. I opened the back door of the Defender and pulled out one of the plastic tubs. Jack was suddenly beside me. "What do you mean, it doesn't exist?"

I handed him the tub. "As in, non-existent. Never been documented."

"How is that possible?" he asked, looking at the tub, then back at me. "I mean, if it doesn't exist, how can you look for it? How can you even know to look for it?"

I stacked another tub on top of the first one Jack was holding. "Well, you see, Professor Tillman believes they're here."

He looked around the woodlands, but the look on his face had sceptical written all over it. "He believes they're here?"

"Correct."

I stacked two tubs on top of each other and lifted them out of the Defender and walked out into the clearing. "Boy, it's warm. I thought Tasmania was supposed to be cold."

Jack followed me. "It is. Normally. I mean, down south it gets cold, but up here it's not too bad. We're in a drought, remember? That generally means dry. Not forgetting the fact it's summer."

I stopped walking and looked right at him. "Are you being facetious?"

He grinned. "Facetious is a little harsh. I think roguish is more flattering, possibly with a dash of sarcasm."

"I'm not a fan of sarcasm."

"Then why are you smiling?"

"Because I do happen to like roguish."

We stood facing each other, both holding two tubs each, both smiling. "What's in the boxes?" he asked eventually.

"My equipment."

Jack's lips twitched. "Your equipment? Really?"

I rolled my eyes and put the tubs on the ground. "My field equipment. I have a backpack, notebooks, texts, notes, specimen jars. A GPS, emergency beacon, thermometer, barometer, satellite phone." Jack's smile got wider when I listed each item. "What?"

He put the tubs he was holding down next to mine. "I dunno. I don't know what I was expecting." He was still smiling but it was as though he was secretly pleased. "You have all the right gear."

"Well, of course I do."

"Most academic types come out with no supplies, no tracking equipment, and no clue, if I'm being honest."

"Did you assume me to be irresponsible?"

Jack seemed to consider his answer before speaking. "Let's just say I had my concerns, but I'm pleasantly surprised."

"I spent many vacations and weekends in national

parks in and around Melbourne as a child and was taught the importance of safety from the very first. As I grew older, particularly now, I do a lot of field study alone. Like when I was in the middle of the Blue Mountains by myself, I was very aware of my isolation."

"Do you always do field study by yourself?"

"Mostly." I shrugged. "I love it. I'm comfortable with my own company enough to spend hours, or days, by myself."

Jack frowned. "Are you bothered by my being here?"

"Not at all. Though I do have work to do."

"Right." He took a step back, fighting a smile. "Then I'll let you do... whatever it is you do when you look for a butterfly that doesn't exist." He took a few more steps backwards, smiling now, before he turned and walked back to the Defender.

Jack Brighton really was a very good looking man, and the playfulness and flirting were exhilarating. The anticipation even more so. I would be very interested in something physical happening between us, and I had no issue in instigating it if I had to. But now was not the time. Professor Tillman had entrusted me with what could be the legacy of his career.

He swore to me the species was here. He'd seen it. Many years ago when he had youth on his side, a keen mind and able body, he'd hiked all over these ranges. It was the late seventies, he'd said. He had no paper or pencil and his camera was out of film. He'd seen one single specimen. That was all. He'd gone home and drawn what he saw from memory, and he'd been back a hundred times in the years that followed. But he'd never seen it again.

Now his mind was still keen but his body wasn't able.

He told me he'd met a lot of lepidopterists over the decades, but none that he trusted. Until me.

In his words, I wasn't owned by The Society. Yes, I worked under the world-renowned Professor Michael Asterly at Melbourne University. Yes, I was his best and brightest student: I published journal articles years before my classmates, and yes, I was one of the best. It wasn't even that I'd specialised in *Lycaenidae*. It was because I wasn't liked by the *scholar squad*, he'd called them. And that, according to Professor Tillman was why he chose me. As it turned out, he never cared much for their opinions either.

When he'd told them he'd seen an Eltham Copper Butterfly in Tasmania, they'd laughed at him. Only it wasn't an Eltham Copper. How could it be when it was not found anywhere near Eltham? Eltham Coppers were so named, they reminded him, because Eltham, Victoria, was the only area in which they were found. But Professor Tillman was adamant. He said it was *like* an Eltham Copper though it had varying distinct marks on its hindwing, like no other Copper in any book he'd found. And that made it a new discovery. A new species.

But he had no proof. And after decades of fruitless searching, he'd passed the baton onto me.

So, with that in mind, I opened the first tub and got to work.

I took recordings of temperature, wind direction, GPS location, aspect, and sun position. Then I took notes on plant types and soil types. I could see why the professor had liked this area for finding Coppers. On paper, it was perfect.

Eltham Coppers liked north facing aspect for warmer weather, they lived in vegetation classified as woodland, and this area was both of those things. If I were a betting man and these butterflies were going to be found in an area outside of Victoria, then I'd say there was a very good chance for it to be here.

I got so carried away with my data collation like I always do, that I forgot Jack was in the Defender. Actually, I kind of forgot he was there at all.

"Hey!" his voice, even far off, still alarmed me.

I spun to the sound of it, to find him trudging through the scrub toward me. "Jeez, you scared me," I admitted with my hand to my heart.

It took him a few seconds to keep walking so he was close enough for a conversation. "You always make a habit of walking off without telling someone where you're going?"

"Well, no. I'm normally here by myself," I explained. I pulled the GPS and satellite phone from my backpack. "I know where I am."

"Yeah, but I didn't know. I finished my paperwork, looked up, and you were gone."

"Oh."

"Scared the crap outta me."

"Sorry." I felt bad about making him worry. "How did you find me?"

He finally smiled. "You were whistling. A tune or something."

"Was I?" I had been told by other colleagues that I tended to whistle to myself when I was lost in my work, particularly out in the field. "I didn't realise."

"Lucky you hadn't gone too far or I wouldn't have heard you." Jack gave a nod back to the direction he'd come, and following his line of sight, I could just make out the white of the Defender through the scrub. "Found anything yet?"

"Not yet. It's mostly data collation at this stage. The conditions are right, though. The elements and vegetation are correct for the habitat of Coppers, though I've not seen any ant colonies or any butterflies, for that matter."

"What do they look like?" he asked. "I mean, I could've seen one by now and wouldn't have known."

"Have you ever paid attention to butterflies?"

His lip pulled down to one corner. "Well, no. Not really."

From my pocket I fished out the photocopy of the professor's drawing and showed it to him. "That's it."

It was a detailed sketch, the very one the professor had drawn all those decades ago. The copper-coloured wings were what gave the specimen its name.

Jack looked from the drawing to me. "It's brown."

"That's a photocopy of an old drawing. The butterfly is copper. Hence the name Eltham Copper."

"Okay, so it's not brown. It's copper." I was surprised he didn't roll his eyes.

"Coppers are part of the *Lycaenidae* genus, and Elthams, in particular are on the endangered species list. I happen to study them in efforts of conservation."

"Endangered?"

"Yes. They're found in only a few very small, decreasing pockets of vegetation in Victoria. So I'm sure you can appreciate the importance of what the professor found."

Jack nodded, all humour gone. "Yes, of course. I didn't realise it was endangered." He seemed to think something over in his mind for a moment. "How do you go about finding them? I mean, it's not like animal tracks. The Tasmanian devils, for example, dig burrows, leave scratch marks on trees and logs, and disturb the topsoil. Or there's leftover meals or scat. Actually, they're messy buggers. Butterflies aren't exactly intrusive."

It was a good question, and one I got asked frequently.

"There are markers, if you know what to look for. The Eltham Copper have a very complex triangular dependency with the *Notoncus* ant and the *Bursaria spinosa*—"

"Sweet Bursaria? The shrub?"

"Yes. Are you familiar with it?"

"Well, yeah. It grows all over these ranges."

Flora and fauna, of course. I started to smile. "Can you identify more specific areas on my map?"

"Sure I can. It's my job."

I leaned up on my toes and kissed him softly on the lips. "You are a godsend."

He grinned. I had no idea one little kiss could make him smile like that. "Maybe we could go over all your maps tonight with dinner?"

"You've set the bar pretty high for date expectations," I teased. "Not sure what you could do to beat last night."

"I'll think of something."

"Then I'd love to."

He leaned in and, with his fingers under my chin, tilted my face up toward his. He pressed his lips to mine, gently at first, then harder, and sliding his hand along my jaw, he urged my lips open with his own. God, how he kissed me.

In that perfect moment, the world stopped turning. Nothing existed but him. He left me breathless and dizzy, and certain of one thing.

There was more on the menu tonight than just dinner.

CHAPTER SEVEN
JACK

I COULDN'T HELP MYSELF. I *HAD* TO KISS HIM. WELL, technically, he put kissing on the table first. Albeit, his was a chaste kiss, but it was still a kiss. And I'd never been one to do things by halves. If I was gonna kiss him and kiss him properly, then it'd be a kiss he'd remember.

And holy shit, what a kiss it was.

When I pulled away, his eyes were unfocused and his lips were red and wet. We were both breathless, but this was different.

He took my damn breath away. "You are sublime."

"Oh." He blushed, and the colour that crossed his cheeks matched the delicious colour of his lips. "No one's ever called me that before."

I ran my thumb across his cheek. "Then they were fools."

Lawson bit his lip. His shyness was charming in a way I'd never fancied before. Normally I'd go for guys who were more a physical match to me—masculine with more brawn than brains—but there was something about this butterfly-chasing genius that really drew me in.

He let out a little chuckle and stepped back, apparently so he could take a few breaths. "Okay, so I seem to have some kind of cognitive dysfunction when you're too close."

I laughed. "Sounds serious."

He put his hand to his forehead, and I might have been worried if he wasn't smiling. "Could be." Then he looked up to the sky. "Should we be heading back?"

I checked my watch. "Probably. It's just after four."

We walked back toward the clearing. Lawson packed everything away neatly into the tubs, and we loaded them into the Defender and headed back to town. He drove for a while, then he asked, "So, what are you planning for our date tonight? Because if we're heading back into Launceston, I'll need some time to transfer my data to my laptop."

"Did you want to head back into Launceston?"

"Well, no. Not really. As nice as a fancy dinner sounds, I have work to do."

"What makes you think I can't get you a fancy dinner in Scottsdale?"

"Well, the table for two in the bakery is going to be hard to beat."

I grinned at him. "Mr Gale, that sounds like a challenge."

He made a happy sound. "I believe it was supposed to. I have high expectations, remember?"

"How can I forget?" I took his GPS from his dash.

"What are you doing?"

"Adding in the address you'll need to get to for the best date ever." I put the GPS back into its dash holder. "Bring whatever work you want to go over too."

"Are you sure?" He looked from the road to me and back to the road. "Not to say I'm not grateful for the offer. But working on a date?"

I looked out the window and tried to play it cool. "Well, you're only here for a week, so the work you're doing is not only important, but you're also on a very limited schedule. If we have to multitask, that's okay with me."

He looked at me again for a long second before turning his attention back to driving. "Thank you. For saying that."

"What? That multitasking is okay?"

"No. For saying my work is important."

"Environmental conservation of any kind is important."

Lawson smiled. "You know, it's already highly likely you'll get lucky to some degree tonight. You don't have to butter me up."

I laughed at that. "Can't say I've ever used dairy spread as a personal lubricant, but I'm not opposed to trying."

His mouth fell open and he stared at me, as though he was half-amused, half-horrified.

"Please watch the road," I said, pointing to the windscreen. "We can't have the best second date ever if we die in a car crash."

I HEARD THE DEFENDER PULL UP OUT THE FRONT OF MY PLACE AND watched Lawson get out. I think it took him a second to realise he was at my house. It was, after all, the address I'd given him. He appeared hesitant to walk up to the garden gate, so I opened the front door. He wore the same navy trousers but had changed his shirt. This one was a short-sleeve button-down with some triangle pattern. And sweet mother of God, he was wearing a bow tie. I had to steady my breath before I could speak. "Hey. You look lost."

He patted down his already perfectly combed hair. "Well, I wasn't expecting... actually, I didn't know what to expect. The address you gave me was out of town, and this is the only house for miles... Then I saw your work ute."

I walked out to meet him, and I could see he was taking in the view. There were mountains to the north-east, a valley to the west. I lived in a tidy three-bedroom timber cottage painted pale yellow with white trim on the veranda that wrapped around all sides of the house. It was old but had character. The best part was, the cottage was on a ten-acre lot in the middle of larger properties, which meant there were no other houses in sight. "So, uh, this is my house."

He smiled up at me. "It's very quaint." He listened for a second. "And very quiet."

"Which is why I love it." I leaned in and gave him a soft kiss on the lips. "Thank you for coming."

He sighed happily before turning back to his rental. "Can you help me carry these?"

I had no idea what *these* were. "Sure."

He opened the back door to the Defender and pulled out one of the tubs he'd had in the clearing earlier today and handed it to me. He grabbed a laptop bag and held it to his chest. "Something smells really good."

"Dinner or the jasmine? Or me? Because I did have a shower."

He smiled at that. "I was referring to the food. The jasmine plant is nice, though. And I haven't smelled you." He paused for a moment. "Yet." Then he looked around me and nodded to the front door. "Are you going to invite me inside, or are we dining out here tonight?"

"Oh, yes, of course," I said, walking down the path to my front veranda. "Someone's very excited to meet you."

"Oh," he mumbled. I stopped on the steps and turned to

him. He looked put off and a little confused. "I wasn't expecting there to be anyone else here."

I smiled at him. "Her name is Rosemary. She promised to be on her best behaviour." I crossed the veranda and opened the door. Rosemary was still sitting like a very good girl where I'd told her to stay. "Come." She padded over to me, then stuck her head out the door behind my legs. "Rosemary, I'd like you to meet Lawson."

How this meeting went was critical for me. If she didn't like him, or if he wasn't a dog person, I'd be very disappointed. It would mean that whatever was starting between Lawson and me would end tonight. I couldn't have a man in my life who didn't accept Rosemary into his. Me and my dog were a package deal.

I was nervous because I really wanted this to go well. I liked Lawson, and I really thought we had a connection, a beginning of something that could be very special. Permanent even, if it was possible to know that after just a few short days. But their getting along was the catalyst on where we went from here.

My worries went unfounded because Lawson broke out in a grin when he saw her, and my dog immediately wagged her tail. She went out to meet him, and Lawson put his laptop bag on the ground, bent down on my one knee, and gave her a good, hearty pat.

The relief and happiness that went through me were unprecedented.

He didn't just say 'oh cute dog' and walk past her. He stopped, put down his bag, and met her on her level. Rosemary gave me a tongue-lolling grin as he ruffled her fur, which was all the approval I needed.

Lawson stood up and brushed off his knee, then looked at me and grinned. "She's gorgeous."

I was pretty sure my smile was about to break my face. "She is." I couldn't help myself. I walked back across the veranda, down the steps to where he stood. I held the storage tub on my hip with my left hand and used my right hand to tilt his face up so I could press my lips to his. Soft and warm, lingering for a moment. "And so are you."

His cheeks coloured and he ducked his head. Even the tips of his ears went red. It did all sorts of wonderful things to my stomach. It stirred even better things in my groin. "I better check on dinner." My voice was gruff so I cleared my throat. "Please, come inside."

Lawson followed me in. My house wasn't anything fancy or big. The living area consisted of one room that was my lounge room at the front, dining room at the back, kitchen at the side. There was a doorway off the lounge room that became a short hall for three bedrooms, one bathroom, and a laundry. It had timber floors, pale yellow walls, and the kitchen was kinda old. I guessed the decorating types these days would call it retro or country chic. Rosemary trotted over to her bed in front of the unlit fire and lay down.

I headed straight for the kitchen, sliding the plastic tub onto the far end of the dining table on my way. Lawson put his laptop next to it and stood at the kitchen counter. He eyed off where I'd set the end of the table for two, wine glasses and candle included. He smiled. "You have a lovely home."

I collected the tea towel off the kitchen bench and gave him a quick smile. "Thanks. It's old, but she's got that old-home charm. I love it." I opened the oven door and took out the dish of bubbling lasagne. I carefully slid it onto the stove top so it could cool a bit. "I hope you like lasagne and salad."

"Perfect. And homemade? I'm impressed."

"So, the second date might live up to the first yet!"

He chuckled. "It's off to a very good start. Though I'll let you know my full assessment when I leave."

It was hard to tell if he was joking because he smirked when he said it, but knowing him, I fully expected him to tell me what I did right *and* wrong. "If there was going to be a test, I would've made dessert."

He looked right into my eyes, almost daring in a way. "I'm sure you can improvise."

He wasn't talking about food.

It made my heart skip a beat and sent a warm thrill through my balls. "I'm sure I can."

He licked his lips and smiled. "So? Should we look over the maps before or after dinner?"

"After."

I took the green leafy salad from the fridge, uncovered it, and spritzed it with dressing before dishing up a decent square of lasagne onto two plates. He carried them to the table, I carried the salad, then grabbed the bottle of red wine I'd bought on my way home, and set it between our plates. I pulled out Lawson's seat and lit the candle while he sat down and got comfortable. "This is very lovely," he said.

"Thank you." Using the tongs, I scooped out a portion of salad onto his plate, then mine, and then poured his wine first. "Did you get everything done you wanted to this afternoon? You were transferring something to your laptop?"

"Yes. I know most people detest data entry, but I don't mind," he said. He took a small mouthful of lasagne and chewed and swallowed appreciatively. "This is very good."

"It's my Nonna's recipe."

"Nonna?" he asked. "Is your family Italian?"

"On my mum's side. My dad's side came here with the convicts."

Lawson smiled and sipped his wine. "My family's about five generations Australian. Before that we came from England and Ireland." He ate another forkful of lasagne and hummed as he swallowed it down. "Tell me about Rosemary."

"She's almost three. I got her when she was about eight weeks old. Full of mischief but the brightest eyes you've ever seen. Smart as a whip. Smarter than me, anyhow."

"And her name?" he asked. "Rosemary isn't a very common name for a dog."

I had to finish my mouthful before I could speak. "There's a thicket of rosemary that runs down the side of the house. The day I brought her home, she ran straight for it and I couldn't get her out of it. She'd roll in it, lay in it, chew it. And I couldn't pick a name for her, but every time anyone would pick her up, they'd say, 'oh, rosemary,' so it kinda stuck."

He smiled as I told my story, then nodded over to where she was asleep in her bed. "She's very spoilt."

"One hundred per cent," I agreed. "She normally comes out into the field with me. If I have a day where I'm out and about in the national parks, she's usually sitting right up beside me. If I hadda known we were gonna be out all day, I would've brought her along."

"Next time then."

"Will there be a next time?" My heart stopped while I waited for his answer.

"Do you not have work to do?" he asked, but he smiled as he spoke.

"Of course. But like I said, helping out on a conservation

study is work-related. If you're busy doing your thing, I can do my own reports and data collation when I'm out. Take photos of vegetation, soil reports, water levels, check on some known animal habitats, check fencing, that kind of thing."

"Okay." He nodded. "I'd like that very much."

Again with the belly somersault. "Me too."

We ate our dinner, of which Lawson devoured everything in front of him. When his plate was clean, he leaned back and patted his stomach. "Wow. Compliments to the chef and to your Nonna. That was delicious."

I grinned proudly. "Secret is in the ricotta."

"I look forward to seeing what you can do for Date Number Three."

I raised an eyebrow at him but could feel the smile spreading on my face. "I thought you were waiting until you were leaving for your full assessment."

He rolled his eyes. "I think we both know there will be another one. I wouldn't mind seeing Rosemary again."

I scoffed. "Thank you very much. I'll never doubt where your affection lies again."

He chuckled, then sipped his wine. "So tell me, why are you single?"

Right. Straight to the point.

He narrowed his eyes at me. "You are single, aren't you? Because the likelihood of a third date balances precariously on your answer."

"I am most definitely single," I answered. "As to why... well, the last guy I was seeing lived in Hobart, and the commute didn't work for him."

"Oh."

"And the guy before that lasted only two dates. The first date, we had dinner in Launceston. That went okay.

Second date, I invited him here. He got as far as the gate before Rosemary started to growl. That was the end of that."

"Dogs are outstanding judges of character."

"They are. I'd trust her judgement before any human I know."

"She likes me." Then he tilted his head. "Was asking me here some kind of test?"

I laughed. "Yes. And you passed with flying colours."

He seemed put out for half a second before the smile he was fighting won out. He sipped his wine, and I did the same. "And commuting or any kind of long distance relationships are out?"

So I wasn't alone in thinking this could be the start of something... Yes, we lived in different states but were most definitely on the same page. I put my wine glass on the table and met his gaze. "For him it was. Not me."

"Good." He nodded slowly before giving me that shy smile that belied his forthright nature. He stood up and collected our plates. "Let's get this cleaned up, then we pull those maps out."

Twenty minutes later, the kitchen was sparkling, a second glass each of wine was poured, and a large map was unfolded, spread out on the dining table. "If you mark on there, I can transfer it to this," Lawson said, showing me the exact same map on his laptop. "I prefer to have both. There's no saying my laptop will work when I'm hours from anywhere, so it's best to have it on both. Particularly for safety reasons."

"Smart," I said with a nod. "Especially if you go out by yourself, like you said you were prone to do."

"I always leave a detailed map of where I'm going with my professor or colleagues if I go solo." He shrugged one shoulder. "I'd be loath for the news headline to read 'Genius is an idiot who gets lost'."

I laughed at that, then showed him the vegetation maps Parks and Wildlife Services had, outlining documented locations of the particular plant he was after. I transferred the info onto his paper map, and he did the digital. Then I added in the locations I'd seen it personally, paying particular attention to the factors he said were important to his species of butterfly. North facing aspect, warmer climes.

Lawson pointed out the area he intended on searching in the morning and wrote down the GPS locations in his online journal. I really admired how meticulous he was. He was particular about the details, and that probably annoyed some people. But not me.

He was standing, leaning over his laptop, and I was standing beside him, where I'd been studying the unfolded map. I looked at him instead. "Still want me to join you tomorrow?"

He stood up straight and turned to face me. I wasn't aware of how close we were until then. Until he looked up at me and I could see the flecks of gold in the blue of his eyes and how long his eyelashes were. His skin was perfect in its paleness, his lips looked redder than I remembered.

"I'd very much like to kiss you right now," he mumbled.

I wasn't sure if he'd meant to say that out loud, but it was like he read my mind. I cupped my hand to his jaw. "I was just thinking the same thing."

"I can tell," he whispered. "You look at my mouth—"

I covered his lips with my own, and he eagerly met my kiss. God, he tasted so good. He felt even better. Lawson wrapped one arm around me and slid his other hand through my hair and slipped his tongue into my mouth. It almost buckled my knees.

I groaned into his kiss and pulled him against me. He came willingly, melting into my arms. He gave himself to me in that moment. In that kiss. He was putty in my hands, and I wanted to mould him, I wanted to take him, claim and make him mine.

All this from just a kiss. My world had tilted on its axis, nothing would ever be the same again.

From just one kiss.

Lawson hummed before pulling back a little. I cupped his face in my two hands and fluttered my eyelashes against his cheek.

"What are you doing?" he whispered.

"Butterfly kisses," I murmured before pressing my lips to his once more.

His eyes danced with something like happiness, but just when I thought he was going to say he should go, he surprised me yet again.

I should know better than to expect anything but the unexpected.

CHAPTER EIGHT
LAWSON

I WASN'T NORMALLY SO BRAZEN TO SUGGEST SUCH THINGS outright, but I couldn't help myself. I wasn't ready for this to end right now; I needed more of him. And from the way he kissed me, I was certain he felt the same.

"I think we should move to somewhere more comfortable."

I took his hand and pulled him toward the couch. I didn't think the bedroom was strictly appropriate. Not yet, anyway. I stopped in front of the sofa, and Jack's nostrils flared. He licked his lips, and sliding his hand around my neck, he crushed his mouth to mine hard enough to push me backwards. His other arm wrapped around my back, and he lowered me onto the couch.

His strength surprised me. Of course I was aware of his height and his huge shoulders, but he simply manoeuvred me as though I weighed nothing—I was suddenly on my back, lying the length of the sofa and he was over me, caging me in with his arms as he slowly lowered his body onto mine. And it was glorious.

His weight on top of me, between my legs, was heavenly.

He kissed me slower this time, deeper, but with no less passion. Every nerve in my body sang. I rolled my hips, grinding against him, and his breath stuttered as he broke the kiss. "God," he murmured; his voice was rough. He kissed along my jaw to my ear and down my neck. "I want more of your neck, but I really like the bow tie." I could feel him smile against my skin.

I reached up and pulled on one end of my tie, unravelling it, and scrambling to undo the top button. "I don't care much for the bow tie right now," I rasped, tilting my head to give him more of my neck. "Not when you do th—"

Then he scraped his teeth across my skin, and he chuckled as my words stumbled to a stop. But his hot breath down my neck and shoulder sent a shiver right through me, and *that* made Jack moan.

"Lawson," he growled. He pulled back, and his eyes were dark but his smirk was nefarious. "If you keep squirming like that, I won't be responsible for what I do to you."

I laughed and rolled my hips, rubbing my erection against his through the fabric of our clothes. From what I could feel, he was in proportion—to say the least. He was big, and he was hard. I writhed against him again because he felt so incredible. His weight, his hard-on...

Jack's huge hand stilled my hip while he pinned me with his body. "Lawson." There was more warning in his tone now. He began to pull away. "This is about to get embarrassing very fast. You have no idea how much you turn me on."

I hooked my foot around the back of his leg to prevent him

from moving. I wanted him right where he was. "This doesn't have to stop," I whispered. I ran my hand down his back, over his arse, and then slowly—so he could deny me if he wished—slid my hand between us and palmed his erection.

Jack whined. He closed his eyes as though he was trying to summon willpower from a higher being.

I'd never felt so empowered. He was half a foot taller than me, outweighed me by twenty kilos, he was athletic and I was academic, yet I was in complete control.

So using both hands, I undid his belt, pulling it roughly through the buckle. Then I popped the button and slid my fingers underneath the elastic of his briefs. His erection was confined toward his hip, so wrapping my hand around him, I pulled his cock free.

His eyes flew open, a mix of lust and abandon stared back at me. "Lawson," he murmured my name before crushing his mouth to mine. I stroked him, gyrating my hips, needing to feel him. Needing more. Needing everything.

Jack pulled back, almost to his haunches, and he undid my trousers. I was transfixed, watching his face as he revealed my cock. He licked his lips and his nostrils flared, and when he gripped my shaft, his eyes met mine, and I just about caught on fire.

"Jack." I don't know what I was insisting on, or begging for. Something. Anything. "Just fucking do it."

His eyes lit up and his smirk was wicked as he aligned our cocks and wrapped his huge hand around us both. I gasped at the onslaught of pleasure, before he kissed me with a fervour I'd never known.

I'd never been wanted like he wanted me.

He broke the kiss and spoke against my lips. "Please

come." He groaned, a pained sound. "Need you to come first, and I'm not gonna last."

His hand, now slicked with precome, slid our cocks together, and the feeling was incredible. Knowing I was turning him on so much was dizzying. I looked down between us, my forehead against his neck, and watched as our cockheads squeezed through his hand—it was the most erotic thing I'd ever seen. It was the most erotic thing I'd ever felt, been a part of, or had happen to me. God, I was so turned on. I couldn't ever remember being this aroused...

"Lawson," he growled, pure sex and wonder. "Need you to come."

And I did. A coil, wound so tight, sprung deep at the base of my spine. I came in spurts between us, groaning through an unspeakable pleasure.

"Oh, God," he whispered in my ear, and his cock pulsed against mine as he came. "Fuck!"

Jack held himself above me with one hand, trembling as his orgasm rocketed through him. His face was the picture of ecstasy and bliss. His eyes were heavy-lidded, his lips parted in a silent cry.

Thick ropes of come covered my stomach and shirt. Jack collapsed on top of me, his weight immense and divine, and he nuzzled into my neck. With him in between my thighs, I shifted a little to get more comfortable. He clearly had no intention of moving.

He nuzzled my neck some more, then kissed lazily up my jaw until he found my lips. He rested against his open palm and snugged his elbow in beside my shoulder. He smiled down at me languidly. His eyes were dreamy.

He sighed happily. "We're a mess. I probably should apologise, but I'm not sorry at all."

I bit my bottom lip to stop from smiling too much.

Though I doubt I had him fooled. "I probably should apologise for being so bold as to insist you join me on the couch, but I'm not sorry at all either."

He chuckled and planted a soft, wet kiss on my lips. "I do like the way you speak. But I will admit, I like it when you swear even more."

"Swear?"

"You said fuck. Actually, you said 'just fucking do it.'"

"I did not!"

"You did too." He grinned and kissed me again. "And it was hot."

I could feel my cheeks heat. "I'm sure I'm aware of what words come out of my mouth. I'm not one to curse. The English language has many thousand words, some much more indulgent and better serving than swear words."

Now he laughed. "You totally swore. Next time I'll record you so I have proof."

"Next time?"

"Please tell me there'll be a next time."

I found myself smiling at his expression. Blinking innocence and hope. "Will it be the best third date ever?"

"Yes," he answered quickly. "Though, just as a gauge, how did the second date go?"

"I'll let you know when it's over."

He laughed into a sigh and smiled as though he couldn't possibly have been happier. "I think you should stay the night."

Oh. My heart squeezed with his words and the look in his eyes. "Well, no. I think I shouldn't. I appreciate the offer, but I have none of my belongings here and I have an early start tomorrow."

"Am I not coming with you tomorrow?"

"If you want."

"I want. You, me, and Rosemary. I thought we had a deal?"

I looked over to find her still sound asleep in front of the unlit fireplace, then back to Jack. "Okay, deal."

"So you'll stay?"

I smiled at his insistence. "No."

He pouted gorgeously. "Then I better make Date Number Three even better."

"Or even Date Number Four…"

He kissed me with smiling lips. "I'm not afraid of working for it."

"It? As in sex? You presume a lot."

"I wasn't referring to working for sex, no. I was referring to working on making you happier with each date." He seemed amused. "If more sex is a reward for awesome date planning, then I'm not opposed. And I'm not presuming anything. I seem to recall you dragging me to the couch to get more comfortable."

I'm certain I blushed. "I believe in asking for what I want. There's no point in yearning for something if you can actually have it."

Jack traced his thumb over my heated cheek. His eyes followed his thumb, then scanned my face. "You are something special," he whispered. "And you can have me anytime you want me."

I leaned up and kissed him. "I think I need to get cleaned up."

He jumped off me with the agility of a cat and walked off down the hall. "Take off your shirt. I'll get you a clean one."

I pulled at the unravelled bow tie, sliding it from around my neck, then undid the buttons on my shirt. I slid it from my shoulders just as Jack came back with a wet washer in one hand and a folded shirt in the other. And he stopped. And stared.

I felt warm all over as he examined me with his gaze, as though his eyes were hands that skimmed over every inch of my skin.

Jack licked his lips and took a robotic step toward me. "Oh wow," he said, now appearing to be fixated on my chest. He swallowed hard and finally met my eyes. "Right, then. Shirt?" He held up his hand with the shirt. "Though I'll be completely honest with you, Lawson, I'd rather you didn't put it on."

He stood in front of me; his height and size never seemed more apparent. I felt slightly vulnerable, I was half-naked and he towered over me, his shoulders dwarfed mine. But he very tenderly put the washcloth to my abdomen, gently washing me clean in slow, deliberate circles.

It was the most adoring, indulgent thing anyone had ever done for me.

He pressed a kiss to the top of my shoulder, and I almost told him I was staying...

Jack took a small step backward and let out a slow breath. "A shirt," he said, his voice low and lovely. "It will be too big, but it's the smallest I've got. I haven't worn it in years."

I took the folded shirt. "Thank you." I slipped it on over my head, and yes, it swam on me.

When I finished pressing it down into submission, I looked up at Jack to find him biting the corner of his bottom lip. "Looks good on you."

"It's far too big." I tried tucking the front in a bit, but it was pointless.

Jack put his fingers under my chin and gently tipped my

face upwards so I would look at him. "I like my clothes on you," he murmured before pressing his lips to mine.

I slid my hand along his jaw, the feel of stubble scratched my skin in the most delicious way, and I deepened the kiss. He let me kiss him this way, deep and slick until he put a hand on my hip and pushed me away. He chuckled, a disbelieving sound. His voice was gruff. "If you intend on leaving, you probably should go now. Before I take you to my bed."

I blinked, staring up at him, and somewhere in my brain a voice was telling me to breathe, breathe, because I'd somehow forgotten how to. I took my lungs full of air and my mind buzzed as a response to the reprieve. I put my palm to my forehead, staving off a dizzy spell.

Jack's eyes were a mix of amused and concerned. "You okay?"

"While it's correct that breathing can be both a voluntary and involuntary process, I'm not certain I've ever actually forgotten to breathe before now."

Jack barked out a laugh, and he smiled with a hint of mischief. "You know, if you're feeling lightheaded, you can always stay."

This time, I stepped back. "Thank you for the offer, but I'm fine. Though I really should be going."

He looked disappointed, which made me happier than it should have, but he nodded. "Fair enough. We still on for tomorrow, though?"

"Yes. I'd like that."

"Me too. And I need to put my thinking cap on about Date Number Three. Is tomorrow night too soon?"

I picked up my laptop satchel and smiled at him. "Tomorrow night is fine."

"Good." He collected the storage tub I'd brought with

me from the table and followed me to the front door. "I'll wash your shirt for you and leave it here for you then."

I stopped by the light on the front porch and turned to face him. "So, Date Number Three will be here again?"

He blanched and the corner of his lip pulled down with uncertainty. "Well, I thought... we can go somewhere else if you'd prefer. I just thought you could bring your work here and get the paperwork done while I cook dinner, that way we have more time..."

I smiled at him, letting him know it was fine. "Sounds perfect."

He beamed a smile that made my heart soar. Then he ducked his head a little and nodded toward my rental before taking the three porch steps with a familiar ease. He opened the back of the Defender and slid the tub inside. I opened the driver's door and leaned in to put my satchel on the passenger seat. When I straightened up, he was standing behind me and he made no apologies about being caught ogling my arse. I raised my eyebrow at him, but he only shrugged.

"So, do I get a score on tonight's date?" he asked. Then he apparently remembered something out of the blue. "Oh, wait! Hold that thought." He dashed off to the corner of his house, disappearing from the light the front porch allowed. He came back holding a strand of jasmine: dainty white flowers on a sliver of green. He stopped in front of me and presented them to me. There was a nervousness to the set of his lips. "For you. A date's not a date without flowers, apparently."

I reached out slowly and took the flowers. "Perfect."

His smile was my reward. "What's perfect?"

"My assessment on Date Number Two." I took a deep breath and looked up at the amazing blanket of stars above us. The silence, the open space, and seclusion of where he lived was incredible. "I'm starting to think all dates with you might be perfect, varying only in their degree of perfection."

He smiled victoriously, happily. "I'm already looking forward to tomorrow." He put his hand to my face and kissed me. "But if you have to go..."

"I do."

"Then goodnight."

I leaned up and pressed my lips to his. "Goodnight."

He watched as I manoeuvred the ridiculously sized Defender out of his driveway. When I looked back to wave, I saw that Rosemary had joined him on the porch. Jack patted her forehead, said something to her, and waved me off.

I drove back to town with an absurd grin on my face. I went to sleep with it too.

CHAPTER NINE
JACK

I PUSHED THE DOOR TO THE BAKERY OPEN, WELCOMED BY THE DING of the bell above the door, then by Remmy. "Oh hey, you! You're in early!" Then she eyed me cautiously. "Well, look at you."

"What?"

"That smile."

I laughed. "Don't know what you're talking about."

"Oh my God." She walked out from behind the counter, never taking her eyes off me. "It's him, isn't it? The bow tie guy. What was his name? Lawson?"

I pulled my lips into a pout. Well, I tried, but they went back to smiling without my consent. "Yes, his name is Lawson. And I still don't know what you're talking about."

Remmy laughed at me and gave me a hug. "Tell me everything."

"We had a second date last night. Having a third tonight. I'm also spending the day with him out in the national park."

She wrung her hands together and buzzed excitedly. "Did he wear a bow tie last night?"

"Yes, he did."

She made some weird, dramatic sound. "Aww, he's so cute!"

"And he's smart, and he's sexy as hell."

"And Rosemary?"

"Loves him."

Remmy's eyes got teary. "Awwwww."

"Actually, Rosemary is spending the day with us too. I think he's a bit taken with her."

"Thank God. I thought he might be a bit timid around her," Remmy said. "You know, he seemed the type to be timid..."

If she was referring to the nerdy, bow tie-wearing, genius look he had going on, she was very wrong. "Ah, Lawson's not timid." I bit my lip. "About anything."

She laughed and gave me a knowing grin. "And that explains the smile." She went back around the counter. "Did you actually want anything or did you just come in here to brag?"

I snorted. "Surprise me. Anything you think we might like to eat today. And something for Rosemary too."

Remmy had a separate small display of bone shaped cookies for her four-legged customers. Made solely with ingredients for human consumption—oats, carrot, peanut butter, honey—Rosemary would eat them as fast as Remmy could make them.

Remmy put some pastries and bread into a paper bag for me. "What are your plans for your date tonight?"

"Not sure yet. Something at home. I'll cook for him again while he gets through his paperwork, which will leave more time for... other things."

"Ah, confident, I see?"

"Well, I don't think I should assume anything when it

comes to Lawson. I get the feeling he'll keep me on my toes." I was back to smiling. "In a good way, of course."

Remmy winked. "Of course."

"Well, I better get going." I took the bag of goods and offered her a twenty, which she refused to take. So, without a word, I walked around her side of the counter, opened the till, and slid the money inside. She rolled her eyes. I gave her a kiss on the cheek. "Don't want to be late."

"Have fun tonight!" Remmy waved me off as I walked out the door. I put the bag of pastries in the Esky I had on the back of the ute. I'd put some fruit in earlier as well, not knowing what Lawson might want to eat today. I climbed into the driver's seat and gave Rosemary a pat for being patient. "One more stop to make."

I bought some takeaway coffees, enough for everyone in the office and one for Lawson too. I slid the two trays on the floor at the passenger side, where they wouldn't spill onto Rosemary. "Don't touch. They're hot," I told her, though I dunno why. It wasn't like she knew what the word *hot* was. But she knew what *don't touch* was, and like a good girl, she didn't give the trays of coffee a second look. "You'll have to wait until lunchtime for your cookies." Her tongue lolled out in her doggy smile. I was pretty sure she knew what the word cookie was. After me, I think Remmy was her favourite human.

I drove to work, handed out coffees, and explained I'd be out doing field assessments again today. No one batted an eyelid, but when Lawson arrived right on eight thirty, there were a few knowing smiles. No one seemed surprised that Lawson knew Rosemary already, or they hadn't realised that it meant he must have been to my house. But when I walked out the door with him and a tail-wagging Rosemary, Karen gave me a ridiculous smile and mouthed "good luck." I cleared my throat, grateful Lawson hadn't seen it.

The day was warm already. Well, warm for Tasmania. The morning summer sun made Lawson look angelic. He wore long pants again, good for getting through long grasses and bushes, and hiking boots, a polo shirt that matched the blue of his eyes, but the lack of bow tie was disappointing. We walked toward his Defender, and I pretended that I hadn't checked him out already, focusing on the day ahead instead. "So, what's the plan of attack this morning?" I asked.

Lawson sipped his coffee. "I'd like to investigate the areas where you have seen the Sweet Bursaria plant. The ones we marked on the maps last night. I have three locations marked as a priority, given the northerly aspect. So I thought we could start there."

I had a bag with me today for my laptop and camera, a shovel and soil sample bags, and some data collating. As much as spending time with Lawson was more pleasure than business, I did actually have some work to do.

I put the Esky into the Defender, hooked up Rosemary's harness to the backseat, and climbed in. "Is she all clicked in?" Lawson asked, scanning the rear-vision mirror.

"Yep."

"Does she prefer the window up or down?"

Lawson asked the question so seriously, but all I could do was smile. He treated my dog like her well-being was important to him, and it made my chest all warm and tight. "Down, of course."

Lawson found the right button on the driver's side door and pressed it, and within no time, we were following GPS directions to his first destination. I could have told him where to go, but I liked that he used initiative and didn't rely on anyone else.

As the rain-deprived highway scenery flew by and Rosemary had her nose out the window, I couldn't help but look at Lawson and smile. "Sleep well?" I asked him.

"Yes, very. And you?"

"Very."

"I think your colleagues at the office suspect there might be other reasons you're accompanying me."

"I think you might be right."

He shot me a concerned glance. "Is that... Is that problematic?"

"Nope."

"How do they know? Have you told them of me... and what we're doing?" His cheeks reddened deliciously.

"No. But you called Rosemary by name, and the only place you could have met her already was at my house."

He frowned. "Oh. Of course. I'm sorry. I hope that hasn't put you in a difficult position."

"Not at all. I am actually doing work today, and they won't even know if I happen to sneak in a little make-out session with the sexy lepidopterist during my lunch break."

He blushed properly this time, heat stains running from his cheeks down his neck in the most wonderful way. He dismissed my compliment with an eye roll. "If I ever find an attractive lepidopterist, I'll be sure to pass on your number."

I laughed. "Believe me, I've found one."

"You're absurd."

"If you need me to do a full case-study on this new, exciting specimen of sexy lepidopterist, I'll be only too happy to oblige."

He squirmed in his seat. "And that would involve what, exactly?"

I was grinning, glad he was playing along. "I think the sexual habits need a full review. I'm enjoying the courting rituals so far. I've seen *some* sexual activity, but I don't think I've even scratched the surface yet. But I'm certain this particular specimen is like nothing I've ever known."

Lawson's eyes went from the road to me, then back to the road. He licked his lips and the colour on his cheeks deepened. He shifted in his seat again and cleared his throat. "Is that right?"

God, at this rate we'd be naked before morning teatime. Needing to pull back the tension a bit, I sighed. "Yep. I'm considering giving David Attenborough a call."

Now he chuckled. "I met him once."

"David Attenborough? Get out!"

"But we're not there yet."

I barked out a laugh. "Did you really?"

"Yes, I did. At a gala in Melbourne. He was most charming."

And so we talked about things he'd done, the people he'd met, and the places he'd been until we arrived at our first destination. I really had no idea someone who studied butterflies could live such an interesting life. It was pretty evident that when he didn't have his head in a book, he was out getting things done. Travelling, taking courses, hiking in far off places, all in search of elusive butterflies.

I had to admit, I admired him. Okay, I more than admired him. I was enamoured with, charmed by, and attracted to him.

I couldn't deny it. If there was a list of things that needed to be included in my perfect guy, Lawson Gale ticked every single one. Hell, he even ticked boxes I didn't know needed ticking.

"You getting out?" Lawson asked, his voice startling me from my thoughts. He didn't wait for an answer. He just opened his door and got out. He had the back door open and was getting his gear out a second later. I unclipped Rosemary, and she climbed out and was soon sniffing her way around the clearing.

"Don't go too far," I told her.

"Do you always talk to her?" Lawson asked, putting two stacked plastic storage tubs into the centre of the clearing.

"Of course I do."

Rosemary chose that particular time to inspect what Lawson was doing. Then he spoke to her, "He talks to you all the time, doesn't he?" She wagged her tail and smiled at him in response, and he tousled the fur on her forehead. "I bet you have him wrapped around your little finger," he went on to say to her. "If you had a finger, that is."

"Are you done?" I asked, when the truth was, I could watch him talk to her all day long. I walked over to them with the laptop satchel. "I'm not wrapped around her little finger. I would say I don't spoil her, but I'd be lying. She's my best mate. Of course, I spoil her."

Lawson looked at me then, an amused smirk on his face. "If you didn't, I wouldn't be here. Well actually, that's not correct. *I'd* be here, but you wouldn't be with me."

I scoffed. "Is that right?"

"Yes. What makes you think yours was the only test upon my meeting her?" He raised a daring eyebrow at me. "If I'd have gone to your house and met your dog and it was apparent she was maltreated, I'd have walked away, right there and then, without another word."

Well, I'll be. "So I passed your test?"

He fought a smile now. "With flying colours."

I grinned, then walked over to stand right in front of him. "We might both be technically at work right now, but would you be opposed to me kissing you?"

Something flashed in his eyes like humour, or a challenge. Possibly both. "I'm not opposed. Actually, I rather like it that you asked permission."

I leaned down until my lips barely touched his. "I rather like that you like it." I kissed him then, with open lips and I tilted my head enough to make it playful and perfect. I pulled away, and his eyes slowly opened to reveal a dazed look.

"I rather like it a whole lot more when you don't stop kissing me," he said.

I chuckled. "If I keep going, then I'll keep going, if you know what I mean."

"Oh."

"And I need to keep some secrets hidden for Date Number Three. I'm going for a hat-trick."

He licked his bottom lip and took a small step back, clearly needing some distance. "I'm sure it'll be perfect. No matter what you decide."

The truth was, I hadn't decided what I was doing for dinner. I had no clue yet. "So, work. We better get started or dinner tonight will be eggs on toast."

He opened the first tub and took out his maps. "I like eggs, just so you know. I can eat the finest dining at black-tie galas, but I'm equally happy with eggs on toast. It's the company that matters."

I was grateful he was distracted by his maps so he couldn't see the goofy smile I'm sure I was aiming at him. "Right, then." I heaved my satchel up on my shoulder. "Work. What are you doing first?"

"Well," he answered, holding the unfolded map out and changing his stance to face north. "I'm going to do a very basic grid formation. I won't be heading any further than two hundred metres in any direction." He then concentrated on his iPad, showing the same map as the paper one at his feet, the same maps we'd dissected last night. He wrote something on the screen, then started to take readings of temperature and barometric pressures or whatever it was he was doing. He was so engrossed in his work, I thought it best to leave him to it.

"Right, then, we'll just be here. Rosemary," I called to my dog. She was sniffing at something thirty-odd metres away, but she was quick to come back when I called her. I told her to lie down under the shade of the Defender, and soon enough she was happily snoozing.

I took photographs of the track we'd driven on, good for condition reports and records. I took soil samples, checking for moisture content. I'd have preferred an auger, but doing it by hand was cathartic. I loved being outdoors, getting my hands dirty, and doing hard, physical work was rewarding. It was hot, and I had worked up a sweat by the time Lawson came back.

"Looks hard," he said, nodding to the hole I was working on. "The ground, I mean."

"It is. We need rain badly."

"Yes, I'm still surprised Tasmania is this dry." He wiped his forehead with the back of his hand. "I understand the entire state isn't prone to high rainfall, but even farmlands in this area which would be typically lush have browned off. Underfoot is very dry."

I nodded. "Department of Meteorology says we should get rain next week. Not that it'll be drought-breaking, but we'll take anything we can get." I noticed then he was still holding his iPad. "How'd you go? Find anything promising?"

He shook his head. "Not yet. I've covered the northeast areas of what we marked out last night. I'll start on the south and west now."

"Need me to help you?"

He gave me a small, thankful smile. "It's fine. It won't take me long, and I'd hate to take you from your hole digging."

I snorted at that. "Soil testing for moisture content, thank you very much."

His smirk in response told me he was only joking. "I'd like to assess a second area after I'm done here. Is that okay with you, or do you need more time here?"

"I'm right to go whenever," I said. "I also packed us a lunch, so just give a holler when you're hungry."

"Oh." He seemed taken aback. "Thank you. That was most thoughtful."

"I try."

"Lunch *and* dinner," he mused. "I'll have to think of ways to repay you."

I raised an eyebrow at him. "While I can think of a few things," I hinted, "I don't actually expect anything in return." I gave our surroundings a quick glance. "This isn't exactly a horrible way to spend my day."

He smiled, and his eyes never left mine. His gaze was intense and somehow playful. "I preferred my suggestion of repayment, but if digging holes does it for you, then I'll keep my suggestions to myself." He turned and walked away, heading toward the line of trees to the south of us.

"I like suggestions!" I called out after him. "You can repay me however you see fit!"

He turned to give me a smile but kept walking. I sighed,

resting on my shovel. Damn. He was just getting more and more perfect.

And it was getting more and more hot. Another half an hour of digging baked earth had me a sweating mess, so I took off my shirt. I wiped my face down with it and tucked it into the back of my pants. I was finished digging and was lying down on my stomach, scooping out a sample of soil at 400mm for collection, when someone cleared their throat.

I looked up to find Lawson standing, watching me. And from what I could tell, he liked what he saw. "I got hot," I explained.

He swallowed hard. "I would argue the fact you were hot before the temperature rose. But I won't lie, you shirtless and lying down in the dirt does improve the aesthetics."

I laughed, and putting my hands on the ground near my shoulders, I jumped to my feet. "Is that so?"

He was staring at my chest and stomach, both covered in sweat and dirt. "Mmm."

I might have flexed a little, just for show, as I took my shirt and wiped myself down again. He didn't even try to hide the fact he was gawking at me. When he finally looked at my face, I was grinning. "So? Did you discover any non-existent butterflies in the southwest section?"

His eyes flashed with something like indignation and he tilted his head. I don't think he liked my question. "No."

"Did I say something wrong?"

"Do you think I'm foolish for taking Professor Tillman at his word and spending my time searching the woodlands of Tasmania for a species that might not even exist?"

"What? No, I don't think that at all."

"Would you mind putting your shirt back on please?" He licked his lips again. "I can't seem to concentrate."

"Sorry," I said, not really sorry at all. Seeing Lawson all flustered did great things for my ego. I pulled my shirt over my head.

"I'm not doing this for the glory of it," he added. "Searching for this species."

"I know that." I looked him right in the eye so he would see my sincerity. "No. I think you're passionate, and you love what you do so much that you *want* to believe Professor Tillman. Because what if he's right? Because what if there *is* a species of butterfly never documented before! And what if you're the one to find it? You're not in this for the glory, even I can see that. You're doing it because if this species does exist, there needs to be research and breeding programs and funding. Finding it is just the beginning."

He didn't speak for a moment, just looked at me like a cryptic riddle in his head finally made sense. "Well, yes." He looked to his feet, then back to me. "No one's ever understood that part of me. Not outside of my work, anyway."

A warmth expanded in my chest at his words. "Then no one's ever paid close enough attention."

"No," he answered quietly. "I guess they haven't."

Changing the subject, I dusted off my hands. "Want some lunch? I'm starving."

We ate our lunch of pastries, bread, and fruits while Rosemary chomped through her doggie cookies, and Lawson started asking me questions about what I did every day. "What do you love about your job?"

"Being outdoors. Days like this: sitting in the shade out in the middle of nowhere. Nothing but peace and quiet and the sounds of birds, crickets."

"What's your least favourite thing?"

"Paperwork."

"Really?"

"I hate it."

"I find paperwork relaxing."

"Relaxing?"

"Yes, it's methodical and predictable. It calms my mind."

"It turns my mind to sludge."

Lawson let out a long breath and smiled serenely. "Well, if this is your office, your view isn't half bad."

"Tell me about your office."

"It's small. Half the size of that of my boss's. I assume it reflects my pay and importance, by comparison also." He smiled, I assumed to let me know he was either joking or he found the humour in the truth of it. "The laboratory is my favourite workspace. Well, not even workspace. Any space, really. But this here..." He looked around. "This isn't too bad at all."

I got to my feet and extended my hand to him. "Come on. Lunch is over."

Lawson allowed me to pull him to his feet, but as I suggested we head to the next area we'd marked on the map, he frowned. "Forgive me if I'm wrong, but I was under the impression that along with lunch there was also making out?"

I laughed at how unashamed he was. "Oh, were you?"

He lifted his chin and fought a smile. His defiance and humour were cute as hell. "Yes. If I recall correctly, you said no one will know if you happen to sneak in a little make-out session during your lunch break."

Now I laughed more genuinely. "Ah, that's where you're wrong." I put my hand to his jaw and lifted his face a little. "I'm pretty sure I said 'a make-out session with the sexy lepidopterist.'"

He rolled his eyes and I crushed my mouth to his. He

was startled by the contact, but I held his face right where I wanted him. He melted against me, sighing into the kiss. I tilted my head just enough to deepen the kiss, and he slid his hands around my back.

God, he tasted so good. He fit against me perfectly, and his arms around me felt divine. His hands clawing at my back felt even better...

Rosemary huffed at our feet, making us break apart. She sat there smiling up at us.

I took a step back and let out a laugh, running my hand through my hair. I was a little embarrassed at how carried away I'd gotten. "I uh, I'm sorry. That got out of hand."

"Don't apologise." Lawson thumbed his bottom lip, and Jesus help me, I almost groaned. He had no idea—absolutely no clue—how sexy he was. "I think Rosemary knew she'd better interrupt." He licked his lip and cleared his throat. "Or it could have gotten very out of hand."

I took a very large, very deliberate step back. "Agreed." I turned and pointed to the Defender. "We really should get more work done." I was grasping at my self-control, and if he hesitated in the slightest, even the smallest bit, I doubted I'd be able to stop myself. My dick was half-hard and at an odd angle, and I really needed to adjust...

His line of sight followed my hand, and he swallowed hard. "Work, yes." Thankfully, he turned and started to collect our lunch leftovers, putting them back into the Esky. He gave Rosemary a pat and shot me a hesitant look, his eyes dark. "I think work is a very good idea."

So we did work, all afternoon. We found the next area I'd shown him on his map last night. It was about a kilometre further up on the track we'd taken into the National Park. He did his grid-walk of the area we'd highlighted, and I took more soil samples, took photos of the vegetation, and of a tawny frogmouth's nest. We didn't track every kind of native animal or bird, but noting locations and activity when I could never hurt.

Lawson found nothing again, and even though he said he expected nothing less, I could tell he was a little disappointed. It was in his eyes, and as he drove us back toward town, it was in the way he fidgeted in his seat and the tic in his jaw.

"Tomorrow's another day, huh?"

He brightened some. "Yes."

Just then, my phone buzzed. It was a message from Remmy. *Call past home. I have something for your dinner date tonight.*

I smiled. "You know, I'm pretty sure Remmy thinks I'm useless." I held up my phone to show him the message.

"You told her about our date tonight?"

"Yes, of course. I called in to see her this morning to collect our lunch, remember?"

He nodded. "Oh, right."

"Well, I didn't actually have to tell her anything. She guessed as soon as I walked in."

He glanced at me, then back to the road. "What do you mean?"

I pointed to my face. "The smile. Gave me away, apparently."

His answering smile was slow spreading. "Oh."

"So she's taken it upon herself to prepare something for our dinner tonight. I told her I had no clue what I was gonna cook, but it had to be special, ya know, because of the perfect date pressure you put me under."

He snorted. "I told you I don't need anything extravagant. It's the company and conversation I scrutinise. Not the food."

"Good to know the pressure is on my personality and not anything else."

Lawson laughed. "Exactly."

AFTER PARTING WAYS WITH LAWSON, I KNOCKED ON REMMY'S front screen door. The wooden door was open to let the breeze in, so I could see inside. I heard little footsteps before I saw the culprit. Luca, all long blond curls and cute dimples, wearing only a pair of shorts, sprang to life in front of the door with a giggle. "UncaJack!"

"Hey tiger," I replied.

Luca roared at me just as Remmy came to the door, wiping her hands on a tea towel. She let me in and Luca launched himself at me. I picked him up. "Jeez kid, you're getting too big! Have you been playing in your mum's garden? You're growing like a tomato plant!"

Luca laughed. "I show you," he said, squirming to get down. I followed him into the kitchen, where he leaned up on his tiptoes so he could reach and pull over a bowl of home-grown vegetables. "These are from my garden." He reached in and took a tomato in one hand, a zucchini in the other. His little fingers barely held them. "I can make ratooey."

"Ratatouille," Remmy gently corrected.

Jeez. The kid was four and was a better cook than me. I guess that's what happened when your parents, French and Portuguese, were chefs. "Make sure you save a seat for me when you do, 'kay?"

The kid beamed before running to the fridge to get himself a drink. He put the jug of juice on the counter, and

Remmy watched on as he poured himself a cup. "He'll hold you to that," she said fondly.

"Good. I'll look forward to it."

"Next week?"

"It's a date."

She smirked. "Speaking of dates…" Remmy went to the fridge and pulled out a tray that had some kind of baking paper pouch on it. "For a perfect date tonight."

"You didn't have to do this," I said kindly.

"It was no problem. I was making it for our dinner, so it was easy to make enough for you." She unwrapped the corner of the paper pouch. "I put that twenty you put in my till this morning to good use. It's rainbow trout with a splash of Thai spices. I wasn't sure if Lawson liked spicy food, so I kept it fairly tame. All you need to do is pop it in a hot oven for twenty minutes. It'll steam in the paper. Then serve with steamed veggies and you're golden."

"You're an angel."

Nico walked into the kitchen. "Ah, the man with the perfect date," he said with a warm handshake. "Good to see you, my friend."

I chuckled. "Well, I'm aiming for three outta three in the perfect date score. I think Remmy's almost got me home with this." I gestured to the trout she'd prepared.

Nico rubbed his belly. "Don't know how I'm not the size of a barn." He kissed Remmy's cheek. "The hardships of marrying a pastry chef."

"Well, I don't know what I'll cook for Date Number Four," I said. "Don't know what will beat fresh trout prepared by a chef."

"I cook for you, UncaJack," Luca said. He was kneeling on a stool at the bench next to me, sipping his cup of juice. "I make ratooey."

"Oh Luca," Remmy said. "UncaJack doesn't want us there on a date, darling."

"I don't mind," I said. "And I'm sure Lawson wouldn't either." Because if he didn't want to spend any time with my dearest friends, then maybe there was no long-term hope for us. "We can have dinner at my place. Only if it's alright with you."

"Can I, Mama? Can I?" Luca pleaded.

Seriously, the kid was so stinking cute with those big eyes and dimples.

I gave Remmy my best grin. "Come on, it'll be fun. And I know you're itching to give Lawson the third degree."

Nico snorted out a laugh. "She is."

"Then let me make dessert," Remmy said.

"You're doing enough!" I tried to reason. I knew Luca cooking meant that Remmy was supervising, and by supervising, I meant doing most of it.

Remmy waved her hand in the air, dismissing my concern. "Ah, it's nothing."

Nico gave me a sympathetic smile. "You know she's not happy unless she's feeding someone."

That was true. "Well, thank you. I'm very grateful."

"Wait until after dinner before you thank us," Remmy said, winking toward Luca. "And I suggest you tell Lawson before you drop him into this."

"Ah, where's the fun in that?" I asked. "Let's see how he likes surprises."

Remmy laughed. "I guess it's one way to see someone's true colours." She handed me the tray of trout. "Here. Don't want to keep him waiting. We'll be at your place at six tomorrow night, that way we can be out of your hair by seven thirty." She waggled her eyebrows at me. Nico laughed, and Luca was busy already lining up his tomatoes and zucchinis along the counter.

I gave Remmy a kiss on the cheek. "Thank you. And I'll see you then."

By the time I got home, I barely had enough time to shower and get some veggies sorted for steaming before Lawson arrived. I heard his Defender pull up and met him at the front door. He'd showered too, and was now wearing brown pants, a faded denim long-sleeve shirt, and his trademark bow tie. He took my breath away. I leaned in and kissed him softly, square on the lips. "Hello there."

He produced a small bottle and frowned. "I wasn't sure if I should bring a gift or token of thanks. I know it's customary for the guest to do so, but I couldn't think of anything that seemed appropriate or that the local supermarket would sell. But I found this, and given it's a local product, and you like to cook, I thought…"

I took the bottle and read the label. It was a locally produced gourmet strawberry coulis. "You don't have to bring anything, but thank you."

He rewarded me with a smile that made my stomach flip. "Something smells amazing."

"Dinner, which I can't take credit for. It was all Remmy's doing. Hope you like a Thai-inspired trout?"

He hummed. "Sounds lovely." We walked inside where he gave Rosemary a welcoming pat, and I thought now was a good time as any to bring up dinner plans for tomorrow night. "Now, I don't want to assume there will be a Date Number Four, but I might have already organised something…"

"Oh?" He leaned against the kitchen counter, completely at ease. "You're that confident to presume a fourth date?"

I shrugged at him. "Confident. Hopeful. Same thing, really."

He smiled and a faint blush covered his cheeks. "I'll have to check my schedule, but I think I'm free."

I chuckled. "Good. Because I have a personal chef lined up to cook here, just for us."

He stared at me. "Are you serious?"

I nodded. "Yep. He's a cutie too. There's a downside, though."

"What's that?"

"We won't be dining alone."

"Oh."

"They've promised to leave early, though. I hope you don't mind."

His blush deepened. "Not at all."

I traced the heat across his cheek with my thumb, then gave him butterfly kisses along his cheekbone. His breath caught, and he slid his hand around my neck and pulled me in for a kiss. Fuck. I pushed him against the kitchen counter, and he deepened the kiss with a groan from the back of his throat.

God, I could kiss him forever.

And just when I took a breath and kissed him again, the microwave beeped and startled us. I laughed at myself for jumping, and Lawson licked his bottom lip. "That would be the rice," I said lamely. I couldn't seem to take my eyes off his mouth. "Which we could totally ignore for a while." I kissed him again, only this time to be interrupted by the oven timer.

He chuckled. "I think the universe is trying to tell us

something."

"Yeah. If I burn Remmy's trout, she'll kill me." So I served dinner, which was outstanding. Lawson made a point of complimenting the rice and steamed beans and baby squash, knowing it was the only thing I'd done. But we sipped wine and made small talk about new government environmental protection laws, climate change, and music, but there was an underlying static, a charge of sexual tension that never went away.

It was in every forkful of food, every lick of his lips, and in every sip of his wine. It was in his eyes when he looked at me, in how his fingers held his wine glass. Even the line of his jaw, his neck, the timbre of his voice. Every single thing he did turned me on.

He took a sip of wine and slowly put the glass on the table. "If you keep looking at me like that, I won't say no to whatever it is you want to do to me."

Oh, fuck.

I couldn't speak for a second. I had to take a breath first. "I can't help it. And I can't even bring myself to apologise. You're sexy as hell, Lawson, and you have no idea what it is I want to do to you."

His cheeks flamed but his eyes darkened. He held my gaze, daringly. "Does it, in any part, involve your mouth on my body?"

All pretences were down and I was done for. Every nerve in my body was a live wire, and my cock throbbed and my balls ached with need. I stood up, my chair scraping on the floorboards. I walked around to his side of the table, and he never even attempted to stand up. He simply sat there and stared up at me with a knowing, brazen smirk and waited for me to make my move.

CHAPTER TEN
LAWSON

Jack held out his hand, which I took and stood up, but instead of leading me to the sofa or to his bedroom, as I'd hoped he would, he pushed me against the dining table. With my arse pressed into the wood, he pushed his body against mine and kissed me like he owned me.

He pinned me where I was with his body and his arms wrapped tight around me. I could feel his desperation in the strength of his hold. It was possessive and pure desire. He swept his tongue into my mouth, owning every part of me he touched.

He was clearly aroused, his erection pressed hard against mine. He ground against me for the friction we both craved, never breaking his mouth from mine.

A passion had sparked between us that I'd never known could exist. I wanted him with every cell in my body.

He was pressing me so hard against the table, it moved under our weight. I lifted my feet and wrapped my legs around the backs of his thighs, just about to beg him to take me to bed.

He gripped his huge hand around my thigh and just

when I thought he was going to hitch my leg higher, even pick me up and carry me to bed, he lowered my foot to the floor. I pulled my mouth from his to protest. I was so turned on, my erection wouldn't recede on its own. I needed him to touch me... "Jack, please."

His lips were plump and wet, his eyes unfocused and filled with a fire I'd not seen before. His chest heaved and his nostrils flared, then slowly, he went to his knees in front of me.

"Oh, God."

He undid my belt, roughly pulling it through the buckle. Then he popped the button and undid the fly like he was about to defuse a bomb. He was taking his time, possibly savouring the moment, and all I wanted was his mouth.

I ran my hand through his hair. "Jack." My tone might have been sharper than I intended.

He looked up at me and smiled. "Yes?"

"Please." I wasn't even ashamed to beg. I was desperate for his touch, his mouth, anything. He pulled the front of my briefs down, finally freeing my erection. But he gave me no relief. I fisted his hair this time. "Just fucking suck me."

He hummed and took the head of my cock into his mouth, finally. The warm, wet heat was exquisite. He sucked me down, tonguing my shaft before pulling off. "I do like it when you curse." He held my cock up and nuzzled the underside. "I can't wait to hear your filthy mouth when I'm finally inside you."

My cock jerked in his hold, and he chuckled again. "That's what I thought." Then he took me into his mouth again, pumping my base with one hand and sucking me hard.

"Oh God. Jack, you're gonna make me come."

He hummed around me, encouraging me to come. With

my hand still gripping his hair, I thrust into his throat and he took me. I tried to warn him, but my orgasm shattered through me and I released into his throat.

The room spun as the perfect moment of bliss and ecstasy consumed me. As the euphoric haze dissipated, I saw Jack was now on his feet, smugly licking his lips. He wasted no time in kissing me, sharing the taste of me. I could barely catch my breath and loved every moment.

I pulled him harder against me, and the press of his still-hard cock at my hip reminded me of his need. I broke the kiss. "Your turn."

"You don't have to," he whispered.

I raised an eyebrow at him. "I want it. Please tell me I can."

He let out a low growl that sounded like desperation. "God yes."

I took his hand and led him to his couch. I pushed him back on it and quickly knelt between his legs. I undid his belt, then the button and fly of his pants. His eyes were dark and his chest rose and fell with rapid breaths. He put his hand to my face like he was lost for words. Not breaking eye contact, I freed his cock. The smell of musk and desire made my mouth water.

I looked down then to see his cock. He was well in proportion, big all over. A good eight inches, solid girth, and veins. "Oh, that's beautiful," I murmured. I licked my lips and leaned down, tasting his precome. Salty and sweet and everything I wanted. I licked his head, tonguing his frenulum, eliciting a strangled groan from him. So I took him into my mouth and sucked him mercilessly.

"Ugh." Jack's hips came off the couch. "Fuck, Lawson. Yeah, just like that." He put his hand on my head, and I hummed to let him know I liked it. "So good."

I swirled my tongue along the underside of his shaft and he grunted, so vocal. Every reaction was my reward. I skimmed my hands along his hips, then up and under his shirt, searching out his nipples. I circled each soft nub before gently pinching.

"Oh fuck!" Jack cried. He took rapid breaths and his cock surged in my mouth, so I did it again and again until he flexed underneath me. "Gonna come."

I sucked harder, and he swelled and spurted into my mouth. I swallowed every drop, humming gratefully as I did.

I let him slip from my mouth, and he was the picture of satiation. His arms now hung limply at his sides, his face serene, and his gorgeous cock, glistening under the light, lay across to his hip. He chuckled lazily. "Wow."

I sat back on my haunches, proud that I'd rendered him undone.

He lifted his hand and beckoned me closer with his finger. So I put my hands on his knees and leaned in to kiss him, but he wrapped his arms around me and pulled me onto the couch with him. He lay us both down, somehow, like I weighed nothing, and he sighed contentedly. Then he kissed me, soft and lingering, before he pulled me in for a sleepy hug. Okay, so Jack was the cuddling kind. I smiled against his neck.

"Stay the night," he murmured.

I repressed a sigh. I didn't want to ruin this peaceful mood. But I also wouldn't lie. "I can't."

Jack took a deep, disappointed breath. "When will you say yes?"

"When it's right."

I felt his confusion in his embrace. "Is this not right?"

"This is very right."

"I'm confused."

I chuckled. "I can't stay tonight."

He pulled back, and the look on his face was indeed confused and, if I were being honest, hurt. "It's okay if you don't want to."

I put my hand to his cheek and kissed him. "I have another early start tomorrow."

"Oh, that reminds me. I have a meeting tomorrow. I can't come with you."

I pouted. "That's a shame. I enjoyed having you around today."

He brightened a little. "But don't forget dinner tomorrow. You'll need to be here early, if that's okay? I think the chef extraordinaire is getting here around six, so you might want to get here around six thirty."

"Should I bring anything?"

He shook his head and smiled. "No. But can I make one request?"

"Of course."

"Wear a bow tie."

"Is it a formal dinner?"

"No! Not at all. Very informal, in fact." He bit his bottom lip and adjusted my bow tie, which, with us lying down, wasn't easy. "I just find them really hot."

I chuckled at him. "Then I shall wear my finest."

He gave me his most genuine, eye-crinkling smile. But he never said anything. He just stared into my eyes and I couldn't look away. The intensity of his gaze, the fire burning behind them, made my heart gallop.

"I should go," I whispered, though my tone held no conviction. If he'd asked me to stay right then, I would have said yes. And I was sure he knew it too. He held the power to make me stay or leave, but he knew my wishes, so instead of getting what he wanted, he didn't push.

"Okay." He kissed me softly again. "Text me when you get back to your room. Or in the morning. Or both."

Reluctantly, with a willpower I didn't feel, I got up and fixed my clothes. I gave Rosemary a pat goodbye, and Jack stood on the porch to see me off.

"Oh, wait!" he said, dashing off the porch steps and running into the dark at the corner of his house. He came back a moment later with his hand behind his back and a goofy grin. He stood in front of me and presented me with a sprig of rosemary. "It's not a date without a flower. Though it's not really a flower, but it's symbolic of me and my dog, so it's kind of appropriate."

I took the rosemary, put it to my nose, and inhaled the earthy scent. "It's perfect."

"The date? Or the rosemary?"

I leaned up and kissed his cheek. "Both."

I drove away watching the man and his dog on the front porch, knowing that something had changed. Something irreversible. Something amazing. Something I wasn't sure I would ever get to have given we lived states apart, but out here in the woodlands of north-east Tasmania, I'd found something unexpected, something completely wonderful.

I FOUND NOTHING IN THE WOODLANDS I SCOURED THE NEXT morning. I found chrysalises of *Zizina labradus* and *Pieris rapae* as I had found in the other areas I'd searched when Jack was with me, but nothing on the Eltham Copper.

I ate just an apple for lunch, washed down with two bottles of water, and searched again until four, walking my usual grid, taking notes on observations, checking undersides of fallen bark and large rocks a thousand times. I'd done countless field searches, so I knew patience was key, though it was hard not to be disillusioned. And frustrated. I was running out of days on this trip. Maybe I should ask Jack to re-evaluate the mapped areas.

Mmm... Jack.

My mind kept wandering back to him, making it difficult to focus on my data. Knowing I was running out of days here and running out of days to spend with him exasperated my frustrations.

It was foolish, I told myself. I'd known him for a matter of days, and what we had together was no more than a holiday fling. Not that it was really a holiday; though I technically was on annual leave from my employer, I was still working.

I came to Tasmania in hopes of finding evidence, or proof at least, of a species of butterfly not yet documented. Instead, I'd found myself the kind of man I'd only dared dream of. Of course he had to live in a different state than me; it couldn't be that easy. I had no clue if he wanted to keep in touch when I went back to Melbourne or how we could even make it work. He said his last potential boyfriend didn't want long-distance, but he wasn't opposed to it. But just how did one factor in scheduled weekends, airports, and hired cars into a relationship?

God. Would he even want that with me? Just how far ahead had I let my heart wander unsupervised?

Like I said. It was foolish.

It was a lot of fun and incredible while it lasted, but foolish nonetheless.

I sighed as I loaded my storage tubs back into the Defender. I thought of Professor Tillman and how many decades he'd searched these areas and wondered if I was wasting my time. Had he simply handed the baton over for me to give decades of my life just like he had done? Was this now to become *my* life's work?

I allowed myself to wallow in my disillusionment on the drive back into Scottsdale. It was a pretty little town, and I could see why Jack loved it. Everyone knew him by his first name, said hello in the street. He could walk into any shop in the main street and have a chat with whomever was working. It was a world away from Melbourne. Not just the community feel, either. The cogs turned slower here, and that wasn't a bad thing.

It wasn't a bad thing at all.

Back at my room, I showered and sat on the bed with only a towel wrapped around my waist. I entered my data findings, or lack thereof, into my laptop. When that was done, I seriously considered going back into the bathroom and jerking off to stave off any embarrassing erections that seemed ever-present in the company of one Mr Jack Brighton. Especially if there would be other company attending.

But part of me didn't want to dull the intoxicating hold he had on me. He made my whole body sing, and I wanted him to get the full reward. So, ignoring my own needs, I got dressed for the evening. Jack had said it wasn't formal, but we weren't dining alone and there was a personal chef.

A personal chef? Who on God's earth hires a personal chef? Who even knows one to hire them?

I was excited and nervous for this evening. Each date had been better than the last, and I had no doubt I'd be staying the night soon. Maybe not tonight, but soon enough. I wanted to give myself to him in that way, and I knew in my bones it was only a matter of time. I wasn't joking when I'd said I'd stay when it felt right. Though it felt right every time I'd been there, and the sexual side of me wanted it badly. But my brain said not yet. I would stay the night only after he beds me, and I liked to sample the menu before savouring the main course.

So to speak.

And speaking of main courses, I should pick up a bottle of wine or two to take. I was musing over red or white, given I didn't know what we'd be eating, when I opened my door to leave.

Mrs Nola Bloom stood in front of me with her fist up, as if to knock. "Oh," she said, putting her hand to her heart. I must have given her a scare. But then she looked me up and down. "Oh, how lovely. Going out for dinner?"

"Ah, yes." She tried to look over my shoulder into my room, so I quickly stepped into the hall and closed the door behind me. "Just leaving now. Running a tad late," I added, an excuse not to get stuck talking.

"Where are you off to?" she asked cheerfully. Then she gave me a sly smile. "Dining with anyone I know?"

I cleared my throat. "Ah, no. It's a work dinner. Heading out of town." That wasn't technically a lie. I did see Jack for my work, and he did live out of town. "I best get going, actually. Was there anything I can help you with? You were about to knock?"

"Oh." She blushed, and I knew right then that she was merely here for the gossip on me. "Just checking to see if you needed anything. You've been getting in late every night and leaving early, I wondered if you wanted a decent, home-cooked meal. Or breakfast. It's part of the price you know. No extra charge."

I put my hand up. "No, but thank you. I've been very busy with work, but I'm managing to eat just fine."

"Right, then," she said, stepping out of my way. "Better let you go. Don't want to keep your dinner date waiting."

I repressed a sigh and considered correcting her—she was, after all, only after gossip to feed the town vines, no doubt—but thought it wasn't worth it. "Thank you."

I walked as fast as was polite and got into my Defender. Next stop was the local hotel, which also served as the local bottle shop. I was loath to walk into a small town country pub, but with no other choice, I parked out front and walked inside.

The smell of stale beer assaulted me first, all bar room chatter died away to leave an awkward silence, but the lady behind the counter smiled. "Hey love, what can I get for ya?"

I ignored the eyes I could feel on me from the men at the bar. "Do you have a wine list?"

She handed over a laminated sheet of paper, and not knowing the first thing about wines, I chose the most expensive white, and the most expensive red on the list.

"Sure thing. I'll just grab them from the storeroom. Be right back," the lady said. She darted through a door, leaving me alone with the five men at the bar who were all staring at me.

"Good evening," I said, uncomfortable under their scrutiny.

One man nodded, one man craned his neck to get a better look at me.

"Dressed a bit fancy for round here," one other man said. This is why I hated frequenting establishments like this. I didn't belong and was clearly made fun of by those who felt their masculinity needed protecting. They looked like they'd walked in from Blokey Farmers R Us, and I wondered if they got their flannel plaid shirts at a discounted rate for bulk buying.

The barmaid walked back in with two bottles in hand. "You fellas could learn a thing or two by dressing up a bit," she said with a wink to me. "George, I reckon Bev'd love to get dressed up to go out for dinner with you looking as sharp as this guy."

"Hey," the man I assumed to be George said. "I have a bow tie."

Another man snorted. "From when? Your wedding?"

The barmaid placed the bottles in brown paper bags in front of me. I handed over my card and paid, taking my wine as George was trying to remember the last time he wore suspenders.

I rushed to the Defender and don't think I breathed until I'd turned down Stanning Road. By the time I pulled up in front of Jack's place, I was feeling okay, until I saw another car parked at the side of his house. I'd forgotten he was expecting company other than myself. I took a deep breath, then another. My nerves were getting the better of me, and for a brief moment, I considered going home. But then I remembered he'd hired a personal chef and that I couldn't leave him in the lurch like that. So with another deep breath, I grabbed the wine and made myself get out of the car.

I walked up the porch steps and could hear chatter inside, and the smell of something cooking was wonderful. Rosemary met me at the screen door before I even knocked. She wagged her tail, and I heard Jack say "I'll get it" before he appeared at the door.

Jack's immediate smile when he saw me made me feel a thousand times better. He opened the door with a tea towel in his hand. "Hello," he said quietly, just for me. He leaned in and kissed my cheek. "You look great."

I looked down at myself. "Oh, thank you. I wasn't sure if the suspenders were appropriate, and the fellows at the bar seemed to think I was overdressed."

Jack frowned for a moment. "Did they say something to you?"

"No, it wasn't a problem." I brushed his concern off. I held up my purchases. "I brought wine."

"Please, come in," he said. He slid his arm around my waist. "There's people I want you to meet."

A man was at the dining table, and I wondered if he was the chef. He was average height, had a healthy tan and curly brown hair. "You must be Lawson," he said. There may have been a slight accent, possibly European, but I couldn't be certain. He extended his hand for me to shake.

"Yes, that I am." I shook his hand, and his smile widened.

"I'm Nico. Remmy's husband."

I turned to find her familiar face in the kitchen. Remmy was standing at the counter, and she quickly rounded the benchtop to put her two hands on my shoulders and kissed both cheeks. "Lawson, so nice to see you again. You met my husband, Nico?"

"Yes, thank you."

"And our chef for tonight..." Remmy waved her hand to the small child standing on a dining chair at the kitchen sink. He was peeling a carrot. "Luca, this is Lawson. Lawson, this is my son, Luca."

"Nice to meet you," I said.

Luca grinned. "Hello."

Jack chuckled beside me and put his hand on my back.

"Luca, tell Lawson who grew those vegetables you're chopping up?"

"I did!" Luca said. He was a gorgeous little boy with blond wispy curls and a cherub smile. "I did grow them all by myself and UncaJack said I could cook the dinner."

I found myself smiling, grinning even. I couldn't explain how relieved I felt. "That's perfect," I said.

Jack gave me a curious look, so I explained, "I was rather nervous about tonight. I wasn't sure what to expect when you said a personal chef." I almost laughed. "But this is... even better."

Jack went to say something, but Luca spoke first. "UncaJack, your carrot."

"Oh," Jack said, walking to stand next to Luca's chair. He smiled at me. "I'm being the apprentice today."

Remmy laughed. "Lawson, can I get you a drink?"

And so began what was to be a night of laughter and stories, surprisingly delicious 'ratooey,' and even better homemade apple pie. Remmy asked me a slew of questions, Nico was quite well versed in world economics, Luca asked me all about butterflies, and Jack's deep, throaty laughter was quite possibly my most favourite sound.

By the time Luca was falling asleep, Remmy and Nico thanked Jack for a wonderful night, bundled their little one into their car, and bid us both goodnight. The silence after they'd gone was a little loud, but when I turned to look at Jack, he was smiling at me. "You were great tonight."

"How was I great?"

He put his hand to my jaw and thumbed my cheek. "Luca thinks you're the best thing ever."

"He's a great cook. For a four-year-old."

"He is." He ran his hand down my neck and over my shoulder, down my chest. Then he said, "And while I thoroughly enjoyed their company, I missed talking to you. I heard you telling Remmy you didn't find anything in the field today."

"No, nothing."

Jack skimmed his hand back along my suspender, up my chest, and over my collarbone. His smile faded as he licked his bottom lip. "Will you stay for a little bit? You don't have to stay the night if you don't want. But please tell me you'll stay long enough for me to take you out of these suspenders."

"I thought you liked bow ties?"

"I do! Well, I did, but that was before you wore suspenders."

I chuckled at that. "Then I'll be sure to wear them more often."

He leaned in as if to kiss me, but stopped. His eyes flashed with concern. "Earlier tonight, when you bought the wine, you said some guys said something to you? Were you okay? Because on Date Number One, you were dead set against going inside."

"I haven't had the best of luck at such places." He frowned and waited for me to continue. "When I was at university, we were doing a field study in a small town. A few of my classmates thought a trip to the local pub was in order, and I guess a few of the locals thought the way I dressed was comical. Or offensive."

"Oh, Lawson," Jack whispered.

"I had a similar experience at a country pub in New South Wales as well. I believe I can safely assume I am the common denominator in all such examples, so I have avoided putting myself into that situation again."

His frown had deepened. "I'm sorry that happened to you. The guys here aren't like that, but next time I'll come in with you and introduce you, and I'll make sure they know you're with me." He slid both his hands around me protectively. "No one would say or do a thing to you."

I ran my nose along his jaw. "I can take care of myself." I squeezed his arse. "Though I'd prefer if you took care of me."

He hummed and moved his mouth over mine. I pulled back a little. "Jack?"

"Yes?"

"My suspenders are still on."

I SMILED AS I PULLED UP OUT THE FRONT OF THE PARKS AND Wildlife office. Jack was standing by a Rural Fire Services truck, talking to a man I'd not seen before, and Rosemary sat happily at their feet.

I'd only left his house eight hours before. Again, I was tempted to stay the night, but I didn't. He took my suspenders off all right. He wanted to take his sweet time with me, but I was so turned on, I begged for his mouth on me.

I swear he drove me crazy just because he could. Because he would rile me up to breaking point until I couldn't bear it another second, and I'd beg and curse at him until he gave me relief.

And I could honestly say, no one had ever taken such thorough care of me. No one had ever treated me like a delicacy. Not like Jack did.

He grinned as he noticed me, waving at me to join him. He was wearing work shorts and a Parks and Wildlife polo shirt, with work boots worn by tradesmen, but oh boy, he'd never looked better. Well, that's not true. He looked better last night when I'd returned the favour of fellatio. He'd looked unbelievable, then, with his head thrown back, his body taut, and muscles flexed as he came... and of course that memory made me blush.

I walked over to where he was still talking to a friend of his. "Good morning," I said.

Jack grinned. "Tony, let me introduce you to Lawson Gale. Lawson, this is Tony Wells. Tony is the local superintendent for the RFS. Lawson's here on official business for the University of Melbourne."

"G'day. Nice to meet you," he said, offering his hand to shake. He was an older man but fit looking. "Jack was just telling me he's heading up into Mount Stronarch today."

"Yes," I replied, hoping I didn't blush any further. "Jack coming with me has been mutually beneficial."

Jack tried not to smile, and I recalled my words.

Oh dear.

"I mean, he gets his work done, I get mine done. Separately. On the same trip, that's all."

Tony, thankfully, seemed unaware of my innuendo. He bent and gave Rosemary a pat on the head. "And Rosemary, CEO, overlooks everything."

Jack laughed. "She does."

After a few minutes of small talk, Tony bid us farewell, said it was nice to meet me, and went on his way. Jack watched the RFS truck pull away, then looked at me and laughed. "Jack coming with me has been mutually beneficial?"

I groaned. "I can't believe I said that."

He was still grinning when he collected his things out of his ute. He added them to my Defender. "You ready?"

"I am. Coffee's in the cup holders."

"Perfect," he said. "I'll just go tell Karen I'll be off then."

I opened the rear passenger door to the Defender and told Rosemary to climb up. I harnessed her in, and a moment later was joined by Jack. He slid an Esky onto the backseat next to Rosemary, climbed into the front passenger seat, and buckled himself in. "So?" he asked. "Where are we going to first, in this mutually beneficial arrangement?"

I slipped the Defender into first gear and headed out on the highway. "Do you plan to remind me of that often?"

He picked up his coffee. "Yes. It didn't help that you blushed."

"All I could picture was your face when you orgasmed last night."

Jack choked on his coffee. "Lawson!"

I shrugged. "I'm not at all embarrassed to admit it was highly erotic."

Jack brushed down his shirt, wiping away spilled coffee. "You're picturing it again right now, aren't you?"

I shifted in my seat. "It really was a spectacular sight."

He reached over and took my hand, lifting it so he could kiss my knuckles. "Do me a favour?"

"What's that?"

"Don't ever change."

After spending the whole morning searching the last areas Jack had marked as known locations of the *Bursaria spinosa* plant in the Mount Stronarch National Park, I'd not found a single trace.

Yes, the plant was there, but there was no trace of *Notoncus* ants. And the Eltham Copper couldn't live without them. There was no evidence of caterpillars, eggs, chrysalises... nothing.

I walked back to the Defender and put my gear in the back but took out the large folded map.

Jack came over. "What's wrong?"

"Something isn't right." I unfolded the map and laid it on the ground. I weighed each corner down with rocks and studied the area. "Either the area is wrong or Professor Tillman was wrong, or if he had seen them here, they're not here anymore."

"He did see them a long time ago," Jack reasoned. "What can change in a species' life cycle over fifty years?"

Well, when he put it like that... "Everything."

Jack's brow furrowed. "Maybe. But the fundamentals can't. Evolution takes longer than a few decades. So tell me, and I'm being serious, what can change? Or what is most likely to change in that time frame. Look at it objectively, Lawson. Break it down into categories and reassess your search."

I stared at him. My first reaction was to tell him not to tell me how to do my job. But he was right, and putting my ego aside, I took his suggestion as a learning tool instead. "Migration patterns. Their diet won't change. They can adapt, yes, but their food source of choice is *Bursaria spinosa* and that *is* available, so it stands to reason they would eat it if they were here. Migration patterns could change, yes. I can't dispute that, but there are no *Notoncus* ants."

Jack considered what I'd said. "Explain the triangle of dependency thing again."

I'd only mentioned that once to him before in the very beginning, and it thrilled me that he'd remembered it. "You have the Eltham Copper butterfly, *Bursaria* plants, and *Notoncus* ants. The butterfly will lay its eggs in the roots of the *Bursaria*. Larvae live within the underground nests of the ants and emerge at night to feed on the *Bursaria* leaves. The ants protect the butterfly larvae while they feed, and in return, the ants feed upon sugar secretions from the larvae. It's a rather complex plant-butterfly-ant-ecological interaction."

Jack tilted his head. "So, maybe it's not the habits of the butterfly that's changed. Maybe it's the ants."

Of course! I smiled at him. "You're very insightful."

He grinned. "Thanks."

"So, in your observations of the parklands in your jurisdiction, have you ever noticed ant colonies?"

"Only about two thousand. But I don't know what the *Notoncus* ant looks like."

"Oh, that's easy. The frontal *carinae* are weakly arched or straight along—"

Jack put up his hand to stop me. "Stop. You're speaking to a civilian. Are they black or brown? Big or small? Do they look like a green ant or a meat ant?"

I smiled at him. "Sorry. *Notoncus* ants are the small black or brown common ant found in open soil or under stones and logs on the ground. Found in your garden, parks, everywhere, really."

"Well, that narrows our search down to the entire state."

Now I laughed. "It does."

"Then why are you so happy?"

"Because I was getting frustrated and disheartened, but this gives my search a new focus."

He cupped my face in his huge hands and kissed me. "So tell me, where do you start from now?"

I sighed and enjoyed the moment before I kissed his palm and looked back down to the map on the ground. "I can discount what I've searched so far. There are no traces of the *Notoncus*. Maybe I should study more on their changing migration habits and favoured climes." I stared at Jack while my mind worked over some long-remembered facts.

"What?"

"You mentioned the *Iridomyrmex*."

"No, I didn't. I can't even say that word."

I snorted. "Also known as meat ants."

"Ah, those I did. Bastards bite."

My smile was slow spreading. "They also inhibit the morphological and behavioural adaptions of the *Notoncus*."

Jack blinked. "And that's important because...?"

"I noticed a few nests not far from the areas I've searched."

"And the *Notoncus* won't go near them?"

I shook my head slowly. "No, they won't."

"So, we need to find areas where there are no meat ants?"

I nodded. "Yes."

"How do you find that?"

"The *Notoncus* will live anywhere. Any type of soil, under rocks, bark, anywhere really. But the *Iridomyrmex* is soil-specific. You've been taking soil samples, yes?"

"Yes. As part of our ecosystem analysis. So we can see patterns of average climate changes, soil degeneration, moisture content, pH levels, vegetation quality, all at a glance."

I picked up the map and folded it. "You," I said, leaning up to kiss him quickly, "are a godsend." I opened the rear passenger door of the Defender and called for Rosemary to get in.

As I was harnessing her in, Jack asked, "Where are we going?"

"To your office. How many years' worth of data have you got?"

"Uh, our records go back fifty-something years."

I was grinning when I threw him the keys. "You drive. I need to research a few things on the way."

"Oh, you're back early," Karen said as we walked into the office.

"Yes, we need to access some archives," Jack said. "They're all electronic now, aren't they?"

"Sure," Karen said, quickly typing something into her keyboard. She turned the screen around, showing banks of data files all sorted by year. "Even photographs have been uploaded."

Jack clapped his hands together. "Excellent. That will save us about a decade." Then he stood back, making a point of looking at me. "Lawson here needs access. We'll be in my office. Could you please bring me the geotechnical reports we have on hand?"

"Sure," Karen said brightly. She gave Rosemary a pat with an odd kissy noise and spoke to her in a baby voice before disappearing down a hall.

Jack led the way into his office. "This way." He sat behind his desk and brought his computer to life. "Hey, Robert?" he called out.

"Yes?" came a voice, I assumed Robert's. A moment later, a short, middle-aged guy appeared in the door. "What's up?"

"Can you remember off the top of your head what type

of soil is predominant in the North Scottsdale Forest Reserve?"

Robert thought for a moment. "I think it's basalt, but I'd have to double-check. We ran that core sample last year, remember?"

Jack nodded. "Yeah, that's what got me thinking." Then he looked at me. "What type of soil did you say the meat ants like?"

"Typically clay or clayey soil."

And for the rest of the afternoon, we cross-referenced years of ecosystem data with photographs, soil reports, and rainfall data. Jack and I sat side by side and worked perfectly together. We almost had a conclusion down when there was a soft knock at the door.

Karen stood there smiling fondly at Jack. He cleared his throat and a light blush covered his cheeks. "Yes?" he asked.

"It's five o'clock," she said. "You two staying or calling it a day?"

"We're almost done here," I said.

Jack nodded. "We'll close up. Thank you, Karen." She waved us off, and she and Robert left, and the office was quiet. Jack tidied the piles of paper in front of us. "Wanna call it a day?"

"Yeah. I think we've got enough to know where to start tomorrow."

"Dinner at my place?"

"I don't want to keep relying on you to feed me," I said. "You've gone to a lot of trouble to impress me with dates."

"I promise there will be nothing fancy about dinner tonight."

"But I'll still be impressed? It is Date Number Five, I believe."

Jack laughed warmly. "I think so, yes."

We packed up our work and closed and locked the office. Instead of saying goodbye, I said, "See you at your place in half an hour."

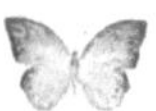

A QUICK SHOWER LATER, I WAS DRESSED FOR A CASUAL DINNER, and I was fairly sure how this night would end. I packed a bag of toiletries and supplies and some clean clothes for tomorrow I could leave in the car if needed. I called into the store on my way and bought some locally mulled honey cider, some local cheeses, apples, and crackers, and at the checkout there was a stand of small posies. They weren't anything fancy, probably lame by most standards, but I picked a yellow collection of daisies, and added them to my purchases.

Fifteen minutes later, I pulled up at the front of Jack's place. Leaving my overnight bag and clothes in the car—in case it didn't work out as planned—I grabbed my bag from the store and made my way up his porch steps.

He must have heard me pull up. "Door's open," he called out.

Rosemary met me with a wagging tail and toothy smile, and I found Jack in the kitchen. He wore old jeans and a faded T-shirt, bare feet, and he looked incredible. He was putting something into a basket.

"I bought these," I said, putting my purchases on his kitchen counter. Then I held out the flowers. "These are for you. You've given me a selection of flowers, so it was only right that I return the gesture."

"Thank you," he said, planting a soft kiss on my lips. He took the flowers with a heart-stopping smile and rummaged through a cupboard until he found what he was looking for. An old jam jar became a vase. He added some water and placed them on his kitchen windowsill. He looked particularly pleased.

I took the items I'd bought from the bag and showed him the cider, and he read the label of the cheese. "So perfect." He grabbed two glasses from a cabinet, a knife from the drawer, picked up the basket, and nodded toward the back door. "This way."

I'd never seen his backyard, so I followed him keenly. His yard was huge; a green field of mowed grass was like a shoreline to a rolling paddock of woodlands. There were shrubs and flowers and a clothesline in the corner with some tea towels swaying in the breeze, but that wasn't what captured my attention.

In the middle of his lawn, he'd laid a blanket, some cushions, and pillows. Jack put the basket he was carrying on the blanket and turned to me and waved his hand at the picnic. "Your dining table tonight."

I was certain I was grinning like a crazy man. I put my hand to my heart, feeling the tempo through my shirt. "This actually couldn't be more lovely."

He sat his huge frame down on the blanket and spread his long legs out, leaning back on his elbow. He patted the space beside him. "I believe you fit here."

I joined him on the blanket and took his face roughly in my hands. I planted a hard kiss on his lips. "I believe I do."

He opened the basket and took out a container of small sandwich triangles. "Hungry?"

I chuckled. "I haven't eaten sandwiches cut like this since I was at primary school."

Jack grinned and held one perfect white triangle out to me. "Vegemite? Or peanut butter?"

"Either is fine."

Rosemary came sniffing over and Jack roused on her. "She'll steal the peanut butter ones if you're not careful."

I patted the blanket between us and called her over. "Lie down," I said, and she did. I gave her a scratch under the ear, and Jack was staring at me, smiling.

He bit into his sandwich. "Are you here for me or my dog?"

"Both. And we shouldn't exclude her. I don't want her to think I'm the reason she's not getting one hundred per cent of your attention."

He ruffled the hair on the top of Rosemary's head, then he leaned in and gave me a peanut buttery kiss. He didn't say anything, just smiled serenely as he lay back down. He shoved a cushion under his head and ate another sandwich triangle. "So, how is this date stacking up so far?"

I looked around as evening settled over the countryside. The sun was behind the house, the sky was a palette of blues and oranges, the air was cooling down what had been a warm summer day. "It's kind of perfect."

He sighed happily. "Glad you like it."

Just then a common white butterfly flitted along the breeze near us. "Ooh," Jack said. "What kind of butterfly is that?"

"A *Pieris rapae*. Or a white cabbage butterfly."

"Is there anything you don't know about butterflies?"

I considered his question. "I think there are always things we don't know. But about the recognised species already discovered, I know all there is to know. Though I'd hate to think we've learned all we can."

He smiled up at the sky as though my answer truly pleased him, and he absentmindedly played with Rosemary's fur.

I poured us two glasses of the honey cider, and Jack

took one gratefully. Then I sliced the apple and cheese, opened the crackers, and fed him alternate mouthfuls. I liked taking care of him. He had, after all, provided four dates where he'd cooked for me, so it was the least I could do.

When we'd eaten enough of our picnic and the bottle of cider was almost gone, we discussed things such as biodiversity right down to music and movies. The sky was almost darkened through by then, but the backlight of the house cast enough light so we could still see.

Rosemary had wandered off after all the cheese was gone, and I lay down with my head in the crook of Jack's arm. We watched the sky become night, and the cider had given me a pleasant buzz.

Jack seemed content to just lay there, but I wanted more. I had come here with the intention of letting him take me to bed, but he seemed equally content to just lay under the stars with me in his arms. And it *was* perfect, but the urge, the desire in my blood wouldn't let me not try...

I turned in his arms and slid on top of him. I let my legs fall on the outside of his, and I leaned on one arm, my face just an inch or two from his.

His smile was surprised and warm. "Oh. Hello."

"I'm testing a theory."

He put his hand to my face and brushed my hair from my forehead. "And what's that?"

"That I can improve on perfect."

I kissed him softly at first, tilting my head just so, for the best angle. He opened his mouth for me, and I deepened the kiss, a charge of warmth filled me when our tongues touched. I put a hand beside his head so I could grind on him, needing the friction, needing to feel his strength underneath me.

He seemed to understand, or maybe he felt the same because he wrapped his arms around me. I was caged by his powerful hold, his hands were warm on my back, and I felt safe, adored, yet I was the one who set the tempo and rhythm.

I rubbed my erection against his through our clothes. The combination of both heat and hardness was both everything I needed and nowhere near enough. I rocked my hips, grinding on his cock, and he moaned into my mouth.

So I leaned back on my knees. He was a glorious sight. His shirt had ridden up enough to show me the skin above his waistband, his lips were flushed and swollen, he was breathless and beautiful.

I undid the button of his jeans and carefully unzipped the fly. I slid my hand underneath the elastic of his briefs and freed his cock. Sweet Lord have mercy, he was heaven on earth. His skin was silver in the moonlight and a drop of liquid shone at his slit. I leaned down and licked him, moaning at my salty reward.

"Oh, Lawson," he murmured.

I smiled at him and undid my pants, and his nostrils flared and his breath caught. It was intoxicating to be in such control of him. I drew out my cock and gave myself a few strokes while he watched. The look on his face was complete awe and pleading. I shuffled up until our cocks aligned, and when I took him into my hand and slid our cocks together, Jack's eyes rolled closed. He whispered, "Oh fuck."

It was kind of clumsy but he didn't seem to mind. In fact, he writhed with pleasure. His hands found purchase on my shirt, my neck, my face, and he brought me in for a hard, deep kiss. When we needed air, he pulled away. "God, you're gonna make me come."

I stroked our cocks harder, using our mix of precome as lube. "I wanted to have you inside me tonight, but I couldn't wait. I needed to feel you now."

He slid his hand along my jaw, his thumb at the corner of my mouth, and I took it in between my lips and sucked on it.

Jack flexed hard underneath me, and his cock surged in my hand. Pulse after pulse of come spilled from him, and the sight, the smell, tipped me over the edge.

The coil in my belly sprang, and the ache in my balls bloomed into pleasure, and I came on him. Jack held me while my orgasm rolled through me, and he caught me as I collapsed on top of him, utterly spent.

There were no other sounds but our breathing and the hammering of our hearts. Jack kissed the top of my head. "I think you kind of rewrote perfect."

I snorted indelicately, still too boneless to do much else. "I think that orgasm just rewrote my DNA."

Jack roared with laughter, the sound echoed loud and warm through my ear pressed to his chest. "That good, huh?"

The haze started to lift from my brain, and I realised I'd just done all that to him outside. Thank God he had no close neighbours. "Um, I've never had sex outside before."

He chuckled and gave me a squeeze. "Me either. I think there's a little devil inside you that likes to come out to play in the bedroom."

I lifted my head and looked around. "Strange bedroom."

He grinned, but then he turned serious. His eyes were dark and deep. "I will have you in my bedroom one of these days."

I put my fingers to his lips, then replaced them with my lips. "Yes, you will."

Before he could reply, I jumped up to my feet and tucked myself back in. "We should go inside and get cleaned up."

I started to pack up our picnic. He was quick to join me, collecting the blanket before leading the way back inside. "I can get you another shirt," he said.

"It's okay. I brought a change of clothes. And an overnight bag..."

It took him a second to catch on. "Are you staying?"

I nodded, and the grin he gave me was something I'll never forget. It made my stomach flip. "I'll just go grab it."

I took my bag from the Defender and Jack met me at the door. I stepped inside, he lifted my chin, kissing me sweetly, then he closed the door behind me.

CHAPTER ELEVEN
JACK

After we showered and dressed for bed, I pulled back the covers and hopped in, then extended my arm out in invitation. He was cute as hell in his chequered sleep pants and plain T-shirt, and he bit his lip as he climbed in beside me.

I turned the bedside lamp off and quickly pulled him into my arms. I snuggled in a bit and kissed the side of his head, and he relaxed immediately.

"Just because you're in my bed doesn't mean I'm going to ravish you," I whispered into his hair. "Not saying I won't either, but the DNA-rewriting orgasm you gave me half an hour ago kind of took the edge off."

I could feel him smile against my chest. "This is just as good. Actually, this is very good."

I sighed, and a contentment settled over me like sinking into a warm bath. Sleep was quick to come for us, and the last thing I remembered was thinking that morning sex sounded pretty damn good.

"Wake up, sleepy head."

I frowned and reached in the bed for Lawson, but I found only cold sheets. I cracked one eye open. He wasn't in bed, he was standing beside the bed with a coffee cup in his hand.

"I made this for you."

I groaned as I stretched out. The weight of my morning wood lay heavily across my hip. "What happened to morning sex?"

He laughed and put the cup on my bedside table. "I have butterflies to find."

It was hard to be frustrated or even disappointed when he was so damned cute. He was basically vibrating with excitement.

"I'll make toast," he said on his way back out the door.

I sat up and sipped my coffee with smiling lips. Mmmm, it was good. "I could get used to this," I mumbled.

"What was that?" he called out from the kitchen. There was a clanging of plates and cutlery.

"Nothing," I replied, smiling at the empty doorway. The truth was, I liked having him here. I liked the sound of someone else pottering about, and I really, *really* liked the fact it was Lawson.

After a bathroom stop, I made my way to the kitchen to find Lawson buttering two pieces of toast. He proceeded to spread one with peanut butter and one with Vegemite without asking me which I wanted and slid the plate toward me. He picked up his own coffee and sipped it. "Hope you don't mind. I made myself at home."

"Not at all."

I picked the peanut butter toast, Lawson took the Vegemite piece, and he smiled as he ate it. "So, will you be joining me again today?"

"Would you like me to?"

"Yes."

A thrill ran through me at his direct reply. "Then I shall join you."

Lawson put the plate in the sink as he finished his toast, and he wiped down the countertop. He was babbling because he didn't know if Rosemary usually had breakfast, but he didn't want to give her something she shouldn't have. He was trying to hide his excitement, but he really was buzzing. "Okay, okay," I said, washing my toast down with coffee. "I'll go get dressed."

He breathed a sigh of relief. "Thank you."

I walked up the hall to the bathroom and called out behind me, "And there's some of Rosemary's favourite treats in the container in the laundry."

When I was showered, shaved, and dressed for a day in the field, I found Lawson standing at the back of his Defender. Rosemary was sitting in the back next to the tubs, and he was running through his inventory with her.

"Your office assistant is a cutie," I said.

Lawson chuckled. "She is."

"I was talking to Rosemary."

Lawson's mouth fell open, but I could see it in his eyes when he realised I'd just called him a cutie. "I'm not her assistant."

"Of course not."

"That would assume her in a position of authority over me."

I leaned against the rear of his Defender and grinned at him. "Have a problem with that?"

He never missed a beat. "The only person I want in a position of authority over me is you." He raised an eyebrow. "I have every intention of that happening tonight, but if you don't help me get to North Scottsdale National Park in the next thirty minutes, it won't be happening at all."

I stood up straight and clapped my hands together. "Right. Who's driving?"

NORTH SCOTTSDALE NATIONAL PARK WAS NORTHEAST OF WHERE he'd searched before, and the only access in was a dirt road, as the name suggested, north of Scottsdale. The areas we'd marked out yesterday on Lawson's maps were estimated areas of silted clay on the town side of the mountain. Still classed as dense woodlands, the undergrowth was thicker. Theoretically, on paper, an Eltham Copper wouldn't inhabit an area like this. But Lawson was adamant. Everything pointed to this location. A combination of the correct soil types, average rainfalls, and temperatures suitable for *Notoncus* ants. From the photographs of the area taken over many years, there was proof of *Bursaria*, but we wouldn't know for sure until we got there.

But more than that, Lawson's gut told him this was where he would find it.

I helped him unpack his tubs and waited for him to get ready. "What will you do if you find a whole... colony of them?"

He didn't even look up. "Colony of what?"

"A colony of the Eltham Coppers that aren't actually anywhere near Eltham."

"A kaleidoscope."

"A what?"

"The collective noun for a group of butterflies is called a kaleidoscope."

"Oh." Then I thought about that. "That's actually pretty cool."

He looked up from his iPad and smiled. "It is."

"Who gets to name the collective nouns? Because they're all very clever. An army of ants, a pounce of cats."

"A flamboyance of flamingos," he added keenly.

"A flamboyance? Who the hell named that? Actually, who the hell *knows* that?"

"I know that."

"Yes, but you're a genius." Then I thought about that too. "Actually, a flamboyance of flamingos is pretty clever."

Lawson smiled. "An array of hedgehogs."

"A cackle of hyenas."

"An ambush of tigers."

"A parliament of owls."

"A congress of gorillas."

"Oooh, that's a good one," I said. "I take it I'm not the only one who finds the collective nouns interesting."

"I used to read them when I was little."

That made me smile. The thought of a little Lawson with his nose in a book, no doubt. "When did you catch your first butterfly?"

"I was four."

"Wow. That's young."

"My grandfather was an enthusiast. He gave me a catching kit for my fourth birthday."

"A catching kit?"

"Yes, you know the green and orange kits with a plastic cylindrical holding jar with a small net."

"Oh, I had one of those. I caught grasshoppers."

Lawson smiled as he scrolled through something on his iPad. "Then the following Christmas, he gave me a proper kit with an actual killing jar. I was very excited."

"About getting a killing jar?"

"It's not the most favourite part, and truthfully it's more humane than the old practices of stabbing an entomological pin through the thorax. And it's only a rarity that any individual butterfly is killed these days. We have such good technology for studying them that we don't need to." He smiled sadly. "I remember when I caught my first monarch, my grandfather made me put it in the killing jar. It was quick, but it was awful to watch. I cried for days."

"Oh, that's horrible." I went to him and put my hand on his arm. "I'm sorry."

He gave me an honest, appreciative smile. "Thank you. But I was five."

"And it drove you to spend your life dedicated to protecting the species?"

He laughed. "It wasn't quite that dramatic, but something like that."

I kissed his cheek. "So, if you do find one of these butterflies, what do you do?"

"Photograph, video, record data." He took a deep breath. "And make some phone calls."

"Is there a Butterfly Justice League or something that sends out a protective detail?" I joked.

He smirked at me. "There is. You're looking at it. Do I detect an inner nerd familiar with Justice League?"

I barked out a laugh. "There is a lot you don't know about me, inner nerd included."

He chuckled again. "I never was one to back down from a challenge." He scrolled and swiped at his iPad screen. "Later though, if you don't mind. Right now, I have much BJL work to do."

"BJL?"

He rolled his eyes. "Butterfly Justice League."

I laughed as I left him to do his thing. I went about my own data collection, taking photos and soil samples. He was quicker in his assessments this time. Still methodical and thorough, but there was a pressure and urgency now. The additional information gave him extra drive, and it compounded his disappointment when he found nothing.

He'd assessed three sites before lunch. He concentrated on the areas of preferred soil type, did his grid thing, and came up empty-handed.

His mood wasn't exactly a happy one as I offered him some lunch. He bit into his apple and frowned as he chewed. "I've found grass blues and common whites, so it's feasible the Eltham might be here."

I knew there wasn't much I could say that would make him feel any better, so I listened to him instead.

"Professor Tillman spent the better part of six decades looking for this particular species. You know what? I don't think I'm cut out for that. I understand patience is key, and I was foolish to think I could find it in a week."

"You've made great progress."

He took another bite of his apple, chewed, and swallowed it down. "Am I supposed to spend every weekend of the next fifty years searching every national park in the state?"

I shrugged. "Yes."

He went to reply but stopped, and his shoulders sagged. Instead he took a deep breath. "I guess so."

"You know it might not be all bad. You'll go back to Victoria but get to come back every weekend you can. I'm not opposed to seeing you on weekends."

Lawson opened his mouth, then promptly closed it. "I don't want to think about that just yet."

"About seeing me again?"

He shook his head slowly. "No. About not seeing you again."

I stepped in front of him and put my hand to his face. "I don't want to think about it either, but we're running out of days, Lawson." I kissed him softly. "When do you leave?"

"In three days."

I sighed, closed my eyes, and pressed my forehead to his.

Three days.

"This is kind of insane, isn't it?" I asked. "I've only known you for a few days."

"Five days. Six days if you include today." His blue eyes met mine, our foreheads still touching. "It's not insane. Insanity is a state of mind which prevents normal perception and/or behaviours."

I chuckled at his clinical reply, but he pulled back so he could see my face properly and shrugged. "Jack, what I perceive of you, and how I've conducted myself in your company is with full mental cohesion." His cheeks stained with colour. "And Einstein would have you believe that insanity is doing the same thing over and over again and expecting different results." He bit his lip and laughed at himself, I think. "But I don't want different results. I wouldn't change a thing."

I kissed him, deeper this time. It wasn't a kiss that was leading to something more. It was simply an I-have-to-kiss-you-right-now kind of kiss. He'd just professed how he felt to me, as only Lawson could. By giving me a clinical definition of insanity and quoting Einstein, of course.

I ended the kiss with a flutter of butterfly kisses against his cheek. "I wouldn't change a thing either," I whispered. "Except for the whole leaving thing."

"Except for that."

WE DROVE FURTHER NORTH, DEEPER INTO THE NATIONAL PARK, THE track now no more than a four-wheel drive fire trail. The terrain went from undulating woodlands to steeper, open forest. The canopy wasn't exactly touching but the under-growth was thicker and made for difficult assessment of possible activity.

But it didn't stop him. I doubted much would. Again, he did his own research and I did mine, though I could hear him whistling or muttering to himself periodically, so I knew where he was at all times.

But he found no *Notoncus* ants, and therefore, no Eltham Copper butterfly.

There was nothing at the second site we went to after that either.

Cloud cover was starting to roll in from the south, which troubled me. After Lawson had thrown his storage tubs into the back of the Defender, he pulled off his hat and wiped his sweaty forehead. "The humidity is rising."

I pointed to the sky. "Those clouds are coming from the south, too."

"And that's not a good thing?"

"Usually means storms."

He sipped his water bottle and moaned. "Please let it rain. It's so dry and hot. Never thought I'd miss Melbourne weather. This here never changes. Back home we'd be onto our third season of the day by this time: arctic southerlies, desert westerlies, monsoon rain. This here is just plain old hot and dry."

I put my hands out and felt the sweat roll down my

back. "This is a perfect summer day." Truth be told, it was stinking fucking hot and dry as a chip.

Lawson rolled his eyes. "What's your favourite season?"

"All of them."

"You can't love all of them."

"I do. In summer, I love winter. In winter, I love summer."

Lawson laughed and threw his water bottle at me. I caught it easily and finished it off. "We'd better get heading back. That road in isn't going to be easy going if this storm hits."

He nodded reluctantly.

"I'm driving," I announced as he buckled Rosemary into her seat harness. "There's something I want to show you. It's not far from here."

I followed the trail further north—the overhung branches scraped up the side of the Defender—and pulled off at a closed gate. "Is that private property?" Lawson asked.

"No. It's all Park's land, but we closed access. It's not locked, but it keeps the innocent people out. Plus, most people who use this road are heading through to Bridport. They don't stop along here." I got out and opened the gate, pushing it into the scrub to keep it open. I jumped back in and drove the Defender through and kept on going.

"Shouldn't we have closed the gate?" Lawson asked, looking behind us. "Rule of thumb in the country is, you leave gates as you find them."

I grinned at him. "I know, but we won't be long."

I drove for maybe a hundred metres, but with the winding and bumpy trail, it was slower going than I'd have liked. When I got to as far as the trail would take us, I stopped the Defender and undid my seatbelt. "We walk from here. It's not far, but we'll have to be quick."

Lawson was excited but cautious. "Should I be worried? Maybe my first impression of you being a serial killer was founded."

I laughed as I got out. I opened up the back door, unclipped Rosemary, and pointed directly ahead. "This way."

We'd only been walking for a little while to a symphony of birdlife when he asked, "How far are we going?"

"Almost there. See the clearing up ahead?" As we entered the clearing, I could see the sky had darkened considerably. "Okay, we need to be quick. This way."

I took us to the right of the clearing where a gully formed before the line of trees. I jumped down into the gully and back into the treed area and held onto Rosemary's collar.

"Why did you stop?" Lawson whispered.

"Look over there, twenty metres through the gully." I nodded ahead. "Listen."

He craned his neck and his brow furrowed as he concentrated. I could hear it, and I waited for him to. His eyes flashed to mine. "What the hell is that?"

The noise was very distinct. Growls, hisses, screams, and screeches. It sounded like there were younglings. My grin got wider. "We can look. But we can't get too close."

Lawson's gaze searched and searched, and I could see the moment he found them because he smiled. "Tasmanian devils."

I nodded excitedly. "And joeys. They're very vocal."

We could see two baby devils rumbling and jumping on each other. They were the cutest things. Black with bands of white across the chest, little tails, and huge jaws.

"There's been a den here for years. The same female comes here to have her babies year in, year out. We've been keeping an eye on them. The bitch has been tagged, but she's healthy, her joeys are healthy, so we leave them be."

Then a third joey pounced onto his siblings and more growling and snarling ensued, followed by more rumbling and rough-play.

I took out my phone and snapped photographs. "I'll send these to the STDP."

"What's the STDP?" he asked, not taking his eyes off the playful joeys.

"Save the Tasmanian Devil Program," I explained. "We give them any information we can. They do some great work."

"Where's the mother?" Lawson asked.

"She'd be sleeping, probably. With one eye open on this lot, I'd say. They're nocturnal mostly, but will bask in the sun." I watched the joeys play. "Cute, huh?"

"Oh, Jack, they're remarkable."

It was silly how his words could cause my heart to skip a beat. But his love for and understanding of what I did made me happier than I could explain.

He put his hand on my arm as he took a small step and leaned so he could get a better look. Thunder rolled overhead, and I looked up at the sky. "Come on. It's time we weren't here."

We climbed up the embankment of the gully, and I headed left, back toward the way we'd come. I only got a few steps with Rosemary when I realised Lawson wasn't with me. I turned to find him stopped, staring in the other direction.

"Lawson, we gotta get going."

Without looking at me, he put his hand up. "Wait one sec..."

I barely heard him over the rumble of the sky. "Lawson—"

But he was already walking in the wrong direction, over to the far edge of the clearing. He stopped and looked up. "What direction is this?"

"Uh, north, I think. Why?"

He was inspecting something near the trees. "Jack! Jack, come quick!"

I ran over to him. He was now crouching down, lifting the bottom of a shrub off the ground.

A *Bursaria* shrub.

He was looking at ants...

Oh, holy shit.

Then he put his hands down and leaned real low to look up under the leaves of the shrub.

Ants quickly crawled over his hands. "Lawson, the ants..."

"They don't bite," he said absently, not even looking. Then he lifted the bottom branches of the shrub and gently poked a pen into the roots of the plant. And as if right on cue, a little copper coloured butterfly flittered out and landed right near his hand. Then another, then another.

Lawson fell back in shock, scrambling to stay off his arse, and put his hand to his mouth, his eyes wide. He glanced at me. "Jack."

I nodded.

One butterfly took flight again, skipping across the air before landing back in the shrub. Lawson took his phone out and his hands were shaking so badly he could barely scroll to his camera. He took some photos, then had the presence of mind to switch his phone to video mode. He filmed it, this tiny little creature, as it stretched its wings and skittered to a different leaf.

Thunder cracked through the sky just above our heads, scaring the crap out of both of us. Rosemary whined. "Shit that was close. Lawson, we have to go. Now. We can come back tomorrow, first thing. I promise."

He nodded, took a dozen photos of the ground, the shrub, the clearing, then another quick succession of shots of the butterfly, just as the rain began to fall.

"Lawson, now. Or that road will be impassable."

He spun around and got to his feet. The rain had begun to flatten his hair and made his shirt cling to his chest, but his grin was huge. "I found it."

I grabbed his arm and pulled him along with me. "Come on."

Together, along with Rosemary, we ran back to the Defender. I jumped into the driver's side and Lawson jumped into the back with Rosemary. I threw the Defender into reverse, and looking over my shoulder, I reversed the whole way out down the trail to the gate.

Lawson had harnessed Rosemary in, then jumped out to pull the gate shut. When he got into the front passenger's seat, he was still grinning. Actually, he was buzzing. He stomped his feet and did some crazy laughing dance in his seat. Laughing with him, or at him, I shifted the gears into first and started down the trail. "Seatbelt," I said gently, as he obviously hadn't remembered.

He clicked his belt in. "Jack, I found it!"

"Lawson, it was incredible. And it's so small. I wasn't expecting it to be so small."

"I know!" he said, nodding excitedly. He was still bouncing in his seat. "Oh my God, I need to call the professor." He pulled his phone out and did a quick scroll of the photos again. His hands were shaking. The energy he was giving off was incredible. Even Rosemary was standing on the backseat smiling at Lawson. He took a deep breath and tried to calm himself before he dialled the professor. He hit Call, put the phone to his ear, looked at me, and grinned. "Professor Tillman? This is Lawson Gale." I couldn't hear exactly what the professor said, but Lawson then added, "You'll never guess what I found today."

There was a second of silence, then I could hear the professor's muffled voice, and Lawson laughed. His excitement was so contagious, even I was smiling despite the torrential rain and shitty dirt road.

"I'll send you some photos, to the email you gave me. You can confirm, but I'm confident it's it. Looks like the Eltham Copper but has five small dots on the hindwing with tapered black edges."

He saw all that detail?

Lawson laughed. "Yes! Yes! I know! It's so remarkable. We're just returning to town now. The weather has turned bad, so once I get to my laptop, I'll forward you what I have... Yes, we're heading back up in the morning, weather permitting, of course."

They spoke briefly before disconnecting the call. He looked at Rosemary, then at me, his grin still firmly in place. "I found it."

I laughed. "So you keep saying."

"I can't believe it."

"Can I ask something?"

"Yes, of course."

"What do butterflies do when it rains?"

He laughed. "They hide. Under leaves, bark, logs, large rocks, anything they can find. That's what they were doing when I interrupted them: trying to get out of the coming rain."

As we came down the mountain, the Defender slipped on the dirt road a few times, and I sighed with relief when we reached the tarmac. Lawson seemed oblivious, because he looked at me and smiled. "Can we please go past my place so I can grab my laptop and a change of clothes?"

"You don't want to just stay there?" Then I added, "With me. I mean I'll come to your place with you."

"I'd rather not. Mrs Bloom is nosey, and I love the privacy your place provides." He waggled an eyebrow at me. "I have plans for tonight, remember?"

"Should we get some wine? I think celebrations are in order, don't you?"

His grin hadn't waned one bit. "I think wine and cele-brations are definitely in order."

AFTER LAWSON HAD RACED INTO THE B&B, HE CAME BACK OUT with a laptop bag and jumped into the Defender, out of breath and rain running down his face. He looked at the clothes sticking out the side of his bag, then smiled at me. "I multitasked."

I laughed and pulled the Defender up in front of the hotel. "Won't be one sec." I braced for the deluge of rain, though it had eased up a little. It was more wind now. I raced for the front doors of the hotel and ordered two bottles of the same wine Lawson had brought home the other night. When I got back into the Defender, he had his phone pressed to his ear and his smile was gone.

"I am advising of my find, not to gloat, but out of professional courtesy. I most certainly will not be sending photographs until Professor Tillman has confirmed what we both suspect is a new species."

Okay then. Someone was having their arse handed to them. I had to admit. Lawson was sexy as hell when he was pissed. I hated that some jerk had ruined his mood, though. It was a monumental day by anyone's standards, and some dickhead was trying to bring him down.

"I'm technically on leave until Monday, so you can do whatever it is you see fit... By all means, please do. You can also tell him to expect a full report from me, which I'm certain he'll love. I'll make a point of dedicating an entire subsection to you and how you've just requested to go against protocol... That's fine, Professor Asterly, but after all the years we've worked together can you tell me what I am?"

Lawson tilted his head as he listened. "Yes, well. That too. But more than being a pain in your arse, I am unbiased to the facts, and I won't be manipulated. It's unfortunate that your emotional reaction is to be hurt, but I can't be responsible for how you feel, Professor... No, that won't be necessary. I'll be in contact with him directly. He can let you know when I will return."

I was almost home by the time he got off the phone. Lawson growled in frustration. "That man is an ignoramus."

"Your boss, I take it?"

"Yes. Ugh. I shouldn't have called. I only did so as a gesture of goodwill, and he seems to think himself invited to come down here. No doubt to have his name associated in some way."

I drove into my driveway and turned off the engine. "Lawson, forget about him. Until he gets here, *if* he gets here. Enjoy tonight, get all your data on file, send it to

Professor Tillman, then tomorrow we can go back and you can get all the data you need." I just wanted to see him smile again. "Wanna go in and upload the photos? Get a closer look?"

It worked because his lips twitched until he smiled. "Yes, please." He leaned forward and looked up at the low, grey sky. "That looks like it's set in."

"I can check the meteorology site. See if you can get back up there tomorrow." From the look he gave me, I was pretty sure he was going anyway, rain or not. "Come on." I opened the door and got out into the wind and rain. I unharnessed Rosemary while Lawson made a run for the door with his laptop.

Inside, we dried off with towels. It wasn't exactly cold, but the temperature had dropped some with the storm. "You warm enough?" I asked.

He nodded, but it wasn't convincing. "I might get changed, is that okay?"

"Sure. I'll see what I can organise for dinner."

When he came out, he was wearing his chequered sleep pants and a T-shirt. He looked completely comfortable and at home. It took the breath from my lungs.

He looked down at himself. "This okay?"

I nodded stupidly. "More than okay."

He looked into the pantry where I stood with the door open. I picked up a packet of couscous. "Well, I can do a Greek lamb and couscous thing, or—"

"Tomato soup and toasted cheese sandwiches," he said, reaching in and taking a can of tomato soup.

I chuckled. "You're a man after my own heart." I took the can from him and kissed his cheek. "You go start on your photos. I'll fix dinner."

He stood in my kitchen, looking all kinds of adorable. "I *will* cook for you one day."

I barked out a laugh. "Yes. Yes, you will."

So he busied himself in the lounge room while I got changed into my PJ's too, heated the soup, and made some toasted sandwiches. The wind howled outside, splashes of inconsistent rain hit the roof, thunder and lightning boomed through the sky. But inside was warm and dry and peacefully, blissfully quiet.

When I walked out with his soup and sandwich, I found him sitting on the floor, leaning against the couch, laptop on his legs, and his eyes trained on the screen with Rosemary asleep against his leg.

It stopped me where I stood. My heart squeezed and my mouth went dry.

Such a simple thing, really. A truly domestic sight that sent a pang of longing through to my core. I never realised it was what I wanted. It never occurred to me that I should yearn for something so basic. Sure, I'd had times of loneliness, but I never thought to myself, *gee, I wish I had someone who would sit on my floor in his pyjamas and do his work with my dog curled up at his side...* well, until I saw it. Now I'm pretty sure I wanted nothing else.

Lawson looked up at me expectantly, oblivious to the profound realisation I'd just had.

I held up his plate. "Dinner's ready. Want it down there or at the table?"

He smiled and my breath caught. Man, I was in trouble. "Down here, if that's okay."

We ate in the lounge room, he on the floor, me on the sofa behind him. The soup was a perfect dinner, homely and all comfort as the weather made a fuss outside. Lawson did what he needed to do while I sat and watched him work. I also played with the hair at the nape of his neck, relishing the wake of goosebumps that followed each trail of my finger. When he declared he'd done all he could do, he pounced on me.

He straddled my hips, resting his arse on my legs, and he planted both hands on either side of my face and kissed me.

And holy hell, it was some kind of kiss.

He rocked his hips back and forth seeking friction. "Jack." He breathed the word into my mouth. "Take me to bed."

I was going to pick him up—I could have easily—so he could wrap his legs around me, but he climbed off and stood in front of me. And waited.

I stood up to my full height, so close our chests touched, and I slid one hand around his jaw and crushed my mouth to his. I could feel his erection poking into my thigh, and he slid both hands over my arse and pulled our hips together. He broke the kiss. "Jack. Bed."

He was getting impatient. And I had to admit, I really liked a bossy bottom. It turned me on to be with a man who wasn't afraid to tell me what he wanted.

I took his hand and led him down the hall to my room. I left the lights off, I could see him just fine. I pulled his shirt over his head and kissed down his shoulder. "You want me inside you?"

He moaned quietly. "Yes." He craned his neck as I kissed back up to his jaw. "God, yes."

I slid my fingertips under the elastic of his sleep pants

and pushed them over his arse and whispered in his ear, "I want to taste your arse first."

"Oh god," he breathed.

I gripped his erection and gave him a few languid strokes. "Get on the bed, Lawson. Face down."

He did as I instructed, stepping out of his pyjama pants and kneeling on the bed before slowly lying down. Lightning cracked outside, illuminating the room. God, he looked so amazing. I stepped over to the bedside table and threw a condom and the bottle of lube onto the bed beside him. He fisted the duvet in anticipation.

I knelt on the bed and pushed his legs apart, running my hands up the back of his thighs and over his arse. I leaned in and breathed a slow warm breath over his hole.

"Jack, fucking hurry up."

I loved that he only swore during sex. But apparently me taking my time with him was not on his agenda. "I can't wait to hear your filthy mouth," I murmured against the skin at the base of his spine. Thunder boomed outside and the static in the room amped its charge.

"My mouth isn't filthy," he replied on a whisper. There was no conviction in his voice.

I spread his arse cheeks and ran my tongue up his crack, pressing into his hole. He fisted the sheets at his sides and raised his arse for me. "Oh, fuck!"

I smiled victoriously. "You like that?"

"Yes, please more."

Thunder rolled far off and lightning lit up the sky through the window. His arse was perfect, illuminated by the storm outside. Pale and round cheeks and a perfect, tight hole. He wanted more, so I gave him exactly that. I fucked him with my tongue and he grunted with every pass. But it soon wasn't enough.

"More."

I flipped the lid on the lube and poured a decent drop down his crack, and slipped my finger inside him.

"Mmm," he hummed, rocking his hips for me.

"You love it, don't you?"

"God yes. More."

I added a second finger and curled them, searching for his prostate.

"Oh fuck," he growled.

There was another curse word. I'm sure he had more in him. So I played with him a bit, stretching him, testing his patience while turning him on. He slipped his hand under his hips, no doubt to grab his cock. "I need more," he said with a tortured groan. "I need your cock inside me."

There was nothing like hearing him beg.

I pulled out my fingers and he responded by raising his hips off the mattress so he could jerk himself. God, he was so hard and so desperate for it.

I rolled a condom down my length and slicked myself up with lube, then added more to his arse. He hummed an impatient sound. "Jack, I need you now."

I knelt behind him and swiped the head of my cock up and down his crack. He rocked back and forth, wanting, needing. "This what you want?"

"Fuck yes."

I did it again, this time pressing in a fraction, only to pull away again, giving him another swipe.

Lawson pushed up so he knelt on the bed and turned his head. An angry, frustrated flush covered his cheeks. "I need you to fuck me. So quit playing with my arse and bury your cock in it."

And there it was.

That filthy fucking mouth.

I put one hand on his shoulder and pushed him back down on the bed, leaving his arse raised. With my other hand, I lined my cockhead to his hole and pushed in.

There was no filthy mouth now, just short gasping breaths that became a long keening sound the deeper I pushed in. "That what you wanted?"

He cried out underneath me. "Yes, yes. Fuck yes."

I pulled out a little, only to push back in deeper, beginning to slowly thrust into him. He gasped and grunted with each breath, the most wonderful sounds. When I was buried to my balls inside him, I stayed there. I ran my hands over his shoulders, down his back, massaging him as I gave him time to adjust. He responded by rocking his hips, wordlessly asking for more.

"Oh God," he murmured. "You're so big."

"And you can take every inch," I said, thrusting into him sharply.

He let out a long low groan, but raised his arse. "I can feel your pulse inside me."

Oh fucking hell. His dirty mouth would be the end of me.

"Jack," he moaned. "Fuck me."

I thrust into him again and again, listening to his whimpers and moans, his whispered pleas for more. I was so close to coming. He felt so damn good, his arse was so warm and slick, but I needed to feel his mouth as well.

"I want to see you." I slowly pulled out. "Roll over."

He quickly did as I told him to and lifted his knees to his chest. I pushed into his welcoming heat in one thrust, watching his eyes flutter closed. His mouth gaped open at the intrusion.

I crushed my mouth to his, tangling my tongue against his. Lawson's hands went to my hair and then my jaw, and he held my face right where he wanted me.

He kissed me deeply until he needed air. "God, you're so far inside me."

Lawson's words made my balls ache. I slammed into him, and his neck corded with strain. I grunted as I spoke. "If you keep talking like that, you'll make me come."

"Fuck yes." Lawson's arms tightened around me. "So good, Jack. This is what I need."

"You need to come first," I said, pushing up to lean on my left hand. I took his cock into my right hand and pumped him. Precome pulsed from his tip, so I ran my thumb through it, slicking his shaft.

"Oh fuck," Lawson cried out. His hands fisted the sheets at his side. I drilled into him, fucking his arse as I pumped his cock. Then his eyes went wide and his mouth fell open. His whole body went taut, and his cock throbbed in my hand before shooting stripes of come across his belly as lightning struck somewhere close.

I pushed every inch into him, spreading his legs wider and fucking his mouth with my tongue while he rode out his orgasm on my cock.

But the need, the urgency was gone, and I could take my time now. When he sagged, sated and smiling, I let go of his cock and leaned over him. I thrust slower, deeper now his body was pliable and relaxed. He put his hand to my face and we kissed as I made love to him. Rocking slowly, savouring every second of being inside him. My climax built, slow and steady, and Lawson held my face as I came.

He gasped as I filled the condom deep within him. "I can feel every pulse," he whispered, his eyes wide with wonder. Then he kissed me as my orgasm rocketed through me.

I collapsed on top of him and he held me tight as my breathing returned to normal. What I experienced wasn't just a physical release. Something inside me shifted as well. I was pretty sure my heart had fallen for him.

I could feel his heartbeat against my chest, and I wondered if—I hoped—he felt the same.

Lawson's fingers traced patterns across my back, and I slowly pulled out of him. I rolled out of bed to discard of the condom, and he pulled up the blanket. When I came back, he smiled at my naked form and held the blanket open for me. I climbed in and he settled himself into the crook of my arm. I kissed the side of his head. "Want a shower?"

"No. Just want to lie here. Fall asleep with you."

I pulled away, and with my fingers under his chin, I tilted his face so I could look into his eyes. "Are you staying the night?"

He smiled at me. "Is that a problem?"

I tucked him back into my arms and snuggled in. "No problem at all."

He was quiet a minute, but I could tell by his breathing he was awake. "So um, sex with you is amazing."

I barked out a laugh. "I could say the same to you."

"Yes, you could."

I was still grinning. "Sex with you is amazing."

He sighed happily. "Thanks."

I kissed his forehead again as the rain fell outside. "It was better than amazing. You're better than amazing."

He froze before he lifted his head to look at me. "So are you."

His face was ethereal in the silver of the darkened room. I swallowed hard. "Tell me I'm not alone in what I feel."

He studied my face, searching for what, I don't know. "What do you feel?"

"That this is something special. That whatever this is shouldn't end when you go back to Melbourne."

His eyes bore into mine. "I don't want this to end."

"Me either."

"Promise me we'll work something out."

Thunder boomed outside, lightning split the sky as the storm raged. Outside, a frenzy whipped around us. Yet I'd never felt more calm, more peace than I did in that moment. "I promise." I fluttered my eyelashes on his cheek, making him smile.

"You're the first person to ever give me butterfly kisses."

"Really? But you're a butterfly expert."

He kissed me softly, lingering, but pulled away with a sigh as he settled his head on my chest. "I came to Tasmania in search of an elusive species. And I found it. But never in my wildest dreams did I expect to find you. And I believe I found a type of butterfly that exists only in my belly which only makes itself known when I think of you. Though sometimes they lodge in my throat when I see you and they make breathing somewhat difficult."

I smiled at his way with words, tightened my hold on him and grinned at the ceiling. "Me too."

With Lawson in my arms and the storm raging outside, my body sated and feeling more content than I could ever remember, I fell asleep with a happy heart and what could possibly be a permanent smile.

I woke to a panic. My phone was ringing, my pager was beeping, and Rosemary was barking. I sat up, grabbed my phone to see it wasn't even five a.m. Lawson was now awake, sitting up beside me, looking confused and disoriented. I answered my phone.

It was my rural fire inspector, Tony Wells. His voice was loud and brusque.

"Jack! We've got a Category Three bushfire. She's in Oxberry. 10k northeast of Scottsdale, but mate, she's heading straight for you."

CHAPTER TWELVE
LAWSON

Jack shot out of bed. "Lawson, you need to get up. Get dressed. We need to leave."

"Why? What's happening?" I asked, getting out of bed. I rummaged through my bag and found some briefs and my jeans. I pulled on a shirt and found some socks.

Jack quickly dressed in long pants and a T-shirt. He pulled on his work boots. "There's a bushfire. I have to go."

"Where to?"

"RFS headquarters. In town."

He was starting to scare me. "Where's the fire?"

"Ten kilometres northeast of town. Oxberry Forest Reserve. Must have been a lightning strike."

I stopped and stared at him. "Jack, the butterflies..."

He let his hands fall to his sides and gave me a sad smile. "Hopefully we'll have it under control by the time it gets that close."

I shook my head. "But Jack—"

"I need you to go into town. Scottsdale has a fire exclusion zone surrounded by kilometres of cultivated farmland. You'll be safe there. Head straight for the community hall.

It's the town's evacuation centre. That's where everyone will be. I need you to go there. Take Rosemary. I don't want her to freak out here by herself."

All I could do was stare.

Jack came over to me and put his hands on my shoulders. "Can you do that?"

I nodded. "I'm scared."

He gave me a quick hug and kissed the side of my head. "I know. But we'll have it all sorted soon. You'll be fine. Just stay in town with the others. The evac centre gets all the newest updates, so you'll know everything as it happens. But if you want to leave for Launceston, go now."

I shook my head. "No. I'll go to the evacuation centre." I knew his house was on the opposite side of town to the forest reserves, but I had to ask. "What about your house?"

"The house'll be fine. Well, if the fires reach here, it means all of Scottsdale is gone, and if that happens, my house will be the least of my worries."

"What about you?"

"I'll be fine. I've done this a hundred times before."

"Jack…"

He lifted my chin and kissed my lips. "I need to go."

He gave me a butterfly kiss that stole my breath. His lip quirked in a smile before he went for the door, but I stopped him. "Jack. Be safe."

He smiled at me. "Always." Then he stopped and gave Rosemary a pat. "You stay with Lawson, okay sweetheart?" He gave me a final look. "Go find Remmy. She'll be at the evac centre feeding people. It's what she does."

And with that, he was gone.

I stood there until I couldn't hear his ute in the distance anymore, frozen to the spot. Rosemary whined at me and it kicked me into gear. I pulled on my boots, grabbed my jacket and my phone, waited for Rosemary to join me, and pulled the front door shut behind me.

"Come on, girl," I said, calling for her to get into the Defender. I didn't bother with the harness. I let her sit in the front passenger seat. I needed to keep her close. I threw the Defender into first gear and roared my way into town.

Scottsdale was well and truly up and awake, even though it was barely five thirty in the morning. Cars, trucks, and people were all out, and already there was a line of cars at the community centre. I slowed down, someone was directing traffic, but I didn't stop.

I couldn't.

I turned off the main street onto North Scottsdale Road and drove like a bat out of hell in the direction of the bushfire.

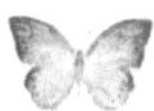

I DROVE BY CARS WHO FLASHED THEIR LIGHTS AT ME, BUT I DIDN'T care. I couldn't just sit there and do nothing. I'd finally found a species of butterfly never seen before, and I couldn't allow it to be wiped off the face of the planet. Not without trying.

I barely slowed down to take the dirt road turn off, and I put my left hand out to brace Rosemary as she tried to keep her balance on the seat. "Almost there," I told her.

As day broke, the clouds were still dark and heavy but the rain had stopped. I could see now why Jack was concerned about the roads after the deluge we got yesterday because they were in pretty bad shape.

The ride was bumpy and we jostled around a bit and slid in the mud, but I could handle it, and the Defender was made for this. I sped past the areas I'd searched the day before, took one corner too fast and slid across the slick muddy road. Instead of hitting the brakes, I accelerated and overcorrected through the turn and we fishtailed out of what could have been a hairy situation.

"It's okay, we're good," I told Rosemary. Or myself. I wasn't sure at this point. My heart was in my throat.

I went past the spot we'd had lunch yesterday and took the Defender onto the road where Jack had taken me. The trees were rain-heavy and scraped up the sides of the Defender, and when I came to the gate, I didn't stop.

I simply ploughed right through it.

"Sorry," I told no one. I'd be up for a new gate. *If Jack forgives me. If I make it out of here alive.*

Bloody hell, Lawson. You get yourself into some crazy predicaments.

I pulled the Defender up to a stop at the end of the trail, and leaving my door open, I raced to the back and opened the rear door. All my plastic tubs filled with files and papers and equipment were there, somewhat tossed about. I picked up the closest one, pulled the lid off, and upended the contents onto the floor of the Defender.

I grabbed the now-empty container, Jack's shovel, which he'd left with me, and ran for the *Bursaria* bush. Rosemary ran along with me, and I wasted no time. I dug the shovel into the ants' nest, putting my foot on the shoulder of the blade and dug it into the nest as far as I could. I levered out a chunk of the nest and dumped it, mostly intact, into the tub.

Ants scurried en masse, but I picked up the tub and ran back to the Defender. I slid it into the back and quickly got the lid closed and locked it. I took another tub, upended the barometric equipment into the back of the Defender. Then I did a second tub, which had pruning gear in it, snatched up a pair of secateurs, and ran back to the *Bursaria* bush.

I searched the underside of the shrub and carefully snipped some branches off where butterflies were seeking protection from the weather underneath. I gently placed them in one tub and secured the lid.

I looked up at the sky then, and in that one moment I took to think, I heard it.

It was distant, far off but frightening all the same.

It was a quiet roar, like a background noise. Rumbling and angry. It wasn't thunder.

It was fire.

I had no clue how close it was. But there was something missing too. There were no birds. Yesterday they'd been so loud, but now there was nothing. I looked up at the sky again. I couldn't see smoke yet, but I guessed if I could see smoke this close, it would be too late.

Realising I was out of time, I picked up the shovel and edged it into the soil around the circumference of the shrub. I needed to try and be gentle, but the urgency didn't permit it. With as much force as I could muster, I pushed the shovel in, as careful of the roots as I could be, trying to get underneath the bulk of root growth. When I'd levered it the best I could, I reached into the stalk of the shrub and pulled.

I ended up on my arse, but the shrub had dislodged and a kaleidoscope of butterflies took to the wing. Some resettled, some fluttered away. "I'm sorry. I'm sorry," I told them. "I'm trying to save you."

Picking up the empty tub, I plonked the roots of the shrub into it and carried it back to the Defender. I slid it onto the floor of the backseat, trying to do as little damage as possible. I raced back to where the first tub and shovel were still lying on the ground, and Rosemary leapt along beside me.

"Your father's going to kill me," I told her.

I collected the tub with the butterflies in it, then everything else I could carry and hauled them back to the Defender. I loaded it all in and shut the back door. I closed the rear passenger door, cringing as some of the *Bursaria* got caught in the door.

I turned to call for Rosemary, but she wasn't at my feet. I scanned the clearing and found her at the edge of the gully.

"Rosemary, come!" I yelled. She didn't move. I patted my thighs and whistled. "Rosemary!" She looked at me, so I knew she'd heard, but she wasn't coming. "Goddammit, we don't have time for this."

Ignoring the huge plume of black smoke billowing into the sky, I ran over to her, fully intending to grab her by her collar or the scruff of her neck if I had to. But as I got closer, she disappeared down into the gully.

"Rosemary!" I yelled, anger and impatience in my tone.

As I got to the embankment, I saw where she'd gone. She was standing near the Tasmanian devil den. "Rosemary, come on."

She barked at me.

"Are you Lassie?"

She wagged her tail.

No one was ever going to believe me.

I ran down the embankment, and as I got closer to her, she started to dig at the den. Then she barked in it.

Something hissed back at her, which couldn't ever be a good thing, and she backed up. One of the little devil joeys came out, gnashing its teeth in a half ounce of might and fury.

"Oh, Jesus."

I couldn't leave it here to burn to death. I didn't know much about Tasmanian devil dens but I knew enough about bushfires, and everything to the depth of a metre of the surface was about to get baked.

Including us, if we didn't get going.

"Fuck, fuck, fuck."

I scrambled back up the edge of the gully, making a mental note to tell Jack that I'd just cursed and it had nothing to do with sex. Which was such an idiotic thought considering I might be rendered to cinder at any moment.

I raced back to the Defender and grabbed the last storage tub. I pulled the lid off and upended the papers inside it, grabbed the lid, and raced back to the gully.

"I have no idea what I'm doing," I mumbled as I flew over the edge and almost fell down the embankment. "Bloody hell. What would Jack do?"

He'd take off his coat and throw it over the joey.

Right. I shook out of my jacket and patted Rosemary to calm her and possibly myself. The joey was still out of the den, and I held the jacket out, slowly stepping in toward it. It backed up a little, growling and screeching. I threw the jacket, but the joey scampered back into the den.

Great. Well, it wasn't going to come back out in a hurry.

Rosemary barked at it, and how she sensed the urgency I'll never know. But she understood. And so did I. "One more attempt, then we have to go, okay?"

Okay, then. "What would Jack do now?" I looked at Rosemary and she looked back at me. I nodded. "Jack would get his arse out of here, that's what Jack would do."

Think, Lawson. What would a Tasmanian devil do?

It would bite the shit out of whatever tried to grab it.

With that as my only game plan, I rolled the jacket

around my right fist as best I could, then got down on my knees at the entrance of the den and did the stupidest thing I'd ever done. I stuck my hand in.

Somewhere in my brain remembered an odd fact I'd heard as a child. *A Tasmanian devil has the jaw strength to pulverise its prey. Even joeys.*

I shook my head and mumbled to myself, "If I survive this, I should have my IQ retested."

The snarling and growling sounds erupted—there had to be more than one—and a second later, a dull, vice-like pressure latched on my fist, so I slowly, slowly pulled it out. Attached by its teeth to the end of my jacket was a joey, no bigger than a kitten, but its grip was like that of a pit bull terrier.

I spun on my knees to the tub and put the joey in it. Not knowing how to get it to let go, I gently pinched the scruff of its neck the way the mother would, and he let go. I quickly put the lid on and rewrapped my hand. I stuck it into the den a second time. There was more growling, then again something latched onto my jacket. I pulled out the second joey and put it in the tub with the first one.

The den was quiet. There was no more noise, no scurrying, no anything. Not from the den anyway. The sound of the fire was louder, closer. I opened the jacket up, and taking the lid off the tub, I covered the joeys and closed the lid again.

I looked up at the sky and saw smoke. Thick black smoke had crept over the trees. "Oh God."

I scrambled to my feet just as something else got Rosemary's attention. Her ears pricked up and she took off up the embankment just as I heard something else.

"Lawson!"

I clambered up the edge of the gully, trying to keep the tub even, but my foot kept slipping in the mud.

"Lawson!"

It was Jack.

Rosemary had disappeared over the top and I knew he'd see her, but I called out anyway. "Down here!"

Jack appeared in bright orange overalls looking a horrid mess. "Oh, thank god," he said with tears in his eyes. He put his hand to his heart before he held it out to me to help me up.

"Take the tub," I urged, holding it up. "Be careful with it."

He got down on his knees and took it, then helped pull me to the top. But he didn't stop. He picked up the tub, handed it to me, grabbed me by the shirt, and pulled me in the direction of the Defender. "Run!"

So I ran.

Rosemary went with Jack, and I struggled to start the Defender, my hands were shaking so badly. Jack reversed like a mad man and I finally got the gearstick into reverse and floored it. He spun his ute around onto the road, backed up a bit, and waited for me to do the same. When I reversed onto the road, I spun the Defender around, rammed it into first gear, and drove the fastest I'd ever driven. Jack's front bumper was right on my tail, he was urging me to go faster. Or at the very least, not letting me slow down.

Then I saw why.

In my rear-vision mirror, the tree line behind us was a wall of black smoke and orange fire.

THE DRIVE BACK INTO SCOTTSDALE DIDN'T TAKE LONG. GIVEN THE speed at which we were travelling, it wasn't too surprising. It was long enough for the adrenaline to nose dive, and by the time I pulled up at the evacuation centre, I was barely holding it together.

There were people everywhere, and Jack's ute screeched to a stop behind me. I fumbled with my seatbelt, then couldn't get the door open at first, and when I did, I almost fell out of the Defender.

Jack stomped toward me. "What the hell were you thinking?!"

Right, then. His adrenaline had worn off too, but instead of falling in a heap like me, he was angry. No, actually, he was *pissed*. At me. And rightly so. Everyone had stopped and stared at our dramatic entrance.

He seemed so big and so intimidating, and his ire was aimed right at me. "For a genius, you can be really fucking stupid."

I nodded and my vision blurred as tears spilled down my cheeks. "I had to save them."

His whole body sagged, and he took huge strides so he could throw his arms around me. In front of all the good people of Scottsdale, he hugged me so damn hard, and all I could do was cry. My hands were shaking and, no, not just my hands. My whole body was shaking.

"I need a blanket here," he called out. He rubbed my back. He whispered against my ear. "You're okay, Lawson. I'm sorry I spoke to you like that. I was so worried, and you scared the hell outta me."

A blanket was placed around my shoulders, and I turned to find a concerned Remmy. She rubbed my arm. "You okay, hun?"

I nodded. I felt rather foolish for letting my emotions

get the better of me. I wiped my face. "Sorry. I think the adrenaline wore off." I stepped back so I could look up into Jack's face. "There were only two joeys. The mother and the other joey weren't there."

"Maybe the mother took the strongest," Jack suggested. Then he blinked. "Is that what you have in the tub?"

I nodded. "We need to take them to someone who can care for them. And the butterflies and eggs. I need to get them into a controlled environment."

Jack fixed the blanket around me, then collected the tub off the front passenger seat. He carefully pulled the lid off to reveal two little devil joeys huddled in my jacket. The people gathered around all oooohed and ahhhhed, but I couldn't take my eyes off Jack. "Oh, Lawson," he whispered. "You went back for them?"

"Rosemary made me. She's really Lassie, did you know that?" She was sitting faithfully at our feet, so I took a second to give her a pat. "It was her idea to save the joeys. She was barking at them and wouldn't come back when I called her, and I would have died before I left her behind."

Jack's eyes shone with tears. I got the feeling he didn't get too choked up all that often. All he did was nod, then gave me a hard kiss on the side of my head. He looked at Remmy. "Can you stay with him? Make sure he doesn't run off and almost die trying to save any more animals. I'll go and see if I can find Paul."

Remmy nodded and gave me a bit of a hug. We watched Jack leave with the tub of devil joeys. "Who's Paul?"

"Paul's a local wildlife rescue guy. He looks after native animals until they're ready for release."

"Oh. Okay."

Remmy gave me a sad smile. "Oh, Lawson, you should have seen Jack. They got the fire contained on the southeast line, so he came here looking for you. I told him I hadn't seen you at all, and he took off like... crazy. He just turned and ran. I guess he knew where to look for you."

Jack was suddenly back with a man who was now holding the tub with the two joeys. Jack gave me a look that said I was in a lot of trouble. "Oh, I knew where to look alright. And when I saw the gate on the reserve had been smashed off its hinges, I knew exactly where to find him."

"I'll pay for the gate," I said.

"Never mind the gate now," Jack said. "That whole area's now nothing but charred ground. There's no gate or fences anymore."

"The fire," I said, looking to the east. The hills were nothing but dark clouds and black smoke. "How was it contained? It didn't look too contained when we were in the mountains. And why are we not evacuating?"

"We pushed the frontline to run up the mountain, making it turn back on itself," Jack explained. "The two kilometres of cleared farming land between the town and the national park protects the town."

Paul, the man holding the joey tub spoke then. "You got these two little critters out?" People had gathered around, all clearly curious.

I nodded. "I think the mother and other joey left or died. I don't know, but these two were all that was there. I'm sorry if I wasn't supposed to interfere, but Rosemary wouldn't let me leave them."

Paul looked down at the dog and smiled. "Always liked your dog, Jack." Then Paul looked at me again. He offered me his free hand, which I shook. "You did real good, thank you. We'll get these two checked over by the vet and cared for until they can be released."

I was getting teary again. "Thank you."

Jack put his arm around me and pulled me against him. "Did you save the butterflies?"

"I hope so." I looked up at him. "I need to leave for Launceston. Now."

Remmy was somehow now holding a cup of tea and a sandwich. She handed them both to me. "Eat."

I took them gratefully. I hadn't realised how hungry I was… Jack went to the Defender and opened the back door. Remmy, Rosemary, and I followed him. There were papers and equipment and books and stuff everywhere. But the two tubs were the most important.

"I collected ants and some live butterflies," I said, speaking around my mouthful of food.

Then Jack opened the rear passenger door to reveal the entire *Bursaria* shrub. "And this?"

"I had to improvise."

Remmy laughed, then looked closer to the floor of the Defender. "Are they ants? Oh God, there's ants everywhere."

"They don't bite," Jack and I said in unison, making us all smile.

"What kind of butterflies are they?" Paul asked.

"Well, they don't have a name…," I said, finishing my tea. "They're a new species."

He stared at me. "Wow. Now I can see why you risked your life to save them."

I nodded, and Jack sighed. I realised this whole me-almost-dying and him-almost-dying-to-save-me might be somewhat of a bone of contention. I frowned. "I am sorry."

He put his hand around my neck and pulled me close. He didn't seem to care it was in front of everyone, so neither did I. I looked up at him. "I need to get the butterflies and eggs to Professor Tillman. He'll have the equipment to save them."

Jack nodded. "I'll drive."

Just then, the clouds opened and rain poured from the sky and people cheered and hugged one another around us. Paul took the joeys, Remmy took Rosemary and ran for cover, and I climbed into the front passenger seat. Jack was already behind the wheel and he leaned over, grabbed my face, and kissed me hard. The windows were all obscured by rain and I doubted anyone saw. I didn't care if they did. "Thank God you're okay," he whispered before putting the Defender into first and driving out of Scottsdale.

THE DRIVE TO LAUNCESTON STARTED OFF QUIET. THE SERIOUSNESS of what I'd done, how I'd put both our lives in danger, was starting to weigh on me. "I really am sorry," I said quietly. "But I had to try."

Jack's hands squeezed the steering wheel. "I hate to think what would have happened if I hadn't found you..."

I nodded slowly. "I know."

"Do you?" he asked seriously.

"Yes. I would have died and Rosemary too because I'd put her in danger as well. She had no choice where I took her, and I'm sorry."

Jack looked at me for a long moment and shook his head. "I'm talking about you. *You*, Lawson. I'm not sure what I'd do if..." He swallowed hard and left the rest of his sentence unsaid.

I held out my hand for his, and when he grabbed hold, I threaded our fingers and squeezed his palm. "Thank you for saving my life today." I lifted his hand and kissed his knuckles. His hands were blackened and dirty, but I didn't care. I kissed them again. "Thank you."

"Just promise me you won't do it again."

I thought about that and licked my lips. "I can't promise because I can't say with certainty that I won't be put in a similar circumstance. If I were to have to choose—"

"Lawson," he interrupted sternly. "The correct answer is I promise."

"I was going to say, if I were ever in a position again where I had to choose between my life and that of a defenceless animal, well, that's really not a choice."

"Thank you."

I looked out the window because I was very certain we were thinking different outcomes.

He sighed, long and loud. "You'd choose the animal, wouldn't you?"

I quickly turned to look at him. "Well, there are many varying factors in this scenario, and I can't hypothesise to one conclusion..."

He started to smile, and I stopped talking. "What?" he asked.

"Why are you smiling at me?"

"Because you're adorable. Incredibly frustrating, possibly infuriating, but completely adorable."

I huffed and sank back in the seat. Still holding his hand, I lifted it to press the back of his hand to my cheek. "And you're kind of wonderful."

We pulled up at the address Professor Tillman had given me when I'd called to let him know what had happened.

He met us out the front of his house, where I made

introductions. It was an older style weatherboard home with perfectly maintained gardens, and a single glass butterfly graced the wall by the front door. "Welcome," he said. "Looks like you've both had quite an adventure this morning. Saw it all on the news."

"Yes, quite." And we were a mess. I was covered in dirt and mud from the gully embankment, and Jack was still wearing his soot-covered RFS overalls. I opened the back door to the Defender and handed the professor the lighter tub. I handed Jack the heavier one, filled with a shovel full of *Notoncus* ant nest. I grabbed the shrub from the back seat.

"Come this way," Professor Tillman said.

We followed him around the side of his home to what looked like a garden hot house, but I smiled when I saw it. "Oh, this is magnificent."

The professor basically had his own butterfly house in his backyard.

"It's not bad," he said modestly, walking inside first.

I dumped the tub with the *Bursaria* shrub in it by the inside of the door, with Jack one step behind me. The professor slid the tub onto a workbench, and slowly took the lid off. He gently lifted out one of the offcuts of shrub and turned it over. There was one butterfly on it, and it spread its wings in greeting.

The professor laughed. "Well, hello to you too."

As it turned out, only four survived. The bottom of the tub was a graveyard for five fully grown butterflies. My heart sank. "I tried to save them all," I mumbled.

Jack rubbed my back. His gentle, wordless reassurance meant so much.

"There are eggs in the roots of the shrub," I said. "Hopefully they survived."

The professor beamed. "You did a remarkable thing today." He went over to the shrub and squatted down beside it. He inspected the mass of roots and dirt and ants for a long minute before he looked up and smiled. "I think you saved the entire order of species, son."

After we'd secured the four remaining butterflies into a holding tank and the eggs had been safely relocated into hatching nets, it was afternoon. I could barely keep my eyes open. After a day of such adrenaline, I was starting to crash.

"We've done all we can do today," the professor said. "You should get some rest. Tomorrow we can decide where we go from here."

I nodded, knowing he was right. "Oh, and Professor Asterly has told me he expects to be let in on the discovery. I told him to politely sod off."

Jack snorted. "I heard that conversation. It wasn't exactly polite."

I shrugged and Professor Tillman laughed. "That's the reason I asked you to find this butterfly, son. That tenacity right there. Not that any other lepidopterist would probably have stared down a raging bushfire to save a butterfly either, mind you. But I knew I liked you from the moment I read your dissertation, which could have been subtitled 'Everything The Butterfly Association's Doing Wrong Because They're a Bunch of Idiots.'"

"You didn't?" Jack scoffed and looked at me with wide eyes. I shrugged.

"Yes, he most certainly did," the professor answered. "Best thing I ever read. I told the commissioner for endangered species something similar back in '78, so I knew you and I would get along just fine."

I found myself smiling at the old man. "Sometimes

people need to hear things they'd rather not hear. It doesn't mean they shouldn't be said."

He grinned. "Exactly."

I fought another yawn, and Jack shook Professor Tillman's hand. "It was a pleasure to meet you, but I better get him home or he'll be asleep on the floor."

"Yes, this day is catching up with me," I admitted. "But I'll be back after breakfast. Thank you, Professor Tillman."

He smiled. "Thank *you*. The butterfly'd be lost if it weren't for you. And please, call me Warner." Then he paused. "And you better get thinking on a name to call it. The butterfly, that is. You found it, you name it."

What? "Oh, no... I couldn't do that. And anyway, I'd have never found it if it weren't for you. Actually, I wouldn't have found it if it weren't for Jack. He took me to look at some Tasmanian devil joeys and that's when I found them. But I wouldn't have even been in Tasmania if it weren't for you."

Warner put his hand up like it was final. "You found it, you name it."

"Then I shall name it the Tillman Copper, after the man who found it first."

Professor Tillman's eyes got watery and he cleared his throat. "Well, then I'll be honoured."

I beamed at him.

As we were leaving, he waved his hand at the shrub I'd dug out of the mountainside and bought with us. "You boys take the *Bursaria*. I've got plenty of it here. Plant this one somewhere, see what it might attract."

I smiled at Jack. "I know the perfect place."

CHAPTER THIRTEEN
JACK - TWO WEEKS LATER

LIFE IN THE LAST TWO WEEKS HAD BEEN INTERESTING AND LIFE-changing, that was for sure. Lawson hadn't gone back to Melbourne. Given the Tillman Copper was granted new species status, much to his boss Asterly's disgust, Lawson was the lead lepidopterist in charge of the find.

When his boss had tried to derail Lawson's role, Lawson had simply contacted the head of the University department, and the chairman of the Butterfly Association and told them both exactly how it was going to go.

He *would be* staying in Tasmania to establish a research and protection study on the Tillman Copper. He *would be* lead lepidopterist, and he *would* have their full cooperation. No questions, no arguments.

So that was that.

I couldn't have been happier. Because it meant he was staying in Tasmania.

I asked him to move in with me. I'd told him I was falling in love with him, and he'd kissed and hugged me in return, telling me he felt the same. *The butterflies he felt when he saw me had morphed into love*, he'd said. *The most remarkable metamorphosis.* His words made my heart sing.

But he'd decided that it was too soon for us to move in together. I understood his reasoning—we'd only known each other for three weeks, after all—but I was a little disappointed.

When I'd seen him that time sitting on my lounge room floor in his PJs with Rosemary asleep at his side, I wanted it on a permanent basis. And when I'd thought he might die in the bushfires, my priorities, and my heart, had never been clearer. But he'd said not yet, and I respected his decision.

He'd found a place to rent in Launceston and was having his things ferried over. And in the meantime, he would stay with me until it all arrived, which it did a week later. The week he was at my house was incredible, even he agreed. We talked, we laughed, we cooked, and the sex was amazing. But he didn't want to rush things and ruin what could be something incredible. He did plant that *Bursaria* shrub near the rosemary by the northern side of my house, though, which in a Lawson-Gale way was almost a promise that he'd be around long-term. If butterflies would take a year or two to roost there or even ten years, it gave me hope that he'd be there to see it.

But Launceston was where his work was, so it made sense for him to live there. I told myself it was a helluva lot closer than Melbourne, and the forty-five-minute drive wasn't too bad. We'd only spent a few nights apart in the second week, and while it allowed me to concentrate on my work, I did miss him.

But he'd invited me, and Rosemary of course, to stay for the weekend, and when I arrived on Friday night, he welcomed me with one hell of an amazing kiss. "How was work?"

"Busy. We've got damage control and regeneration plans to implement," I said, kissing him again. The week after the bushfire, I'd taken him back to the place he'd found the Tillman Copper. The whole area was a razed, blackened landscape. Nothing was left, and it was a sobering reminder of how close he'd come to being killed. "Will be flat out for the next twelve months. How about you?"

He gave me an eye-crinkling smile. "Great. There's something I want to show you tomorrow."

"Don't want to show me tonight?"

He shook his head, and taking my hand, he led me to his bedroom. "Nope. There's something else I want to do tonight."

"Oh yeah? What's that?"

"You."

AFTER HE'D COOKED ME BREAKFAST, WE GOT DRESSED AND HE took me back to Warner Tillman's house. I'd been here a few times, but Lawson had been here every day. He walked around the side of the house with a familiar ease when Warner called out to us. "In here, boys."

Lawson went straight inside, with a skip in his step. He was so excited, and seeing him lead his own team and push for the ecological betterment of a species was a spectacular thing to witness. "Anything yet?"

"Any minute now."

I looked between them. "Any minute *what* now?"

Lawson pulled me over to a glass case where inside was

a net with a cocoon attached to it. "What you're looking at is the chrysalis of the Tillman Copper. We're about to witness what no other person in the world has seen. The very first Tillman Copper to emerge, imago."

"Emargo-what?"

"Imago. It's the final and fully developed adult stage. When a caterpillar emerges as a butterfly."

I smiled at him. It was kind of like him. I was finally getting to see him in his element, doing what he was born to do. He'd spent years as a caterpillar, with his head down, working hard and going unnoticed. But now... now he had wings, and the world could see he was truly a magnificent man. I kept that analogy to myself, though. For now.

Then, as if right on cue, the chrysalis moved and started to split. A small copper coloured butterfly entered the world, imago.

It was incredible.

I looked at Lawson then, at his face, at the look of wonder and amazement in his eyes, and what he saw in the butterfly, I saw in him.

Lawson Gale, imago.

imagines

CHAPTER ONE
LAWSON GALE

THE LANDSCAPE LOOKED BLACKENED AND DEAD, CHARRED BEYOND any possibility of resurrection. After six months, I would have thought I'd be used to it, but no. It still gave me a moment's pause.

I almost died here. Rosemary too.

Jack almost died here when he'd come to save me.

And that caused my heart to squeeze.

Against all odds, though, like Jack promised it would, there were small signs of new life, new green shoots in the scorched earth. While some trees had sprouted new life, some were nothing but vertical pillars of charcoal, waiting for wind or time to crumble them to nothing.

This land had been cauterised.

All *Bursaria* shrubs were gone; the Tillman Copper butterfly's only known natural habitat in this area had been singed off the face of the planet.

We still had our captive specimens, and they were breeding well. But it wasn't the same. It would never be the same.

Jack came up from the edge of the gully. I could tell by his face but asked anyway. "Any luck?"

He shook his head. "Nah. There's been no activity here since the fire."

I sighed heavily, taking in the cloying scent of burnt earth. Still, after six months, it was all I could smell.

"You hate coming back here, don't you?" Jack asked, putting his hand on my back.

I nodded. "It's not my favourite place."

"You know, for tens of thousands of years, the Indigenous people used bushfires as a way to encourage new growth." Jack's gaze never left mine. "It's a cycle, and it means new life will grow. It's winter now, so it's slow going, but come springtime, this place will come alive again."

"Not for everything. And that's what I hate the most. I hate the loss. I get the regeneration argument, and I understand bushfires can serve a purpose, but it did nothing to help that poor Tasmanian devil mum and her babies."

"The two you saved are doing well, so Paul tells me."

"It didn't help the butterflies."

Jack pulled me in for a hard hug. "You saved them, remember?"

"Not all of them."

"You did more than anyone else, Lawson. You're not responsible for the bushfire. You are responsible for saving an entire species of butterfly. The Tillman Copper exists because of you."

After a moment of silence, I looked up at him. "Take me home."

He let go of me, pulled on the lapels of my winter coat, and drew me in for a kiss. "My home or your home?" Before I could answer, he added, "You know, it'd save us all this time deciding if you'd just move in with me."

I rolled my eyes, but a smile won out. It wasn't the first time we'd had this discussion, and I doubted it'd be the last. We walked back to his ute. He called Rosemary, who had gone sniffing about, and buckled her in once she'd jumped up onto the back tray. We climbed in, and Jack expertly reversed down the old track. It was much easier now with the lack of trees and shrubs.

"One day, Mr Brighton. One day."

"But not now," he said. I could feel his disappointment in the air between us.

"Are things not perfect enough right now?"

He looked from the road to me. "Yes. But they could be even perfecter."

"Perfecter isn't a word."

"Not yet it isn't, no," he said. "Because you haven't said yes yet. Once you're living with me, it'll be a real word."

I rolled my eyes again but reached out my hand. He slipped his palm into mine and I brought his hand to my lips. "One day."

"I'll hold you to that."

I smiled at him. "I should hope so." We were quite a ways back to town, then I asked, "So, have you thought more on what you'll do for time off?"

He was due to have two weeks annual leave; it was winter and it was the quieter time of the year. "Not really. Might just stay at home, get stuff done around the house. I think Remmy and Nico were looking at doing some work around their house, though last I spoke to them, they weren't sure." Jack sighed. "Unless I could convince my super hot boyfriend to maybe come away with me for a day or two. I know he's busy with his work right now, and he's doing some pretty important things. Not to mention he's finishing up his doctorate externally because of his commitment to research. I haven't asked him yet, though, because I don't want him to say no."

I was smiling at how nervous he was. At how adorable he was. "You should ask him."

His eyes went wide. "Really?"

"Yes. His work might be important, but so is his boyfriend. I doubt he'd say no," I said, playing along. Then I added, "And it helps that butterflies are typically dormant in winter."

Jack's grin was huge. "Yes, that helps."

"Jack?"

"Yeah?"

"You still haven't asked me."

He laughed. "Lawson, come away with me for a day or two, or five, or whatever. We can go wherever you want. Melbourne, to see your family, or to New Zealand for some skiing."

"I don't think skiing is really my thing. Though I'm happy to stay at a chalet, drinking wine and reading books in front of a fire. I can be your official ski bunny."

Jack laughed. "I've never had a ski bunny before."

I lifted his knuckles to my lips for a smiling kiss.

I DID LOVE BEING AT JACK'S HOUSE. IT WAS PEACEFUL THERE AND felt like home. I did want to live with him, but the sensible part of my brain insisted on not rushing. If this was a permanent thing—and I did think it could be—then there was no need to risk moving in together before we were ready.

And the very last thing I wanted to do was ruin what we had.

Winter had well and truly arrived in Tasmania. The wind was biting, the clouds hung low, and the sun seemed like it was on half-watt. And I loved it. It meant big coats and scarves, boots and woolly socks. It also meant wood fires and blankets on the sofa, cuddles and sleepy TV, and stews for dinner.

And Jack loved my lamb and dumpling stew. Like "devoured it all and asked when I could make it again" kind of loved it. So while he was chopping wood in the backyard, I set a fresh stew to simmer and made him a cup of tea.

When he came in with his arms full of logs and kindling, his nose was red and his cheeks flushed. He stacked his burden by the wood fire and pulled his beanie off, and my god, he smiled at me in a way that made my heart stutter.

I held up his steaming tea. "I made you a cup."

He took the tea and sipped it gently. "Mmm," he hummed appreciatively. He put the cup on the counter, then encased me in his arms, giving me a hug. It made me hum. "I love it when you hug me like that."

He nudged his nose to my ear. "Like what?"

"Like it feeds your soul."

He chuckled, warm and breathily. "It does." He pulled back and looked into my eyes. "That's exactly what it does."

"I love you, Jack," I said. I'd told him a hundred times in the last six months, and it still gave me a thrill to say it.

He pressed his lips to mine softly. "And I love you." He reached over and lifted the lid on the pot of dinner and peeked inside. "And I love your stew."

It made me laugh. "So, have you given more thought to this holiday we're taking?"

"I'll have to get online and have a look," he said, settling back against me, smiling down at me. "I wasn't expecting you to say yes, actually."

"Well, you go look. I'll finish dinner. My laptop's on the table. Just use it to Google whatever you want."

I set about making dumplings for the stew, and Jack disappeared into the lounge room. Just as I was finishing up adding the balls of dough to the stew, Jack called out. "Uh, Lawson? You got an email."

"Who's it from?"

"I didn't open it."

I slid the casserole dish into the oven. "Well, open it."

I set the timer and washed my hands. I was wiping them on a tea towel when I walked back into the lounge room.

Jack was squinting at my laptop screen. "It's from the Cairns Butterfly Conservatory."

I frowned. "What does it say?"

He held my laptop out. "You read it."

I sat beside him and took my laptop, reading the email.

Dear Mr Gale,

We have followed your work closely, with regards to the Tillman Copper...

I scanned through the rest of the email, then read it again, slower this time.

"Lawson, what is it?"

"I've been invited to assist on a study of the Ulysses butterfly."

Jack blinked. "Is that good?"

"I don't know. It's in Cairns, Far North Queensland, Jack."

I could see the moment it dawned on him. "How long does a study take?"

"It says the initial invitation extends to two weeks."

"Can you leave your work right now on the Tillman?"

I nodded slowly, thoughtfully. "Two weeks is fine. Everything is established, and Warner could supervise…"

Jack frowned. "When would you leave?"

I stared at him. Clearly he'd missed my intention. "Correction, Jack. When would *we* leave is a more pertinent question."

It took him a second, then a smile pulled at his lips. "We?"

I chuckled. "I think I just solved our holiday destination problem. We're not going to the snowfields. We're going to the tropics."

CHAPTER TWO
JACK BRIGHTON

GETTING ORGANISED TO GO ON A TEN-DAY WORKING VACATION with Lawson was as funny as it was frightening. To say he was pedantic was an understatement. He had lists. Lots of lists. He had lists for his work equipment—which I understood—but he also had lists for everything else. Including me.

When we asked Remmy and Nico if they could babysit Rosemary, or dogsit as it were, for the duration of our trip, Lawson insisted on giving them a list of foods Rosemary preferred and desired exercise routines. Mercifully, Remmy accepted the list seriously, thanking Lawson but smiling at me.

She found him adorable.

So did I. But the list thing was driving me insane.

I was more of a "pack on the day you leave" kind of guy.

When I told Lawson that, he couldn't speak and his eye twitched.

We compromised by, for his sake, me packing earlier than the morning we were to fly out to Melbourne and, for my sake, not needing a list.

He had work to finish up with Professor Warner Tillman on Friday, and I told him I'd meet him at his place in Launceston. We were flying out to Melbourne on Saturday morning, so it was logical I drop Rosemary off at Remmy's on my way Friday afternoon and meet him at his place in time for dinner.

I let myself into his house. I had a key like he had a key to my house. It made sense, given that we might arrive at each other's houses while the other was at work. Yes, having each other's keys was kind of a big deal, but it felt right. So did having some clothes at his place, and not just a toothbrush, but all toiletries. I had some books of mine on his coffee table, like one of his reference books sat on mine. I liked the fact there were reminders of him in my house, and I really liked the fact there were pieces of me in his.

And I had to admit, I *really* liked the direction our relationship was going.

Which is why I was nervous about the envelope I brought with me, the one I slid onto his kitchen counter. The exact same one that matched the letter addressed to him in a pile of unopened mail near the fruit bowl.

Lawson was an enigma, that was for sure. Insanely particular about some things—such as his lists and his data collation and his appearance—but then there was his messy pile of unopened mail and his ability to run late to almost everything.

Leaving the envelope on the kitchen counter, I took my bags into the bedroom and smiled when I saw his perfectly made bed and, at the foot of it, all his perfectly lined up bags, storage tubs, and research gear. Then I looked into his walk-in closet, and I briefly wondered if he was injured at all when the clothes-bomb went off in there.

Just thinking about him made me smile. And hearing

his car pull up out front made me smile even harder. Well, it wasn't really a car. It was a Land Rover Defender. Yep, that's right. The hire car he bitched and whinged about when he first got here was the exact kind of vehicle he chose to lease. And he loved it.

He came in carrying a heavy bag of something and, looking all flustered and gorgeous, slid it onto his dining table. I stood back and watched him, just for a moment. The winter suited him, being all coated up and wearing a woollen beanie, his cheeks and the tip of his nose were flushed pink. He looked good enough to eat.

He turned to me, sighed, and walked over, greeting me with a kiss. "Hello. Was your trip okay?"

"It was fine."

"And you got Rosemary dropped off okay?"

"Yep."

"Was she sad?"

"Nope. Remmy had made her fresh doggie cookies, and Luca was already showing her his winter garden. They had their heads down in the dirt, tails up in the air, and I barely even got a goodbye."

Lawson smiled, then unwrapped his scarf, pulled off his beanie, and undid his coat. He dumped them all on the dining table and started to rifle through the bag he'd brought inside with him. "Sorry I'm late. I had to organise all my research gear to be collected in the morning. It's getting shipped ahead of us and will be in Cairns when we get there. It's so much easier than trying to take it myself. Then I called into the deli on my way home and grabbed us some dinner. I didn't fancy cooking or going out. Is that okay?"

"What are we having?"

He held up a takeaway container. "Mediterranean vegetable lasagne, greek salad, and a chianti."

"Perfect."

He slid the lasagne onto the kitchen counter when he noticed the envelope I'd left there. He picked it up. "What's this?"

"It's my letter from pathology. I see you haven't opened yours either."

"I got it yesterday," he said quietly. "I thought I'd wait for you."

"And I thought we could open them together."

Lawson nodded. "We could."

He was clearly nervous, and truthfully, so was I. We'd discussed this at length and agreed that full blood tests were a natural step forward for our relationship. He didn't want to use condoms anymore. He said he wanted me and nothing else inside him.

Now, I'd never *not* used protection, ever. But I'd never been in love with someone like I was with him before either. I also couldn't see myself wanting anyone but him. And when he put it like that, about me being the only thing inside him, I couldn't argue.

So we'd gone together to have blood tests, and the results sat, unread, folded in white envelopes. Lawson was still holding mine, nervously licking his lips and turning the letter over in his hand, so I picked up his. "Why are you so nervous?"

"I don't know. Because this can't be undone, and I want this but I'm also equally fine with it if we don't. Don't ever use condoms, that is."

I would have chuckled at how cute he was if he wasn't being so serious. I stood before him, leaned against him until he was backed up against the kitchen counter, and lifted his chin. "Lawson, we've both been tested before and it was fine. This is just a formality, really. A peace of mind."

He looked intently into my eyes. "Jack, please know that whatever the results are, nothing will change how I feel about you."

I kissed him softly. "Same, Lawson. I love you, that won't change."

He finally smiled. "Thank you."

"How about you read mine, and I read yours?"

He frowned for half a second, then nodded. "Okay." But just as I'd slid my finger through the envelope seal, he said, "Wait!"

I froze. "What?"

"Should we eat dinner first?"

I barked out a laugh but quickly realised he was being serious. I knew him well enough to know he needed some time. I took the envelope from his hand and, along with the one I was holding, slid them back onto the kitchen counter. I kissed him again, soft and lingering. "We can worry about that later."

So, we ate our dinner, then ended up on the sofa under a fleecy throw blanket, wine glasses in hand. "I know reverse cycle heating is convenient, but I do miss my wood fire," I mused.

"There's a lot to be said about wearing sweatpants and socks and snuggling with you under a blanket," he said, sipping his wine. He bent his leg and slid his socked foot along my thigh under the blanket.

I chuckled. "True. It is nice."

"It'll almost be a shame to go to Cairns. Though I'm not opposed to seeing you all sweaty, wearing next to nothing."

"You can see that here. Anytime you want."

He laughed and hummed an impatient sound, then

without breaking eye contact, he downed the rest of his wine in one mouthful and put his glass on the coffee table. He stood up and held out his hand. "You shouldn't put explicit imagery in my mind. I have no self-control when it comes to you."

"Explicit imagery? All I said was that you could see me half-naked and sweaty here. You were the one who mentioned the half-naked and sweaty first."

Lawson rolled his eyes. "Your argument is subjective."

I snorted out a laugh, put my wine glass next to his, and stood up. I gripped his jaw and tilted his face up so I could flutter my eyelashes along his cheek. I only did it because it made his breath catch. I waited for his eyelids to slowly open, revealing unfocused eyes. "I'm going to take you to bed, Lawson."

He swallowed hard and nodded. He waited two beats of my heart before sliding his fingers over my hand that was still pressed to his jaw. He squeezed my fingers, and without a word, he led the way to his room.

He walked as far as his bed, then turned to face me. There was worry in his eyes. "What about the test results?"

I opened the top drawer of his bedside table and took out a condom and the small bottle of lube. I threw them onto the bed and kissed him softly. "Not until you're certain."

I could feel the relief roll off him.

I smiled. "Now, I want you naked, on the bed, on your hands and knees."

He let out a slow breath and his pupils blew out. But he did exactly as I asked, and I gave him everything he demanded.

"Are you nervous?"

"No."

"Why aren't you nervous?"

"Because I'm not."

"How can you not be?"

I snorted. We were in the backseat of a cab, having just arrived in Melbourne, on our way to his parents' house. "Lawson, I'm completely fine. You, on the other hand, seem to be very worried. Is that something I should be worried about?"

"No, of course not. It's just that..."

"It's just what?"

"Well, I've not taken anyone home to meet my family before."

Oh. "Are you worried they won't approve of me?"

His eyes went wide, horrified. "Oh, good gracious, no. They'll love you, I'm sure of it."

"Then what's the problem?" But as I asked this question, it dawned on me what the answer was. "You're worried about what they'll see in you."

Lawson opened his mouth, promptly shut it again, then sighed dramatically, and I knew I was right. "You don't understand. I've never been with anyone... I care deeply for in their company. I don't know how to act accordingly. Mackellar and Paterson never had such problems, of course. Their partners are lovely, but they're very... heteronormative. If you know what I mean."

He was so endearing. "Lawson, they know you're gay, right?"

"Yes, of course."

"And you told them we're together?"

His eyebrows knitted. "Yes, you know I have. You've spoken to my mother on the phone."

"Exactly. So you have nothing to hide and nothing to worry about. I'm not about to grope you in front of your parents. We don't have to hold hands or anything. We can even sit at opposite ends of the house if that's what you're worried about."

He cringed. "Would you be offended?"

"Not at all."

He scrubbed his hands over his face, then patted down his hair. Something I noticed he did when he was nervous or flustered. "Maybe my worries are unfounded. And completely my own. I'm sorry, I shouldn't have said anything."

I took his hand and kissed his palm. "Lawson. I'm sure it'll be fine." The truth was, I had no idea if it would be fine or not. They were, after all, geniuses in their chosen medical fields, and I was, well, not as educated as them. But I loved Lawson, and that was all I had to offer. If that wasn't enough, then that said more about them than it did about me.

Not to say that I didn't hope they would like me and welcome me into their family, given I had every intention of being around for a long time, but if they didn't, then that was that. I wouldn't beg or change who I was.

"Have you met someone's parents before?"

Lawson's question threw me by surprise. "Not since high school. I dated a guy from a different high school and I met his parents, but we were just kids."

"What about when you were at university?"

I shook my head. "I went to uni in Sydney, as you know." We'd talked about all this before. "I never saw anyone seriously enough to bring them back to Hobart to meet my family."

"Will I? Meet your family, that is."

I smiled. "Yes, of course. Well, you've chatted with April a few times on the phone. She thinks you're lovely. We can drive down to Hobart one weekend, and I can finally take you out on a proper date."

"Proper date?" He frowned. "Are you implying that the dates we've had aren't proper? Because I would take great personal offence to that. That picnic in your backyard is unsurpassable."

I smiled at him. "We might wear suits and eat the very best food."

He sat back in the seat, his worries seemingly forgotten. "You made peanut butter sandwiches and we drank mulled cider under the stars. I'd dare a Michelin-star chef to top that."

The taxi pulled up to a house, a modest but well-kept weatherboard home, and Lawson patted down his hair. "Right then, here we are."

We paid the fare, grabbed all our luggage and by the time I turned to face the house, a woman was standing on the front veranda. She had shoulder-length, grey wavy hair, wore a long flowing skirt and a peasant-style top, and looked like she'd walked straight out of Woodstock. I thought that couldn't possibly be Lawson's mother. I was expecting a well-to-do, straight-backed woman—more like Lawson—not a hippie. But then she extended her arms and cried, "Lawson!"

Lawson grinned at her. "Mum!"

I was stunned. Then she raced down the path and threw her arms around me. "And you must be Jack!"

CHAPTER THREE
LAWSON

I couldn't help but smile as my mother embraced Jack on the footpath, then dragged him by the arm up to the house.

"No, that's fine," I called out after them. "I'll get our luggage."

Jack gave me a happy, slightly terrified glance over his shoulder as my mum hauled him in through the front door. I grumbled as I towed the two suitcases up the front path, then struggled to get them up the few steps. Thankfully my brother Paterson was soon there, taking Jack's suitcase from me. "Welcome home," he said warmly.

I straightened and smiled. It really was good to see him. "Thank you. I'm glad you're here today."

"Wouldn't have missed it." He put his hand to the front door, but before opening it, he stopped and turned to me. "It's about time we met this Jack fellow I keep hearing about. I'm almost certain he was attached to Mum as she blurred through the house just now."

I ignored the fact my face grew hot. "Yes, well. I've been terribly nervous about bringing him here."

Paterson laughed and clapped his hand gently on my

upper arm. "What on earth for? The level of embarrassment that Mum and Dad will put you through is only slightly horrific. She's probably already showing him your baby photos. We probably should go save him."

I sighed, and we pushed our way inside. Paterson and I left the luggage tucked away in the corner of the living room and went in search of Jack. He was, as expected, in the sunroom sandwiched between my mother and father, looking completely overwhelmed. And in that moment, any foolish notion on my behalf of displays of affection in front of my family dissolved. I walked directly to him, positioning myself between Jack and my mother, and slid my arm around his waist, making him take a small step back. I gave my mother a stern look. "Breathing room, please."

Her face, which was positively beaming, softened. She put her hand to my cheek. "Look at you, my sweetest Lawson. Protective and so in love."

A part of me died inside, along with my pride and humility. Someone laughed, and when I looked up, I saw Mackellar sitting at the table, not even attempting to hide her glee at my discomfort. I could probably consider it payback for when she first brought her then-boyfriend, now-husband, James, home to meet our parents. James hid his smile behind his cup of tea. Bree came in from the kitchen, carrying a tray with more cups and a pot of tea, and she gave me a reassuring smile.

Everyone was looking at me, so I patted down my hair and swallowed down my nerves. "Introductions, if you will. Jack Brighton, this is my entire family, all at once. Which I apologise profusely for." I started left to right. "My brother-in-law, James. My sister, Mackellar. My brother, Paterson; his wife and better half, Bree. My mother, Hyacinth, and my father, Darren. Everyone, this is Jack Brighton."

Gentle hellos echoed around the sunroom, and Jack seemed to take it all in stride. He turned to Mum, who now had her arm linked with his. "Hyacinth? As in *Asparagaceae Hyacinthus*?"

My mother positively glowed. "Ah, a man who knows his genus botanical names! But no, I'm so named after my mother's favourite character from *Watership Down*, Hyzenthlay."

Jack's eyes flashed with something that looked like a memory. "Ah, Richard Adams. I loved that book when I was a kid."

And with that, my mother was besotted with him. With hearts in her eyes, she ushered him to the table. "Come, sit down and tell us about you."

Dad put his hand on my shoulder. "How's life treating you south of the Bass Strait?"

"It's good, Dad."

"And your Tillman Copper? How's the breeding program going? We're all so very proud of you, Lawson."

My chest warmed through. "Thank you. Everything is going splendidly."

We settled around the table for a wonderful lunch of homemade soup and fresh-baked bread and good conversation. I told of all my findings with the Tillman Copper, and everyone asked Jack questions, including him in their conversations, and there was much chatter and laughter. Seeing Jack interact and laugh with my family made me incredibly happy. I hadn't realised how much his acceptance by them, and his acceptance of them, meant to me.

My family wasn't strictly *normal*. I knew that. I'd been told my entire childhood that we were weird. My mother was never part of the school-mum clique: too alternative for their liking. She didn't dress like them. She certainly didn't think like them. Some days she'd give us the day off school so she could take us into the countryside where we could read in open parks, feeling grass between our toes and the sun on our faces with books in our laps. She told us we'd learn more about life from reading poetry about the earth and love, life and death, than sitting in a classroom all day every day.

She was right. Even as Paterson and Mackellar went on to medical school, they would still take their books to the park, take their shoes off, and spend their days studying in the sunshine. Though I preferred the shade in summer, I found it cleared my mind to read with my back to a tree and my feet in the grass with the occasional butterfly to say hello to.

And growing up, once a week my father would pick a different country and we would search the library on traditional foods and customs. Then we would each help to prepare and cook that country's staples the traditional way and we would discuss their history and culture over the meal. None of my childhood classmates did any such thing, and they quite often reminded me I was not like them. My mother would just hug me and tell me we were the Weasleys in a world of Muggles.

She said there was magic in our individuality. Though over and above everything else, we were taught to be free-thinking and empathetic. And over time, we learned to embrace our individuality.

I know people didn't always agree with my opinion, or my choice of attire, or my sexuality. But everyone in this room loved and accepted me without question. Including Jack. I found myself smiling at him as he told everyone of the two Tasmanian devil joeys I'd saved, and when I felt someone watching me, I turned to see my mum's eyes on me. She was teary and smiling.

"So, tell us, what are your plans for Cairns?" Mackellar asked when Jack's story was done.

Jack answered first. "Well, I imagine Lawson will be busy doing his lepidopterist thing mostly, saving another species no doubt." He put his hand on my knee and squeezed gently. "Though I'm not opposed to spending a few days on the beach or in the national parks. Both, preferably."

"I won't be spending all my time at the conservatory." I gave him a smile. "I'm sure you can spend one day with me in the butterfly house. Then if we go into the Kuranda State Park, you can show me what you do."

The smile he gave me was as warm as the summer sun.

My mother sighed. "Oh, I wish you two could stay a little while longer."

It was then I looked at the clock. "Oh goodness." *Must I be late for everything?* I stood up. "We really should be going."

A few short minutes later, we'd said our goodbyes to my brother and sister and their partners, and Mum and Dad walked us out. My mother had her arm linked through Jack's as they walked ahead of me and Dad. I tried to hear what they talked about, but it was whisper quiet. My dad laughed softly. "Don't worry, Lawson. He's fine. Actually, he's better than fine."

I looked at him and stopped walking. I wasn't aware my father's approval would hold so much weight. "You think?"

He laughed and put his arm around me, walking me forward to where Jack and Mum were standing by the front garden gate. "He makes you happy, Lawson. That's all I need."

As we reached them, my mother put her hands to my face. "My dearest Lawson. I'm so happy for you."

Oh, bother.

"Don't be embarrassed," she said. "Young love is a beautiful thing."

Sweet heavens above. Thankfully the taxi pulled up, and I briefly considered stepping in front of it, if it would mean my mother would stop humiliating me.

Jack and my dad loaded our luggage into the boot. Mum kissed my cheek. "He's wonderful," she whispered.

"I know, Mum."

Before she could respond with anything equally mortifying to Jack, I stuffed him into the taxi and waved my parents off. When we'd reached the end of the block and I could finally breathe, I took Jack's hand. "I apologise for anything my mother may have said to you that you felt was inappropriate or too personal. She has no filter when it comes to, well, most anything."

Jack surprised me by laughing. "Oh my God, Lawson. I love your mother!"

I stared at him. It's quite possible I blinked.

He just laughed some more. "I was expecting some private school headmistress type, but she couldn't be further from that."

"Why would you think she was like a headmistress?"

"Because you were nervous about me meeting her and worried about touching me in front of her."

"Only because she'd be planning our wedding."

"She already is. Well, that and our sex life. She told me that you were a late bloomer and to be patient with you, if need be."

I stared at him and felt nauseous and horrified. I couldn't speak.

Jack leaned in and whispered in my ear. "I told her patience was not a virtue you were overly fond of in that regard, and that if you had been a late bloomer, you certainly weren't now."

I think I blushed from my hairline to my toes. I let my head fall into my hands. "I'm so sorry," I mumbled.

He kissed my neck, just below my ear before he took my hands from my face and kept our fingers entwined. He gave me a perfectly dimpled smile. "Don't apologise. Your Mum's a hoot. She's so much more than I was expecting. She protests for civil rights and animal rights, she eats organic foods, she's crazy intelligent. And she raised three pretty cool kids."

"You like them?" I asked. "I mean, Paterson and Mackellar?"

"Hell yes. And your dad. You're all so different but very much the same. I don't even know how that works, but seeing you all together makes perfect sense."

I squeezed his hand. "Thank you. It means a lot to me that you like them."

"Of course I like them. How could I not when they each remind me a little of you?"

I chuckled at that, relief and those enigmatic metaphorical butterflies coursed through me.

"Oh, and by the way," Jack added casually. "Your Mum said she wouldn't be too opposed to a wedding in Scottsdale, as long as we promised to spend some time in Melbourne on our way to our honeymoon."

I sank down in my seat. Horrified. Mortified. I squeaked an apologetic sound.

Jack just laughed and kissed the back of my hand. "It's okay, Lawson. I'm not opposed to it either."

CHAPTER FOUR

JACK

We boarded the plane and settled in for the three and a half-hour flight. I was excited for this trip. Yes, going away for ten days with a boyfriend of just six months was risky, but I had no doubt that Lawson and I were solid.

No doubt.

He was pedantic about so many things, but he was a relaxed traveller. Despite our very first encounter when we met on a plane and he was flustered, this time he was deep breaths and smiles. Well, he read and re-read his research papers, making notes and highlighting, his forehead creasing in thought every now and then. I put on headphones and scrolled the comedy movies until I found something worth watching and let him do his thing.

I understood this was a working vacation for him, and I was perfectly okay with that. I'd never been to Cairns before, and I was looking forward to it. Warmer weather, white sands, and crystal blue oceans, flanked by pristine rainforests. Not to mention the Great Barrier Reef.

After the in-flight meal, I took out the holiday destination brochure from the back of the seat in front of me. I read about the scenic railway, the Skyrail cableway, snorkelling.

"Find anything interesting?" Lawson asked, closing his notepad.

"Sure! Lots to do."

"I wish I could commit to more time with you, but I'm not sure what's expected."

"It's fine. I agreed to come along with you knowing full well that you'd be working. Just promise me two half days out of the ten."

His lips twitched. "I'm certain my schedule will allow that. Anything, in particular, you'd like us to do?"

"I can think of a lot of things," I murmured so only he could hear.

"Any tourist things," he amended, his cheeks pink, "such as sightseeing?"

"Well, more like hiking and snorkelling."

Lawson settled back in his seat. "An outdoorsman. How could I forget?"

"Of course, I'm not opposed to indoor activities. Or even doing indoor activities outdoors."

Lawson flushed a shade of red I'd only seen in nature.

I quirked an eyebrow at him. "Anything I should know?"

He licked his lips. "About what?"

I glanced quickly at the lady on the other side of him. She had earphones on and wasn't paying attention to us. "About doing indoor things outdoors."

Lawson's breath caught, and that was all the reaction I needed. He didn't have to answer.

"Did we by chance book the private courtyard suite?"

THE ROOM WAS A TIKI-THEMED CABANA-STYLE ROOM WITH A HUGE king-size bed, a spa, a kitchenette, and yes, a private courtyard. The hotel had a gorgeous pool with palm trees, lit with nightlights, and the beach just a block away. I could hear the waves crashing as I opened the glass sliding doors.

But it had been a long day, and Lawson's blinks were getting a little longer, and he did those cute squinty-blinks he did when he was tired.

"Let me order in a late supper," I suggested. "We can have a bath. It's big enough for two. Then bed. You've got an early start tomorrow."

His unpacking seemingly forgotten, he walked over to me and gripped my face, bringing me in for a quick hard kiss. "I'll go run the bath."

Supper eaten, clothes packed away, and all Lawson's research gear accounted for, we slipped into the biggest spa bath ever. He'd even added some bubbles, and it was absurdly comfortable and relaxing. He sat at one end, me at the other, and I picked up one of his feet and started to massage.

He groaned an obscene sound, but closed his eyes and sank lower into the water. He mumbled, "So good."

When I was done with that foot, I collected his other and gave it the same treatment. He was sighing out sex noises. "Didn't realise I was so good at this."

He didn't open his eyes. "You win all the awards." Then he cracked one eyelid. "What did you stop for?"

I snorted and started my ministrations again, kneading my thumb into the arch of his foot. When I'd had enough of that, I lowered his foot back down. "Want me to do your shoulders?"

He lifted one eyelid. "That offer has sexual undertones."

I laughed. "You're too tired for sexual undertones. Turn around, sit between my legs, and I'll massage your shoulders and neck." I held up both pruned hands. "No wicked intent, I promise."

Lawson smiled sleepily but slid over in the tub to settle in between my legs. I kneaded my thumbs into his shoulders, and after about twenty seconds, I think he started to purr. Or snore. It was kinda hard to tell.

I slowly eased him forward, rousing him awake. "Come on. Let's get you to bed."

I pulled the plug and helped him out of the tub. I dried him off the best I could and then did myself before leading him to bed. He was so sleepy and pliant it was cute. I pulled back the covers and climbed into bed after him. I pulled the blanket up over us, settled him into the crook of my arm, and kissed his forehead. There was something to be said about intimacy that wasn't sexual. Sure, I could worship his body with my own for hours on end, and I quite often did, but I could also care for him and make sure he was safe and adored too. Lawson had come into my life so unexpectedly, and I had fallen haphazardly head over heels in love with him.

And as he nuzzled into me, trying to get closer to me even in sleep, I had no doubts he loved me too.

I drifted off to sleep and dreamed of running through fields of long grass chasing butterflies with Lawson, and we were laughing in the sunlight, and then we were the butterflies flittering over pockets of air, weightless and carefree. Then we were fucking and I was buried inside him and he was so warm and wet...

Wait, what?

I jerked awake to find the room lit with the sunrise and Lawson smiling wickedly around my cock.

He was fully dressed, bow tie and all, and I was stark naked and half-asleep but almost ready to come. "What are you doing?" I asked, my voice thick with sleep, rolling my hips for him.

He hummed and pulled off. "You took care of me last night. Now I'm taking care of you." He didn't wait for me to reply, he simply took me into his mouth again and used his hands to fondle my balls and trace my arsehole, then pump me until I couldn't hold back any longer. He moaned when I came, swallowing down everything I gave him.

I was utterly boneless, heavy as lead, and my head was spinning. He appeared above my face, his swollen lips smiling victoriously. "I ordered breakfast for you. It'll be delivered at half seven." He planted a kiss on my lips. "Have a good day." And he was gone.

I smiled at where his face had been and dozed in a sated slumber until room service delivered breakfast.

I SPENT THE DAY WALKING ALONG THE ESPLANADE ENJOYING THE sunshine. It was weird for me to be wearing shorts and a T-shirt in the middle of winter, but it sure was a nice break from the Tasmanian winter we'd left behind. I spent the afternoon by the hotel pool, lazing on a lounge chair, reading, dozing, relaxing. I couldn't remember the last time I'd spent a day doing this little.

It was glorious.

By the time I wandered to our room, I was warmed

through like a stone in the sun, slightly sun-kissed, and my skin felt tight from the salt water from the pool. I was surprised to find Lawson there. "Oh, I hadn't realised the time," I said, kissing him soundly. It was almost five. The still-present sun fooled me into thinking it wasn't that late. "Have I ever told you how glad I am that butterflies aren't nocturnal?"

Lawson smiled and kissed me again. "You haven't actually told me that, no."

"Well, I am. It means you spend nights with me and not them."

"Are you jealous of butterflies?"

"Insanely."

He laughed. "How did you spend your day? You look like you spent the day in the sun."

"I did. It was great. Winter in the tropics is just like our summer back home. I walked along the beach, ate fish and chips by the water, and spent the whole afternoon by the pool. Salt water and sunshine. It was lovely." I took his hand and led him to the sofa. "Tell me everything you did today."

"I met Piers Bonfils, director of the Cairns Butterfly Conservatory. He's the man who emailed me, inviting me to come."

"What's he like?"

"He has contributed to the *Annales de la Société Ento-mologique de France*, so yes, he's quite renowned. He was on the Committee of the Association of Lepidoptera in France before he came to Australia."

Lawson sounded impressed, and I figured this guy's resumé was something to be respected.

"What kind of team does he have?"

Lawson smiled and squeezed my hand. "Can we talk

over dinner? I'll tell you everything, but I'm starving. I didn't eat lunch today."

"Oh, of course. Room service or dinner out? Which would you prefer?"

"I'm sure we can find a café on the esplanade."

"Perfect. Let me grab a quick shower, just to wash the salt water off me. I feel a bit sticky."

Lawson's right eyebrow flickered up as did the corner of his mouth. "Or you could leave it so I can taste it later."

I laughed. "Or we could take a night swim together after dinner? Then afterwards you can taste me as much as you want."

He gave me an insufferable sigh and a smirk. "If I must."

A quick two-minute shower later and I came out of the cubicle to find Lawson at the vanity. He sprayed deodorant under his arms, then washed his face. "I'll shower after our swim," he said, slipping a clean shirt on.

"What? No bow tie?"

"No time. I'm starving. Hurry up and get dressed."

I threw on the closest outfit I could find and pulled the door shut behind us. I knew Lawson well enough to know that he was grumpy if he didn't eat. We got to the footpath and I pointed to the quickest route to the esplanade. "This way."

We found a little café on the waterfront. Lawson ordered the grilled chicken salad and then proceeded to eat most of the fries off my plate. I laughed at him. "Want half my burger too?"

He sat back and patted his belly. "Not now."

"So tell me, what's up with the Ulysses butterfly, and why did the gorgeous Lawson Gale need to cross the country for it? I mean, I do understand you are the best lepidopterist there is, but…"

He ignored my compliment. "The Ulysses isn't breeding successfully."

I thought about that for a moment. "So you came all this way to put them in the mood?"

He chuckled. "Kind of. Well, they are breeding, but it's not viable."

"Did you try serenading them? Dinner first? No wait, tell them all they're serial killers and dazzle them with your intelligence. Totally worked for me."

Lawson laughed. "It did. However, I don't think butterflies and you have that much in common."

I feigned offence. "I'll have you know, I give the best butterfly kisses."

He hummed, and happiness seemed to radiate from him. "You certainly do."

"So, if I were a butterfly, what breed would I be?"

"Hmm." Lawson tilted his head and considered this. "You're more of a dragonfly. The *Calopteryx virgo* to be exact. Strikingly beautiful."

I smiled at that. "But you're a butterfly?"

"Probably."

"You are," I confirmed. "So why can't I be the same as you?"

"Do you need to be the same as me?"

"Yes. How can we be compatible if we're not?"

He gave me a fond smile. "Fair enough. If you were a butterfly, you'd be a White Dragontail."

"Why?"

His eyes never left mine. "Well, again, incomparable beauty, transparent wings, and they usually copulate for hours at a time."

I barked out a laugh. "Is that right?"

"Absolutely." He had that playful, amused spark in his

eyes. "You said, rather adamantly, that I would be a butterfly."

"Yes. It's true. Now, I'm not up to date on their copulation habits, but metaphorically speaking, you come across as an unassuming, shy guy, but you really do have wings. You just don't show them to many people."

He looked at me like he couldn't tear his eyes away. He swallowed hard.

I gave him a smile. "When you were explaining to me what imago was, I kept thinking it was just like you. You'd shown me your true self, and Lawson, it was a remarkable sight."

His nostrils flared, his eyes were dark with lust, and he swallowed again. "Jack, you need to take me back to our room. Now."

I looked around for our waitress and put my hand up to get her attention. "Bill, please."

When we left the café, Lawson slipped his hand into mine. We hadn't really been anywhere together that warranted holding hands. If we walked down the street in Scottsdale, one of us was usually holding a bag of produce or Rosemary's leash. When we were in Launceston, we were usually at his place or at professor Tillman's butterfly house. Sure, we went out for dinner occasionally, but we'd park close to the restaurant. We rarely walked anywhere far enough to hold hands.

He squeezed my fingers. "Is this okay?"

"It's more than okay."

He walked with a skip in his step back to the hotel, and

when we passed the pool, I pointed to it. "Wanna take a dip?"

"After."

"After what?"

He fit the key into the lock and pushed the door open. "After what you're about to do to me."

He walked in first, unbuttoning his shirt as he went. He tossed it onto the floor and kept walking into the bedroom. He stopped in the doorway, looked right at me while he undid the button and zipper on his pants. "Waiting for something?"

Fucking hell.

I stepped inside and locked the door behind me just in time to see his pants being flung to the floor.

"I'm starting without you," he said, his voice tight.

When I got to the bedroom door, I found him on the bed, on his back with his knees bent. His right hand gripped his cock, his left rubbed over his hole. A bottle of lube lay next to him on the bed.

"Lawson," I breathed his name.

He slipped a finger inside himself. "Jack, you're not naked and you're not inside me."

I pulled my shirt over my head and toed out of my shoes. I pulled my socks off and slid my shorts over my hips. I was already hard. Seeing him laid out before me like that, offering himself to me, turned me on like nothing else could.

I gave myself a few strokes but then had to pull on my balls to stave off my orgasm. Jesus. I wasn't going to last at this rate.

Lawson writhed on the bed, jerked himself, and added another finger to his slicked hole. "Jack," he bit out. "You're still not inside me."

I knelt on the bed and took the foil packet he'd put near the lube. I rolled the condom down my length and Lawson moaned. I knew if I left it a moment longer, that filthy mouth of his would—

"Jack, I need your cock in me when I come. If you don't fuck me soon—"

And there it was.

"Take your hand away," I ordered and moved into position between his thighs.

He gripped the backs of his knees and I pressed the blunt head of my cock to his hole. "Just fucking do it," he ground out.

I pushed into him, in one full thrust.

His eyes went wide, his jaw bulged, and he gritted his teeth.

I knew he could take it. And not just take it but love every second. "Is that what you want?"

He nodded and breathed, his body relaxing. "God yes." I slowly rocked my hips, giving him time to adjust. "Fuck me, Jack. Make me yours."

God, his words were fuel to a fire I was trying to contain.

I couldn't help it, I couldn't stop. I slammed into him, deeper than I'd ever been, and his mouth fell open; his neck corded. He gasped and moaned. "Yes, like that."

Leaning back on my haunches, I took his cock in my hand and pumped him while I fucked his arse. Lawson put both his hands on his head, pulled at his hair, and shook his head. Precome was leaking from his slit, and he bucked his hips. He was hard and close to coming, so close.

"You like being filled with my cock," I grated out. "And soon it'll just be me, nothing else. And when I come, you'll feel it."

Lawson's whole body jerked, his arse tightened around me, and his cock swelled in my hand before spilling come onto his belly.

He was glorious.

When he sagged beneath me, I let go of his spent dick and leaned over him so I could kiss him. And I kept kissing him. What had started out as hard and fast fucking was now slow-and-sweet lovemaking.

Lawson fisted my hair and rolled his hips, taking every inch of me in every unhurried thrust. He broke our kiss but spoke against my lips. "I can't wait to have your come inside me."

And that was all it took.

My orgasm exploded at the base of my spine and bloomed through my whole body. Pleasure burned in my veins, and Lawson held onto me: he wrapped his legs and arms around me as I filled the condom inside him.

I didn't know if I passed out, but I kind of came to with Lawson gently stroking the hair from my forehead and planting soft kisses to my nose. We were a sticky mess but neither of us seemed too keen to move. He hummed contentedly. "Hmm, how about I get a cloth to clean us up, then we go for that swim?"

I smiled at him. "How about you stay right here, and I get us the cloth, then we go for that swim."

A slow spreading smile covered his face. "Okay."

I kissed his lips and slid out of bed. I disposed of the condom, grabbed a washcloth, and wet it before cleaning him up. I threw his swimming trunks onto the bed and pulled on my boardies, then we headed out to the pool.

"Oh," I said on our way out. "I forgot about the courtyard."

"What about the courtyard?"

"Doing indoor activities outdoors, remember?"

Lawson put his hand on the pool fence gate and raised one eyebrow at me. "Pool's empty?"

I laughed. "Maybe the pool's a little too public. I don't fancy having a criminal record for indecent exposure, if you know what I mean. I think the courtyard might be more private, yet still outdoors."

He tilted his head in that adorable way he did when considering all the facts presented to him. "Good call." He swung the gate open, threw his towel onto a pool chair, and dived cleanly into the water.

He surfaced, glistening wet and smooth, looked up at me, and grinned. "Getting in, Jack? Or do you intend to stand there and stare at me all night?"

"I dunno," I answered, looking right at him. "The view's pretty good from here."

He laughed and smoothed back his dripping wet hair. "I'm sure it is. But the *view,* if that's what we're calling me, is interactive in the water."

I threw my towel next to his and dove, not as gracefully as him I'm sure, into the water. I came up close enough to him, but as soon as I found my feet, he launched himself at me. He threw his arms around my neck and kissed me, and I slipped my hands around his back.

I had no idea that a wet-Lawson was such a hot-Lawson. He broke away with a smirk. "I'm going to do some laps. Care to join me?"

I shook my head slowly. "You go ahead. I'd much rather just enjoy the view."

So he turned and glided through the water with strong and languid strokes, and I stayed with my back to the end of the pool, watching him.

Until I got bored with that. And when he swam up to

touch the end of the pool, I pounced on him. He came up spluttering out a laugh. "What was that for?"

"I prefer the interactive view."

He folded his legs around my hips, locking his feet behind my back, his arms wound around my neck. "Ever kissed anyone underwater?"

I shook my head. "No."

"Neither have I."

I laughed, but apparently that was not the right response. He gave me his stern face, his no-nonsense, you-might-be-bigger-than-me-but-I'm-the-one-in-charge face. "Jack, take me to the deep end and kiss me underwater."

Have I ever mentioned I'm a sucker for a bossy power bottom? "Your wish. My command."

CHAPTER FIVE
LAWSON

PIERS BONFILS WAS A PASSIONATE FRENCHMAN. HANDSOME, LATE fifties, with eyes the same colour as his dark-grey hair, and a lighter grey goatee. He was tanned and fit and walked with a fluid grace that was borne of his confidence and ego.

I liked him. He spoke his mind, a trait I admired in anyone, and had the intellect to back up his arguments. But he also listened with an open mind, never afraid to learn. And that was a rarity, especially in my field.

He had met my old boss from Melbourne, Professor Asterly, a few times, and although he appreciated the man's input to lepidoptery, he never much liked the way he played the political game to further his career.

"Asterly can deny it all he likes," Piers said, his accent thick, "but the truth is, he disliked me because of who I choose to bed. Nothing to do with my career. I assume he's the same with you?"

I blinked in surprise. We were having lunch in his office, not discussing our private lives in a bar or something. "I uh. Um."

Piers smiled knowingly at me. "It's fine with me,

Lawson. I will never hide the fact I'm gay. Neither do you. I thought you would understand."

This was not a conversation I was strictly comfortable having. "I am, gay, that is, and I do understand. Only I separate my personal life from my professional life. I would never want details of Professor Asterly's sexual habits, and I expect the same courtesy."

He smiled as though I charmed him. "Ah, we are of different generations, young Lawson. You are of an age where it is accepted and no one bothers you, you know? But I had to fight for it and not hide who I was, even if it could cost me my job. Asterly always thought he was better than me for this reason. The wolves were always at my door, and he was given research grants as rewards."

"I was unaware of this," I said, pushing my water away. "Though I would hardly be surprised. He never warmed to me. I assumed it was because I spoke my mind and refused to pander to everything he said."

Piers laughed. "This is why Professor Tillman sought you out!"

"Well, yes. Professor Asterly was not happy."

He threw his hands up and said some rather choice words in French. I knew enough to piece together what he meant. But he offered me a smile. "Serves him right."

I folded my sandwich wrapper neatly in half, then half again, pressing it down flat. Piers was watching me with a smile. "So tell me, Lawson. What is your expert opinion thus far on the Ulysses?"

"I agree with your findings. Everything you list is accurate, and there are no discrepancies in your data."

He nodded slowly. "I should hope not."

"It would be counterproductive of me to assume your figures and percentages are correct without checking for myself. If I took your data as gospel and there was an error, I'd never find the inconsistency."

"True."

"Given the data is sound, we need to determine external factors, as I'm sure you're very aware."

Piers smiled and scrunched up his sandwich wrapper. "Yes."

"The fact the butterflies can breed and are willing is encouraging. Why the caterpillar survives but the butterfly dies is the concern."

"Your first thought?"

"External factors, such as climate and diet, would be my first guess. Given the butterfly house is and has been a constant temperature and humidity for years without incident before now gives me reason to lean toward diet."

"Ah, but nothing has changed in their diet."

"With all due respect, Professor Bonfils, that's where you're wrong. Because something *has* changed. Those butterflies are telling us something has changed. We just need to figure out what it is."

I GOT BACK TO THE HOTEL ROOM FEELING DISGRUNTLED AND irritated. Though Jack was there with a welcoming smile and a hug that held healing qualities. I could feel my worries dissipate in the few seconds he held me in his strong, warm arms.

"You've had a crap day," he stated. He could tell. I nodded against his chest. "Tell me about it."

"Are you sure?" I asked, still with my face pressed into his shirt. "Because I feel the need to rant and I fear it will be misdirected at you."

I could hear the quiet rumble of his laughter through his chest. "You ranting in all your passionate glory is one of my favourite things."

I finally smiled.

"Let me guess," Jack said. "Bonfils is an idiot."

I sighed. "Well, not exactly. He just has idiotic views."

Jack's whole body vibrated when he chuckled. He tightened his arms around me. "What did he say?"

"Normally he's very receptive and open to ideas, but he's refusing to see reason. I understand he's frustrated and upset with what's happening to the Ulysses, but"—I pulled back a little so I could look up at his face—"how can someone who has dedicated his career to the betterment of lepidoptery be so ignorant to the plight of his very cause?"

"How so?"

I huffed out a sigh. "The Ulysses is in decline. The breeding program is failing, and he is unwilling to believe external environmental factors are at play. 'Nothing has changed.'" I imitated the Professor's accent. Then I growled out my frustration. "He's a scientist. How can a scientist ignore facts? I told him he was wrong."

Jack smiled. "Of course you did."

"Something has changed. Those butterflies are telling us something has changed, but he won't listen to them."

"How does one listen to a butterfly?" Jack wasn't placating me. He was serious, as though he really wanted to know the answer.

"We watch. We learn. We study their habits, movements, habitat. The butterfly house is a controlled environment, and for many years, it's worked exceptionally well."

"Is it the air quality?"

I smiled. "I've tested that. The air filtration system is

well maintained and there have been no recent changes. The humidity is perfect."

Jack frowned. "Then it has to be diet. If their habitat hasn't changed, the air and humidity are fine, then it has to be diet."

I clawed my face. "Oh my God, Jack, if you can see that and I can see that, why can't he?"

"You've suggested this?"

"I told him it had to be the likely contributing factor."

"And he refutes it?"

"He simply claims it can't be because nothing has changed."

"Well, that's stupid."

Despite my frustrations, I laughed. "I may have said that also."

Jack put his hands on the tops of my arms. "Would you like a glass of wine?"

"I would love one." I leaned up and kissed his lips. "Then you can tell me what you did today."

I collapsed onto the sofa, feeling better already, and Jack walked back from the kitchenette with a glass of wine in each hand. He handed me one and sat side-on to me with one leg folded up underneath him, giving me his undivided attention. "Sure you don't want to vent some more?"

I sipped my wine and shook my head. "No. I want to hear all about your day."

"Well, I walked the esplanade again, though I'm not too keen on going in the ocean. There are warning signs listing all the things that bite in there, so I think I'll stick with the pool. I did some laps, had a lunch of fresh seafood."

"And you're bored," I deduced.

He gave me a smile. "A little. I'm used to being busy all

the time, and yesterday it was great to be lazy, but by lunchtime I was itching to do something constructive."

"I'm sorry."

"What for?"

"It's because of me we're spending your holiday time up here, and I'm busy working. That's not fair on you."

"I like being here with you. And anyway, I was thinking of heading up to the national parks office tomorrow and introducing myself. You know, one park ranger to another."

"Is there some kind of code you guys go by?"

He laughed and sipped his wine. "Only that we're smarter than the av-er-age bear." His impersonation of Yogi Bear was disturbingly good.

I couldn't help but laugh. "Do all park rangers make Yogi Bear jokes?"

He grinned and put on his Yogi voice again. "Ah, that's Mr Ranger, sir, to you, Boo-Boo."

It really wasn't that funny, but all I could do was laugh. If that was his intent—to make me happy after my frustrating day—it sure worked.

"What did you feel like for dinner?" he asked eventually.

"What? No pic-a-nic baskets?"

He chuckled warmly. "A picnic on the beach is a great idea."

So, half an hour later, I was changed into shorts and a T-shirt, and Jack was carrying a bag from the supermarket. Tonight we feasted on roast chicken, fresh baked bread, marinated artichokes, and olives. And wine, of course. We found a quiet place on the sand and sat down, facing the beautiful Pacific Ocean just as the sun had almost disappeared behind us. "We should have brought a blanket," Jack mused.

"No. This is perfect."

He held out a plastic cup we'd bought from the supermarket and grinned. "Not exactly high class."

I chuckled. "This is better than high class. This is us."

He opened the wine and poured some into my cup, then into his own. He held his plastic cup up to mine and repeated my words back to me. "This is us."

The night was dark, but the esplanade was lit well enough that we were hidden by night from most of the passers-by. We ate some dinner, using our fingers, feeding each other, and laughing at the mess we'd made of ourselves. He was so much fun, and I hated the idea of him being bored on his own during the day.

"Come with me tomorrow," I said, "to the butterfly conservatory. I have one or two things that need attending in the morning then in the afternoon we can go up to the park. How does that sound?"

Jack grinned in the faint light of the esplanade. "Sounds perfect."

THE LOOK ON JACK'S FACE AS HE WALKED INTO THE BUTTERFLY conservatory was one I'd never forget. His eyes were wide with wonder, identical to his smile. "Oh my God, Lawson. This is incredible."

And it was. I agreed.

The butterfly conservatory wasn't just a lab or a butterfly house where we kept pupas and chrysalises. There was a huge atrium with a climate-controlled rainforest where butterflies were free to flutter and roam as they would in the wild. It truly was an amazing setup and one I could only hope to achieve back in Tasmania.

I'd explained procedure and what not to do, and Jack's excitement was adorable and contagious. "And we can go inside it?" Jack asked.

I chuckled and opened the door. "Yes, of course."

Once inside, we walked over the wooden bridge and moved to the centre near the water feature. "Okay, just lift your arms out and stand still," I urged him. I took a half-cut orange from a feeder and put it in the palm of his hand.

"What are you doing?"

"Just wait."

He did as I instructed. "Oh my God," Jack squeaked as a Ulysses butterfly flittered over to him, landing on his chest, then another on his shoulder. "What are they doing?"

"Be careful. They're the last two breeding pair left here."

He remained stock still, but his gaze shot to mine. "Last?"

I nodded slowly. "Unfortunately, yes."

"I didn't realise it was so dire. When you said there was a breeding problem..."

"It's more of a longevity issue. They breed just fine. But they're dying soon after imago."

Jack frowned and watched the butterfly for a quiet moment. "My God, it's beautiful." He looked at the butterfly now on the orange in his hand. "It's huge. I wasn't expecting it to be so big!"

"They like you," I said with a laugh. "Well, they like your shirt."

He shot me a look. "You told me to wear this one today."

"Because it's blue. They're attracted to the colour blue."

A green birdwing butterfly landed on his forearm. He made a funny face that was part comical, part awe. "Holy shit, it's big. I can feel its feet, and it tickles."

"He's tasting you," I explained. Then I hummed. "I have

to say. I've never been jealous of a butterfly before."

Jack laughed, and I put my hand up to his outstretched arm, trying to tempt the butterfly onto my fingers. We both stood breathless, watching as the butterfly flittered from him to me and back to him. When our gazes locked again, we both smiled at what had just passed between us. It was a strangely private moment. Quiet and reverent. Personal.

Then Jack looked over my shoulder to something behind me. "There's a man watching us."

"Oh?" My first thought was that someone might not appreciate two men being caught in a questionable moment. "Is he angry?"

Jack frowned. "No. Sad."

I turned around then to find Professor Bonfils. "Oh, good morning, Professor," I said, relief washing through me. "I hope you don't mind I brought Jack in this morning. I wanted to show him the reason we're in North Queensland and why he's not skiing in New Zealand."

It took a moment for him to smile, which was an odd reaction.

So I quickly added, "I can assure you I've taken every precaution with quarantine."

Piers held his hand up as a peace offering. "It's fine, Lawson." Then he nodded to Jack. "Professor Piers Bonfils. It's a pleasure to meet you. Is it Jack? I'd like to say I've heard all about you, but I haven't. Lawson didn't mention he had a travel companion."

I didn't care much for the professor's tone but Jack smiled good-naturedly. "Jack Brighton. I would shake your hand, but Lawson told me not to move. And that's okay about me being a surprise; I don't expect Lawson to talk about me at work."

I frowned. "Well no. I don't cross-contaminate my

personal and professional lives."

Jack appeared as if he was trying not to laugh, though I couldn't understand why. So I added, "And Jack is more to me than a travel companion."

Piers gave me a tight smile. His accent was particularly thick when he said, "I could see that." Then his face softened, as though he'd remembered his manners. "I was watching when the butterflies first landed on you." He turned his attention to Jack and the two butterflies still on his shirt. "Magnificent creatures, no?"

Jack gave him one of his disarming smiles, dimples and all. "They're remarkable."

Piers' peculiar tension seemed to dissipate as he told Jack about this particular Ulysses, and when there was a brief pause in the conversation, I interrupted. "If you don't mind, Professor, I'm just going to check the water samples." I gave Jack an apologetic glance as I left them to talk.

I entered the lab area and quickly set about checking the samples I'd taken on day one and day two. I'd taken petri dish swabs to see if the issue was bacterial, and I had sent samples to the CSIRO for analysis. I was doing everything that Piers had already done, but I had to see the data for myself.

All pH levels were fine. All bacteria was fine and well within the healthy range.

With a final check of emails, I printed off the CSIRO soil report and read through their findings. All readings were normal. Potassium levels were toward the higher range of normal, but nothing stood out as problematic.

It was frustrating, but by process of elimination, it was still something. If it wasn't the air or the water affecting the Ulysses, it had to be diet.

I was more convinced.

Piers appeared at my side, startling me. "Oh!"

He gave me a sad smile, then nodded to the report in my hand. "Find anything new?"

"No. Nothing really."

He nodded slowly. He appeared uncomfortable or distracted.

"Everything okay? Where's Jack?"

Piers looked back to the atrium. "Oh, he's still with the butterflies. He's quite fascinated."

I smiled.

Piers studied me a moment. "That look on your face. You love him."

"That's hardly professional and quite frankly not up for discussion."

He waved me off. "Oh, Lawson. It's perfectly fine. Don't be embarrassed. If anything, I'm envious."

"Of my relationship with Jack?"

He bobbed his head in a so-so manner. "More so his relationship with you."

Oh.

"*Oh.*"

He laughed, embarrassed, and shook his head. "It was foolish of me to think... Anyway, he's a very lucky man."

Oh dear. This was terribly embarrassing. "He is a lucky man. As am I. But if you invited me here on the proviso or the assumption that you and I would be compatible... in that manner, you were quite incorrect."

"Not entirely," he said. He looked properly abashed, and I found myself forgiving him.

"Then why *am* I here?"

"For your intellect, to see what I cannot," Piers answered. "You have a proven track record to examine and process. Though you've spent three days repeating data analysis that I assured you was correct. Now you're leaving today to do tourist sightseeing. You keep saying it's the diet, but it cannot be."

Okay, so maybe he wasn't completely forgiven. Piers' passion and temper were not mutually exclusive, and I was only tolerant of so much. "Professor Bonfils, the reason I am here at your request is to help determine possible causes of the decline in the Ulysses. I'm not here to agree with you. If you want someone to pat you on the back and tell you you've done all you can do, then you chose the wrong person. I'm here to help you save this species. If you'd rather I left, tell me now and I'll go. I don't want to waste your time. But I can tell you right now, this butterfly is dying. If you'd rather see it face extinction than admit you could have done more, then I'll have no part of it. If you want to help me help you, then respectfully, sir, take your head out of your arse and help me."

He did his angry-Frenchman-hand-waving thing. "I think I can see why Professor Asterly doesn't like you."

"I don't care what Asterly thinks of me. I don't care what you think of me. I'm not here to be liked, Professor. I'm here to do a job."

His eyes flashed with defiance and possibly amusement. "Despite my best efforts to the contrary, I do like you."

"Thank you. And I respect the work you've done here. It is incredible, and I'm not disparaging your life's work. Quite the opposite, actually. But we need plans and we need them actioned. I'm only here for a limited time."

"Well, about that," Bonfils replied cautiously. "I told you my interests in you being here were only partially personal. If I were to offer you a position here, full-time, to work as co-lead, would you be interested?"

CHAPTER SIX

JACK

Lawson was quiet on the drive to the Kuranda National Park. Granted, it was just around the corner, but he spent the entire time in the car either frowning or scowling, chewing on his bottom lip.

"Everything okay?"

"Hmm?" He looked surprised I'd spoken. "Sorry, I was a million miles away."

I drove the car into a spot in the tourist parking lot. I shut the engine off and looked at him. "I asked if everything was okay?"

"Oh, yes. Well, not really."

"What's going through that brilliant mind of yours, Lawson? Is it the butterflies? Or something else?"

He swallowed hard and shook his head. "It's nothing. Let's go. I'm quite excited to be here."

I looked out the windscreen to where the sign to the Kuranda National Park greeted us. Something was bothering him, but if he needed time to process, then I would give him that. "I'm excited too! We could spend days here, and given we have half a day, we better get moving."

We paid our entry fee and opted for the guided tour, which was an amphibious vehicle that took us into the rainforest floor, exploring the amazing trees and ferns, all the tropical and citrus fruits, then onto the river where we could explore the rainforest from the water. It was incredible, but I really wanted to spend time with Lawson, just us. I wanted to see him experience this rainforest, this new environment, and watch his every reaction.

After the guided tour, we took the Skyrail up to the top of the mountain so we could walk back down, just the two of us.

And I wasn't disappointed.

I could practically hear his mind turning, his love for learning new things shone in his eyes. I mean the rainforest was incredible: damp paths underfoot, dense green foliage, tall trees, and a whole symphony of sounds.

"It's an extraordinary place, isn't it?" I couldn't keep the wonder from my tone.

"Yes, quite," he replied, stopping to look up at the canopy of a particular tree. "Very different from your parks in Tasmania."

"Well, on the west coast of Tassie, we have rainforests similar but not tropical like this. I'll have to take you to the Franklin-Gordon Wild Rivers National Park. Now *that* is something to see." I reached over and put my hand on the trunk of the tree he was looking at. "Wanna know what this is called?"

"Sure."

I grinned. "It's the *Idiospermum australiense* or the Idiot Fruit."

He gave me a disbelieving look. "You're joking?"

"No, I'm not joking! The fruit seed is highly poisonous. No birds or animals will touch it."

"Except for the idiot it was undoubtedly named after."

I laughed. "Probably."

He gave me a smile that didn't quite sit right.

I had planned to give him time, but maybe he needed some prompting. I debated not saying anything, but I hated the fact he was miserable. "Lawson, did Professor Bonfils say something to upset you?"

His gaze shot to mine, and the look on his face told me all I needed to know. He blinked nervously. "Why do you say that?"

"Because you're an open book. I thought it might have just been the butterflies, but that's not it. Something's been bothering you since we left the conservatory this morning. I figured it was him because he went off to speak to you, and you've been quiet since."

"Oh." He chewed on his bottom lip and stared off into the forest.

"Lawson, is it the fact he's attracted to you?"

His eyes bugged out and his mouth fell open, which would've been funny if he didn't go a little pale. "I never encouraged... I didn't know..."

I pulled him against me and hugged him, and chuckling, I kissed the side of his head. "I know. But it was pretty clear from the moment he saw you with me that he was disappointed."

The truth was, Lawson was oblivious to the reactions of most people around him. It would have been obvious to most people that Piers found Lawson attractive, but just not obvious to Lawson.

"I'm sorry," he mumbled.

I pulled back, keeping my hands on his arms. "What on earth for? You've nothing to apologise for."

He sighed and his frown deepened. "He told me he was

jealous that I had a friend such as you. I told him, indisputably, you were more than just a friend, and if his intentions in asking me to come here were romantically inclined, he was very mistaken."

I tried not to smile, but I lifted his chin so he'd look at me. I pecked my lips to his. "Thank you. Though I had no doubt. I trust you, Lawson. Implicitly."

The corner of his lip pulled down. "There's something else."

A cold trickle of dread seeped into my chest. "What's that?"

"I wasn't going to say anything, but I can't… I won't keep secrets from you."

The trickle became a pool.

"He's asked me to join his team. Permanently."

"What?"

"Professor Bonfils has officially requested I join his team on a permanent basis here, in far north Queensland."

I blinked. "Oh. What did you say?"

"Nothing. Before I could answer, he told me to think about it."

"What about your Tillman Copper?"

"Exactly. My work there is very important. I won't leave my own team." He stared into my eyes. "I don't want to leave you, either. You're very important too."

Relief coursed through me. I couldn't deny it. He slipped his hand into mine and gently pulled me to keep walking. "Come on. We better get heading back." He lifted my hand to his lips and kissed my knuckles. "You can tell me more botanical names on the way."

I FELT KINDA DETACHED AFTER LAWSON TOLD ME THAT HE'D BEEN offered a job here. I was pissed off and scared too because I'd just found the most incredible man, and I could see myself with him forever. In Tasmania. Where we lived. I mean, we didn't live together, per se, but it was only a matter of time. We both knew that.

Or had I assumed that? Were we even on the same page? I thought we were, but now I wasn't sure.

When we got back to the information centre, I was still talking about the *Epiphytes*. They were an amazing plant, in particular, the *Drynaria rigidula* and the Northern Elkhorn. And it was easier for me to keep talking about the ecosystem of plants rather than think about Lawson leaving.

"Well, you certainly know what you're talking about," a woman said. She wore a park uniform, her blonde hair in a ponytail, and a high-wattage smile.

"Oh, hi. Yes, flora and fauna. It's what I do," I said, extending my hand out to her. "Jack Brighton's my name."

"Cassie O'Hearn." She had a firm handshake, and I liked her immediately.

"Lawson Gale." Lawson introduced himself politely. "Jack works for Parks and Wildlife in Tasmania."

"And Lawson's here on a professional invitation from the butterfly conservatory." Then I added, "So, technically, flora and fauna is what *we* do."

Cassie's eyes lit up. "Excellent!

"Maybe you can tell Lawson about the *Dendrocnide moroide*," I suggested to her. "Because he thinks I'm making it up."

Lawson rolled his eyes. "I believe him about the idiot fruit because... well, I don't doubt some idiot ate it and died after being told not to eat it. But a tree that has glass on the leaves?" He gave me a doubtful look. "I'm not gullible."

Cassie laughed. "The Stinging Tree. Rest assured it's very real, and I don't recommend you go near it."

Lawson frowned at her. "He wasn't pulling my leg?"

Cassie shook her head with a smile. "No. The leaves may look harmless, but they're covered with microscopic hairs made of mineral silica: the chief constituent of glass. If you brush against the hair-like tips, they break off and embed in the skin and release a poison irritant. The sting's effect is severe and lasts for months."

Lawson made a face. "That's what Jack said. I'm starting to see why most tourists believe almost everything in Australia is trying to kill you."

She laughed again. "So, you're here from Tasmania?" she asked, looking at me this time. "That's pretty cool. I help look after the Tasmanian devils here. We have a breeding pair, and the newest pups are a handful."

"Oh, can I see them?" Lawson asked excitedly.

Cassie beamed. "Sure!"

We followed Cassie out into the wildlife park, and as we walked to the enclosure, I told her how Lawson had almost died when he saved two joeys from the bushfire. She stopped at the enclosure fence so she could hug him. The look on his face was priceless.

Cassie laughed and looked to a particular spot in the enclosure. "Over there," she said.

The devils were out of the den. Given the late afternoon, it wasn't too surprising. Lawson put his hand on my arm. "Look, Jack, there they are!"

I put my hand on his lower back. "They're bigger than the ones you saved."

"They might be this big by now," he said wistfully, not taking his eyes off the playful joeys.

If Cassie had any problem with mine and Lawson's displays of affection, even as passive as they were—a gentle touch, a reassuring hand—she certainly didn't let on. In fact, we chatted as we watched the devils rumble and tackle each other.

Just then, another staff member joined us. He introduced himself as Gary, and Cassie explained further, "Gary's one of our vegetation experts." Then she nodded to me. "Jack here's with the Tassie Parks and Wildlife."

Gary's eyes widened, as did his smile. "How're ya finding it up here?"

"It's beautiful."

"Sure is," he agreed. "How long you stayin' for?"

"Another week." I introduced Lawson and mentioned his work with the conservatory. "He has a week to find out what's affecting the Ulysses, save the species, and ensure the entomological ecosystem remains in balance."

Gary and Cassie laughed. Lawson rolled his eyes. "It's hardly that exciting."

"That's a pretty remarkable job," Cassie said.

"It is a remarkable job," I agreed.

"It's one I should get back to," Lawson said, glancing at his watch. "I told the professor I'd be back before he leaves for the evening."

"Ah, how is Professor Piers going?" Gary asked.

"You know him?" Lawson asked.

Gary nodded. "I deal with him a bit. We supply organic fruit and plants for his butterflies."

"Oh, of course," Lawson said. "Piers is okay. He's very passionate about his work. And I'd imagine he won't be too pleased if I'm late."

I took our cue. "Yes, we should be going. Thank you, Cassie, for the private tour."

"Pleasure," she said cheerfully.

Gary put his hand out. "Hey, if you're looking for something to do during the day, I run guided walking tours. Not many people find the biodiversity of our flora as exciting as me, but you might like it."

"I'd love it!" I agreed. "And actually, I have a few hours to spare."

"Excellent!"

We said our goodbyes, and I was quite excited about my little guided excursion into the forest tomorrow. I'd almost forgotten about Professor Bonfils' offer to Lawson and for the reason of the trip in general until we got back to the conservatory.

We found Professor Bonfils sitting dejectedly at his lab desk, a sad frown etched into his features.

"What is it?" Lawson asked as we approached him.

Piers nodded to a tray in front of him, and we took a closer look. On it was the body of a dead Ulysses. Its bright blue wings folded, its inquisitive, curious light extinguished. "Our last breeding pair is gone."

Lawson's shoulders sagged, his whole frame seemed smaller. "Oh no."

I took Lawson back to our hotel room. He was understandably quiet and sad. I put my keys on the table and cupped his face. "Tell me what you want. Do you want to talk? I know it helps you think straight talking through things."

He sighed and leaned into my palm.

"Lawson?" I said gently. "Tell me what's happening to the Ulysses."

He closed his eyes. "It's dying. The species. In captivity, in the wild. Not just here, but worldwide. We don't know why."

"You think it's diet related?"

He nodded and looked up to me. "It has to be."

"Tell me why? Tell me how it's possible for just this species. No other butterflies are affected, so tell me what's different about this butterfly?"

He started to smile. "You really want to know?"

I nodded. "Start with the basics. You said this was happening worldwide. Where else is the Ulysses found?"

"Papua New Guinea, Indonesia, Solomon Islands."

"So basically, the tropics of the Pacific."

Lawson gave a nod and sighed. "Larvae feed typically on kerosene wood, citrus, and *Euodia*. Imago, they eat from blossoms of the doughwood plant."

"Okay, so what's happening to these plants to impact the butterfly?"

"By all reports, from various universities and the CSIRO, nothing. There has been some decline of the *Euodia* tree in deforestation, but that doesn't contribute to the fact they're dying in captivity."

"Okay, then, so tell me what's unusual about their deaths. It seems odd to me that they're making it to adult stage and then dying."

"Exactly. Typically parasites that may affect a butterfly species will render eggs unfertilised, or the egg casings are simply not viable."

"What is the main factors in adult Ulysses' deaths?"

"Heat stress, pesticides, predators such as snakes, frogs, birds."

"None of which can contribute to the butterflies at the conservatory."

Lawson shook his head slowly. "No. Everything is organically grown and certified, from the national park, actually, and the conservatory is climate controlled. There are no predators."

"And it's only the Ulysses. No other butterfly?"

Now he sighed. "Just the Ulysses."

"It has to be botanical."

"That's what I said."

"Does Piers not agree?"

"He's tested the soil, the leaves. As have I. There are no significant changes; we've tested for every disease we can think of. Potassium was marked a little higher than usual but still well within the normal ranges. I've wasted three days re-testing when I should have been doing something else."

"Like what?" I asked. "What could you have done to avoid that butterfly dying today?"

He put his head down. "I don't know."

"Lawson, you had to start from the beginning. There's no point in studying a contaminated control sample."

"Maybe I should be here," he mumbled. "Full-time, trying to save this species."

My heart stopped.

His frown deepened. "The Tillman Copper is thriving; the Ulysses is not. My time would be better spent here."

"Oh." I nodded slowly. "You're right. It would be."

He put his forehead on my chest. "Though I can't bear to think of leaving you."

I rubbed his back. "We'll work something out," I said, not feeling the conviction I'd hoped he heard. "If it comes to that."

He looked up at me, his eyes imploring. "If I did decide to move here, would you support my decision?"

"Of course I would. I'd hate that you were so far away, but we could make it work. I told you before, distance isn't a problem for me."

He settled his head against my chest and slid his arms around me. "Thank you."

I gave him a squeeze. "You're welcome."

"I'm hungry."

I snorted and lifted his chin so I could kiss him. "Then I shall feed you."

He let his forehead fall to my shoulder, and I kissed the side of his head. "Room service?"

He burrowed into my neck and hummed. "I wasn't talking about food."

CHAPTER SEVEN
LAWSON

I don't know what it was about having Jack's arms around me, but it brought something out in me that I hadn't experienced with anyone else. Every time he embraced me, I felt safe and sheltered, in every sense of the word.

He also spurred a yearning, a deep physical desire within me. I wanted him to have me, claim me and own me. I wanted to be his, to fulfil every need he had, and to be thoroughly at his mercy.

His sweet, sweet mercy.

"Come with me," I murmured against his lips. "I want to show you something." I took his hand and led him to the bedroom. I urged him to sit on the bed, and I went to the drawer I'd put my underclothes in. "Now, please don't be mad."

I took out the two white envelopes I'd brought with us from home. The envelopes from the pathology lab concerning our bloodwork.

Jack's eyes went wide when he realised what they were. "Oh. You brought them with you?"

I nodded slowly. "I don't know why I wasn't ready before, but I am now." I swallowed hard. "If you are."

He still sat on the bed, his eyes were filled with worry. "I'm sure. Are you sure you're sure?"

I gave him a smile and sat down next to him. "Never been surer." I held up the two envelopes. "Do you want to read mine or yours?"

"Mine."

I handed him the envelope addressed to him and slid my finger underneath the seal of mine. I pulled out the folded piece of paper and opened it. Jack did the same, and we read our reports at the same time. My blood work was all fine, and I watched Jack as he read through his. He looked up and smiled, then handed me his report. I gave him mine, and after seeing his report was all fine as well, we sat in silence for a moment.

"What now?" he asked.

I took the letter from him, stood up, and set them both on the bedside table. Then planting my knee on the bed, I swung my leg over him to straddle his hips. "Jack, can I tell you something?"

He had to look up at me, his hands bracing his weight behind him. "Of course."

"I don't know if I will explain this adequately," I started, sliding my hand along his jaw. "I want to be yours."

He smiled in confusion. "You already are."

"No, I want to be only yours. I want you to make me yours, make me belong to you. In a way that no one else ever has."

His nostrils flared, his eyes flashed with desire.

I bent down and kissed him, tasting his mouth before I pulled away. I put both hands to his face and spoke against his lips. "Jack, I want to take you inside me, all of you, and only you. I want you to come in—"

Jack crushed his mouth to mine and flipped me over so I was on my back and he was between my legs. He drove his tongue against mine and kissed me so hard my brain lost all coherent thought.

I could feel his erection, hot and hard, against mine through our clothes, and then he was frantic about removing them. He sat back on his haunches and pulled at my shoes, giving me a chance to catch my breath. Then he undid my trousers and pulled the hems at my ankles to slide them off my legs. Then my underwear, then my shirt, until I was naked before him.

He took in every inch of my body and licked his lips. "Oh, Lawson."

Not that I minded being on display for him, being studied and ogled, not when he looked at me like he wanted to devour me. But one thing wasn't right. "You're still very dressed."

He pulled off his shirt, tossing it over his shoulder. Then he climbed off the bed and took his boots off, and while he undressed, I leaned over to the bedside table and collected the bottle of lube.

No condom.

My blood warmed at the thought of what we were about to do.

I flipped the lid on the bottle and Jack's head turned at the sound. "Put that down. That's my job," he said. His gruff voice sent a shiver through me. I snapped the lid shut and took a hold of my erection, giving myself a long, slow pull. He crawled onto the bed, up my legs, and stopped when his mouth met the tip of my cock. He locked gazes with me, let his tongue out, and licked the tip as I jerked myself off.

Then he slid his lips over my cockhead as I pumped the base, and he sucked me hard. I rolled my hips, urging him to take more of me, but he pulled away.

"Goddammit, Jack. Don't stop."

He smirked at me and continued crawling up until his mouth met mine in a hard, deep kiss. My cock forgotten, I gripped his hair and spread my legs, lifting my hips to meet his. He wrapped his hand around my knee and hitched my leg higher and ground his erection against me.

"Jack," I growled. I was fast running out of patience.

He pulled back so he was resting on his haunches. His thick cock jutted forward, almost right where I wanted him. He took the lube, slicked his fingers, and rubbed them over my perineum.

"Mmm," I hummed, raising my hips for him. "More, Jack."

He slipped a finger inside me, and I relaxed into it, knowing what I really wanted wasn't far away. Then he added another finger, sliding in and out of me, and I pushed down on him, needing more. "I need you inside me," I groaned out.

Jack leaned over me, still fucking me with his fingers. "I am inside you."

"Your cock, Jack. I need you to fuck me."

He grinned. He found something about my cursing during sex amusing. "There it is." He kissed me as he withdrew his fingers. "I know you've had enough games when you start to swear."

I considered cursing, and I considered demanding that he drive into me, but all I could do was beg. "Please, Jack. Please."

He poured lube onto his cock and slicked himself properly and wasted no time in positioning himself at my hole. He leaned over me once more, his eyes above mine. "Are you sure?"

I cupped his face. "Yes."

And so he pushed into me. Thick and breaching, hot and hard, and everything I needed. It was pain and pleasure, too much and nowhere near enough. Jack's eyes were closed, and his jaw clenched tight as he pushed all the way inside.

"Look at me," I whispered.

His eyes shot open and he groaned. "Lawson, you feel so good like this."

I brought his lips to mine. "So do you."

He moaned out a cry when he was all the way inside me, and he shuddered. "Lawson, I don't know how long... I can't last like this..."

"Then don't." I ran my hands over his face, taking in the depth of his restraint in his eyes. "Do what you want, fuck me if you need."

He pulled back and slammed into me. "Do you want to be mine?" he asked.

I nodded. "Please."

"Only mine?"

All I could do was nod.

He was annexing me in the most incredible way. Driving into me, filling me, and taking what was his. He hooked his arms underneath my shoulders, buried his face in my neck, and fucked me. Such a brutal tenderness; my cock rubbed between our bellies as he slammed into me but he held me like I was made of glass. Every fibre in my body, every strand of pleasure, every part of me belonged to him.

He bit my earlobe, then sucked on my neck, scraping his

teeth against my skin. "Prove it to me," he rasped, and it set off a reaction I couldn't stop. My body responded, a chord struck within me.

My orgasm buckled me, pleasure detonated like a bomb, and I came. My cock spilled between us, my whole body strung tight. I gripped onto his shoulders and arched my back as the waves of pleasure almost became too much to bear.

"Oh fuck, Lawson." Jack's voice was tight and strained. I opened my eyes to see him watching me, his gaze wide and filled with wonder. "I'm gonna come inside you."

I put my hands to his face and watched as his orgasm crashed over him. His eyes rolled back, his jaw strained and neck corded as his cock swelled and he came so far inside me.

In that moment, we were one. Physically, emotionally. I could feel his heartbeat pulsing inside me, through his chest, and it beat in time with my own. Resonating, completing, everything.

I'd never felt anything like it.

Jack shuddered as his orgasm subsided. I ran my hands through his hair and pulled his face back from my neck so I could kiss him. Deep and consuming, he thrust one final time and groaned in my mouth. His arms tightened around me and I knew without any doubt, he felt the same.

He slowly pulled out of me and rolled us onto our sides, pulling me close and wrapping me up in his safe embrace. "I love you, Lawson," he whispered in my ear. Then he cupped my face and looked into my eyes. "I love you, Lawson Gale."

I nodded, and my emotions crumbled. Like my heart was exposed to him and he cradled it with such tender hands, like a gift. I blinked back tears and all I could do was nod.

He froze. "Are you okay?"

Then I laughed through my tears. "So much better than okay."

Jack finally breathed and tucked me into his side, squeezing me. "Oh, you scared me."

"I'm just a bit overwhelmed," I admitted.

"That was very intense." He ran his hand over my back in reassuring patterns for a few moments, giving me time to breathe. Then he said, "We should get cleaned up. If you like, I could run you a bath, then I can order you some room service for dinner."

He was so protective, so nurturing. I felt completely adored and secure, and I had to admit, I loved letting him take care of me. I sighed contentedly and looked up to his perfect face. "I love you too."

He chuckled and put his huge hand on my face. "You're…"

"I'm what?"

"You look like you've been thoroughly had."

I smiled. "I have been. Every inch of me, thoroughly and completely, in the very best of ways. I'm not sure my skeletal system is back to solid form yet, so the bath may have to wait."

He kissed me with smiling lips. "Then let me get a cloth. You stay right here."

He peeled himself away from me and slipped out of the bed. I stretched out, feeling the most delicious aches in all the right places. Jack came back a moment later with a warm, wet flannel and took his sweet time wiping me down, following each caress of the cloth by a soft kiss and a hum of appreciation.

When he was done, he kissed the top of my shoulder. "Feeling like that bath now?"

"Mmm."

"Lawson, can I ask you something?"

"Of course."

"Do you have any regrets? About what we just did... no condom?"

"No regrets at all. Why? Do you?"

He barked out a laugh. "Uh, no."

"And you feel okay? Not sore?"

"I feel incredible. Do I not look like I feel incredible? Because I've never felt this sated. I'm not actually that well versed in physics, but I do believe you changed my bones from a solid to a liquid."

He chuckled, somewhat smugly.

I waited for him to look into my eyes. "Why do you ask?"

His smirk was salacious, and his eyes flashed with a heated look I was becoming quite familiar with. "Because I want to do it again."

I ARRIVED AT THE CONSERVATORY TO FIND PIERS STUDYING A microscope, speaking to one of the lab assistants without looking up. They gave me a smile as they walked past. "Good morning."

"Quite," I answered, making Piers look up.

"Ah, Lawson. Good morning. How was your evening?"

The mere mention of last night brought with it a slew of memories and visual flashes of just how my night went. Sweaty bodies, quiet whispers, grunts and moans that felt so real a shiver rippled through me. Followed by a blush. I pretended to be distracted and focused on the microscope. "Very good. What are you studying in the slides?"

"The scales of the Ulysses that died yesterday."

"Find anything?"

He shook his head.

It was then I noticed the dead Ulysses on a tray behind him. It was fully intact. "Is that...?

Piers nodded. "The final remaining Ulysses was found dead this morning."

I sighed. Maybe Piers was right. Maybe my time was better spent here. The Tillman Copper was thriving and would do so whether I was there or not. The Ulysses, however, needed all the help it could get.

Moving here, away from Jack, was not what my heart wanted. But I couldn't, in good conscience, turn my back on a threatened species.

"Where is Jack today?" Piers asked, rescuing my mood somewhat.

"I just dropped him off at the park. He's spending the day doing what Parks and Wildlife officers do."

"He's a good man," Piers added. "I'm sorry if my being forthright with you earlier was unwelcome. I didn't mean to question your loyalty to him."

"He is a good man," I stated, probably with more finality than was necessary. But I was done discussing personal matters with Piers. That's not what I was here for. "So I've been thinking about the Ulysses. Are you familiar with entomotoxicology?"

Piers frowned. "The analysis of toxins ingested by arthropods that have fed on carrion?"

"Yes. Primarily it is testing on maggots and beetles that have fed on human remains to test for toxins in the body at the time of death."

"How is that relevant here?"

"Bioaccumulation." The blank stare he gave me told me he wasn't familiar with this. So I explained, "Bioaccumulation occurs when an organism absorbs a toxic substance at a faster rate than that at which the substance can be lost by catabolism and or excretion."

"I know what bioaccumulation is. What are you suggesting, Lawson? They're being poisoned?"

"My suggestion..." Then I corrected myself. "My professional opinion is that we surrender the Ulysses specimen to the CSIRO for entomotoxicological analysis, *specifically* toxicology reports."

His face resembled a cartoon character's. He went a furious red like a rising thermometer, and I half expected steam to come out his ears. "Surrender it?"

I stood my ground. "Yes. They have the proper testing facilities."

"They'll destroy it. To run such tests, they'll need to destroy it."

"They'll have to, yes."

He shook his head. "No. We can learn more from it as it is. I can pluck a few scales from the underside of the wing to analyse under a microscope, but to suggest they pulverise it..." He finished by shaking his head again.

"Professor—"

"No. These are the last species in captivity anywhere in this country. And you're suggesting we allow them to put it in a blender?"

Well, that was a crass way to put it. "Yes." I looked at the dead Ulysses in the tray. "You'll learn nothing from it as it is."

"We can run tests here. And we have! Dozens of tests."

"That found nothing."

"I thought you said it was their diet? What, now you've changed your mind?"

"No. Something they're eating is killing them. And entomotoxicological analysis would determine that. It's not like I'm asking to take a living specimen and euthanise it. It's already dead."

Piers stared at me for a long moment. "Arguing will get us nowhere."

"Then don't argue with me."

"What if you're wrong?"

"I'm not."

He waved his hand in the air to signify he'd had enough of this conversation. "Then get me proof. If you can prove something is affecting the diet of a species found in several different countries, poisoning them, then I will agree to the CSIRO testing."

So, for the rest of the day, I sat in the lab, researching, studying, thinking. I scoured the internet for any information pertaining to toxins that might possibly attribute to the cause and effect I was suggesting. I read research papers on bioaccumulation, biotransformation, bioconcentration, biodilution. By four o'clock, I was well past hungry, and my vision was blurry. I paused only a moment to rub my eyes when my phone buzzed in my pocket. It was Jack.

"Hello," I answered, sounding tired, even to my own ears.

He, on the other hand, sounded excited. "Lawson, I think I found something you might wanna come take a look at."

"Jack, I'm very busy. I'm sorry. The last Ulysses died,

and Piers has said the only way he'll allow the testing I want done is to find proof."

"That's what I'm saying, Lawson. That's what I think I found! I think I know what's killing your butterfly. You gotta come over here. Bring Piers, he can have a look too. See whatcha both reckon."

The enthusiasm in his voice made my heart race. I had no clue what he could possibly have found in relation to a dying species of butterfly, but Jack was very clued in when it came to all things flora and fauna. He was excited about something, and that was enough for me.

I stood up and grabbed my keys. "Piers? Piers!"

The professor came out of his office. "What is it?"

"We need to go. You wanted proof. Jack thinks he might have found it."

CHAPTER EIGHT
JACK

I waited in the car park for Lawson to arrive, and I was practically buzzing. He pulled up right by me, and I started explaining before he was even rightly out of the car. "I spent the day with Gary, the guy you met yesterday. Well, this morning we went into the forested area where the public doesn't get to go, and he was telling me about how for the last few years the wet season hasn't been... well, wet. Well below average rainfall. And he was telling me about cane toads and how they're rampant with the drier weather."

By this, Piers was out of the car, and I'd gone to the boot of the rental and took out the plastic tub with Lawson's water testing gear in it. I handed it to Lawson and continued, "He said the water pools are smaller, more concentrated, and the cane toad tadpoles are even toxic. The waterways are making some critters sick. We need a good wet season and she'll be right then."

"Jack, where are we going?" Lawson asked.

I took the tub of specimen jars and closed the boot. "I'm

getting to that." I nodded to the staff-only gate to the side of the main entrance and started walking in that direction. "Anyway, then this afternoon, we went back to the orchard."

"The orchard we visited yesterday?" Lawson asked.

"Yep. Anyway, Gary and Elsie—she works here too—were telling me about the water reticulation system, how it drip-feeds the trees. We had a look at the tank and that's when I saw them."

I stopped at the gate, waiting for Gary to open it. "Saw what?" Lawson asked.

"Cane toads."

The door swung open revealing Gary and Elsie, the two park staff members I'd spent the day with. I quickly made introductions and we walked over to the old ute the staff used to drive around the park.

"Cane toads?" Piers asked. "What's the significance? They're everywhere."

"Correct," I agreed, putting the tubs into the back of the ute. Putting my hands on the tray back, I jumped up, then extended my hand out to Lawson first, helping him up, then Piers.

"Where are we going?" Lawson asked again.

"The orchard," I answered.

Gary jumped in behind the wheel and drove us slowly down to our destination. I looked at Piers, who didn't look all that comfortable riding in the back of a utility. It was kinda bumpy and windy, but there wasn't enough room for us all to fit in the front. Piers was holding on to the side like he might die any minute. I figured distracting him might help. "Piers, where does the conservatory get its fruit from? That it feeds the butterflies?"

"Uh, here. And another organic orchard on the other side of town."

Lawson, not bothered at all with riding in the back, cocked his head to the side in that thoughtful-processing way he did. "Are you saying there's a correlation to the decline of the Ulysses and the cane toad?"

I nodded and grinned. "More specifically, the tadpole of the cane toad." They both stared at me, so I elaborated. "I know it sounds crazy, but think about it. Where are the Ulysses butterflies found? Tropical Queensland, Solomon Islands, Papua New Guinea, and parts of Indonesia. Where are cane toads found? Queensland, Solomon Islands, Papua New Guinea, and parts of Indonesia. The Ulysses butterfly lays its eggs on the *Melicope elleryana* tree, yes?"

Lawson nodded. "The doughwood tree, yes."

"And where does the doughwood tree like to grow?"

Lawson was beginning to smile. "Near water."

"And what lives in the water pools at the roots of the doughwood tree?"

"Cane toad tadpoles," Lawson answered.

I smiled at him. "And what did Gary say was highly concentrated and toxic?"

Lawson was beginning to smile. Piers looked sceptical. "How does this affect the Ulysses?"

"Bioconcentration," Lawson answered, grinning now.

I beamed at Piers but pointed at Lawson. "That big word he said."

We arrived at the orchard and Gary slowed the ute to a stop. I jumped out and stacked the tubs atop one another while they climbed down. "The water tank is over this way."

As we walked over to the storage tank for the reticulation system, Lawson further explained. "Bioconcentration is a term that was created for use in the field of aquatic toxicology. And if the cane toad tadpoles are increasing the toxicity of the water, as Jack suggests, it stands to reason that only the Ulysses is affected because only the Ulysses inhabits the doughwood."

We stood, looking at the tank, Gary included. The tank was pretty big: six-metre circumference, one metre high, and open at the top. We could see down to the bottom. It was essentially a rainwater catchment tank. The park administration buildings' roof runoff was gravity fed to the tank. The water was then drip-fed to the orchard trees.

Lawson turned to Gary. "Are we free to take water samples?"

"By all means," he answered.

So, Gary and I stood there and watched as they took water samples in specimen jars and even managed to catch some tadpoles.

"Cane toads are generally land-dwellers but they lay eggs in water," Gary said for everyone's benefit. "They're a real bloody pest. We cover this tank, but it doesn't stop 'em. They were introduced to Australia to eradicate some kind of beetle, but they ate everything else except for the damn beetle. They've infested waterways all across the top end of the country. Almost killed off water monitors and quokkas over on the west coast and have no predators. A mate of mine lost his dog to toad poisoning."

"How do you deal with them here?" I asked.

"We try to trap 'em and euthanise 'em. We're organic here, we have to be."

"Yeah, back in Tassie we have the European white snail. Different pest, and certainly not on this scale, but same principle."

Lawson and Piers were finished with their water samples, so we moved to the trees themselves. Ulysses favoured citrus, so we went to those first. Lawson collected bark, leaf, and fruit samples. He collected another water sample of the drip feed irrigation near the trees, and of course, documented it all accordingly.

I thought Piers might have been reluctant to agree with my theory; he seemed a bit standoffish. But then he asked Gary, "And the fruit collected for the conservatory comes from here?"

Gary nodded. "Yes."

Piers frowned. "And the doughwood trees in our butterfly house?"

"Sourced from the forest. We sell the saplings to raise money. There was a push a while back for the public to plant doughwoods when the decline of the Ulysses was first announced." Gary spoke in a no-nonsense manner. He knew his job. I liked him.

Lawson stood up from his collection of specimen jars. "Can you take us into the forest?"

Gary looked at his watch. It was getting late. "We'll have to be quick."

So we grabbed the tubs and climbed into the back of the ute. Lawson smirked at me when Piers opted for the passenger seat, and once we were seated in the tray back and Gary was driving us further into the forest, Lawson leaned in and gave me a quick kiss.

"I believe I've said this before, but you're a godsend."

"Maybe it'll lead to nothing," I said modestly.

Lawson shrugged. "Maybe. But I've spent the whole day studying and researching all kinds of biotransference, biocontamination, biotoxicity... but something was missing. I couldn't piece it together. Then you mentioned this, and it fits, Jack." He gave me a smile that made my ribs feel too tight. "At any rate, if it's not the toxicity from the tadpoles, it's something like it. At least this should allow Piers to agree for me to send samples to the CSIRO for testing."

"What do we do if it *is* the tadpoles?" I asked. "They've been trying to find ways to get rid of the cane toad for decades without any luck."

Lawson seemed to think it over a while. "I don't know."

He seemed saddened by the idea, and my first instinct was to rescue him. "Hey," I said, putting my hand on his leg. "But if it is, then at least we'll know. Then contingency plans can be put into place. We can act, and there'll be a better chance at saving them, right?"

He stared at me until his smile won out. "You know what I love most about what you just said—and for the record, I loved all of it—but the way you say *we*. *We'll* know, *we* can act. I love that you're including yourself in this, not only because it's important to me, I understand that, but also because it's important to the conservation of a species."

I nudged his elbow with mine. "True. But mostly because of you."

He gave me one of his shy smiles, my favourite kind. But before he could speak, the ute slowed to a stop and Gary got out. "This is as far as I can drive. We're on foot from here."

Lawson quickly jumped out. "How far is it, and what gear should I bring?"

"You won't need your sat phone or anything like that," I elaborated, knowing what Lawson meant. "This is where we came this morning. It's only a hundred metres or so but it's not exactly easy going. We'll just grab some more samples, then we'll have to leave. It's getting late."

Piers looked at his watch, while Lawson, Gary, and I all looked at the sky. It was funny how different we were. I mean, I understood why Piers might have fancied Lawson, truly I did. He found his intelligence attractive, and his love for *Lepidoptera.* But Lawson was so, so much more than that.

Lawson slid his backpack on regardless, then picked up the one tub that had the empty specimen jars in it. "Right then. Which direction?"

"East," I said with a smile because I knew Lawson would get it. He turned due east and started walking, while I'm sure Piers was more of a left or right kind of guy.

I had to wonder how long it had been since Piers had set foot in the field. Or if he had, ever. It wasn't that I didn't like the guy. I just didn't like the fact he kept blocking Lawson from trying to move forward with his help on the Ulysses. Why ask him here if he was just going to say no to every suggestion? I mean, if Lawson did decide to stay on here and help, he and Piers would argue every day. Lawson certainly wouldn't back down. I didn't think he knew how to take a backwards step.

Then again, maybe Lawson liked to be challenged. Maybe he liked the heated professional discussions and debates. Maybe he liked someone who challenged him on an intellectual level...

Lawson stopped walking. "Jack?"

"Yeah?"

"Is this the spot you saw this morning?"

There was a bit of an embankment that housed shallow pools of surface water lined with doughwood trees. I'm pretty sure Lawson knew it was where I'd meant to bring him. I nodded.

"You okay?" he asked quietly.

"Sure," I said, faking a smile.

He eyed me cautiously for a moment, but Piers and Gary were right behind us. Soon enough, Lawson and Piers were taking water samples, tadpoles, a leech or two, bark and leaf samples, soil samples, and discussing things like equilibrium partitioning models and other things I couldn't pronounce, let alone follow.

"Guys," Gary interrupted their discussion on particulate toxin ratios. "We need to get going back. Park'll be closed soon, and without permits, you have no insurance to be here."

Lawson conceded and packed everything into the tub. I held my hands out. "Want me to carry it?"

He graced me with a smile. "Thank you." He handed it to me, then opened the backpack. He pulled out a bottle of water and handed it to Piers, who I hadn't realised was kinda sweaty. Then Lawson quickly took out a notepad and pen, some digital thermometer thing, and proceeded to jot down some notes.

"What are you writing?" Piers asked after taking a mouthful of water.

Lawson didn't even look up. "Temperature, humidity, location. Standard stuff."

I couldn't help but feel a bit proud of him. Gary gave me a smile before he turned to head off back the way we'd come. Piers followed Gary and I waited for Lawson.

"You good?" I asked after he slipped the notepad back into his backpack.

He slung the backpack on and settled the bag on his back, then we started the hike back to the ute. "Never better. Though I would like to come back, trek further into the forest if we can."

"Sure. Though we'd better organise the proper permits."

Gary dropped us back at the information centre where the rental car was parked. I picked up the three tubs stacked on top of the other and loaded them into the backseat. "I'll sort out those permits before they close," Lawson called out, dashing into the administration office.

I went to follow him, but Piers stopped me. "May I have a word?"

"Sure."

He looked around, embarrassed. "I take it Lawson told you I had expressed an interest in him joining my team here."

I nodded slowly. "Yes, he did."

"He hasn't exactly answered."

"Are you telling me this because you want me to try to sway his decision in your favour?"

"No, no," he said quickly, then I'm sure he mumbled something in French under his breath.

"Because if you did, then you really don't know Lawson at all."

He nodded slowly. "He is a feisty one."

"He's also very good at his job, and he's rarely ever wrong. Maybe you should listen to him."

He seemed offended. "I hope you know I mean no ill toward yourself and Lawson."

"I know. I also know that you expressed interest in his joining more than your team."

Piers put his hand up. "I admit it was true. But he told me, in no uncertain terms, his only interest in that regard lies with you. I told him you were a lucky man."

Okay, I officially didn't get this guy. Was he confronting

me about my relationship with Lawson? Or was he congratulating me? "Piers, what is it you want from him?"

"I want him to help save the Ulysses."

"Then listen to him. You know, before when I said Lawson's rarely wrong, that was true. But you know what else he is? Level-headed, and his eyes are always on the end result. If he *is* wrong, he simply takes the new information on board, learns from it, and moves forward. He has no ego when it comes to his job. You can call him the best and brightest and he'll agree with you, but that's not ego. That's a fact. He doesn't care for fame and glory. I mean, he found a new species and named it after someone else. That right there tells you the kind of man he is."

Piers nodded. "I know."

"So if he does decide to stay here to help you with the conservation of the Ulysses, it's because he thinks it's the right thing to do. Not because of anything you or I say."

Lawson came out of the office holding some papers. He held them up victoriously. "Permits for tomorrow granted!"

He handed them to me and I read the first part. There were only two names on the form. Me and Lawson... and it was an overnight stay permit.

"Overnight?"

Lawson blinked. "Well, the cane toad is primarily nocturnal, is it not?"

"Well, yes."

"And I assumed Professor Bonfils would not rather camp out overnight?"

Piers glanced at me, then smiled at Lawson. "You would be correct."

Lawson tilted his head in an of-course-I-am way then grinned at me. "It also means I can spend all day analysing our samples with Piers and sending away for further test results, while you organise our camping gear."

I grinned at him. "Sounds like a plan." Sounded better than just a plan. A night in the tropical rainforest with just Lawson and me sounded perfect.

Lawson pulled out the car keys. "Right, then. Let's get these samples back to the lab."

CHAPTER NINE
LAWSON

I got to the lab early, excited to start my day. Professor Bonfils was there already, as I assumed he would be.

"Good morning." He looked behind me. "Where's Jack?"

"He dropped me off. He needed the hire car to get some camping gear for tonight," I explained. "I hope you weren't offended by my not including you. I assumed you'd prefer not to camp out, sleeping on the ground."

He chuckled good-naturedly. "You assume correctly. No offence taken. My days of field work, as such, and nights on hard earth are well behind me." He seemed thoughtful for a moment. "I think Jack might prefer my absence also."

I withheld a sigh and bit my tongue. Jack had told me of the conversation they'd had while I was sorting out camping permits. While I did think Piers had accepted that I'd rejected his advances, Jack wasn't sure. In fact, he wasn't sure what Piers' intentions were at all. I'd reassured him the professor was simply eccentric and probably most accustomed to luring any younger man he wanted with his French accent and confidence. Jack had laughed.

"Possibly. Though Piers, please understand his concerns

are of my wellbeing, not a reflection of any insecurities you think he might have. He asked if I was comfortable working with you, and I said yes. If I wasn't certain of your professionalism, I wouldn't be here."

Piers fought a smile. "You are one of a kind, Lawson Gale."

"Thank you. Now let's get these samples processed."

So that's what we did. For hours, we sat side by side documenting, citing, researching, collating. It was therapeutic and productive. Piers called his associate at the Cairns CSIRO, a lady by the name of Jamine. They'd collaborated before, so when he asked if she could process some findings on behalf of the conservatory in the interest and conservation of the Ulysses butterfly, she not only agreed but said she'd fast-track the reports.

By the time Jack arrived, a little after three in the afternoon, we were ready to ship our samples and preliminary findings off to the CSIRO for further, more comprehensive testing.

"How'd it go?" Jack asked. "Can you determine anything yet?"

"The soil samples have the higher potassium levels that the soil we tested here has," Piers said. "It could be a direct correlation to the introduction of the toxins into the water."

"That's good, right?" Jack asked. "I mean, not good that the soil is affected, but good for the theory that it's all linked."

"Yes." I gave him a smile. "Did you get everything we might need tonight?"

"Yep. It's gonna rain later, apparently, so the girl at the camping store threw in an extra canopy tarp for free."

I almost laughed. I could just imagine Jack talking shop with the sales assistant, making her laugh and charming her enough to give him something for free. He probably even offered a sightseeing tour of his national parks if she ever finds herself in Tasmania. "I'm sure she did."

Jack beamed, then looked at all the individual bagged, sealed, and labelled samples, slides, and the paperwork that went with them. "Is this everything you have to take over?"

I nodded. "Yes. Fingers crossed we get some kind of feedback. Any kind, at this point, is all we can ask for."

Piers put two insulated boxes on the counter, and we carefully stacked our samples into them. Before I sealed the second box, Piers came back holding a square, clear plastic container. Inside it was one of the Ulysses that had died. I knew he was reluctant to surrender the specimen for research, but in his heart he knew it was for the right cause. We needed to see if there were any traces of the toxins in the butterfly. It was the only way to know for sure if we were on the right track.

I took the container. "Thank you, Piers."

"It is for the best," he replied. "I will keep the other one, but if they require it, then I'll… then I'll surrender it also."

I put my hand on his upper arm. "You're doing the right thing."

Jack carefully lifted one of the insulated carry boxes. "We good to go?"

I picked up the second box. "Yes. They're expecting us."

Thankfully the drive to the CSIRO laboratories didn't take too long. We were greeted by Jamine in the front office, and Piers made introductions. She was younger than I assumed, appeared Polynesian, though I never asked, and wore a white lab coat. She was friendly enough, and excited by the prospect of finding anything to help in the conservation of the Ulysses. I liked her immediately. Piers and I followed her into the restricted area, while Jack offered to stay in the waiting room.

"Okay," she started, looking at her clipboard. "We will start with the water samples, testing for bioaccumulation factors, and see what readings we get. Then we'll move onto the plant samples, checking for degrees of transference, then finally the animal samples. You said you collected tadpoles, leeches. And there's a butterfly sample?"

"Yes," Piers answered. "The last butterfly to die at the conservatory."

"We're hoping there's a correlation between the deaths of the Ulysses and toxins from the tadpoles," I stated. "Looking for bufadienolides specifically, the toxin from the tadpoles."

Jamine looked from her clipboard to me. "You think there's transference to the food source via toxins from tadpoles permeating the water?"

My answer was resounding. "Yes."

She looked at Piers. "And you?"

He took a breath and seemed to think about his answer. "I will admit, I didn't at first. But I do now. I think it's plausible, yes."

"I'm going back out tonight," I admitted. "I'm hoping to collect more water and doughwood samples from different locations. If the Ulysses is dying in the wild, then we need broader samples."

Jamine nodded. "For conclusive results, yes."

I had no issue with that. "So, we start here. If it's positive locally, then we take it further. Regionally. Nationally. Internationally."

"Well," Jamine said, going back to her clipboard. "It wouldn't be the craziest thing we've found." Then she looked at us both and gave us a blinding smile. "Leave it with me."

When we left the lab, we found Jack in the waiting room. He threw the magazine he was reading back on the table and stood up. "How'd it go?"

"Good, hopefully. Jamine's going to fast track it," I answered. "Reading anything in particular?"

"Nah, just a guy I went to school with got a write-up. It's nothing." He brightened. "So, we ready to go camping? If we want to make good headway into the forest, we're gonna need to make a start or we'll run out of sunlight."

I grinned at him. He was clearly looking forward to a night in the great outdoors, as was I. Piers threw his hands up with a laugh. "Okay, okay, you two, enough with the love-eyes. But please drive me back to the lab first."

A SHORT WHILE LATER, WE WERE HIKING INTO THE FOREST. GARY had graciously driven us as far as the ute would go, and Jack had packed everything expertly into the backpacks we now lugged through the dense undergrowth. We each carried a tub of specimen jars, clip-seal bags, and identification forms, and it was hard going. It was humid, and the uneven forest floor didn't exactly make for easy hiking.

Jack used his GPS and compass and led the way, and I followed. He weaved the way down to a gully, which was dotted with water pools. He put his tub down and surveyed the puddles and trees. "Well, they're pretty dried up now, but I'd reckon this'd be almost a creek with decent rain."

I put my tub alongside his and took out the folded paper map from my backpack. I found where we were. "Yes, see here?" I pointed to the area on the map. "There's a blue line that runs east. But it's certainly not a creek now."

"Nope." Jack opened the first tub and took out some specimen jars. "But it's supposed to rain tonight, remember?"

"It rains most nights in the rainforests. Funnily enough, that's why they're called rainforests."

Jack let his hands fall to his sides and he stared at me. "Are you being sarcastic?"

"I was going for roguish."

He laughed. "I'm the roguish one, remember?" He shoved a specimen jar at my chest. "Now, go get your toxic water samples. I'll take samples of the roots and leaves."

He trudged off, and I quickly took my water samples and even captured another tadpole. I documented the jars, cataloguing each sample, and we went further on, deeper into the national park, and took more samples before the setting sun got the better of us. "We should set up camp," Jack suggested, looking around the small clearing at the top of the dry creek bank. "You wanna do the fire or the tent?"

"Fire."

Jack rolled his eyes and dumped his backpack. "Thought you'd say that."

I had a campfire roaring by the time Jack declared the tent was ready. I collected the small skillet and found the food Jack had packed. Vegetable pasta salad, which I understood perfectly. The clip-seal bag of flour, however, had me confused. "Uh, Jack?" I held up the bag. "I take it this is actually flour and we're not suddenly drug mules."

He laughed and climbed out of the tent. "Yes, it's flour."

"What for?"

"You'll see. I'm making dessert. Is the pasta salad still cold?"

I felt the outside of the container. "Yes. Um, what dessert can you make in the middle of the forest with a resealable bag of flour?"

Jack rifled through the insulated food bag and pulled out what he needed. A tin of Carnation Milk, some portions of butter I suspect he borrowed from the hotel, and a bottle of water. "And the pièce de résistance," he declared, holding up a small bottle. "Golden syrup."

He added the butter to the bag of flour first and re-zipped the seal. He rubbed it in the bag, then added the wet ingredients until he effectively had a dough. He added it to the skillet, wrapped it in foil, and shoved it into the coals of the fire. "And while it bakes, we eat the pasta. I wasn't too keen to have meat in the insulated bag," he mumbled as he rummaged for the forks. He held one out to me victoriously, and I took it with a smile. "So pasta salad with Mediterranean vegetables it is."

"And a true Aussie bush damper for dessert," I added.

He smiled as he took a mouthful of pasta. He looked particularly handsome with the fading sunlight and flickering firelight; a sight I would never tire of. "So," he said as we ate, "thought any more on the possibility of staying on here in Queensland?"

I chewed and swallowed slowly, giving myself a moment to get my thoughts clear and my words even more so. "Truthfully, I haven't yet decided. My heart says no..."

"But your conscience is telling you yes."

I sighed. "This species is dying. The Tillman Copper is doing okay, and the breeding program is well established.

Once the vegetation has regenerated in the woodlands near Scottsdale, they can be released. I'll need to monitor that, of course, but for now..."

"I get it, Lawson," Jack said quietly.

"It's only an idea I'm considering. I can't really make a decision until we get results back from the CSIRO." I frowned. "I don't want to leave you. Please tell me you understand that."

He met my gaze and offered me a knowing smile. "Of course I do. I get it, Lawson. I really do. And like I said before, I have no problem with long-distance relationships. If we need to travel to see each other, with you up here and me back in Tassie, then that's what we do. Simple as that."

"That's why I love you," I murmured. "Well, that, and your damper-making skills."

"Oh!" he cried, reaching for the skillet. He carefully pulled it out of the fire and, with a towel, lifted back the foil. He poured in the golden syrup and recovered it. "Two more minutes."

We finished the pasta salad, then Jack dished up two steaming plates of what he called 'cocky's joy,' an old-fashioned Australian bush dessert. Simple and utterly delicious.

"Oh wow," I said around a mouthful of syrup-sweetened damper. "This is amazing."

Jack laughed as he ate. "I knew you'd like it." We ate the rest in silence, and Jack was looking around the darkening campsite. "So, how long till we see cane toads?"

"Soon."

He nodded slowly. "So... Do we have enough time for a lesson in biotransference?"

I wasn't sure what he meant. "A lesson? What do you want to know? I thought I explained; it's the result of biological substances being absorbed by another living organism."

Again, he nodded slowly, though this time he smirked. There was a smouldering darkness in his eyes that I knew well. "Oh, I know what it is all right, but I thought I could give you a practical lesson, perhaps."

"Oh." Heat pooled in my belly. "*That* kind of lesson."

Twenty minutes later we had dinner cleaned up and squared away and we were stretched out on the thin mattress in the tent. Fully dressed, making out, kissing, touching, gripping, and grinding.

I broke the kiss and offered him my neck, which he quickly adored with kisses and teeth. "I thought you wanted to do this outside?"

"It's gonna rain," he murmured against my skin.

He was right. The humidity was high and thick with the need to break for rain. Or maybe it was just how hot it suddenly was in the tent.

"I've been thinking about this transference thing," he continued, finding his way to the hollow between my collarbones. He settled himself on top of me properly, grinding his erection against mine. I tried to unbutton my shirt, but his hands were quick to stop me, and he pinned my arms at my sides. His lips were swollen, his eyes burned with desire. He spoke against my mouth. "And how it applies to when we make love."

I understood his meaning. Now we made love without condoms, every time he came inside me, it was a transference. God, I could barely speak. "I think I need a reminder."

His salacious grin was my reward. I thought my blood might catch fire.

Jack let go of my arms and knelt astride me, then reached for a backpack, I assumed for lube. I seized the opportunity to unbutton my trousers and roll over onto my stomach. I lifted my hips and pulled my pants down just enough to expose my arse to him.

"Lawson, what are you doing?"

I put my forehead to the mattress and slid my arms above my head. "I want you to have me, Jack. Just like this. Right now, as I am."

He paused a moment. "I don't want to hurt you."

"Do you have lube?"

"Yes."

"Then just do it. Now, Jack. I really need this."

"Let me stretch you first."

Even the thought of anything else inside me right this minute besides what I wanted most drove me crazy. And not in a good way. "Jack, please just fuck me. I don't want fingers, I want your cock. Inside me. Now."

The sound of his zipper in the silence sent a warm thrill through my bones. I heard the pop of the lube bottle lid, a delicious wet noise, and he slicked himself. I arched my back, raising my arse. I didn't need to see what he was doing. I could hear it, and it somehow made the anticipation even better, hotter. The slide of cool liquid down my crack didn't quell the fire in me. It seemed to fan the flames.

With his left hand planted beside my head as he leaned over me, he slid his hot, hard cock along the cleft of my arse.

I was all out of patience for games. "Jack."

Then his blunt cockhead was pushing inside me, and it was far too much and still not enough. He whispered in my ear. "That what you wanted?"

It was a keening sound that escaped me, and he froze.

"Yes," I managed with a groan. He was so big and breaching, yet I relished the burn, the intrusion. The feel of him inside me was everything. "Give it to me."

Jack let his full weight press on my back, his mouth at my ear, his hands gripped my hips, and he started to rock back and forth. "Mmmm," he moaned as he thrust slowly in and out of me, deeper with each pass. He took his time with me, eventually pushing harder and faster. "I won't last long. You feel too good."

"Then this might be a lesson in bioaccumulation," I said breathily. Jack's bubble of laughter became a groan, and he quickened his pace. "See how many times you can come in me."

My words brought him undone, and he slid one arm underneath my chest and held me as he came. I could feel everything... he was everything.

Jack slumped on top of me, his body wracked with the aftershocks of his orgasm, and eventually his breathing returned to normal. His words were warm against the back of my neck. "I never want to move," he mumbled.

"Then don't."

He nuzzled the hair at my nape. "You didn't come."

He normally made it his mission to bring me to orgasm first, and it was strangely satisfying that this time he hadn't. As though my sole purpose was for his pleasure. "Next time."

He hummed a nonsensical reply, but after a moment, he rolled off me, but keeping his arm wrapped tight around my chest, he manoeuvred me so I was his little spoon. He slipped out of me, just as the first spatters of rain began to fall on the tarp above the tent.

I felt bereft at his absence inside me, and as though he felt the same, he snuggled into me. He was sleepy, sated. "So, about that bioaccumulation..."

CHAPTER TEN
JACK

Sweet mother of God, he felt good. And that filthy mouth of his was my undoing, again. I wanted to stay inside him forever. I wanted to keep him in my arms forever. The rain got heavier and the sound of it, the warmth of Lawson against me, was lulling me to sleep. The rainforest sang a different song in the rain. Fewer birds, more frogs, drumming out a tempo that was oddly soothing.

Through the tent I could see the campfire become dimmer as the rain doused its flames and little by little our only light was gone. I closed my eyes and I remember thinking *I'll just snooze for a moment. I'll just close my eyes for a second before we go out looking for cane toads in the rain.*

I woke up with a fright. It was dark, and something was wrong. I was alone. Lawson. Where the hell was Lawson? Then I noticed how heavy the rain had gotten outside, thumping down on the canopy tarp above the roof of the tent, and I had no clue what the time was. I fumbled in the darkness for a lamp and switched it on. Lawson was most definitely gone. So were his boots, the second lamp, and one of the tubs.

Shit, shit, shit. I didn't mean to fall asleep.

"Lawson?!" I called out.

I checked my watch. 11:47 p.m.

"Lawson?!" I yelled, pulling on my boots and a poncho raincoat. I pulled the hood over my head and went out into the torrential rain. "Lawson?"

"Yes, I'm over here," a voice called out.

I turned to the sound and could see him then. Well, I could see the light of the lamp through the dense trees. Pure relief washed over me like the rain. "What the hell are you doing?" I yelled out and walked toward him.

He grinned, wearing a rain poncho, but was still soaked to the bone. "Taking samples. Toads love the rain."

Jesus Christ. I called out, "Please tell me you're wearing gloves."

He held up his free hand. "Of course I am."

I pulled on the hood of my poncho so it shielded more of my face. "It's pissing down." I slid in the undergrowth on my way towards him; a mix of mud and dead leaves made for slippery footing. Eventually I got to where he was and I didn't have to yell. "Why didn't you wake me?"

"You were sound asleep. I could hear the toads, so I thought I'd get up and take a look. I haven't been out of eyesight of the tent."

I knew he wasn't foolish. He was a competent hiker. "Well, I'm out here now. What are we doing?"

His smile became a grin. "I want to go further up this trough, follow the edge of the creek." He pointed north. "I didn't want to get too far from camp, but now you're up..."

"Want me to head south?" I asked. "We'd cover twice the ground."

"Sure." He opened the tub and gave me two specimen jars. "Don't go too far. The ground's slippery, so be careful."

I rolled my eyes. "Are you lecturing me on terrain safety?" He laughed, and I shook my head at him. "How can you be so happy? It's midnight, it's pouring rain, and we're standing in a rainforest surrounded by cane toads."

His answer was simple. "Because it's midnight, it's pouring rain, and we're standing in a rainforest surrounded by cane toads."

I couldn't help but laugh. "I think I deserve a midnight, rainforest, rainy kiss." I pointed to my mouth.

He happily obliged, planting his lips on mine. "Don't touch the cane toads."

"Yes, boss," I said, instead of rolling my eyes. Only an idiot would not know that cane toads were poisonous.

And with a final smirk from Lawson, we went our separate ways. The sooner we got this done, the sooner we'd be back in the dry tent working on that bioaccumulation theory...

I never knew science could be so much fun, and I certainly never knew it could feel so damn good.

I almost felt the need to track down my year eight science teacher and apologise. With a snort at my hilarious thought, I jumped down into the shallow gully to collect some more samples. The fresh water from the rain in the pools would dilute the toxins, we would assume, but samples must be taken to compare. This was the boring part of science. I much preferred the practical, private lessons on the transference of *biostuff*, and knowing Lawson was out there with *my* biostuff still inside him made my chest bloom with warmth that expanded to my groin.

God, I was never going to have enough of him now.

I sat the lamp down in the mud and collected a sample of the water. On closer inspection, or maybe it was because the water level had increased, I could see a string of toad eggs along the edge. Scooping up as many as I could, careful not to touch them, I screwed the lids on, pocketed them, and set about going back to find Lawson.

The small slope was slippery as hell. My boots sunk into the mud and I cursed the weather and all of Far North Queensland as I clambered up to the top. My pants were now pretty much wet right through, and I was cursing that too as I made my way back to where I'd left Lawson.

It wasn't long until I saw his lamp, and I headed straight for it. It was still raining—a torrential downpour, in fact. The forest protected us a bit, but it was still heavy. If we had this much rain in this amount of time back home, we'd be two feet underwater. I slipped in the mud but thankfully didn't fall, but then I cursed about that as well, mumbling to myself, "Who the fuck can live in this?"

"Oh, hey," Lawson said. He was crouching down, looking at something on the ground, but he smiled when he saw me.

"What are you looking at?" I called out, not five metres from him, but the rain was heavier, louder.

He laughed. "Two cane toads copulating."

Of course, that's what he's watching. "Is cane toad porn a thing?"

"I certainly hope not. It's disgusting."

"Don't get too close," I warned. Jesus, he was right near the deep edge of the gully that was fast becoming a creek. "Can you take a step this way?"

Lawson stood up, and as he did, the ground underneath

him gave way. The entire bank of the gully, Lawson, his lamp, and the cane toads were gone.

"Lawson!"

I lunged after him, but it happened all too fast. One minute he was there, and the next he wasn't.

"Lawson!"

I got to the edge, careful of my own footing, and heard a groan. I hung my lamp over the edge and saw him. "I'm all right," he said weakly, spitting out dirt and muck, wiping his mouth with his sleeve.

He was on his back, about two metres down, covered in dirt and mud from where the bank had given way. His lamp was out or under the dirt or under water; I wasn't sure. It was dark down there.

"Can you move?" I asked, trying not to panic. "Stay there, I'll find a way to come down."

"No, it's okay," he said, starting to get up. "Ugh!" He picked up a clump of dirt from his chest and threw it. No, it wasn't a clump of dirt at all. It was a cane toad. Fuck.

"Lawson, are you okay?"

He got to his feet awkwardly, slipping in the mud and sloshing in the water. "Yes, yes. I'm fine."

I sat my lamp beside me and lay down on my stomach, reaching my arm down toward him. "Take my hand."

When he put his hand in mine, I'd never felt so relieved. With every ounce of strength I had in me, I lifted him to the top. He was covered in mud and gunk, but I didn't care. I threw my arms around him. "God, you scared me."

"Scared you?" he asked meekly.

I put my hands on his muddy face. "Are you okay?"

He nodded. "Just a little shaken. The ground just gave way."

Instinctively, I pulled him further away from the bank. "The rain must have weakened it. Come on, let's get you back to the tent."

He certainly didn't argue. I grabbed the lamp, took his hand, and led him back to camp. At the front of the tent, I pulled his rain poncho off over his head so most of the mud and gunk wouldn't come inside with us. His trousers and boots were caked, but there wasn't much I could do about that. I pulled him inside and sat him on the bed.

But before I could take his boots off, I noticed him lick his lips, then again, and he made a face like he tasted something bad. "Lawson? What is it?"

"Tastes like metal. Like mud and sludge but metallic."

Oh no.

I noticed the mud smeared down his face and neck was streaked with white. A milky-like spray over his mouth...

Oh no, no, no.

I grabbed a bottle of water and screwed the lid off. "Wash your mouth out. Don't swallow. Spit it outside."

He tipped the bottle to his mouth, swished, and leaned over through the door to spit it out. When he sat back upright, he swayed and closed one eye. "Oh, my Lord," he said feebly. He put his hand to his head. "Oh, my head." Then he put his hand to his chest, over his heart, and his breathing became laboured.

"Lawson, we need to get you to hospital. Now."

He didn't answer. He just slumped to the side and almost fell off the mattress. I caught him and tried to hold him up. "Lawson!" I shook him gently. He tried to open his eyes but couldn't. "Lawson?"

Nothing.

I let go of him so he slouched to his side on the bed, and I grabbed the backpack with the phones and keys in it. I fumbled for my phone and dialled 000. "Ambulance, please." The dispatch lady was quick to respond, and I gave her all the information I could: cane toad poisoning by ingestion, unresponsive. But the thing was, we were in the middle of the rainforest, a good half-hour trek from the track Gary had dropped us off at. There was no way an ambulance was going to rush to the tourist car park, then wait for God knows how long until I could walk us out of here.

Thankfully the dispatcher had her wits about her. "I'll put a crew on standby, call us again when you're almost there.

"Will do."

I shoved the phone in my pocket, slung my backpack on, then dragged Lawson to a sitting position. He was floppy and kept falling to the side. I had no idea how I was going to carry him out of the jungle and hold a lamp in the pouring rain in the middle of the night and find my way to the track, let alone the car park. But I certainly couldn't give up. I heaved him over my shoulder and crawled out of the tent. I grabbed the lamp and stood up in the rain. He moaned over my shoulder. "Lawson, baby. I got you. We just need to go for a little walk."

I took a second to get my bearings and headed off in what I was sure, what I hoped, was the right direction.

The ground was slippery, I could hardly see, and I couldn't wipe the rain from my eyes. Lawson wasn't heavy, by any means, but he was dead weight over my shoulder, and I had to step over tree roots and up and down natural step formations on the path. It wasn't even really a path. Walking *into* the forest had been easy. It had been daylight, it had been dry, and I hadn't even considered the footing.

Walking out of the forest was a different story altogether.

After what felt like a lifetime, I stopped, sure I'd taken a wrong turn. Nothing looked familiar in this light, or lack thereof. I considered changing direction, but Lawson moaned. "Hang on," I said, not knowing if he could hear me. I worried about the blood rushing to his head and to his heart. I worried about what that would do to the toxins already in his body.

I had to move quicker.

Instinct told me to keep going. I really had no clue if I was going in the right direction, but something told me I was. And after an eternity, the forest cleared to a track, the very track that Gary had dropped us off at. *Oh, thank God.*

The ground was flatter, the tyre tracks making it easier to walk. There was a proper path to follow, at least. I picked up my pace, trying to shuffle Lawson a little to make him more comfortable. He groaned. "Almost there, baby. You're okay. Gonna get you some help."

I fished my phone out of my pocket. Not slowing down my pace, I dialled 000 again. After explaining who and where I was, I was assured an ambulance was on its way. The dispatcher asked me to stay on the line until the ambos arrived, and I had to admit, I was grateful for the company.

My legs burned, my back hurt, but my heart... my heart was in limbo. That unsure place between hope and breaking, being scared to death and never feeling more alive.

"He's gonna be okay, isn't he?" I asked into the phone.

The dispatch lady, whose name was Cheryl, gave me her professional, noncommittal answer. "You've done everything right. ETA for the ambulance is five minutes, they'll assess him and get him straight to hospital."

"No one's died from cane toad poisoning, have they?" I asked.

"Not in Australia, I believe. Dogs and cats, yes. Other native wildlife, yes. Humans, I'm not sure. The hospital has been notified."

"It sure is dark out here," I said, not even realising the rain had stopped until that very second. My breath was short and I choked back tears. "He has to be okay. I don't know what I'd do if he's not."

"Mr Brighton."

"Jack."

"Jack," Cheryl said calmly, "just keep on moving. Can you hear sirens? See any lights?"

I listened for a moment. "The forest is really loud." God, it was deafening. Crickets, cicadas, frogs, toads, birds... I thought most birds were mostly diurnal. Maybe it was the blood pumping in my head that made everything seem so damn loud. I pulled the phone away from my ear so I could concentrate, and...

In the distance, I could hear them.

"I can hear the sirens," I said into the phone, and pulling strength from a place I didn't know existed, I started to run. Lawson moaned again. But then I caught a glimpse of red-and-blue lights and headlights. "I can see lights!"

I heard Cheryl telling someone—not me, maybe the ambos—that I had a visual of lights, they should be seeing me any moment now.

I broke into the clearing that was the car park, just as the ambulance arrived. "I'm here," I said, to Cheryl, to God, to anyone.

The ambulance made its way over to me and stopped. I'd never been more grateful to see anyone. Then they were lowering Lawson onto the gurney and I was telling them what happened while they were strapping him on and checking his eyes, and I was bundled into the back of the ambulance with him, and then everything was quiet.

And I could finally breathe.

My body ached, my chest burned.

"You okay?" the paramedic asked me, looking up from Lawson.

I waved him off, stuck the heels of my hands into my eyes, and willed myself not to cry. Taking a few deep breaths, I gathered myself to finally get a good look at Lawson.

And I immediately wished I hadn't.

There was a line of foamy drool running down the side of his mouth, escaping under the oxygen mask. His shirt was ripped open, he had ECG pads stuck to his chest, but his face was pale. Too pale.

He looked... dead.

"Is he...?"

The paramedic wouldn't answer me. Instead he spoke into some kind of radio mouthpiece, giving readings and stats I couldn't follow. The driver replied, "ETA, one minute."

I slowly reached out and slid Lawson's hand into mine. "Is he going to be okay?"

The paramedic finally afforded me a sorry look. "His heart rate isn't good, but there's a cardio specialist—"

Lawson abruptly coughed and vomited, and the paramedic launched into action to ensure Lawson wouldn't choke. The ambulance came to a stop, the back doors flew open, and there was a flurry of noise and movement, nurses and doctors, bright lights and too much noise.

Then they raced Lawson inside and I was still standing there, alone, confused, scared. Numb. The world seemed to spin without me, and it was like I couldn't move.

A kind face appeared in front of me. A heavy-set man in scrubs with blond-and-pink hair, an eyebrow ring, and an empathetic smile put his hand on my arm. "Are you with him?"

I nodded.

"You were the one who brought him in?"

I nodded again.

He tried to gently pull me toward the emergency doors. "Come on, let's get those scratches looked at."

Scratches? I looked down at myself. I had scratches up my arm which I didn't recall getting, and there was blood soaked through my muddy trousers at the knee. I didn't recall that hurting either.

"My name's Lyle," the nurse-guy said. "You wanna come inside? We'll get you looked at, then we'll see what we can find out about your friend."

"His name is Lawson," I said. "He's my boyfriend. Well, he's more than that. He's the guy that changed my life. He's everything to me, and I can't go in there because what if he's not okay? What if I go in there and he's not doing so great? Because if I stay out here, then no one can tell me he... no one can say that he's not..." I swallowed hard and shook my head. "I don't think I can go in there."

Lyle rubbed my arm. "Oh, sweetie. He's in the very best hands." I looked at him then, into his eyes, and whatever he saw in mine made him frown. "What's your name, honey?"

"Jack."

"Well then, Jack. I need you to come with me." This time he pulled on my arm and I went with him.

Being led through the emergency department was like an alternative reality in slow motion, the fluorescent lights, the nurses and doctors all moving without sound. There was a disconnect somewhere in my brain.

I found myself sitting on a hospital bed in a sterile cubicle. I watched as Lyle swabbed the scratches, cleaned and dressed them. I still couldn't feel anything. Then Lyle was asking me questions about how I felt. Did I feel nauseous, have blurred vision, shortness of breath? Was I allergic to anything?

I shook my head. "Nothing. I need to see Lawson."

Lyle nodded but just continued with his assessment, writing down notes. He didn't understand. "I need to see Lawson."

He began to shake his head.

"Is it because I'm not family? Is it because we're gay? Would it make any difference if we were married because—"

Lyle put his hand on my knee. "Hon, you can't see him right now because the doctors are working on him. They need space and calm to do their jobs. If you go in there, you'll disrupt the space and calm, and they won't be able to do their jobs. Being gay don't change anything, not for me. You listen to me, sweetie. I promise you I will keep you posted. You will know all there is to know. I will find out all I can, okay?"

He looked at me with such sincerity, I could only believe him. I nodded.

"Good," he said with a smile of satisfaction. Then his eyes focused above my right eye. "Now, let me take a look at this cut up here."

Until then, I hadn't been aware of any cut above my eye and instinctively tried to touch it, but he held my hand. "Nuh-uh, no touching. Not until we've cleaned those hands."

Then I noticed that my hands were covered in dirt and mud, and there were scrapes across the knuckles.

Oh.

"So, you banged yourself up pretty good," Lyle noted, wiping a cotton swab above my eyebrow."

"I didn't realise," I mumbled.

Lyle nodded like that was expected. "You've been through a bit tonight, huh? Did you really carry him all the way out of the national park? In the dark?"

I nodded. *Of course, I did.*

He gave me a sad smile. "That'd explain the state you're in. Want some Panadol?"

I shook my head. I couldn't feel anything.

Other nurses came in, then a doctor. They all fussed and talked stats, but I didn't pay any attention. I couldn't focus at all. I stood up off the bed and Lyle and the doctor put their hands on me to stop me. "You need to stay here," the doctor said.

"I need to find Lawson."

Lyle frowned. "I'll go and see what I can find out. You stay here so I know where to find you. I'll be real quick."

He disappeared through the curtain. The doctor shone his penlight in my eyes and asked me all the questions Lyle already asked, and I sat there for I don't know how long. Forever, it felt like. Then Lyle came back and put his hand on my knee. "Okay, so he's stable."

I let out a breath, instant tears welled in my eyes. "Oh, thank God. Can I see him?"

Lyle shook his head. "He's not in the clear yet, Jack. The

toxins cause all sorts of stress on internal organs, primarily the heart, so they're monitoring him pretty closely. He's still unconscious. They're running all types of blood tests and watching his brain activity. They've got him in the ICU. I can take you to the waiting room because you'll only be sitting up here waiting, so you may as well sit there and wait. You'll be closer, but you won't be able to see him until the morning, at least."

I nodded, feeling the first flicker of hope. "Thank you."

Lyle filled in some more paperwork, and I was soon following him through a warren of corridors and elevators until the sign on the wall read Intensive Care Unit. Lyle pulled some chairs without armrests into a line. "That's the closest you'll get to a bed. At least it's padded," he said. He disappeared for just a second and came back with a folded blanket. "Get some sleep. It's three o'clock in the morning."

I nodded, but apparently that wasn't enough. Lyle made me sit down then lie down the best I could. He put the blanket over me, asked if I was okay one last time, gave me a gentle pat on the shoulder, and was gone.

I closed my eyes, just a blink, because I wanted to stay awake in case Lawson woke up. But the next thing I knew, there were voices and a gentle hand shaking my arm. I opened my eyes to a strange woman's face. I had no clue where I was, who she was, or why my body ached from head-to-foot.

"Sorry to wake you. Lyle said you'd want to be there when Lawson woke up."

"Lawson," I mumbled, then tried to get up. My body protested, every muscle, every bone, but I pushed through it with a grimace as I got to my feet.

"This way," the nurse said. "It's still early, but I can take you in for just a sec."

I followed her with my heart in my throat, and she stopped at a door at the end of the long room near the nurses' station. I peered in, and there he was. Lying in the bed, propped up into a half-reclined position. There was a doctor at his side, but I couldn't take my eyes off him.

He was still pale, his eyes half-open, he had oxygen tubes up his nose, and he looked like he'd been to hell and back. Then he saw me and cracked half a smile, which set me in motion. I was through the door and at the side of his bed—opposite his doctor—in four long strides, and without really thinking, I wrapped my arms around him and pulled him against me. Literally, almost pulled him completely off the bed. "Oh, my God, Lawson, I've never been so scared," I mumbled into his neck.

"Okay, sir," the doctor said, pulling on my arm. "You need to let him go."

Lawson squeaked, and I quickly propped him back up in bed. "I'm sorry. I'm sorry," I said, patting him down, trying to make sure I hadn't hurt him. "I just... I just..." Then the tears started. Relief and every emotion I couldn't name right then flooded through me and burned hot in my eyes. I put my forehead to his.

Lawson put his hand to my cheek. "Jack."

I pulled back and wiped my eyes, then kissed the side of his head. The doctor cleared his throat, making me look at him. "Sorry," I mumbled, not really sorry at all.

"You're the one who saved his life," the doctor stated.

Lawson closed his eyes and smiled. "He has a habit of doing that."

"He has a habit of almost dying," I said with an incredulous laugh. "Anyway, I didn't save him. I just got him here so you could do the saving part."

The doctor smiled at that. "He's very lucky."

"Is he going to be okay?" I asked, taking Lawson's hand. He had a cannula taped to the back of it, so I had to be careful.

"Right now, he needs rest. We'll run more tests later, but being conscious and alert is promising." The doctor looked at his watch. "I suggest you get some sleep."

With that, he was gone. I leaned down, took Lawson's face gently in my hands, and kissed him. "I love you. Go to sleep. I'm not going anywhere."

His eyes remained closed, but the corner of his lip lifted in a smile.

I pulled a chair over to the side of the bed, sat down, and carefully took his hand. I tried to stay awake just to watch him, but my eyelids betrayed me.

The next thing I knew it was daytime.

CHAPTER ELEVEN
LAWSON

I felt awful. Worse than awful. Like I'd been hit by a bus. A fleet of buses. Like each bus had backed up and mowed me down again, in fact. I couldn't actually pinpoint which part of me hurt the most. Every part of me ached and stung. My bones felt like razors, my lungs burned with every inhale, my head ached like a white-hot poker was embedded in my brain. Even my skin hurt.

I blinked until my eyes would stay open, and then I saw him.

Jack.

He was in a chair beside the bed, sound asleep, leaning forward with his head near my hand. It took every modicum of strength to lift my arm and touch his hair with my fingers. He stirred, then shot up. "Lawson," he croaked. "Oh, thank God you're awake. How're you feeling? You scared the crap outta me." His eyes welled with tears. "Jesus, you scared me."

He had a gauze bandage above his eye. "You okay?" Wow, it even hurt to talk.

Jack laughed and squeezed my hand. "I'm fine. So much better now you're awake."

Then I realised he had scrapes on his knuckles. "You've cut your hand And above your eye."

Jack shrugged it off. It seemed he couldn't take his eyes from my face. He leaned in and pressed his lips to my forehead, then he cupped his hand to my cheek. "How are you feeling?"

"Awful."

He frowned. "I'll go get the doctor. Be right back."

I closed my eyes again for just a moment, and when I opened them again, Jack was standing beside a tall woman in a white coat. "Mr Gale," she said with a smile. "Nice to have you with us." She leaned in and shone the light of hell into each eye.

I clamped my eyes shut in response. "If you're checking retinal dilation, would you mind not piercing my brain?"

I heard Jack's snort of laughter. "Oh yeah. He's okay."

"No, I'm not," I disputed, still with my eyes closed. "Everything hurts." I suddenly felt nauseous. "Ugh."

The doctor told of side effects, speaking of pain, severe headaches, nausea, just to start with. "I'll be back soon. Lawson needs to rest, but we'll need to do liver and kidney function tests."

"Can he have anything for the pain?" Jack's voice was like a homing beacon. "He said everything hurts. There has to be something you can give him."

Their voices muffled, and I drifted into sleep. But the feeling of queasiness never waned, and I woke up with a start, needing to vomit. Jack, who was now sitting beside the bed again, lurched forward with a sick bag. I dry heaved into it, producing nothing but bile, reminding me that my entire body had been through a mince grinder.

I fell back against the bed, and Jack soon had a damp cloth to my forehead, wiping down my face. I closed my eyes but lifted my hand for him. He knew what I meant because he threaded our fingers, and I fell back asleep.

The next time I woke, it was because there were people talking close by. A familiar voice, and I blinked again and again to try and focus. I realised belatedly that my drowsiness must be chemically induced. But Jack was still sitting beside my bed, talking into his phone.

"Oh wait, he's just waking up." He held the phone to his chest and smiled at me. "Hey. How're you feeling?"

"Better."

"They gave you something for the pain and nausea."

I smiled. Well, I think I did.

Jack held up the phone. "It's your mum."

"Oh."

"Want to speak to her for a second?"

I nodded. "Sure."

"Okay, Hyacinth, I'll just put him on. He's drowsy and he can barely keep his eyes open, but here he is."

Jack put the phone to my ear and held it there. "Oh, Lawson," my mother cried into the phone. "We've been so worried."

"'S okay, Mum." I smiled again at Jack. "Jack's looking after me."

"He carried you out of the rainforest on his back. In the dark and in the rain. I don't know what we'd do if not for him. You would have died out there."

It took a minute for her words to connect in my brain. "Yeah. He's kind of wonderful." The words felt like molasses in my mouth.

Jack took the phone back, and I was going to tell him to put it back to my ear but I couldn't stay awake.

"Yes, Mrs Gale. He's nodding off again. I will. Of course. Yes, I'll call you later. Okay, bye."

Then warm lips pressed again to my forehead. "That one's from your mum." Then he softly kissed my lips. "And that one's from me."

THE NEXT TIME I WOKE UP, JACK WAS THUMBING SOMETHING INTO his phone. "Hey."

His gaze shot up and he sat forward in his chair. His phone forgotten, he took my hand. "Hey. You look a bit better."

"Drugs are good."

He laughed quietly and put the back of my hand to his face. For a moment he closed his eyes and when he looked at me again, he sighed. "Oh, Lawson."

He looked exhausted, and the white strip of bandage above his eye had some spots of red on it. His knuckles were scraped and there was another gauze strip on his arm. "You okay?"

He nodded slowly. "I'm perfectly fine. Worried about you, mostly."

"Sorry."

He gave me a sad smile. "Do you remember what happened?"

I thought back. My memories were a little hazy. Whether that was drug-induced or because of the toxin, I didn't know. "The bank of the gully collapsed."

Jack nodded. "And you and two cane toads went with it. From what I can tell, they somehow fell on or near your face and secreted toxins into your mouth. Doctors said it must have been a direct ingestion for you to be so ill. I told them you wiped your mouth as you got up, and there was milky stuff in the mud smeared all down your chin and neck."

"I remember... the taste was... metallic and... putrid."

"If you're tired, close your eyes," he murmured. "I'm not going anywhere."

I shook my head a little. "What have they given me?"

He afforded me a smile. "They had to do some tests first, to see what your kidneys and all that could handle. But something for pain and vomiting. I can't remember what they called it."

I squeezed his hand, feeling my strength drain away. "What time is it?"

"Five-thirty in the afternoon. I'm probably supposed to be leaving soon but I think they took pity on me." He bit his lip and even blushed a little. "I might have told them we were engaged to be married so I could stay with you. Hope you don't mind."

Even half-sedated, his words sent a thrill through me. A machine next to me beeped erratically. "I don't mind," I said.

Jack looked at the machine, and the smile he gave me was knowing. And smug. "Mmm, this ECG machine right here tells me you rather liked the idea."

A nurse appeared and walked straight over to the machine, reading something. "Ah, you're awake, Mr Gale. Is Jack here making you excited, or is there some other reason your heart rate spiked?"

I didn't need to answer. The heat across my cheeks said enough. Jack laughed, and the nurse patted him on the shoulder. "Be gentle with our patient, please, Jack." She made some notes in a file, then on a computer, and smiled to herself as she walked out.

Jack lifted my hand so he could kiss my knuckles. "ECG

machines don't lie."

"Shut up."

He laughed louder this time, then stood up and kissed my lips. Of course, the ECG beeped again, but I could only smile.

"Ah, he's awake," a familiar voice said. I looked to the door to find Piers holding a bouquet of flowers.

Jack sat back down, but never let go of my hand. "Yes, he's more alert this time."

"This time?" I asked. My brain was so foggy.

"Piers came in this morning," Jack explained, "when he heard the news."

Piers walked into the room and put the flowers beside my bed. "Yes, Gary came by asking if I'd seen you. He went to your camp today and found it deserted and everything left askew like you'd abandoned it in a hurry. He was concerned when he saw the embankment had washed away."

"So Piers called your phone," Jack explained further, "which I had here in the backpack. I told him what happened, how sick you were. And he came by to check on you."

"And brought Jack lunch," Piers declared loudly. He waved his arm with that dramatic flair he used so well. "This boy has not left your side. He refuses to leave, so I had to feed him or he'd starve."

Jack smiled at Piers, and it was clear whatever animosity had been between them was now gone.

Piers gently patted my shin. "You look better, Lawson. Before you looked like death, but now you have some colour."

"I feel a little better. Hazy, a little slow, but I'd rather that than the headache I woke up with." Jack rubbed my hand, which felt really nice and reminded me that my skin didn't hurt anymore either.

"The doc said you'll probably have headaches for a while," Jack said. "And you'll be weak and tire easily."

I smiled. "Feels about right."

"Well, I'm glad you're feeling better," Piers added.

Then I thought of something he'd said a minute ago. God, my mind really was slow... "Our campsite? The samples we took, the data..."

Piers smiled. "Gary collected everything, camping gear, samples, and whatnot, and brought it in. I have all your work catalogued and waiting for you. I didn't want to touch it without your permission."

I tried to wave him off but my hand—the one Jack wasn't holding—felt like lead. "Please, do what you will with it. I'd rather we not waste any more time."

Piers gave a hard nod. "I'll start on it first thing. But now, Lawson, you need to rest. I can see you're in very capable hands. I'll be back tomorrow."

He waved us off, and Jack smiled at where Piers had stood. "You and he are more amiable?" I asked.

"He means well," Jack said. "He was worried about you, but he said he's very glad you have me." He shrugged. "Kinda can't argue with that."

I smiled and took in a deep, steady breath. I wasn't sure which parts of me were starting to hurt again. Under the chemical buffer of drugs they'd given me, there was a current of pain just waiting.

Jack seemed to understand. He picked up the pain-relief push button. "Want me to press this?"

I shook my head. "I don't want to sleep again just yet."

"Tell me what you want?" He took my hand. "If it's within my power..."

"Food."

Jack snorted quietly before a grin spread across his face. He stood up and softly kissed my forehead. "Let me go see what I can find out."

Twenty minutes later, he was spoon feeding me a broth soup. Clear liquids apparently, and under normal circumstances, I'd have probably objected—and Jack turned his nose up at it—but it was the best tasting soup I'd ever had.

I could only stomach half of it, getting incredibly full all of a sudden. I left the jelly and cup of tea for later, but I was suddenly exhausted and achy all over. Jack asked if I wanted him to push the pain-relief button. I gave a nod and closed my eyes. I felt his lips on my forehead before sleep claimed me.

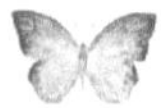

I WOKE UP FEELING SO MUCH BETTER AND TO A FRESHLY showered, smiling Jack. "Good morning!" Again with a kiss to my forehead.

"Morning," I said, my voice croaked.

"How are you feeling?" He asked, with a hopeful look on his face.

"Better." I sat up, feeling every protesting muscle. "And I'm starving."

"That's a good sign." Jack propped up my pillow and pressed the automatic lever on the bed so I was more comfortable sitting up. "I think I heard the breakfast trolley. Surely you can have some proper food today."

"I hope so."

"If they say no, I'll sneak you in some."

"No you won't," a nurse said as he walked in. He had a stripe of pink hair and metal rings pierced into his face in random places.

"Ah, Lyle," Jack said happily. He stood up and shook hands with him. "Good to see you again."

"Just came in to see how the patient is," Lyle said, looking to me. Then he spun on his heel and looked at Jack. "Well, patient*s*." He inspected Jack's face and hand and arm. "You healed up quite nicely. And you, darling"—he turned back to me—"had this man just about beside himself." He did something with the machines and checked my saline bag, then leaned in and winked at me. "You know, in case he didn't tell you, he said he'd marry you if that's what it took for us to let him stay with you."

I felt the colour return to my face, and Jack cleared his throat and gave me an apologetic look. "Uh, yes," I replied. "He told me something of the sort."

"Just as well," Lyle said with a cheery grin. "'Cause there's a line-up of girls and guys who'd be happy to take him up on his offer."

Now Jack blushed. I gave Lyle my best attempt at stern. "Thank you, but I should think he's spoken for."

Lyle just laughed. "You can have yourself a light breakfast, my good man."

"Oh, thank goodness, because I'm starving."

I was sure the toast was stale, and maybe the toast was cold, but it was all good. And I was certain the hot tea was brewed in heaven. Jack watched me devour everything with an amused, enamoured look on his face.

It was only once I'd eaten that I'd taken a moment to think about the morning. "You left last night?" I asked him.

"Yeah, I needed to shower. To put it bluntly, not even

my charm and good looks could mask the fact that I stunk." He offered me a small smile. "And you were sound asleep. I was back first thing."

"Have you eaten?" I asked. "I should have asked before I mowed through my breakfast."

Jack snorted. "Yeah, grabbed a coffee and toastie from Maccas on my way."

"You said you'd marry me. And you told them we were engaged? Did I remember that?" My memory of yesterday was all but a blur.

Jack held my gaze, even though I was certain he'd rather looked around the room or anywhere else than at me. He swallowed hard. "I did tell them that, otherwise they might not have let me stay. And I would. Marry you." He lifted his chin, as if defiant and proud and nervous. "I would."

The ECG machine started to beep like crazy, and Jack laughed as Lyle came in to investigate. "I need to have these removed," I said, pulling at the circle pad stuck to my chest. "They're giving all my secrets away."

Lyle laughed. "I'll speak to the doctor."

"Lyle? I'd like to have the catheter removed and the saline as well. If I'm allowed. And I'd really like to go home today."

"No promises," he said, walking out in search of my doctor.

"Do you feel up to it?" Jack asked when we were alone.

"I'm sick of being hooked up to everything. I'm certain the doctor will wish to see if I can keep food and water down before they agree to discharge me, but I feel okay. I'm tired, and I'm sure I could manage pain medication on my own. And I'd really like to shower. And shave. And brush my teeth. I feel disgusting."

Jack put his hand to my face and swept his thumb across my cheek. "You're still exhausted, though. I can see it in your eyes. Don't rush yourself, my love."

It was as if him mentioning being tired put me under a spell because a wave of weariness washed over me. Maybe it was the big breakfast I'd eaten. Maybe it was all the talking, but I blinked slowly. "I am tired."

He pressed his palm into my cheek and traced my eyebrow with his other hand. "Then sleep."

So I did.

I WAS RIGHT ABOUT THE DOCTORS WISHING TO SEE IF I COULD EAT and drink, and by mid-afternoon, I was fast out of patience. I was, however, unhooked from all machines and urine bags and allowed to shower.

Lyle offered to help, but Jack was quickly on his feet. "Need me to help instead?" Then he must have realised how keen he sounded because he followed it up with, "I mean, I can look after him. Here, and when we leave eventually, I'll be the one who's helping him, so should I learn here first?"

Lyle fought a grin but gave him a side-eye. "All right. But no funny business, you hear?"

Jack gave him a Scout salute.

"And you press the assistance button on the wall in the bathroom if you need help, okay?"

Jack collected the shaving bag, made sure I had towels waiting for me in the ensuite bathroom, then helped me stand up. He held my arms and watched my feet. "Just take it easy. If you need to rest or stop, tell me."

"I'm okay." We shuffled to the bathroom, and Jack started the water while I caught a glimpse of myself in the mirror. I was taken aback by how pallid I looked, accentuated by the bruise-like smears under each eye. "Good Lord, I look awful."

"You've been through a bit, don't forget," Jack added. "And anyway, you look perfect to me."

I turned to look him in the face. "No funny business, remember?"

He chuckled quietly. "Believe me, that's the last thing on my mind right now."

I undid the hospital robe and let it fall to the floor. "The very last thing?"

"Yes." He took my arm and supported me as I walked under the water spray. "How about we just worry about you getting well first, huh?"

The water felt heavenly. Divine, even. I washed my hair, scrubbing the grit of dried mud from my scalp, cleaned my body and face the best I could, and let the hot water run over me. I must have swayed a little because Jack was soon holding my arm. "Okay, that's long enough," he ordered.

Then I was sitting in a bathroom chair and he was drying me down with a towel, gently, lovingly. I didn't have the energy to argue with him about drying myself, but it was also a very tender moment between us.

Then Jack knelt before me with my pyjama bottoms in hand. He fed one leg in, then the other, then pulled me to my feet so he could pull the pants all the way up. It just so happened that my groin was right near his face. He looked up at me and licked his lips. "Okay, so it's not the very last thing on my mind." He stood up quickly and let out a deep breath. "I'm only human, okay?"

I chuckled quietly, secretly pleased I still had an effect on him. "Not sure I have the strength for it right now anyway."

He pulled a T-shirt on over my head, and I fed my arms through the armholes. Then he scooted my chair over closer to the basin. "Can you brush your teeth from there?"

I nodded, so he drew a strip of toothpaste onto my toothbrush and handed it to me. Brushing your teeth after a few days of not being able to was a little piece of minty-fresh paradise. I almost felt human, apart from feeling exhausted and achy, but I was led to believe that was to be expected.

When I was done with my teeth, I scrubbed my hand over my scruffy jaw. "I don't think I could be bothered shaving." The truth was, I was already exhausted again.

Jack chuckled. "I like the three-day-old growth on you. I say leave it."

I motioned for him to come closer with a curl of my finger, and when he was close enough to kiss, I nuzzled my cheek to his. "You like that?"

He made a strangled groan sound, and took a step back. I took that response as a yes. "Back to bed with you," he said. "And no teasing."

Jack helped me get settled, and I was almost dozing off again when the doctor came back in. "Good news," he announced. "You can go home. All your results have come back clear. On the proviso that if the headaches get worse, any dizziness, nausea, you get yourself right back in here."

"Of course," Jack answered, nodding.

"I'll get the discharge paperwork ready. No kissing any more cane toads, ya hear?" the doctor joked.

I snorted. "I'll keep that in mind."

He walked out and literally had to sidestep Piers as he was walking in. "Oh, look at you! So much better."

I gave him a smile. "I feel better."

"Did I hear you're allowed to leave?" he asked.

"Yes. Thank the heavens."

"That is good news." Piers grinned. "And I have even better news…"

I suddenly wasn't so tired. "What's that?"

"Jamine contacted me, little over an hour ago. The CSIRO has results on the samples we took over."

"And?"

"And they're going to do a lot more testing, Lawson, because you were right. The Ulysses is dying of bufadienolides poisoning, directly related to the biotransference from the tadpole of the cane toad to the doughwood tree, on which the Ulysses larvae and pupa feed. Levels are low, but enough to affect the caterpillar, so the butterfly weakens soon after the time it reaches imago."

I sagged against the mattress, relief coursing through me. "Oh, that is fantastic news."

"Yes! But it is just the beginning!" Piers said. His excitement would have been contagious if I weren't so damn tired. "There is much to be done. Now we know the cause, we need to implement strategies and plans. But having the CSIRO on board is hugely beneficial—"

I was sure he could have talked for hours. "Piers, I'm not staying."

The smile left his face and the air left his lungs in a resigned sigh. "I assumed as much, Lawson. After you were so ill and Jack took such good care of you, I figured you'd go back to Tasmania."

"There's still a lot of work to be done on the Tillman

Copper," I added, feeling the need to justify my decision. I glanced at Jack. "And it's where my home is."

Jack grinned, and Piers nodded. "I get it. Love is a beautiful thing, blah blah blah."

I chuckled. "Something like that." A quiet fell over the room for just a moment. "Piers, I would officially like to offer my services, though. If you need to discuss or even think-tank with someone, I insist you call me. I'd still like to be involved, to help, although from a distance. Not here."

Piers gave a grateful nod. "I will hold you to that."

"I can recommend some names of people who may be able to assist you."

"Indeed. But for now, you should rest."

Jack shook his hand. "We'll drop around to collect our camping gear tomorrow or the morning after. I'm sure Lawson will want to see the lab one more time before we leave."

"Then I shall leave our farewells until then," Piers added with a flourish, a wave of his hand, and he left.

Jack walked slowly back to my side and traced a line over the back of my hand with his finger. "You don't want to stay here? In Queensland? I'm sure there's a lot of work you could do..."

I took his hand and threaded our fingers. "No. I want to go home. Back to Tasmania. Where I belong, with you and Rosemary."

Jack looked so happy he could burst. "I'd like that too."

I kissed his knuckles, then leaned back on the inclined bed and sighed. "I really miss Rosemary. Have you spoken to Remmy?"

"Of course. Rosemary's just fine. Luca's tilling his vegetable garden, so Rosemary has been helping every day."

Jack brushed my hair off my forehead. "Remmy was very worried about you."

I smiled up at him, feeling the weight of exhaustion settle over me. "I miss her as well. I know she and Nico are your friends, but they've come to be dear to me too." I think I was mumbling, so tired, I just had to close my eyes for a minute.

Jack kissed my temple. "They love you too."

CHAPTER TWELVE
JACK

Leaving the hospital with Lawson was the best feeling ever. He was exhausted, and he still looked pale. He was to manage the headaches and body aches with Panadol and Advil, which he was loath to take, but he did—which told me he wasn't as well as he pretended to be.

When we got back to the hotel, I propped him up on the sofa with pillows and a blanket, and he dozed for a bit. I watched him while he slept and contemplated just how much he'd changed my life.

Six months ago, I was intrigued, bewitched even, by this butterfly man. Now I was in love with him, impossibly so. Impossible because there was no going back from this. I was a changed man. My heart belonged wholly to him, and I knew, without a doubt, it always would.

God, I thought I'd lost him this time for sure. And it really put things into perspective for me.

When he'd gone back to save the Tillman Copper in the path of the raging bushfire, I thought I might lose him then too. But looking back, I could see now that was adrenaline.

This time it was fear.

God honest, heart-stopping fear.

I thought he was dead. I thought I'd lost him forever, and I'd never been so terrified in all my life.

And to see him now, sleeping all peaceful and safe on the couch in front of me, made me truly understand that I couldn't live without him.

And that scared me too.

In a good way. In a life-affirming kind of way. In a my-life-is-forever-changed kind of way.

I resisted the urge to touch him, even just to stroke his hair or his beautiful cheekbone, in fear of waking him up. So I tidied up our clothes, did some washing, getting everything ready for our flight home the day after tomorrow.

Lawson was keen to go tomorrow if we could change flights, but the doctor suggested another full day of rest would be best, so that was that.

I ordered some room service for our dinner, knowing he'd probably wake up starving again, and went into the bathroom to freshen up. When I came back out, Lawson was sitting up on the sofa, bleary-eyed but smiling.

"Did I wake you?" I asked him. "I was trying to be quiet on the phone to reception."

He shook his head. "It's fine. You ordered dinner?"

"Yep. I put in a special request for plain vegetable and chicken pasta. It might be a little bland, but I thought the protein and carbs might do you good."

"Sounds perfect." He slowly got to his feet and walked gingerly over to me. "Thank you for looking after me. For saving my life, for being you."

I brushed my lips against his. "You're most welcome."

He looked at me all dreamy with a loving smile, then added, "I really need to pee."

I laughed. "Need me to help you with that?"

He gave me a sly smile as he shuffled to the bathroom. "I think I can manage."

After dinner, which he devoured, we curled up on the couch together, me being the big spoon, to watch some TV. He yawned, then sighed heavily, and was already struggling to keep his eyes open. "Sorry," he murmured. "I know this isn't how we planned to spend our holiday."

I gave him a gentle squeeze. "I'm just glad you're okay."

He wiggled his butt against my groin. "Yes, but still... I'm sure I'm not that sick that I can't enjoy some—"

I put my hand on his hip to still him. "Ah, that's not helping. And you heard what the doctor said."

Lawson grumbled. "Well, yes. Complete rest for the next few days."

"And I'm sure that means no strenuous activity. And believe me, the way we have sex is quite the workout."

He chuckled. "But I could just lie there, face down, and you could—"

"Lawson, that's really not helping." Jesus, the visual of that, the feel of him against me, and my dick was well and truly awake.

"You really won't have sex with me?"

"Not until you're feeling better."

"I'm fine," he protested but followed with another yawn.

I kissed the back of his head and wrangled my way from behind him to get off the couch first. Then I took his hand, "Come on, bedtime."

And even if he really desperately wanted to have sex right now, there was just no way. He could barely lift his head as it was, let alone keep his eyes open. I got him into bed, slid in beside him, and he snuggled into me like a koala. He took a deep breath, let it out slowly, and was already sound asleep.

I woke up to find Lawson's side of the bed empty. Maybe that was the reason I woke up, I don't know. I heard him in the kitchen area, popping pain tablets from the blister pack. A quick check of my watch told me it was just past seven in the morning.

"Morning," I said. "Didn't realise it was so late." I'd normally be up for an hour by now.

He was standing at the glass sliding doors, looking out onto the morning, freshly showered and shaven, with a bottle of water in his hand. He was back in his sleep pants again, though, which told me he wasn't feeling too good. "Good morning," he replied, giving me a warm smile. "I was sick of lying down, sorry."

"Headache?"

He nodded.

"Anything I can do for you?"

He held his arms out, waiting until I fit myself right where he wanted me. He slipped his arms around my waist and let me pull him against me. I rubbed gentle circles on his back and he sighed. "There is something you can do for me."

"What's that?"

"I hope you don't think I'm being brazen by saying this, but you asked me once to move in with you and I foolishly turned you down. I thought I was doing the right thing, for us, by giving us some space while we found our feet together. And now I feel I may have missed my opportunity."

I pulled back so I could look into his eyes. "You want to move in with me?"

He made a face. "Yes. But it would only be proper if you asked me again. I can't bear the thought of imposing just because it's what I want now. I have no idea if you're still offering, but it would only feel right if you asked me again."

I was grinning. I couldn't help it. He was such a dork. "Lawson Gale, would you do me the honour of living with me?"

"And Rosemary?"

I amended my statement. "Lawson Gale, would you do me the most incredible honour of living with me *and Rosemary*?"

He smiled serenely. "There's nothing I want more. It would make my life perfecter, isn't that the word you used?"

"Yes! I told you it'd be a real word." I gave him a crushing hug, then remembered that he was unwell. I set him back on his feet. "Oh, sorry."

He laughed and patted his shirt down. "It's quite all right."

I cupped his face in both my hands. "Feel better now?"

"Perfecter." Lawson gave me a smile and leaned into me. "I don't want to be apart from you, not for anything. Not only did you save my life, but you've been everything and more while I've been ill. It's made me realise I don't want to waste another minute."

I kissed his forehead, then his lips, then pulled him in for a gentle hug. "Me too. I don't know what I'd have done if you didn't make it. Because truthfully, in the ambulance on the way to the hospital, I thought you were going to die." I shuddered at the memory. "I've never been so scared."

He tightened his hold on me. "I'm sorry you had to see that. I can't even imagine what would have happened if it were you, Jack, that went down that embankment with those cane toads. I'd have never got you up the embankment, let alone carry you out of the forest." He pulled back and his frown was so utterly sad. "I can't even bear to think about it. And now we're two for two. First the bushfire, and now this. You've saved me twice."

I kissed him softly. "How about we don't try for a hat trick, okay?"

He finally laughed. "Well, I can attest to not trying to die again, that's for certain. But I'm sure there'll be other butterfly expeditions—"

I put my finger to his lip. "The correct answer is 'yes, Jack.'"

He chuckled. "I'd love some breakfast. But can we go to the restaurant? I don't want to be cooped up inside any longer than I need to be."

"Of course. Let me grab a quick shower."

Ten minutes later, I was ready to go, and Lawson had changed into some shorts and a shirt. He still looked tired, though I guessed the headache tablets had kicked in. "Ready?"

"Starving."

I chuckled, thinking that was his new state of being. We ate a breakfast of fruit, toast, and tea, and even though his energy levels had improved, he still tired easily. "How about we spend the morning lazing in the courtyard, then this afternoon, if you're up for it, we can go see Piers at the conservatory?"

He gave me a grateful smile. "Sounds perfect."

Whether he felt up to it or not, by mid-afternoon, Lawson was determined to visit Piers. I took his stubbornness as a sign that he was feeling better. Something I'd learned through all of this was that a sick Lawson was agreeable to almost everything. A feeling-better Lawson was getting back to his feisty self.

But I understood his frustration. No one liked being sick and dependent on someone else, so even though I thought he might be rushing it, I didn't want to dampen his mood. He simply washed two Advil down with some juice and grinned. "I'm good to go."

And going back to the conservatory did brighten his mood. As soon as we walked into the lab, Piers met us with an enthusiastic greeting. He put both hands on Lawson's shoulders and gave him the once over. "How are you feeling? You look better." Then Piers glanced at me. "He looks better, no?"

"He does. But he insisted on dropping by, and I know it'll be easier and quicker if I just agree and help him rather than argue, because we all know he's just going to do it himself anyway."

Lawson considered this for a moment, then conceded. "True."

Piers laughed. "Ah, it is good to have you both here. Come and look."

It almost looked like a different lab. There were charts, folders, spreadsheets, data, laptops, and a smartboard, and Piers showed Lawson each one, in turn, pointing out the data Lawson had collated, and they discussed numbers and pH levels and bio-somethings, while I didn't even pretend to understand.

"Isn't it fascinating?" Piers asked with a flourish. Lawson quickly agreed, and I nodded. Though what was really fascinating was the difference in attitude in Piers. Where before he was frustrated and angry at getting nowhere, now he was excited and driven by results. If I had wondered at Piers' ability to keep the ball rolling, I certainly didn't now. He was all over it.

"We're expecting a good wet season," Piers said. "First decent one in four years. It will flush out existing pools and toxicity levels. So we should see significant improvement in the Ulysses environment in the next few seasons. In the meantime, we're considering special gardens and plantations specific to the doughwood. We'll have safeguards, of course, now we know the cane toad tadpole is to blame. Thanks to you, Lawson.

"And we've presented our findings to the environmental departments in Papua New Guinea, the Solomons, and Indonesia. Though Indonesia has had good rainfall, so they're not seeing the results we have. It seems we might be able to secure some breeding pairs from them once we are sure we have resolved our situation the best we can."

"That is terrific news!" Lawson said.

"Yes. Come see this," Piers added quickly.

I put my hand up like a stop sign. "I'll go find Gary and sort out the camping gear. You two will be a while here, no doubt." They both nodded like it was a given. "I'll be back soon. And Piers? Would you mind getting Lawson a stool to sit on or something?"

Lawson gave me a half-irritated, half-thankful scowl. Piers threw his hands up like he couldn't believe he didn't think of that. "Yes! Of course, silly me. Where are my manners?"

I left them to it and went in search of Gary. He'd been kind enough to pack up all our camping gear that we'd had to leave behind in the middle of the forest. I caught him as he was zooming past on a quad runner with some kind of wood and tarp contraption on the back. He pulled up to a stop as soon as he saw me.

"Hey," he said warmly. "How's Lawson?"

"Better. Recovering, though it's slower than he'd like."

"I bet. I've got all your camping gear back in my shed. I can grab it for you now if you like? All the tubs and work gear I left with Piers." He nodded in the general direction of the conservatory.

"Well, I have no real way of getting it all back to Tassie anyway, plus I've got all my own camping gear. Could anyone around here use it?"

"Sure they could!" he replied brightly. "We have camping expeditions into the forest with tourists, school groups, research students. I'm sure it'll get put to good use, if you're sure?"

"Positive." Then I took a closer look at the weird looking apparatus he was taking somewhere. "What is that thing? Are they buoys?"

He snorted and got off the quad runner. "Yep. I got thinkin' about those tadpoles, you know, the ones we have in the water tank for the orchard filtration system."

I nodded. "And?"

"And I got to lookin' on some cane toad site online. A team in Brissie designed a kind of funnel trap and a bait that attracts the tadpoles. Some kind of pheromone thing. Anyway, I contacted 'em and got approval through my boss to get some of the bait. But I rigged this trap up myself after looking at theirs. Wasn't too hard." He held it up and showed me the underneath. It was indeed some kind of funnel trap that sat on the water surface. "Little buggers go in here and can't get out. They reckon they caught tens of thousands in a just a few days."

"That's awesome!" I said, looking the device over. "Lawson would love it!"

Gary smiled proudly. "Guess it certainly can't hurt. Who knows? If we try it here, it might help this team in Brisbane with a trial."

"That's incredible," I said. I liked Gary. We were a lot alike. Both outdoorsy, better with our hands than with our brains. "I better get back. But hey, if you're ever down south and want to see how the Tasmanian Parks and Wildlife do their thing, I'd love to show you around. I really appreciate everything you've done for us."

"Will do," he said. He shook my hand, got back on the quad runner, and went on his way.

When I got back to the lab, Lawson was sitting on the stool, and he and Piers were both studying a laptop screen filled with tables of numbers. Lawson looked up and smiled, and I rubbed his back. "How're you feeling?" The fact he was sitting on the stool while Piers was standing told me enough.

"Okay. Tired."

I kissed the side of his head. "Just spoke to Gary. He showed me a funnel trap he made himself for the retention tank at the orchard. There's some kind of bait he found online that attracts the tadpoles and kills them."

"Yes," Lawson said. He gestured to the screen. "We were just looking at that. Can you believe the bait they're testing is from the cane toad's own poison?"

I barked out a laugh. "Actually, I can believe that. I've seen what that poison can do."

Lawson gave me a sad smile. "Indeed."

"Apparently the pheromone they extract attracts only the cane toad tadpole, not any other frog species," Piers went on to say.

Lawson still hadn't stopped looking at me. "Did you get everything sorted with Gary?"

I rubbed his back again. "I did." He was still tired, I could tell. "You ready to go?"

He gave me a small nod. "Yes. I can't believe how utterly exhausted I am. We did nothing but lie about reading all morning." Then he seemed to reconsider what he said. "Well, Jack read. I mostly slept."

I rubbed his back some more. "The doc said it'll take a while. You need to take it easy."

The look he shot me said *I am taking it easy*, and Piers chuckled. "Well, Lawson and Jack, I must say it has been a true joy to have you both here. I owe you both an immeasurable debt. I hate to think where we'd be if you hadn't made the connection between the toxin bufadienolides and bioaccumulation and transference."

"It's my absolute pleasure," Lawson said. "And I have no regrets about not staying on." Before Piers could be offended, Lawson added, "Because I know it's in very capable hands."

We bid Piers farewell, with him promising to email Lawson often with updates, or to call if he needed, and we headed back to the hotel. Lawson leaned his head against the headrest and smiled sleepily at me. "No regrets on not staying?" I asked.

He shook his head a little. "None."

I grinned at him as I drove. "Me either."

"I miss Rosemary. I miss the quiet of your house, the smell of your bed. I want to go home, Jack."

I took his hand and gave it a squeeze. "Tomorrow. By this time tomorrow, you'll be on the sofa with Rosemary at your side, and I'll be in the kitchen cooking you my Nonna's lasagne."

"Sounds perfect," he mumbled, almost asleep in the car. "So tired."

When we got back to the hotel, I managed to get him into bed, took his shoes off, pulled his trousers off, but left his shirt and undies on. I pulled up the blanket, kissed his forehead. "Love you," I whispered and let him sleep.

By the time we got all of Lawson's tubs and work gear organised for freight back to Tasmania and then into the airport ourselves, I could tell he was already lagging. We'd only been up for a few hours and I'd done all the packing and lifting, but he was still weary. "Want me to get you a courtesy wheelchair?"

He shot me a horrified look. "No! Of course not!"

When we boarded the plane, he sank into his seat and snoozed for most of the flight. But when we arrived in Melbourne, he was having trouble staying awake. "Want a wheelchair now?" I asked. "We have to walk to the other end of the terminal, Lawson. It's not worth ending up back in hospital, is it?"

He pouted but didn't argue, and that was answer enough for me. I asked a stewardess if we could please have a wheelchair, and without any trouble, we had one. I pushed him through the terminal to our gate, and he never said a thing. When we finally took our seats on the plane to Launceston, he let out a heavy sigh.

"You okay?" I asked.

He blinked slowly, barely awake. "Yeah."

I took hold of his hand. "Remember the first time we met, it was on this flight. Melbourne to Launceston."

He smiled. "Yes, you laughed at me, then trampled me into the aisle."

I barked out a laugh. "I did not! Anyway, I seem to remember you calling me a serial killer."

He closed his eyes and squeezed my hand. "The foundation of all perfect relationships."

I chuckled and was going to say something else, but he was already asleep.

THERE REALLY IS NOTHING LIKE COMING HOME. EVEN THE BITING Tasmanian cold didn't dampen my spirits.

Lawson snoozed the entire drive from Launceston to Scottsdale. When I'd asked him if he wanted to go to his place or mine, his answer was immediate. "Yours. Ours. Take me home, Jack."

My heart almost beat right out of my chest.

And my smile got bigger as I turned down Stanning Road. I was taking him home—mine, his, ours. We'd worry about getting his things moved later, but for now, he needed rest and recuperation. And if he stayed at home, then Rosemary and I could look after him.

It seemed Remmy had other ideas.

As my house came into view, so did four cars, all parked in my front yard. Remmy and Nico's car was there, and I knew she had to be the one behind it.

I drove up to the house and pulled on the handbrake. I knew she only had the best of intentions, but Lawson really wasn't up for a welcoming committee. At least they'd have the fire going, I reasoned. I climbed out of my ute and walked around to Lawson's door. He was still asleep, so I gently shook his arm. "Hey, Lawson, baby, we're home."

He startled awake and looked bleary eyed at the house. With my hand under his elbow, I helped him out and up the front porch steps. It was only then he seemed to notice the cars in the front yard, and as I opened the door, a loud and warm 'welcome home' cried out from the lounge room.

God, everyone was there. Rosemary, of course. Remmy, Nico, Luka. My mum and step-dad, my sisters, and Lawson's parents. A huge sign stuck to the wall read "Welcome home and thanks for not dying" which made me laugh.

Lawson was shocked, to say the least, but he was all smiles as his mum and dad hugged him. Hyacinth had her hands to his face, but I was distracted by Remmy almost tackling me into a fierce hug. "Oh my God, Jack. Is he okay?"

"He's fine, Remmy, thank you. Travelling has just taken it out of him, that's all."

I turned to find Lawson bending down and giving Rosemary a half pat, half cuddle, and she was wriggling herself crazy. I gave her a scratch behind the ear. "Hey, you're supposed to greet me first," I pretended to rouse on her.

Lawson gave me a smile. "She loves me."

I slid my arm around his back. "Yes, she does."

Then Lawson's parents hugged me. "Thank you for everything," his mum said.

"It was nothing," I replied humbly.

His dad put his hand on my shoulder. "It was everything."

Then I noticed my parents and sisters watching. I rubbed Lawson's back. "Come on, I want you to meet my folks."

Lawson didn't budge. He mumbled, "I'm not really dressed appropriately to be meeting your family."

He was wearing his navy trousers and a pale blue button-down shirt and looked more than fine to me. "You look great." He made a face. I leaned in and whispered, "They'll love you no matter what you wear."

Reluctantly, he let me lead him over to where my family were standing back. "Mum, Dad, this is Lawson Gale. Lawson, this is Robert and Katherine Brighton. And my sisters, April and Poppy, who you've spoken with on the phone."

My dad, or technically my step-father, but he was the only dad I really knew, was first to reply. He shook Lawson's hand. "We've heard so much about you, it's good to finally meet you, son."

"So very nice to finally meet you," Mum said, taking his hands. "We heard about how sick you got in Queensland, and Remmy said she was having a little welcome home party. I hope you don't mind?"

Lawson quickly answered. "No, I don't mind at all. I'm very glad to meet you both. I'm just sorry I'm not exactly dressed for first impressions." He patted down his hair, which was a nervous thing he hadn't done in a while. "It's been quite a long day."

I took his hand. "Excuse us for a second," I said, leading him to the hall. "We'll be right back."

There was silence behind us, but Remmy saved the situation. "Right, then. Pot of tea is on. Who wants cake?"

I took Lawson into my bedroom and sat him down on

the edge of the bed. "What are you doing?" he asked, looking up at me.

"You're not comfortable," I stated. "Take your shirt off."

His eyes bugged out, but I went to my wardrobe and pulled out one of his shirts. I handed it to him. "Here. Put this on." Then I went to my dresser drawers and took out one of his bow ties. "You'll feel much better if you're dressed the way you feel most comfortable."

His eyes got glassy, and for a moment I thought he might cry. "Thank you." He slowly pulled on the shirt and did up the buttons. It was just plain white with long sleeves, but it was freshly pressed. He took a little longer to finish buttoning up, as though his arms were tired, so I popped his collar up and he let his arms fall to his sides while I tried to tie his bow tie. It had been years, and I was never really any good at them. It was a yellow bow tie, one he'd left here ages ago. "I wondered where I left this one," he said quietly.

When I met his eyes, he was staring up at me with such love. I folded his collar down, leaned in, and kissed him. "I kinda suck at doing ties of any kind," I said, "and it's crooked, and one side is bigger than the other, just a little bit, but still. Not exactly symmetrical like how you do them."

He stood up, his eyes never leaving mine. "I don't care. It's perfect."

"You uh, haven't seen it."

"I don't need to."

"You sure you feel okay?"

He nodded. "Yes. Tired, but otherwise fine. We best not keep them waiting. And I believe there's tea."

I kissed him one more time for good luck. "And cake."

I took his hand and led him back out to where our

friends and family were sitting around the dining table, drinking tea. I eyed the almost-gone cake. "There better be some of that left," I said.

"Hummingbird cake," Remmy said, quickly cutting me a huge slice. "Your favourite."

I pulled out a chair at the table for Lawson to sit on, which he took with a shy smile. I only realised a little too late that it was in between my mother and his. I gave his shoulder a squeeze and pulled out a stool from under the kitchen bench. Remmy handed me the plate of cake, but I needed to grab a spoon, and Remmy quickly cornered me in the kitchen.

She looked panic stricken. "I didn't realise he was still so ill. He looks awful. If I'd known... Jack, I'm sorry. This party is probably the last thing he wanted..."

"He's okay. Just tired. Well, he's better than he was, that's for sure. And this party is perfect, thank you."

She frowned. "How did your first holiday together go, apart from the almost dying part? I mean, first holidays away together are a make or break thing..."

"He wants to move in with me."

Remmy bit back a squeal but still had to cover her mouth. "Oh my God," she said from behind her hand. "I'm so happy for you."

"Me too."

Then I heard Lawson's mum say, "Oh, Lawson, honey, seriously, you should have studied medicine and not be out traipsing through the wilderness almost getting yourself killed by bushfires or toxic wildlife."

His dad laughed. "If he did study medicine, Hyacinth, he'd be off in some remote part of the globe helping village children in Peru. Or Cambodia. Or Uganda."

I couldn't help but laugh. "That's so true. He totally would be."

Lawson sipped his tea just as Rosemary padded over to him. She knew better than to approach the dining table, but I couldn't bring myself to rebuke her. She rested her head on his thigh, as though she somehow knew he wasn't feeling too great. He stroked her forehead and she closed her eyes, and I found myself smiling at them. Remmy nudged my side and gave me a knowing smirk before she reclaimed her seat at the table. Luca clambered all over her lap and I ate my cake while everyone chatted and talked, told stories and laughed.

My sisters claimed Lawson for their own, and I could tell by the way they smiled at him that he had totally charmed them. My mum watched on fondly, and with her cup of tea in hand, she stood beside my stool at the kitchen bench. "He's lovely," she said.

"He is."

She sighed contentedly. "I'm so glad you found him."

"Well, I was watching him when he slid down the embankment. I didn't exactly have to find him."

She rubbed my hand. "No, Jack. I mean, I'm glad you found someone who makes you so happy."

"Oh." I pretended I wasn't embarrassed. I met her gaze so she could read the seriousness in mine. "He does, Mum. He's moving in with me."

She gave me an eye-crinkling smile. "Well, it's always good to live with someone, find out all their bad habits before you get married."

I choked on my tea, and we caught ourselves a few glances from around the table. I dabbed a serviette to my mouth. "Jeez, Mum."

She simply smiled in that knowing way mothers do. "I

can see how you are with him, love. The way you look at him, and how he looks at you. And his parents are lovely. Having met them before meeting him, he wasn't at all what I expected."

I chuckled. "He's not what I expected either."

She squeezed my hand. "Hey, Jack," Poppy called out. "I was just telling Lawson of that time in high school—"

"Please don't," I said, cutting her off. "Whatever story you're about to tell, I'd rather you just stop right there."

April clapped her hands together. "Aww, come on Jackie, it was funny."

I sighed. "Please don't call me that." It was then I looked at Lawson; he was fighting to keep his eyelids open. Mum saw it the same time I did, then Lawson's dad did too.

I put my cup down and was just about to go to him when my mum stopped me. "Okay, well, we better get going," she said. "We've got the drive back to Hobart ahead of us."

"Oh yes, we should be going too," Lawson's dad said, giving a subtle nod to Lawson. "You boys have had a long day."

Remmy agreed, and I walked her, Nico, and Luca to the door. "I'm sorry, Jack," she said. "I feel so bad. The poor guy!"

I pulled her in for a hug. "Thank you. And no more apologies. The welcome home party was lovely, and the *thanks for not dying part* was a nice touch."

She gave me a shrug and half a smile. "I thought so too."

I waved them off with a laugh and a promise to call into the bakery tomorrow.

I hugged my mum and dad and sisters and thanked

them for making the effort to come visit. "We'll come to Hobart next time. I promise."

Mum hugged me the hardest, and Dad clapped my shoulder. "You need to look after him," he ordered with a smile. "Poor kid looks beat."

"I will."

Lawson thanked them for coming, telling them he was very pleased to meet them, but his blinks were getting longer and longer. His parents left the same time as mine did, but they were staying in town and flying back to Melbourne the next afternoon.

I had no doubt we'd see them again bright and early but didn't begrudge them for wanting to spend some time with Lawson. "We'll bring out breakfast," Darren offered.

"I'd love that," I answered. "We haven't had a chance to grab milk or bread or anything really."

So with plans made, they drove off, leaving the house in a silence that felt like a comfy blanket. I took Lawson to bed, undressed him, and tucked him in. It was still too early for me to fall asleep, so I did some tidying up, some laundry, then planted myself on the floor with Rosemary.

"It's good to be home, hey, girl?"

She replied with a tongue-lolling smile and a wag of her tail.

"You want Lawson to come live with us?"

She wiggled her butt.

"You'll have two daddies, huh? How does that sound?"

She huffed, and I swear she was smiling.

"Yeah, sounds pretty good to me too."

CHAPTER THIRTEEN
LAWSON

I WOKE UP TO THE SMELL OF FOOD AND THE SOUND OF VOICES AND laughter. I had no idea what time it was, and I took a moment to assess how I felt. There was an ever present ache in my head, like a band that tightened inside my skull. I was still bone weary, which was absurd because I'd just slept for God knows how long.

I sat up and put my feet to the floor, giving myself some time to adjust. I reached for my phone to find it was almost eight. Bother. I'd slept for... I couldn't even remember what time I went to bed.

I pulled on my trousers, relieved myself in the bathroom, brushed my teeth and washed my face, then went in search of Jack. I found him in the kitchen with my parents, laughing about something to do with stewed fruit. I'm not sure I wanted to know.

Jack got to his feet as soon as he saw me. "Oh, you're awake! Want some tea? Your mum and dad brought out some of Remmy's breakfast specials and some bread and milk, so I can make you some toast?"

I gave him a smile just before Mum put her hand to my face. "You look so much better."

"I feel better," I admitted. I looked over her shoulder to Jack. "Tea, please."

It was lovely to spend some time with my parents, it really was. They were worried about me, as were Paterson and Mackellar. And I think they had a newfound adoration of Jack after he'd carried me out of the rainforest. They liked him before, but now I highly doubted he could ever do wrong in their eyes.

He doted on me, making sure I had everything I needed. When my parents left, he put me on the couch with snacks, drinks, phone and laptop, books, TV remote, all within reach. Rosemary sat by my side the entire day, the fire well stocked and blazing, while Jack went into town to catch up on a bit of work, call in to see Remmy, and grab some groceries. I only dozed once or twice.

On the second day, Jack left me in bed, and I spent the day a little more upright and only dozed once. I also notified the real estate agent of my intent to vacate my rental, which was an overwhelmingly wonderful feeling.

I couldn't even remember why I ever thought not living with him was a good idea.

It was unusual, though, being in Jack's home without him. All his belongings, all his personal effects, his entire life was in this house. It was a curious feeling, being surrounded by him but not having him here.

He did leave work a little early so he could be home with me, though after two weeks off it was hardly feasible. But he was adamant. He was also devoted to my wellbeing, my recuperation, though I couldn't convince him that I was well enough for sex.

I was feeling better every hour, and he was attentive to

my every need. Except that one.

By the fourth day, I'd tended to all my emails, I'd spoken to Professor Tillman on the phone, and to Piers, who both assured me all was going well. I'd sat by the *Bursaria spinosa* we'd planted near the rosemary, in hopes of spotting a Tillman Copper. Not that I expected to, especially in winter when butterflies were more docile, but as a lepidopterist, I hoped. The shrub had taken well, the ants were building a nice nest underneath it... but no butterflies. Yet.

I decided I'd cook dinner for Jack and settled on lamb souvlaki and couscous salad. I'd also decided I'd had enough of his abstinence, so I was freshly showered, wearing my normal trousers and shirt, but added the bow tie and suspenders. Because, well, because Jack had a thing for suspenders...

He greeted me with a warm, humming kiss. "Something smells great."

"Me or the food?"

"Both."

"It's almost done."

"Good, because I'm starving. How are you feeling?"

"Better. I didn't nap at all today."

Jack grinned. "Are these"—he trailed his fingers over the suspenders, over my collarbone—"for any reason in particular?"

My hopes soared, and those elusive butterflies that only existed in his presence flooded my belly. "Is that smile indicative of your willingness and intent to bed me later?"

He gave me a blank stare. "What?"

"You won't touch me. You won't have sex with me."

"Because you're unwell, Lawson. No other reason."

"But I'm not unwell anymore."

He put his fingers to my chin and lifted my face so he

could stare into my eyes. "My abstinence is not a reflection of anything but your physical wellbeing. You know I love you. You know I love being intimate with you." His eyes flashed with a spark. "And wearing suspenders is a low blow. You know how much I love taking them off you."

I smiled victoriously. "That was the reason I wore them."

He kissed me briefly, then put his finger to my lips. "Dinner first, then you can tell me about your day, and then we'll see if you feel up to it."

I never thought I'd be one to feel antsy without sex. Lord knows I'd endured dry spells to rival the Sahara. But I needed him in ways I'd not needed anyone before. Yes, I needed him emotionally, but I also needed him physically as well.

I was craving him.

"What is it?" he murmured, cradling my face in his hands.

"I need to feel connected to you. I thought there were always two different kinds of connections: physical and emotional, but I've just realised that when you make love to me, I get both. I need to feel that. I need to feel reconnected and I need you to..."

He pressed himself against me and he whispered in my ear, "You need me to what?"

I closed my eyes and spoke the words against his neck. "To make me yours again. I feel disengaged since the accident, detached almost. But when you're inside me, I feel... centred."

He sucked back a breath. "Lawson?" His voice was rough and thick with desire.

"Yes."

"Turn the hotplates off." I grinned and he bit my

bottom lip, gently pulling it between his teeth. "And don't be so smug about it."

I quickly shut dinner off, and when I turned around, Jack held his hand out. Without a word, he led me to his bedroom, our bedroom, and stopped. He stood right up close and slipped a finger under one of my suspenders and slid it off my shoulder. He licked his lips, his eyes smouldered, and the butterflies in my belly took flight. With just as much dedication, he slid the other suspender from my shoulder and watched it fall to my side. Then he tilted my head back, then ghosted his lips across mine. "I need to use the bathroom. Don't go anywhere."

It took me a second to realise he'd gone. I'm not sure I'd breathed the entire time and my head buzzed. I undressed quickly, leaving my clothes in a pile on the floor, too impatient to fold neatly. I took the lube from the bedside drawer and climbed on the bed, laying on my belly. Without waiting for him to return—I simply couldn't wait a second longer—I slicked my own fingers and slid them along my arse crack, over my hole, and pushed one fingertip inside myself.

I heard Jack's gasp from the bedroom door. "Lawson." His voice was strained.

"I can't wait. I need this, Jack. I need you."

I heard the rustle of fabric as he undressed. The zipper undoing sent a thrill through me, and I raised my hips and pushed a second fingertip inside myself.

"Fuck," he rasped out.

I turned my head at the sound and saw him naked, staring at me, stroking himself. "Jack, please."

He smirked and knelt on the bed. "Remove your hand," he ordered gruffly.

I did, and he took my leg closest to him and manoeuvred me so I was on my back instead. Then, still gripping my ankle, he pulled me closer to him so he was now between my legs. "I need to see your face," he murmured. "I need to kiss you while I fill you."

My cock jerked at his words and he smiled. I wrapped my fingers around my shaft and Jack's nostrils flared. I let my eyes wander down to the hair on his chest, down to his almost-defined abs, and further down to his proud erection. His cock was fully engorged, the cockhead purple, precome at the tip.

He slid his huge hands around my thighs and lifted my legs toward my chest, then leaned over me so his lips were almost touching mine. His thick and heavy cock slid along my perineum, teasing. I tried to push onto him, but he held me still. "Jack, I've not the patience for teasing right now."

"I can tell you're feeling better," he said with a smirk. "Because you're back to being feisty and bossy in bed." He gripped his cock and pressed against my hole, but didn't push in. He loved driving me to the brink and never seemed satisfied until I cursed and demanded he do certain things to my body.

"Jack, I swear, if you don't fuck me right now."

His eyes flashed with triumph. "You'll what?"

I reached down between us and slid my fingers past my balls. "I'll do it myself."

Jack gripped my hand and pinned it to the mattress by my head, and in one thrust, he pushed into me.

He was bigger than I'd remembered.

"Fuck," I gasped, blinking and trying to breathe.

Jack's eyes smouldered. His voice was gruff, his lips against mine. "Is that what you wanted?"

I nodded and groaned as he settled himself inside as far as he could go. As far as I could take him. He let go of my hand and gripped my hair instead. He kissed me as he pulled back, almost all the way, then slowly slid back in. Over and over.

It was everything I needed. Feeling owned by him, claimed and taken. There could be no doubt I was his when he took me like this.

He broke the kiss, trailing his lips down my jaw to my neck. And he never stopped fucking, reminding me with every thrust that I was his, and he was mine. He increased his tempo, speeding closer and closer to the precipice. "Lawson," he rasped. "Need you to come." I shook my head, and he pulled back so he could look into my eyes. "I need you to come first." He thrust slower now, as if he wanted to stop but couldn't.

"Not this time. I just need you to come inside me."

He moaned and he closed his eyes, and I could feel him swell deep within me. He put one hand at the top of my head, his other cupped my jaw, and he arched fully with a guttural moan as he came.

He surged inside me, spilling his seed, and he cried out with a final shudder as his orgasm subsided. He collapsed on top of me but nuzzled into my neck. "My God," he mumbled. Once his breaths had calmed, he kissed that spot below my ear that made me shiver. He kissed up my jaw to my mouth. His eyes were glazed over, sated and happy. "Feel better?"

I took stock of every inch of my body, my mind, giving a little roll of my spine. "I feel superb."

He kissed me with smiling lips. "I can tell. You're almost purring."

I chuckled. "Helps that you're still inside me."

He kissed me and rolled his hips. "I never want to leave."

"Then don't."

He ran his thumb across my cheek. "Are you not tired?"

I shook my head. "Not really."

"Good. Because you didn't get off, so there needs to be a round two."

I hummed, liking the sound of that very much. "We never did test our theory on bioaccumulation."

Jack laughed and slowly slipped out of my body, quickly wrapping me up in his arms instead. "I'm going to need about twenty minutes and some food."

"Should we venture out to the kitchen?"

"If we have to."

Neither of us moved, just enjoying the peaceful moment between us. "Thank you," I said eventually. "For not denying me. I felt quite out of sorts, and it didn't really occur to me what it was. But I needed this intimacy between us. It was rather difficult to articulate, but I just needed to be yours again. And you did exactly that. So, thank you."

"You were out of sorts. But you feel okay now?"

I nodded and kissed his chest. "Much better."

Jack sighed. It was a contented sound with a hint of understanding. He gave me a hard squeeze and another kiss to the side of my head. "Just so you know, Lawson, my love, you are mine, and I am yours. But if you ever need reminding, I won't ever deny you." He pulled back so he could put his hand to my cheek and kiss me.

"I love you, Jack. Now and forever."

He smiled. "Thank you."

I kissed him softly. "Let me get you some dinner, then we can further our research on biotransference and accumulation."

Jack laughed. "All the bio-somethings there are?"

"All of them."

TEN MINUTES LATER, I'D FINISHED COOKING OFF DINNER, resurrected the couscous and served two plates to the table. I went back to the kitchen for a bottle of water and two glasses when Jack came in from being out the back with Rosemary. She'd needed to go, so he'd followed her to grab some more firewood, which he stacked next to the fire. Then he walked over to me, windswept and his nose an adorable red from the cold, with a sprig of rosemary and a wild daisy from the grass. He slid them into a small white vase and presented them to me with a proud smile. "For you. It's been too long since I offered flowers."

I took the vase gratefully. "They're perfect." I put them to my nose and inhaled everything that reminded me of Jack—earth and outdoors, sweet and unpretentious, and all that was good in the world—and smiled up at him. "Thank you."

We sat at the table and ate our dinner, with the small vase between us, and Rosemary asleep in front of the roaring fire. If perfect was a moment personified, this was it, right here.

And when we were done, Jack took my hand and led me back to bed. I was sleepy, not in an unwell-exhausted way, but in a warm and happy way. Jack lay me out on the bed and showed me every way he adored me, and I'd almost felt foolish for needing his reaffirmation of how I belonged to him earlier. He made those butterflies in my belly take flight and dance on every nerve ending; he made my heart morph into something that would belong to him always.

And I'd never doubt again.

SIX MONTHS LATER...
LAWSON

I LEFT PROFESSOR TILLMAN'S BUTTERFLY HOUSE IN LAUNCESTON after spending the day with the Tillman Copper's latest newly emerged kaleidoscope, with a printed off email in hand, and headed straight for Jack's office in Scottsdale.

Karen greeted me first. "Lawson, so good to see you!" She looked flustered. "But Jack's not here."

"Oh, is he out in the field or something?"

"Um, uh." She was a terrible liar. "He's gone home for the day, actually."

"Oh, was he unwell?"

She side-eyed me. "Not exactly."

I wasn't quite sure what to say to that. "Okay, well then, I'll just meet him there. I guess."

She grimaced, then tried to smile. "Okay." As I walked out, I could already hear her clambering to pick up the phone.

Well. That was very odd.

I drove home, wondering what on earth Jack had gone home for and why Karen was being so secretive. Jack's ute was parked where it always was beside the house, and I pulled in behind it and went inside.

Jack met me in the lounge room like he'd raced to greet me. Rosemary skidded to a stop beside him, both looking ridiculously happy.

"Good afternoon, Doctor."

I smiled at his greeting. Since I'd gained my doctorate, he'd taken to addressing me as such. I think he got off on it, to be honest. "Hi. I called into your office, but Karen told me you were here."

"Oh yes, she just called..." He swallowed hard when he'd realised he'd said too much. His ability to lie rivalled Karen's. His eyes went to the papers I was holding. "What you got there?"

"Well... it's a letter from the New South Wales Lepidopterist Society..."

"And?"

"It's more of a formal request, actually."

"A request?"

"Yes, you see, they read my journal entry on the Ulysses last month, and of course they know of my work with the Tillman Copper."

"And?"

"And there's a butterfly, the *Pasma tasmanicus* or the Two Spotted Grass Skipper, as it's more commonly known, and it's typically found at altitudes such as the Blue Mountains or Mount Kosciuszko. It's bivoltine, however, researchers are claiming there's been no summer brood this year."

Jack stared then nodded slowly. "And they want you to look into it?"

I smiled and handed the letter over so he could read it. "Yes, hence the formal request."

He read the first line. "Doctor Gale." He looked up at me. "Sounds formal."

Yes, there was definitely a doctor kink.

He went back to reading and I waited for him to finish. He looked up and tilted his head. "Did you call them?"

"Yes."

"And? When did they want you to go?"

"As it's summer and the wildflowers are in full bloom, it would make sense to go soon. Winter would be redundant, as the snow over Kosciuszko would make things rather difficult. Especially if we were to camp out."

"We?"

"Of course."

His lips twitched before becoming a smile. "Really?"

"Yes. After the last few incidents, I don't think my parents would approve of me going alone."

A huff of laughter escaped him. "That's probably true. I don't want to think about what trouble you could find in the Snowy Mountains by yourself."

I rolled my eyes. "I thought with your position with the national parks, we might gain special access."

"Ah, so you're only inviting me for my perks, huh?"

I chuckled. "Well, yes. And your ability to save my life if needed."

"Well, there is that."

He handed the letter back to me. "I could put in for some time off. I mean, the survival of a species might very well depend on it."

I stepped in and leaned up on my toes so I could kiss him. "You're wonderful."

He buzzed with a cute little smile. "I know."

"So, do you want to tell me what you and Rosemary were doing outside?"

His eyes widened. "What?"

"You both came inside as I pulled up. And I assume it's what Karen failed to lie about when I called in."

He took a deep breath and let it out slowly. "It isn't quite ready yet, but I wasn't expecting you until around five."

My curiosity was piqued. "What is it?"

"Close your eyes."

I did, and he took me by the hand and led me out the back. I was confused as to where he'd taken me because I thought we'd gone right, but we should have run into a fence by now. But I trusted him so I kept my eyes closed. When I was in the spot Jack deemed correct, he stopped me. "Okay, open your eyes."

We were standing to the right of the house in the next paddock, where the fence had been taken down. There were four wooden pegs in the ground with string lines between the pegs, outlining a rather large rectangle. "I wasn't finished pegging it out when you got here."

Was he building another house? "What is it?"

He put his hand up in a one-sec notion, raced over to the back of the house, and came back with some papers. He handed them to me.

It was a legal document with our local council insignia blazoned across the top, with the words Development Application in bold.

The applicant — Mr Jack Brighton.

Proposed Development — a butterfly house.

Status — approved.

My gaze went from the papers in my hand to Jack. "A butterfly house?"

He nodded. "Your very own."

I walked into the outlined footprint of the butterfly

house and looked around. My heart swelled with emotions I couldn't name, my eyes burned with tears. The butterflies in my belly flooded my throat and I couldn't speak. It was the most incredible gesture, the most extraordinary gift. Tears spilled down my cheeks, and Jack was suddenly alarmed.

"Is it okay? If you don't like it..."

I laughed, because how on earth could I not like this? "It's perfect," I tried to say through my tears.

"Oh, thank God," he said, laughing with relief. He threw his arms around me and pulled me in for a hug. "You like it?"

"I love it. It's more than I could ever ask for. *You* are more than I could ever ask for."

"I had some help with the design I submitted. Warner, of course, and Piers too, they both drew up their ideal designs and helped me with requirements. We'll need to get a specialist architect, I'd reckon, but the plans I submitted are approved pending proper—"

"Marry me."

He stared, his mouth open. "What?"

"Marry me," I repeated before I could lose my nerve. He was still staring, so I explained, "Jack, there are species of *Lepidoptera* all over this world, but there are none—none—like those I experience when I'm with you. You are quite possibly the most perfect man, with the kindest heart, and you make me strive to be a better person. And this here—" I looked around us, the Tasmanian countryside, Rosemary off sniffing around the garden, this perfect piece of life. "It's everything I want for the rest of my life. I want to grow old with you, right here. Marry me, Jack. Please."

Jack put his fingers under my chin, and taking a deep breath, he leaned in and fluttered his eyelashes along my cheekbone before kissing me softly on the lips. He shivered, and when he opened his eyes, they were glassy with tears, and he nodded. He could barely speak. "Yes."

EPILOGUE
JACK

TWO YEARS LATER

It was a glorious Tasmanian summer day, barely a cloud in the sky. I was at Remmy's helping her with the finishing touches on the menu because Lawson insisted we had to spend the day apart.

It wasn't right to see each other before the wedding, he'd said.

He was probably right, not that I was superstitious at all, and truthfully neither was he. But it gave us some time to spend with our families before the big event. My sisters and parents were with me at Remmy's. Lawson's parents and his brother and sister and their partners were at home putting the final touches in.

Not that they needed to. Everything was perfect.

We'd spent the better part of two years making sure everything was spot on.

It was really a very simple affair. Uncomplicated and perfect, Lawson said.

"This is the sweetest menu I've put together," Remmy said as she took the last batch of pastries out of her oven. She had done the majority of the baking at the bakery but she was never happy unless she had extras and a few special bits and pieces.

"What do you mean?" Mum asked. "I thought Jack said it was a simple menu."

"Didn't he tell you?" Poppy chimed in. Poppy was sitting at the dining table while April was doing her hair, curling or straightening, I couldn't tell the difference, to be honest.

Mum frowned. "Tell me what?"

"Jack and Lawson wanted to replicate the menu of their first date," Poppy said, fluttering her eyelashes. "Such romantics."

"It was special to us," I added, needing to defend myself. "And it's not *simple*, it's just not fancy fine dining. It's what Remmy put together when I said I'd met a guy I wanted to impress." I could feel myself blush, so I stopped talking.

"It is sweet," Remmy said. "And perfect for you both." But then she turned total traitor and blabbed to my entire family. "It was so cute. He set up a table for two with a little vase of flowers in the bakery after closing time, and I made a basket of things for them to share. Lawson was swept off his feet; never stood a chance, the poor boy."

"It wasn't flowers. It was a flow*er*. Single. Not plural."

"Getting a single flower sometimes means more than getting a whole bouquet," April said with a wistful sigh.

"And those are the flowers they're having for their wedding, in their lapels, on the table," Remmy added, throwing me right under the bus. "There were five dates, five different types of flowers."

My mum put her hand on her heart. "Awwww."

April counted on her fingers. "White Milligan's daisy. Jasmine. Rosemary. Yellow daisy, and the *Bursaria*, of course."

"I know!" Poppy cried. "It's like the sweetest thing ever."

"Are you guys done?" I asked. Pleaded. Whatever. "Anyway, the *Bursaria* wasn't from a date. It's the shrub Lawson planted at the side of our house. It's a wedding. It's supposed to be romantic."

Just then, the front door opened and Dad came in first, followed by Nico and Luca, with a freshly groomed Rosemary.

"She wanted to roll in the duck poo," Luca announced with a grin.

"Almost did too," Dad added. "Walked out of the groomer's place, took three steps, and aimed right for a big streak of—"

Mum put up her hand. "We get it."

I bent down and gave Rosemary a pat and ruffled the fur on her forehead. "You look real pretty, Miss Rosemary. Got a big day today, huh?"

She gave me a tongue-lolling grin then proceeded to sniff out Remmy's cooking in the kitchen. Yeah, she knew who had the good stuff. She padded over to Remmy, sat down in front of her, and waited for a fresh-baked treat. Remmy made baby talk to her but promptly rewarded her for being a such a good girl.

My dad, or step-dad, but really my only dad, nudged my elbow with his. He gave me a small, patient smile. "You ready?"

He wasn't asking if I was ready, like showered and shaved. He was asking if I was ready to be married, if I was ready to change my life forever, from *me* to *we*. "I really am."

Nico clapped my shoulder. "Then go suit up, my man. If all us men here gotta be miserable—" He shot a faux-panicked glance toward his wife. "I mean *happily* married..."

"Yeah, you better mean happily married," Remmy fired back at him playfully.

Nico sauntered over to her and slid his arms around her, trying to pick at the pastries. She batted his hand away. "No touching."

I left them then, took a shower, shaved, and dressed in the suit I'd picked out. I kept waiting for the nerves to kick in, but they never did.

When we were all suited and frocked up, we made the convoy down Stanning Road to my house. I still wasn't nervous. I just wanted it to be done. I wanted to be married already. I wanted to start my official forever with Lawson as soon as possible.

The plan was that we'd arrive at the house at four, and I'd walk in last, walk straight up the aisle to a waiting Lawson. So I waited inside the house and gave everyone plenty of time to take their seats. When I couldn't stand it any longer, I looked at Rosemary and gave her the nod. "It's time, girl."

I walked out the back with her and went to the side where the butterfly house stood. It had taken a good six months to plan, six months to build, and twelve months to establish what it was today.

I paused at the threshold for a deep breath, then opened the door, and Rosemary and I stepped inside.

There inside the butterfly house was Mum, Dad, April

and Poppy, Remmy, Nico and Luka. On Lawson's side were his parents, Paterson and Bree, Mackellar and James, and they all turned to look at me.

The only person missing was Professor Warner Tillman. The old man had passed away a year ago. Lawson had been devastated and had not only lost his mentor but a dear friend. Lawson swore his legacy would live on, and I'd never been more grateful that Lawson had named the butterfly after him. The Tillman Copper would indeed live on.

But I couldn't take my eyes off the man at the front. Lawson. Looking incredible in his charcoal suit and bow tie, of course. He grinned when he saw me, and then I noticed the butterflies.

Dozens of Tillman Coppers fluttered above our heads. Lawson's butterfly house was now the largest living display of the Tillman Coppers in the world. When Warner Tillman had passed away, they'd moved the study to Lawson's facility. He bred many, and they flourished enough that he could release them.

We'd been on a few expeditions to find, research, save some butterflies all over the country, but these little copper-coloured butterflies would be not only Warner's legacy, but Lawson's too.

And the fact they were an integral part of our wedding was perfect. The celebrant standing near Lawson put her hand out and a butterfly landed on her, making her laugh. Luka had one land in his curly hair, and Hyacinth was trying to entice one onto her palm. Lawson had one on his shoulder, but he didn't seem to notice. He just stared at me.

I started to walk to him then, with Rosemary at my side. When I reached him, he held out his hand and I took it, sliding his palm into mine, in a feeling that was entirely of coming home. Rosemary sat at our feet, looking up at us both like she knew good and well what was going on.

The celebrant started her spiel then, only stopping every so often to appreciate a butterfly as it skipped across the air in front of her. Paterson's laughter interrupted her once, but he'd had a butterfly trying to land on his eyelid. It was an incredibly personal, private ceremony, with our closest family and friends. And butterflies, of course.

With our hands clasped, we exchanged plain silver wedding bands, and I promised to love and honour, cherish and adore him all my days.

Lawson's smile made my heart beat double time. "You'd once said you'd watched me become imago, getting my wings and being who I was born to be. But I could say the same about you. You keep telling me I've made you happier than any other time in your life, and I am grateful and humbled... and I, too, am witness to you becoming the man you were meant to be." He took a breath and squeezed my hands. "In entomology, we have a term we call *imagines*. It's the plural of imago. And if imago is one butterfly reaching its full potential, then surely we, together, would be imagines. I will love and honour you, cherish and adore you for all my days, Jack. Nothing would bring me greater joy than to be your husband."

I had to blink back tears, though I'm sure no one was fooled. I nodded. "And I yours."

The celebrant lifted her arm to show a butterfly on her sleeve, and with a smile, she declared us husband and husband.

Something shifted inside me, settled into place, and we kissed, sealing our ceremony done. We were quickly surrounded by our families with warm hugs and laughter while butterflies danced around our heads.

"I better go check on dinner," Remmy said, disappearing out the doors. We all followed her, leaving the butterflies to settle for the afternoon. We sat at our dining table and ate various pastries from baskets like we'd done on our very first date. We drank locally mulled cider too, then Nico's Portuguese tarts, laughing and celebrating.

We were heading to New Zealand for our honeymoon in a few days, and talk soon turned to that. "But there are earthquakes in New Zealand," Lawson's mum said.

"Or avalanches!" my mum added.

"It's not snowing," Lawson informed them. "And I'm not *that* accident prone. The bushfire wasn't exactly an accident, and the whole incident with the cane toad was simply a set of unfortunate circumstances..."

"And the time on Mount Kosciuszko?" Paterson furthered. "What was that?"

"It was slippery underfoot."

"And the time in the Blue Mountains?" Mackellar added with a smile.

Lawson lifted his chin. "Well, luckily for Jack—"

"Luckily for Jack?" his dad barked out a laugh. "Luckily for *you*!"

Lawson sighed and I leaned in and kissed him, trying not to smile. "I'll always be with you."

"Because the National Parks and Wildlife Service have banned him from visiting alone," Darren said.

It was all said in good fun, and the jibes at Lawson's run of bad luck whilst out in the field had long been a running family joke. But still, I put my arm around him and defended his honour. "I'll have you know, he's very capable and responsible."

Lawson gave me a look of love and thanks, then preened to his family. "Thank you, Jack."

But then I added, "Well, except for the bushfire thing."

"Uncle Lawson!" Luka came running in from out the back, Rosemary at his side. "Uncle Lawson, I think your butterflies have escaped."

"What?"

We shot up out of our seats and raced outside, but the butterfly house was fully sealed. There's no way any could have gotten out.

"No, over here," Luka cried. He was standing at the side of the house, waving us over. "Here they are."

It was the *Bursaria spinosa* shrub we'd planted after the bushfire. For three years it had thrived on the northern side of the house with the rosemary that Rosemary still loved. Lawson had kept an eye on it, the *Notoncus* ants had built a colony, but there had never been any butterflies...

Lawson crouched down in the dirt, still wearing his suit, and examined the foliage. He bent lower and inspected the roots of the shrub, then bent right down so his hands were in the dirt and he was looking at the undergrowth.

He pulled back, looked up at me, and grinned. That kind of heart-stopping grin that he only gave to me and butterflies.

"What?" I asked, though I was pretty sure I already knew.

He stood up slowly and looked at all of us waiting for him to speak. He barked out a happy laugh and put his hand over his mouth. "We have Tillman Coppers. In the wild. Here. *My* butterfly. In the wild at my house."

Everyone cheered, and I collected him in a crushing hug. "I knew you could do it."

He mumbled into my neck. "On our wedding day!"

"Like they somehow knew."

He nodded, and when he pulled back, he had tears in

his eyes. "Like Warner sent them here as a wedding gift. Do you think that's possible?"

I smiled and kissed him softly on the lips. "I think he's up there somewhere in the biggest butterfly house he could have dared imagined and sent them here to you, today of all days."

Lawson got all teary. "Thank you."

I noticed then that our families had left us alone to have this moment in private. Lawson put his fingers to my tie and adjusted the knot. He still had watery eyes, though it wasn't a sadness. More of an overwhelming love. "You look so handsome today," he whispered.

I ran my thumb over his jaw. "So do you."

"I wish Warner could have been here."

"He was," I said. Then I looked to the shrub and the roosting butterflies. "He is here."

"How do you always know exactly what to say?"

I shrugged. "I dunno, Lawson. You did pretty well with your vows today. I thought we agreed on no personal vows, then you surprised me with the whole speech on imagines?"

"Did you like that? I thought it was fitting for us."

"I loved it. And it was very fitting. If you were imago on your own, then we together are imagines."

He stared into my eyes and smiled. "Oh, Jack, that is where you're wrong. I was, could never be, imago on my own. If I ever did reach imago, it was only ever because of you."

I put my forehead to his and held his jaw. "Lawson Gale—"

"Lawson Brighton-Gale," he corrected with a smile.

I grinned at that. "Doctor Lawson Brighton-Gale."

"Yes, Jack Brighton-Gale?"

Dear God, I loved the sound of that. I put my fingers under his chin and lifted his face. I put my eyelashes to his cheek and gave him butterfly kisses until he sighed. "We better get inside. Our families are waiting."

"Must we?" he asked dreamily. He glanced behind me to the setting sun, to the colours of the sky, then back to me. "I wouldn't mind starting our forever out here, just us. The sunset, the silence, just us."

"You forgot the butterflies."

He put his hand to his stomach and shook his head slowly. "Oh, no. I didn't."

Now I kissed his lips. "Imago?"

He shook his head again and smiled. "No. Imagines."

~ THE END

DELETED SCENE
JACK

WHEN JACK GOES WITH LAWSON AND PIERS TO DROP OFF THE SAMPLES AT THE CSIRO LAB.

IT WASN'T THAT I DIDN'T TRUST PIERS... IT WAS THAT... WELL, okay. I didn't trust him entirely. He had never exactly been encouraging of Lawson's theories and findings, to what end was anyone's guess. I just wanted to ensure the samples got to the CSIRO without incident. I wanted Lawson's work to be received, respected.

So the three of us had made the trip to the CSIRO building in Cairns. And as Lawson and Piers went through to the lab area, I took a seat in the waiting room. It was then a face on a years-old magazine on the side table caught my attention. I couldn't believe it...

God, I hadn't seen him in years.

But that face was unforgettable. Well, one face was.

There were three men standing together at some rural meeting, but the one guy in the middle hadn't changed in years. Still ruggedly handsome, still had that killer smile.

I'd spent *personal time* with him during our uni days in Sydney. Meaning we'd spent a lot of time in bed together. He was a country kid, far from home, as was I. We had a few classes together, both of us environmental science students, two out of towners, both spreading our gay wings for the first time.

He'd disappeared during our third year, apparently had to go home, back to the farm, and never graduated. I hadn't seen him since. But he'd obviously done all right for himself. The magazine was a *Beef Farmers Association* edition titled *Farming in the Future*.

I hadn't thought of him in so long.

I flipped the magazine open and started reading about farming the remote Outback deserts in the twenty-first century. Wow, he'd really done well for himself.

In all our time together, he never spoke much about his life back home. Every time conversation turned to family, he'd clam up, and I could read cues well enough to know it was a subject best left alone. Not that we were that close. Truth be told, we didn't do a great deal of talking when we were together... I knew he was from some huge property in the middle of the desert, but I really had no idea just how big. Jesus Christ, his property was about the same size as all of Tasmania. Okay, so maybe not quite that big, but jeez... I had no idea.

The article went on to talk about using technology and how this new generation of farmers were doing this better, smarter than their fathers before them. It was an interesting read. It was such a blast from the past! I couldn't believe out of all the waiting rooms, out of all the magazines, I had to see this one. The magazine itself was a few years old, worn and tattered, and I wondered how he was doing now.

But it wasn't long before Lawson and Piers came back out. Lawson was smiling, that happy, heart-stopping smile and any past lovers were soon forgotten.

"You ready to go camping out?" Lawson asked excitedly.

I threw the magazine back on the pile, stood up, and matched his grin with my own. Spending the night in the middle of the forest with Lawson sounded bloody perfect to me. "Sure am."

~FIN

IMAGO

Red Dirt Heart

CROSSOVER BONUS STORY

BLURB

A RED DIRT HEART AND IMAGO CROSSOVER ~ THE STORY OF WHEN RED DIRT AND BUTTERFLIES COLLIDE.

When Charlie Sutton's neighbour Greg is notified by the Queensland government that they intend to run a pipeline through his property, Charlie vows to help him fight it. Then Travis remembers seeing butterflies at the creek near their joining fence line - the same butterflies they couldn't find in any Australian butterfly book. Hopeful this might be their only chance to stop the development, they seek the help of a specialist.

Lawson Brighton-Gale receives an email request to identify a butterfly in the Outback, only to discover it's not an Australian butterfly at all. But that's not all he discovers. The name on the request is familiar to Jack. An old friend from his university days, who also happened to be his old friend with benefits, Charlie Sutton.

Lawson and Jack's trip to Sutton Station certainly doesn't go to plan, and what they take back to Tasmania isn't just butterflies, but a cocoon of possibilities.

CHAPTER ONE
CHARLIE SUTTON

Travis and I sat at Greg Pietersen's dining table along with Greg, his wife, Jenny, and Alan, Greg's neighbour to the north.

I was Greg's closest neighbour to the west, and over the years, Greg and Alan had become both friends and allies. They were the reason I was on the Board of the Territory's Beef Farmers Association, and together the three of us were, apparently, the faces of Farming the Future in the Northern Territory.

Greg had been a mate to my old man too, and he'd been the one to come help look for Travis when Trav'd found himself lost overnight in the desert. So one phone call from him was all it took for Trav and me to be sittin' there over a cuppa with our serious faces on.

"It's bullshit," Jenny said. "They can't just do what they damn well please."

Greg gave his wife a smile. "Seems the government can do what they please, love."

I stared at the letter on the table while chewin' on my lip, tryin' to think.

"It doesn't belong to anyone," Alan added. "The Artesian Basin is an underground water supply that feeds half the Territory and Queensland into New South Wales, even South Australia. It's not theirs to take."

"The water don't belong to anyone," Greg agreed. "But the property they wanna run a pipeline through certainly does."

No one spoke for a bit, while we all let our tempers simmer down and our thoughts settle into order. The thing was, I was really pissed about this. No, the bloody government hadn't declared they'd just drop a few hundred kilometres of pipeline through Sutton Station, but they did tell Greg they'd put it through his place. And that was something I just couldn't rightly let happen.

I would defend his property like it was my own.

"Have you spoken to Melville?" I asked. Melville owned property to the north of Greg, and he was no friend of mine.

Greg's eyes met mine, and he shook his head in disgust. "The old bastard's happy to sell it off. His kids don't want his place, and he can't work it like he should. I reckon he was as happy as a pig in the proverbial when he got his letter."

I had to unclench my jaw so I could speak. "I wouldn't be surprised."

Greg's nostrils flared. "I don't want their bloody money, not a goddamn cent. What they're proposin' to pay us off with isn't worth shit anyway."

"Then we fight them," Alan said. "In court. The Supreme Court if we have to."

"They'll just wait us out to bleed us dry," Greg mumbled. I'd never seen him so resigned, like he was beat already. "They'll be expecting that and'll simply tie us up in red tape until we can't afford to stay."

I shook my head. "This ain't over yet. Not by a long shot." I tapped the table with my finger. "It'll be a cold day in hell when I let some pen-pushin' government idiot tell me what they will and won't do with my land, and I sure as shit won't let 'em tell you what they're gonna do with yours."

Jenny squeezed Greg's hand, and I gave her a smile. I could hear their boys playin' in the room next door, and I could only imagine what trouble Milly was getting' up to at home with Ma.

I lifted my chin and set my jaw. My mind was made up. "Jenny's right," I said. "It is bullshit, and they won't do what they damn well please. This is our land, this is our kids' land, and it'll be over my dead body that they try and take anythin' away from my daughter."

Greg smiled properly for the first time all day. "There's the Sutton I know."

I noticed Trav then, staring out the window like he was a million miles away. He had that busy-thinkin' line between his eyebrows. "Whatcha reckon, Trav? We'll find some way to fight 'em, yeah?"

Trav looked right at me. "Absolutely. Oh, we'll fight them all right." Then he sat forward in his seat and stared right at me, his blue eyes as intense as I'd ever seen 'em. "Charlie, you remember the other week we were out fixing fences along the northeastern paddock? What did we see in that creek that I couldn't find in no book?"

I nodded. "Yeah, I remember." Then I clued in to what he was getting at, and I began smiling. I turned to Greg. "If we're gonna fight these bastards, then we need to beat 'em at their own game. And I reckon Trav might've just figured out how."

CHAPTER TWO
LAWSON BRIGHTON-GALE

"Jack?" I'd just opened and read an email that was quite interesting. I picked up my laptop and closed up the butterfly house, going in search of Jack. It was a Sunday, and he'd been busy tending to the gardens and pottering around while I was holed up in my lab. I found him in the kitchen, slicing apple and cheese, one of his favourite snacks for TV watching. "Oh, there you are."

"Hey," he said with a smile. He looked at my laptop. "What's up?"

"I just received an email from Piers Bonfils."

"Oh, how's he going? The Ulysses still breeding okay?" He held a small slice of apple to my lips, which I took into my mouth. Then he frowned. "It is okay, isn't it? The Ulysses, it's not dying again, is it?"

I finished chewing the apple and swallowed. "Oh no, all is well in that regard."

Jack slid some crackers straight from the box onto the plate of apple and cheese. Then he tossed a small square of cheese into his mouth. "So, what's up?"

"There's a fellow who wanted help identifying a butterfly. He took photographs and sent them to Piers. Piers confirmed it was definitely worth looking into, but he was simply too busy with the Ulysses, so he recommended me." I turned the laptop around and showed Jack the photograph. "It's a *Charaxes brutus*, the White-barred Emperor, by the look of it. Very remarkable."

He studied the picture for a moment, then me. "Is it endangered?"

"It is on a watch list, but that's not what makes it remarkable."

He raised an eyebrow. "What makes it remarkable?"

"Because it's only found in Africa."

Jack's eyes widened. "Africa? He wants you to go to *Africa*?"

I smiled at him. Lord knows, he was probably envisioning me being eaten by a lion or hippo. "No, the Northern Territory."

"Oh." He huffed out a breath in relief. Then he mumbled, "Thank God for that."

I ignored that and went back to the email. "Do you know a Charlie Sutton?"

Jack choked on a piece of cheese.

How odd.

"Are you all right?" I patted him on the back.

"Yeah, yeah," he said, swallowing hard. "That's just a name I haven't heard in a long time."

"Well, I take it you do know him. May I ask how?"

He nodded slowly. "We went to uni together."

"And you were sexual partners," I deduced. "Your reaction said enough."

Jack made a face and went a little red. "Well, yes, but that was a long time ago. We were at uni. You know how that is."

I chuckled at his horrified expression and stole another piece of his apple. "Well, yes. You have no reason to worry, Jack. Or to be embarrassed."

"It just kind of came from nowhere," he said, back under control now. "Remember when we were in Cairns that time at the CSIRO building and I sat in the waiting room and was reading a magazine article? I said it was of a guy I went to uni with. Well, that was him. Some big-shot farmer he is now. Well, he was. That magazine was a few years old even back then."

"I think I remember that," I answered, when the truth was, I hadn't a clue.

Then a look of confusion crossed Jack's features. "If the email is from Piers, what on earth does Charlie Sutton have to do with anything?"

"The butterfly was found on or near his property."

Jack gave a piece of cheese to the patiently waiting Rosemary. "Oh. The African butterfly?"

I nodded and smiled at the idea of going on another butterfly hunting expedition. "What are the chances of you taking some time off work for an Outback adventure?"

"Well, if you think I'd let you wander off on your own into the desert where the deadliest snakes in the world call home, you've got another thing coming."

I resisted the urge to roll my eyes. Barely. "Not forgetting the fact I'll be meeting a man who you've slept with."

Jack pouted, most adorably. "That too."

"Excellent. I'll reply in the affirmative, yes?"

"Uh, I guess."

I sat myself on the sofa with my laptop and replied to Piers. By the time Jack sat down beside me with his plate of snacks and two glasses of wine, I'd already had a response. I took the offered wine glass and gave him a grateful smile. "I have contact details. Piers said this Charlie fellow said it was urgent. Should I call him now?"

Jack bit his lip and nodded, so I took out my mobile and called the number in the email. It answered on the third ring. "Hello? Sutton Station," an older female voice said.

"Yes, good afternoon. My name is Lawson Brighton-Gale. I was hoping to speak to a Mr Charlie Sutton."

"Can I ask what it's about? If you're selling something, I'll save us all some time and stop you right there."

I almost laughed. "No, I'm not selling anything. I'm a lepidopterist."

Silence.

So I elaborated. "I'm calling about the butterflies."

"Oh! Oh, sorry, yes, he'd be real interested in speaking with you. Please just hold on and I'll go find him. He was out the back." There was a dull clunking noise followed by the sound of a screen door slamming, then a faint, "Charlie! It's a man about the butterflies!" Then silence for a short while, more footsteps, and then a gruff, warm voice spoke into the phone. "Hello, this is Charlie Sutton."

I smiled at Jack. "Hello, Mr Sutton. My name is Lawson Brighton-Gale. I have received your email from the Cairns Butterfly Conservatory. Professor Piers Bonfils thought I might be able to offer some assistance."

"Ah, yeah, we found a kind of butterfly we couldn't find in no book, and we were hoping it was some kind of new or endangered species?"

"Well, from what I can assess by the one photograph, if it's the butterfly I'm thinking it is, it's neither new nor endangered."

"Oh." He sounded disappointed.

"But there's never been one found in Australia, Mr Sutton."

"Really?"

"Yes. From the one picture, I would be confident enough to name it. Though I was hoping you would have more photographs you could send me. I'd like to determine if it is indeed a White-barred Emperor before I trek a few thousand kilometres to see it for myself."

"Oh sure!" He was excited now and talking to someone else, asking them about the photos. I gave him my email address, and as we waited for them to arrive in my inbox, he asked, "So, you'd need to come out and take a look?"

"Yes. Is that a problem?"

"No, no, not at all. If it is one of those White Emperors—"

"White-barred Emperor," I corrected.

"Right. If it is one of those, then what happens next?"

"I would confer with the Lepidopterist Society of Australia."

"And?"

Hmm. "Mr Sutton, may I ask why the urgency? You're very keen for this finding to be in your favour."

It sounded as though he ran his hand over his face. "I'm gonna be honest with ya, Mr Brighton-Gale. We're running outta time. Ya see, the government wants to run a pipeline through my neighbour's place, right where we found these butterflies. Or close enough to 'em. And we were hopin' if these butterflies were special enough, it just might stop the pipeline."

Just then, my laptop pinged with an email from Sutton Station. I clicked on the attached photographs. "I've just received the photos," I said, in case Mr Sutton was beginning to question my silence.

The pictures weren't perfect, but I could see enough. The butterfly itself looked like a *Charaxes brutus*, though I was more interested in seeing what plant the butterfly was on. That would tell me more. I pointed to the green foliage on screen and looked at Jack. "What kind of plant is that?"

He studied the photo for a moment, squinting and frowning. "It looks like *Grewia insularis*. It's a species of flowering plant in the *Malvaceae* family, but I'd need better photos to be sure."

I didn't really need to know any more. If there was a White-barred Emperor in Australia, the only type of plant the caterpillar would feed upon was the *Grewia insularis*.

"Mr Sutton, those specific plants in the photograph, do you have those anywhere else on your property?"

"No, we don't. Not that I've seen. These were along a creek on Greg's property. We were fixin' fences and stopped to water the horses when Travis saw them. The butterflies, that is. That's when he saw the *butterflies*. They're kinda big, and we thought they were little birds at first, so he took some photos, and when we got home, he couldn't find them in any Australian butterfly books."

"Because they're not Australian. They're African. And Mr Sutton, if you're agreeable, I'd like to come and see them for myself."

"That'd be real great, Mr Brighton-Gale."

"I should tell you now, I'll be bringing my husband along with me."

A brief pause. "Husband?"

"Yes. Is that a problem?"

He snorted into the phone, then laughed. "Uh no. No problem at all."

"Good. Because I believe you know him. His name is Jack Brighton."

CHAPTER THREE
CHARLIE

Jack Brighton? Well, holy shit. That's a name I hadn't thought of in a hundred years. After we'd exchanged contact details and the butterfly guy had told me he'd be in touch when they were coming, I called Greg to let him know what was happening. Then it was dinner time, then bath and bedtime for Milly, and by the time we were ready to hit the hay ourselves, I still hadn't told Travis.

"What is it, Charlie?" he asked after I closed our bedroom door. He was sittin' on the edge of our bed, all long-legged-like, with a smug smile. "I know you've got something you don't want to tell me."

I leaned against the bedroom door and sighed. "It's about the butterfly guy."

"What about him?"

"Actually, it's about his husband?"

"He's gay?"

"Well, I dunno. But he's married to a guy, so he ain't exactly straight, Trav."

Travis chuckled. "Fair enough. What about his husband?"

"I know him."

"So?"

"From Sydney. We went to uni together. A lot, if you know what I mean..."

I could see the second he put the pieces together. Me. Sydney. Uni. He'd once said my uni days sounded like I'd slept with the entire gay population of Sydney, and I'd joked that I thought some were possibly straight... Yeah, that kind of we-went-to-uni-together.

Travis raised one of his eyebrows in a perfect arch. "A lot?"

I cringed. "There weren't many that were repeats, if you know what I mean. But he was one of them."

"One of the guys you slept with *a lot* when you were at uni is coming here? With his husband?"

I frowned and nodded. *God, this was a bad idea.*

Travis stared at me for a good long second before he busted up laughing. He laughed so hard he fell back on the bed, and then he laughed some more.

I stalked over to him and knelt on the bed so I was straddlin' his thighs. "It's not that funny, Trav."

He could hardly speak he was laughing so hard. "Oh my God, Charlie. It's hilarious."

I poked at his chest. "It's not funny. It's embarrassing. They're coming here, and it's gonna be awkward as hell."

He waggled his eyebrows and grinned. "Maybe his husband'll suggest a foursome?"

I took a hold of his hands and roughly pinned them to the mattress above his head and leaned down so my nose was almost touching his. His eyes were full of mischief and heat. "No one touches you but me. And the only man who'll ever touch me is you."

He hummed. "I do love it when you get all possessive."

Still pinnin' his hands to the bed, I rearranged us so I could spread his legs with my knees. I rocked into him, our jeans makin' the most delicious friction. "How possessive do you want me to get?"

Trav grinned like he'd won first prize. "I want you to ride me like you stole me, Charlie."

I laughed and kissed him when there was a tiny knock on our bedroom door. Not tiny-soundin', but tiny as in the hands that did the knockin'.

I bit back a groan and climbed off the bed. Before I opened the door, I did a double-check that me and Trav were both respectable enough for innocent eyes. I pulled back the door to find Milly in her PJ's, her reddish, copper-coloured hair in loose curls down her shoulders, and her offsider in her arms. "What's up, pumpkin?"

Milly looked up at me with her huge brown eyes. "Nugget can't sleep."

I looked at the wombat. He blinked at me, did his nose-twitchin' thing, and I swear the little bugger smiled. "Are you sure it's Nugget that can't sleep?"

Milly nodded.

"Want me to read him a story?" I asked.

She grinned, just like the one Trav'd given me earlier, and ran into our room. She barrelled up onto the bed, never letting go of Nugget, and landed herself right in the middle of our pillows. Milly grinned. Nugget grinned. I sighed, and Travis laughed.

"What about your bed?" I asked. "I'm pretty sure four-year-olds are old enough for stories in their own beds."

Milly just snuggled down and pulled the blankets over Nugget. They both looked at me expectantly. Waiting. Nose-twitching. Smiling.

It was hard to be mad when she was so stinkin' cute. "Okay, Milly-moo. Which book?"

Trav walked out with his pyjamas in his hand, smiling from ear to ear. And so, instead of one-on-one daddy time, the four of us—me, Trav, Milly, and Nugget—spent the next hour reading *A Wombat's Diary* fifty-seven times.

Now, I know it's not the same as bein' intimate with my husband, and that was something I'd truly never tire of, but nights spent in bed reading picture books to a giggling gorgeous girl and a snuffling, wiggling wombat would forever be my favourite.

Trav carried a sound asleep Milly back to her bed, and I took a disgruntled Nugget, who burrowed right back in beside her when I put him in her bed. Some kids had a teddy bear or a blankey. Milly had a Nugget.

Trav leaned in and kissed her forehead, I turned out the lights and closed the door as quiet as I could. Ya know, in all my years of sneakin' in around Ma tryin' to get away with shit I shouldn't have been getting' away with, I never did know the art of bein' quiet until Milly was born.

Puttin' her down to sleep was like puttin' a ticking bomb to bed. Trav was always better at it than me; those big skilled hands of his could carry a glass grenade without breakin' a sweat.

We tiptoed back to our room and Trav closed the door and both of us breathed in relief. He took my face in his hands and kissed me with smiling lips. "She's the most precious thing, but damn, how can she not need sleep?"

I pulled off my shirt, then undid my jeans and kicked 'em into the hamper in the corner. It was late now, and the playful mood between me and Trav had simmered to a quiet, sleepy air instead. And that was okay too.

We climbed into bed, and I found my comfy spot

nestled right into Travis' side, his arm around my shoulder, my face on his chest. "So," he started before pressing a kiss to the top of my head. "What's the plan with the butterfly guys?"

"Well, I told them we were outta time, so they said they can get here on the weekend."

"Wow, that's fast."

"Yeah, hopefully they can identify the butterfly and get whatever paperwork they need to get done so Greg can stop the pipeline."

Travis gave me a squeeze. "Let's hope so." We were quiet a while and my eyelids and mind were heavy with sleepin'. "Do you reckon we'll need to camp out with them?"

"I already pre-warned George and Ma we might need to do that, yeah."

"For how long, do you reckon?"

"Dunno. How long does it take to find a butterfly? Didn't take you long."

His chest vibrated as he laughed. "It'll be getting colder soon. Means campfires and joined sleeping bags."

I smiled and sighed as Trav's arms tightened around me. "Sounds good."

"Do you reckon the butterfly guy and your ex'll mind if we get some personal time in while we're camp-side?"

I snorted. "He's not my ex. We were never... like that."

"Friends with benefits?"

"Barely even friends. Just... benefits."

Travis chuckled and kissed the top of my head. "I'm looking forward to meeting him."

I put my head up so I could see his face. "Does it bother you? That someone I've had... benefits with will be here?"

Trav just shook his head and grinned. "It's my ring on

your finger, Charlie. It's our daughter asleep down the hall, and it's me you beg for and my name you whisper." He sighed, content and sleepy. His accent was always thicker when he was tired. "I know damn well who you belong to. And you do too."

CHAPTER FOUR
JACK BRIGHTON-GALE

I'D NEVER BEEN TO ALICE SPRINGS BEFORE, AND FROM THE VIEW out the aeroplane window, it looked very red and flat. Not to say that it wasn't beautiful, I'd just never seen anything like it. Red, red dirt stretched flat to the horizon in every direction.

We collected all of Lawson's research gear from the airport cargo, signed for everything, collected the rental—which was a Defender, of course—and called ahead to Sutton Station. We let them know we'd arrived and were heading straight out so they could expect us in three hours.

Who the hell lived three hours from the nearest town? *God.* No wonder Charlie ran amok when he got to Sydney.

I drove, following the GPS directions, which admittedly said as much as 'turn right onto the Plenty Highway and follow for three hundred kilometres.' Lawson did some more reading up on the African White-barred Emperor butterfly. When I slowed down to turn into a driveway with a sign marked Sutton Station, Lawson shut his iPad off and looked out the window.

"Wow."

I chuckled. "It's strangely beautiful, isn't it?"

He nodded. "I thought our house was isolated."

That made me laugh. "Our ten acres wouldn't be a speck out here."

After a while, Lawson looked at the GPS. "Did you take a wrong turn? I thought he said his driveway was directly off the highway."

"This *is* his driveway."

He peered out at the isolation. "Good Lord."

In the distance I could see a patch of green trees and finally some sign of life in the form of a manmade building, which as we got closer, I could see were actually several buildings. A house, some sheds, stables, water tanks.

It was strange to feel a little nervous. We'd tried to search Charlie Sutton online, and while there were many posts on his business and farming acumen, his position on some Territory Beef Farmers board, and a few photographs to go with those sites, there was nothing on his private life.

I had no clue what to expect.

I pulled the four-wheel drive up at the house and took a deep breath. It was a nice looking farmhouse, with a front veranda and a bullnose roof. It looked well lived in and very well loved. "Well, this is it."

Lawson gave me a quick smile and opened his door, so I did the same. Just as I was getting out, the front door of the house opened and a man walked out. He wore faded jeans, an old KingGee shirt, boots, a hat that was more holes than hat, and a smile I recognised immediately.

Charlie Sutton.

He came down the steps and crossed the small lawn area and stuck out his hand as he walked. "Jack," he said. "Long time, mate."

"Charlie." I shook his hand. His hands were as hard as his grip, calloused and warm. By this time, Lawson was beside us. "Charlie, this is my husband, Lawson."

Charlie offered him the same smile he gave me, and Lawson shook his hand. "Nice to meet you. Thank you for having us."

"Thank you for comin'," Charlie said. "How was your flight? Makes for a long day, yeah?"

"Yeah," I answered. "Left Launceston at six this morning." I checked my watch. It was almost four in the afternoon. "The flight was fine, and the drive out here was prettier than expected."

Charlie was just smiling at me like it was good to see me. Then he clapped his hands together. "Right, let's get your things inside and I'll show you to your room."

Just then, a young lady appeared and Charlie introduced her as Nara. We all said our hellos, and without prompting, she helped herself to taking our luggage and Lawson's research tubs. They probably could have stayed in the rental, but Lawson always liked to double check everything, so we hauled them inside too. "Milly won't put pants on," Nara said to Charlie. He sighed but nodded like he expected nothing less. And I wondered idly if this Nara was Charlie's wife. Just because he slept with guys didn't mean he couldn't fancy women as well. And then I wondered who the hell Milly was and why she was opposed to pants.

Charlie pulled out a suitcase, looked at us, and grinned. "It's a madhouse here some days. Come on in."

The house itself was beautiful. Old wooden floors and traditional wood panelled walls painted white. This house had history and warmth and felt like a home. Charlie showed us to a spare room, with a double bed and a stand-alone wardrobe and dresser, and a window with a light curtain blowing in the breeze. Nara had already put the tubs in the corner, so we dumped our belongings as well and followed Charlie back out to the living room, where an older woman met us. "This is Ma. She's the boss."

She wiped her hands on her apron before offering to shake hands. "So nice to meet you. And I'm not really the boss. Charlie is, but—"

"But he does what she says. We all do," said an older man as he walked in. "George," he declared himself to be. He had a slow meandering way about him, a kind smile, and a strong, weathered handshake.

Then a door shut somewhere, followed by quick footsteps, a weird scratching sound, and laughter. We all turned to the hallway just in time to see a young girl with long reddish-brown hair running in but getting grabbed and hauled up onto the shoulder of a blond man. She squealed in delight just as Charlie darted to the side and caught what at first I thought was a football. But it had little scurrying legs, huge claws, and it snuffled and snorted. "No you don't, you little..." Charlie said as he wrestled with it, and when he uprighted it in his arms, I could see he was holding a wombat.

Then I looked back at the man holding the girl. He was a very handsome man, tall with striking blue eyes and a huge smile. "Sorry about that," he said with an American accent. "I've been trying to get her dressed and her hair brushed since lunchtime."

He held out his hand, but it was Charlie who made the introductions. "This is my husband, Travis."

Husband? So he married too, huh?

"Trav, this is Jack." I shook his hand and ignored the knowing smirk he gave me. "And this is Lawson."

Travis shook Lawson's hand too, then put the little girl

down, but held onto her shoulders. "And this is Milly. Milly, who is wearing a tutu because she refused to wear anything else, and I only pick the battles I can win."

Milly looked up at me, then at Lawson. She had a cherub's face, with huge brown eyes. "Hello."

"Hello," Lawson and I said together.

"My name is 'Melia Sutton," she replied, smarter than her years, no doubt. "And Daddy's got my Nugget."

Charlie held up the wombat. "This would be her partner in crime." The wombat blinked and snuffled. "Or as we like to call them, Seek and Destroy."

Wait... *Charlie's a father?*

Milly put her hands up to Charlie and he gently handed the wombat over. Milly held onto him dearly.

"May I pat him?" Lawson asked. "He sure is cute."

Milly nodded, and Lawson crouched down, so he was more on their level, and scratched Nugget on the forehead. "Why do you wear that?" Milly asked, nodding to Lawson's bow tie.

"It's a bow tie."

She smiled. "It looks like a butterfly."

"It does," Lawson agreed with a laugh.

Her eyes got really big as she remembered something. "You will look for the butterflies?"

Lawson nodded. "Yes, I will."

"Do you catch them?"

"Sometimes."

"I catch lizards. Sometimes their tails fall off."

Lawson fought a smile. "Do you keep them or let them go?"

"Daddy makes me let them go. I feed them bugs. Nugget eats apples and carrots and does square poop."

Everyone stifled their laughter. Travis put his hand on

Milly's shoulder. "Milly, honey, why don't you go put Nugget to bed and wash your hands."

"But Dada..."

Dada? If Charlie's her Daddy, and Travis is her Dada...

"No buts."

Travis must have used a tone she knew wasn't good to argue with because she pouted and walked out of the room.

"Sorry about that," Charlie said. "Like I said, it's a madhouse some days."

"It's all right," Lawson said. "She's positively adorable."

Charlie snorted. "Yeah, well, don't be fooled. She's as pigheaded as—"

"As you, Charlie," Ma finished for him. Then she smiled at us. "Now, I'm about to start dinner. You boys eat everything?"

"Everything," I replied.

"Is there anything we can do to help?" Lawson asked.

Ma looked at us like that was funny, and George snorted. "Only if you got a death wish, son." Charlie grinned and Travis laughed.

"Thank you, but if I need help, I'll be sure to ask for it," Ma said, giving us a wink before she disappeared. George followed her, leaving Lawson and me with Charlie and Travis.

"We're both her fathers," Charlie said to me. "I could see you tryin' to figure it out."

I felt myself blush a little. "I uh, I wasn't sure. But wow. Fatherhood, huh?"

"It's been a helluva road," Charlie said, giving Travis a smile. "But there ain't nothin' like it."

"We've got a Border collie named Rosemary," I offered with a shrug.

Charlie laughed, and he seemed to study me a while. "You look good, Jack. It's been a long time."

"It has. And you too. Life's been pretty good to you, I can see."

He looked up at Travis and smiled. "Won't hear me complainin'." Then he nodded toward the front of the house. "How 'bout we take a walk. I can show you around the homestead and tell ya what we know about this butterfly."

Lawson brightened at that. "Sounds great."

As it turned out, Travis fell into step with Lawson, and Charlie and I followed. We walked toward the stables first, and Travis and Lawson were quickly talking about soil quality and filtration principles, particle ratios and something else I couldn't follow.

Charlie and I were further behind them now, and it gave us a little privacy. "Those two look like they could talk forever," I said, nodding toward our husbands.

"Trav loves talkin' science."

I chuckled. "Then he and Lawson will get along fine."

"So, been married long?"

"Two years. How about you?"

"Almost five."

"Wow."

"Yeah, happened pretty quick, considerin' I didn't think I'd ever find anyone out here."

"It's amazing what you find when you're not looking, isn't it?"

Charlie smiled, stopped walking, and looked out across the paddock. "Yes, it is. Even when it lands on your doorstep and refuses to go back to America."

I laughed. "I thought you were supposed to be the stubborn one."

His grin just got wider. "I met my match, that's for damn sure. How about you?"

"Lawson is... everything I'm not. If there was a case of opposites attract, then we'd be it. I dunno how, but it just works. We have ecology in common, natural sciences, and conservation is a passion. Our old uni professors'd be proud."

"They'd be shocked," Charlie amended with a smirk.

"You never did graduate," I mused, resting my forearms on the fence to what looked like a round yard for breaking in horses.

"Yeah, I did. I went back. Trav made me. There was no way I could leave here, so I did it by correspondence."

"That's really good, Charlie. Glad to hear that." I looked at him, then to the vast space before us. "I seem to recall you once saying you wouldn't ever come back here."

He gave me an eye-crinkling smile. "Nah. This stuff right here"—he kicked at the red dirt at our feet—"is in my blood. There's no leavin' it now."

The sound of Lawson laughing made us both turn toward him. There was Travis, doing some arm motion like he was trying to start an invisible lawnmower, and Lawson was still laughing. Charlie snorted at the sight, and he looked at his husband like he was seeing him for the first time.

Then, embarrassed, like he knew I'd caught him in a private moment, he changed subjects. "Wanna see something?"

"Sure!"

He put his fingers in his mouth and let out a helluva whistle, then looked at me and grinned. Lawson and Travis walked back, and Travis was holding two carrots, green leaves and all. He handed one to Charlie. "Don't tell Ma."

I heard them before I saw them. The sound of hooves, and Charlie climbed through the fence. Two horses came into view in a cloud of red dust, and Charlie just walked out toward them.

"Is that safe?" Lawson asked.

Travis chuckled but didn't say anything, he just watched.

The horses came in at a full gallop. Charlie raised his hand, and both horses pulled up to a stop just a metre from him. Their chests heaved, their heads bobbed, and dust swirled at their feet, and Charlie never even flinched. The taller horse, a chestnut-coloured one, stomped its foot and reared its head, snorting at him.

"Oh, that's enough outta you. Trav's got yours," Charlie said to it. Travis climbed through the fence then and was met by what I guessed was his horse.

"Hey, boy," Travis said, giving him a scratch on the forehead. He fed him the carrot and gave him a quick check over.

Charlie, on the other hand, was having a quiet word with his horse. It was much smaller, mottled in colour, and one I wouldn't exactly call pretty. "This is Harriet," Charlie said. "One of the smartest stock horses I ever saw." At first glance, I'd have said he was being patient with his horse, but the more I watched them, the more I felt it was Harriet who was being patient with Charlie. He fed her the carrot and scratched her behind the ear. She nodded in thanks.

"I'll feed them early, yeah?" Travis asked.

"May as well," Charlie answered. Then he looked at me and Lawson. "We were gonna ride out tomorrow."

A horrified Lawson opened his mouth, then snapped it shut. "Ride?"

Charlie smiled. "Well, we *were* thinkin' of it because we

just don't do it as much as we'd like, but it's not gonna work. So the plan I thought would suit us all best was Trav and I'll drive out first, you guys follow us out with your gear. Now, I dunno how long you'd be expectin' it to take, but we can camp out overnight if need be."

"How far out is the site where you located the butterfly?" Lawson asked.

"It's about three hundred kilometres east of here," Travis said. "Technically, it's on Greg's property next door to us." He led both horses into the stables.

"You'll meet Greg in the morning," Charlie said. He climbed back through the fence. "So if we leave here around six a.m., we'll get out there around nine. How does that sound?"

"Perfect," Lawson answered. "I hope you don't mind, but I have some maps and location information I'd like to go over before we leave."

Charlie nodded. "No problem. After dinner when the table's cleared away, we can take a look at whatever you need."

Lawson was pleased by this. "Excellent. And I certainly hope we find the answers you're looking for."

Charlie clapped Lawson on the shoulder as we turned to walk back to the house. "So do I."

Lawson looked at Charlie as I followed. "Would you really ride your horses for three hundred kilometres?"

"Sure. Bein' out there on horseback, just me and Travis, is... well, it's kinda like what some'd call a date night." Charlie stopped walking and looked as though he might apologise for what he just said, but instead he just shrugged. "We don't get much alone time these days, what with Milly and all."

Before Lawson could respond, the front door opened and Milly ran out. "Daddy, Ma wants you inna kitchen."

Charlie turned to me and Lawson. "Duty calls. I'll leave you two to get freshened up. I reckon dinner'll be on the table in about half an hour." Then Charlie picked Milly up and tucked her under his arm like a giggling football, and they disappeared inside.

Lawson stood there and watched them for a moment. "You okay?" I asked him quietly.

"Yes, of course." He offered a tight smile.

Then Milly appeared on the veranda again. "'Scuse me, mister," she said, looking at Lawson. "Can you show me the butterflies on my Dada's 'puter?"

He smiled genuinely at her. "I would love to." He leapt up onto the veranda beside her, and she told him how Ma and Nara didn't like the butterflies in their veggie garden as they walked inside.

I found myself smiling at the screen door when Travis came up beside me. "You good?"

"Oh, yeah, fine," I answered. "Dinner's not far away, apparently."

"Awesome." Travis gave me a high-wattage smile. "Oh, in case Charlie didn't tell you already, rule number one is don't be late for dinner. Well, there's the rules about shirts and shoes too, and cussing of course, but I don't reckon you need to worry about that."

I chuckled. "No, I don't reckon I do."

CHAPTER FIVE
TRAVIS CRAIG

I HAVE TO ADMIT, WHEN I FIRST MET THIS LAWSON FELLA, I took one look at his bow tie and perfect hair, and heard him speak all proper-like, and thought *oh boy*. Actually, my first thought was, I hope he finds this butterfly soon because he sure didn't seem the type to last long out here.

But then I got to talkin' with him when we gave Charlie and Jack some time to catch up, and it didn't take me long to figure out he was one smart cookie. And then I watched him when he was with Milly, explaining to her how butterflies did their thing. She took him to the garden out back and showed him where those plant-eating caterpillars got into Ma's veggies, and Lawson listened to her like it was the most important thing he'd heard all day.

I respected him after that.

Then after dinner, Lawson laid maps out over the table and got his iPad out, and he and Charlie went over them, marking GPS locations and talkin' topography and soil types. He had a tub of equipment he said he took with him everywhere, full of things like a barometric reading thermometer, a satellite phone, and some other gadgets.

Charlie was all excited to show him the cattle tracking collars we had installed, showing him on screen that we could see wherever the herds were in any part of the 2.5-million acres we owned. Lawson was amazed, and they talked about how technology and science integration was fundamental. All the while, Jack just stood back and smiled at their entire interaction.

Now, Jack was something else entirely.

He was a big fella, and it was pretty easy to see he worked outdoors a lot. He had that natural strength that showed in his shoulders and arms. He had dark hair and a charming smile, and in that regard, he reminded me a lot of Charlie. I could see why they fell into each other's company all those years ago.

I hated to admit that I didn't particularly like knowin' this other man had experience of an intimate nature with Charlie. There might not have been any emotions involved, but Jack had been with Charlie in bed. He'd been naked with him, touched him, kissed him, tasted him. Looking between them now, I had to wonder which one of them topped. Had Charlie been the one to fuck Jack, or had Jack been inside him?

"Isn't that right, Trav?"

Huh? *Shit.* "What? Sorry, I was a million miles away." I flashed them all an apologetic smile, but I didn't think Charlie was fooled.

He tilted his head and eyed me cautiously. "I was just tellin' them of the time you came off Shelby and busted your knee up pretty bad. Spent a day and night out in the desert in the middle of summer."

"Oh, I'm glad you were found." Lawson gave Jack a look. "And it's a little reassuring that I'm not the only one who has had a run of bad luck. Though I couldn't even imagine being out here in summer. It's hot enough now in autumn."

"A run of bad luck?" Jack asked Lawson, his eyebrows near his hairline. He looked at me and Charlie and smiled as he spoke. "We've had encounters with bushfires, cane toads, sprained ankles in the Snowies, and—"

"And I don't think they need to hear any more," Lawson said, raising his chin. "I assure you, I'm most prepared when on expeditions. The cane toad poisoning was hardly my fault, and Mount Kosciuszko was simply unfortunate footing. Admittedly, the bushfire was foolish, but the Blue Mountains incident was a freak of nature, really."

Charlie chuckled. "Well, if it's any consolation, the snakes out here are gettin' ready for sleepin' at the moment, being autumn and all."

"Snakes?" Lawson gaped.

Just then, a pyjama-clad Milly appeared in the doorway with Ma. "Bath's all done," Ma said.

Charlie went over to them. "Aw, thanks, Ma. You didn't need to do that."

"My pleasure. I knew you boys'd be busy. Can I get anyone a cup of tea?"

We all said, "No, thanks," but then Lawson said, "If it's not any bother, I would love a bag of fruit scraps or rotten fruit if you have it. If not, it's fine."

Ma stared at him like he'd lost his mind. "Uh..."

"We'll need it tomorrow," Lawson explained, "for the butterflies."

"Oh. Course. I'll see what I can find." Ma gave us a nod, bid us a good night with a promise to see us bright and early.

Charlie picked Milly up, and she put her head on his shoulder, clearly tired. "Story time?" he asked her quietly.

She nodded with sleepy blinks, so Charlie gave me a smile. "Won't be long."

We all watched him leave, then Lawson asked, "Travis, may I trouble you for any more of the photographs you took of the butterfly?"

"Oh, sure. I'll just grab my laptop." I'd sent him all the ones I thought were pretty good, but if he wanted to see every photo I took before heading out there in the morning, I had no problem with that. I grabbed my laptop while Lawson and Jack folded up the maps and cleared away the table, but as I was walking back in, I found Nugget wandering the hallway, probably wondering where everyone went. I scooped him up and brought him with me. "Here," I said, handing Nugget over to Jack.

Jack was a bit surprised, and it was pretty obvious he'd never really held a baby before. Or a wombat. But he soon settled Nugget on his back, and both of them seemed happy with this arrangement. "Wow, he's heavier than he looks."

"Yeah, he's like a brick," I agreed.

"Milly picks him up like he weighs nothing."

That made me laugh. "She's never known life without him."

Jack looked at Nugget and made a thoughtful face. "How old is this little fella?"

"He'd have to be six." Jack looked surprised by that, so I explained. "He's small. The vet said he's perfectly healthy, but he's just a runt. Said it could be from when we found him; his mum was on the side of the road, been hit by a car. We don't know how long he wasn't fed for."

Jack frowned at the wombat. "But he's fine now?"

"Oh yeah. Been a pain in our ass ever since. But we wouldn't have him any other way." Then I thought about that. "Well, I coulda done without the foot-bitin' thing he had going on for a few years. But he and Milly are as thick as thieves."

Jack gave me a smile, the genuine kind that made me like him whether I wanted to or not. "They're both as cute as hell. You're very lucky."

I nodded. "We know."

"Travis," Lawson said. He'd been studying the laptop screen so long I'd almost forgot he was there. "Can I ask you about these?" He pointed to the ground in one of the photos, and we got talking about that for a while. He was probably asking questions I couldn't rightly answer to the degree he wanted, but he was getting more excited. Until he looked up at Jack, who was standing, leaning against the table, rocking a wombat to sleep in his arms, and I reckon I saw the moment Lawson melted into love all over again.

I recognised it because I'd looked at Charlie exactly the same way every time I saw him holding a newborn Milly. It was an overwhelming thing that detonated in your chest like a bomb, filling every part of your entire being with a need to love and protect.

Jack seemed to sense our eyes on him because he looked up and smiled with a shyness that belied his size. "He's almost asleep," he whispered.

Charlie appeared in the door. "Milly's finally out." Then he noticed Jack and Nugget, and he smirked. "Come through here. You can put him to bed."

Lawson and I watched them walk out, and Lawson gave me a slight smile before closing the laptop. I wondered if he was okay with meetin' Charlie or if he had the same trepidation I had about Jack. I didn't know why I felt such jealousy, if that's what it even was. It wasn't rational. It wasn't... I didn't even know what it was.

It was stupid, that's what it was.

Lawson gave me a nervous smile. "I know Charlie would think it was me doing him a favour by coming all this way, but I can assure you, the contrary is true. Thank you for inviting us into your home with your family, and thank you for allowing me the opportunity to study these butterflies. I'm truly grateful." He never broke eye contact and he was strangely intense, even though he clearly had no clue how he came across. "But if you don't mind, I'd like to call it a day."

"Not at all. Might wanna set your alarm for five."

Lawson gave a nod and left me feeling even worse. There I was thinkin' resentful thoughts about Jack, and Lawson was nothing but polite and thankful. Charlie walked in, took one look at me, and took my hand. He led me out, turning the lights off as he went. Jack must have gone to bed too, because the house was dark except for a line of light from under their bedroom door. Charlie didn't stop, though. He walked me into our room and closed the door behind me.

"Trav, what's wrong?"

I almost laughed. There weren't no point in denying anything. He knew me too well. "It's stupid."

"Nothin's stupid if it's how you feel." His eyes were imploring, searching mine for answers. "Talk to me."

"I keep thinking of you being with him."

Charlie's eyes went wide. "With Jack? What happened to the Travis tellin' me 'It's my ring on your finger and I know damn well who you belong to.'?"

"That was before he was here. And before he was a real person. A good-looking, real person, I might add." I sighed. "He's been with you. He's touched you, tasted you. He's heard the way you whimper and seen how your eyes roll closed when you come."

He blinked.

"It's stupid and I don't like feeling like this, but I can't help it. I thought I'd be okay with it. I *was* okay with it. Until I saw him. Then he was a real person."

Charlie put his hand to my face. "It was a long time ago. I can't change my history." Then he leaned in all close, took a breath and nudged his nose to mine, giving me an almost kiss. He murmured, "But Trav, if he's one grain of sand, then you're the entire fucking desert."

I tried not to smile and failed. I leaned into his hand. "Thank you. And I dunno why I feel like this."

He leaned against me, pushing me against the door, and kissed my neck up to my ear. "Because the way I whimper when you're buried inside me is just for you. And if I roll my eyes closed when you make me come, it's because you make me. Not anyone else. Never anyone else."

I ran my hands over his ass and pulled our hips closer, grinding our erections together through our jeans. "Charlie."

He slid his hand between us and palmed my dick. He spoke against my lips. "Wanna hear me whimper, Travis?"

I kissed him and pushed him toward the bed. The backs of his legs hit the frame, and I turned him around, fixin' to kiss the back of his neck and grind my hard-on against his ass. Reaching around, I undid his belt. He raised his hips for me. "Fuck yes."

I hummed and undid his jeans, slipping my hand inside and gripping his cock through his briefs. I shucked his jeans down over his hips, then pulled his underpants down to his thighs. I bit down on his neck as I wrapped my hand around his length and pressed my erection against his ass crack. Charlie let his head fall back onto my shoulder and he moaned. "Trav. Please."

"Get on the bed." I stepped back, giving him room to turn around and sit down, and by the time I'd grabbed the lube, he had his boots off and was tugging at his jeans. I grabbed the denim and pulled them off his legs. He grinned and did away with his undies and threw his shirt across the room.

I toed out of my boots, watchin' as he got himself comfortable, lying back with his head on the pillows and his legs spread wide, giving his own cock a slow pull. I was gonna take my time, maybe tease him a little, but then he licked his lips. "Trav." He took the bottle of lube and slicked his fingers, then slipped his hand down between his legs. He groaned when he fingered himself.

I stripped in a flash and quickly found myself on my knees, between his thighs. I watched as he fucked his own fingers until I couldn't bear it. "Take your hand away."

He did as I said but used his slicked fingers to coat my cock, pumping me and positioning me against his hole. "Just do it, Trav. You want me to whimper, then fucking make me whimper."

I pushed against him, that brief resistance giving way until I slid inside him. His eyes went wide and his mouth fell open and a whining sound escaped him, so I leaned over him and covered his mouth with mine.

And whimper he did. That glorious sound he made with every thrust, with every slide of my cock inside him, reachin' deeper and deeper. Part of me wanted to shush him; part of me wanted Jack to hear him.

Charlie gripped my ass, urging me to go faster, harder, until my orgasm crashed over me and I came inside him. I crumpled on top of him, too caught up in my own pleasure, my own head, to consider Charlie.

And he wasn't havin' none of that. He rolled us over and

pushed me onto my stomach. I was face down on the bed, and he got to his knees and grabbed the lube. I knew what he was about to do.

I wanted it.

I lifted my ass and stretched my spine, relishing in the warm buzz of pleasure still flowin' through my veins. Charlie straddled my thighs, poured cool lube down my crack, then pressed his cock against my willing hole. And he pushed in. No preparation, no stretching.

Just how I liked it.

When he was fully buried inside me, he gave me a second to adjust, then put his lips to my ear. "As I belong to you, you belong to me."

He pulled out and slammed back in. I couldn't explain the noises that escaped me. The grunts, the pleading. He fucked me like he owned me, and in many ways he did. In every way, he did.

And with a final thrust, he filled me completely and spilled inside me. Shuddering and jerking as his orgasm took hold of him. He collapsed onto my back, kissing my neck. He nuzzled his nose into my nape. "Shower?"

"Yeah."

Now if Jack and Lawson hadn't heard us in the bedroom, surely they had to hear laughing in the bathroom.

CHAPTER SIX
LAWSON

THE RIDE OUT TO WHERE THE BUTTERFLIES WERE WAS AS LONG AND bumpy as it was beautiful. Charlie had explained that we were to follow them. Our convoy of two vehicles would head east toward the neighbour's property. He explained they normally flew the helicopter over, but with this many people, it couldn't happen. Strangely enough, I didn't mind the drive.

I'd always thought myself to be more of a mountains guy or even partial to the ocean. I'd never even considered the desert to be anything but heat, dust, and flies, but there was a beauty here that I couldn't find words for.

I doubted I'd survive a summer here, though, and I was grateful for the cool morning. After an age, we came to a fence line. It ran like a rickety spine up the scorched red back of this land. Land that baffled me as to how anything survived out here. How Charlie and Travis ever farmed this dirt was a mystery to me.

We followed the fence north for a while, until a four-wheel drive came into view on the other side of the fence. I saw, then, a man who stood by his vehicle, next to an open gate. Charlie drove through, we followed, and we both came to a stop.

"This must be Greg," Jack mused, shutting down the engine. He was mid-forties, maybe, with blond-grey hair. Charlie and Travis were already out and shaking hands with him, their friendship evident by their smiles. Jack and I got out of the Defender. The autumn heat here was as hot as a summer day back home.

Greg greeted us with a warm handshake and the kind of smile I was starting to think was an Outback thing. "Welcome to Queensland," Greg said, "where the good folk live. Not like them Territorians." He gave a pointed nod to Travis and Charlie with a good-natured grin. "Thank you both so much for coming."

"It's no problem at all," I reassured him. "I'm excited to see these butterflies. I hope they are what I think they are."

Greg gave me a hard nod. "Me too. Charlie tell ya 'bout the pipeline they wanna run through here?"

"He did, yes." I understood why I was here, without any doubt. They'd been very honest about it from the start. Their interest was not in the butterfly like mine was. Their interest in the butterfly was in hope it might stop the government staking a claim on Greg's land. I cared not for motive. I had my eyes set on the finish line, and that was to find a butterfly in a country it shouldn't be found in. I smiled at Greg and clapped my hands together. "So, if we'd not like to waste anymore time, let's go find them."

Greg grinned at me. "I like you already, son."

We each took our respective vehicles in a convoy further northeast into Greg's property. There was still red dirt as far as the eye could see, but there were more patches of greenery, thickets of khaki against the red under the bluest sky I think I might have ever seen.

"It's very beautiful, isn't it?" Jack asked, breaking the silence.

"I was just thinking that very thing." I gave him a smile. "I'm getting excited about what we might find today."

Jack laughed. "I can tell. You're doing that knee-bouncing thing."

I tried to keep my leg still. "I am concerned, though. What if it's not what we're hoping to find? That is, what will become of Greg's farm?"

Jack reached over the console and took my hand. "Whatever we find today is not your responsibility. If it's not the African butterfly, then there's nothing you can do to change that. You're here to simply identify, catalogue, and report."

I took comfort from the gentle squeeze of his fingers and went back to watching the landscape.

Finally, we came to a stop in front of a line of trees atop a bit of ridgeline. There were eucalypt trees, but also the *Grewia insularis*. It was a smallish treelike shrub with yellow flowers that I'd only seen in photographs. Finding that plant spiked my excitement because it was the only plant the White-barred Emperor laid its eggs upon and a favoured plant of the caterpillar to eat. It was also a significant find in its own right. That nervous excitement was now becoming a full-body, jittery feeling.

"Wow," I said, walking over to the edge of the ridge, which I could now see was a creek bank. If it could be called a creek. There was barely enough water in it to constitute a trickle.

I didn't realise Charlie, Travis, and Greg were standing beside me until Charlie spoke. "What's wow?"

I took a leaf of the *Grewia insularis* between my fore-finger and thumb, rubbing it, then smelling the oily residue it left on my skin. "This plant," I started, then turned to look for Jack. He was pulling my research tubs from the back of the four-wheel drive. "I'll need Jack to verify—he's the botanical one—but I do believe this plant is a new find. In Australia, anyway."

"This plant?" Greg asked. "It runs north, right along this creek for miles."

"Well, if it is the *Grewia insularis*, it's only typically found in Africa and on Christmas Island. What it's doing here in the middle of the Australian Outback, is anyone's guess."

"But it'd explain why an African butterfly would be found here, though, wouldn't it?" Travis asked.

I nodded. "Indeed, it would." Their smiles became grins, so I added, "But let's not get ahead of ourselves just yet."

Jack walked over to the shade of the gum tree and put the tubs down in the dirt. He pulled the lid off the top one, fished out my digital barometric reader, and handed it to me. We'd done this together so many times now, we had it down to an art. I took my usual readings and made notes while Jack started in on the plant. He photographed, measured, documented, took foliage samples, flowers and fruits included. While he sat himself in the shade and referenced the plant with known botanical sites online, I went about searching for a butterfly. Crouching down to inspect the underside of the foliage, I checked the closest shrub for evidence. I found some old egg casings, which I collected, and there was evidence of chrysalises, but no butterfly.

I stood up and looked down the embankment. It was a mix of shale and red dirt, only four feet deep at this point. The water was just a few inches deep and maybe a metre wide.

Charlie, Travis, and Greg left us alone to do our work, mostly. "You can walk down the embankment," Charlie said. "It gets steeper further north. Becomes more of a rock face, but you can get down here easy enough. Those plants are down there too."

He was right. The bank was easy to climb down where we'd parked our vehicles, and I could see the ridgeline was taller further off in the distance, rising up several metres from the creek below it. "How far did you say this creek ran?" I asked Greg.

"About fifty miles or so. It's spring-fed from the Artesian Basin."

"And these plants are found right along that distance?"

He nodded. "Pretty sure it's them. The cattle don't touch 'em, so I never paid much attention to 'em, to be honest."

I picked up the three research tubs and called out to Jack to let him know where I was going. "Jack, I'm heading north up the creek."

He put the iPad down. "I'll come with you. I'm still waiting for an official ID on the plant. Don't know how long it will take."

I jumped down the small ledge and waited for Jack to join me. He took the two top tubs from me, and we walked further up the creek bed with the others following not far behind us. It was maybe half a kilometre up when I stopped. I put the tub into the sand and took out my camera. The creek was a little wider here but still only a few inches deep, so I simply walked to the other side. The embankment was steep, a geographical timeline spanning a million years in lines of red shale and sand. But there were also shrubs dotted along the cracks, fed by the creek.

I crouched down to inspect the underside of the leaves

and found what I was looking for. A caterpillar. Chrysalis casings, more caterpillars. I took a run of photographs and must have disturbed a branch at just the right time because there was a flutter of brown and white, and I was suddenly face-to-face with a butterfly.

About a six-centimetre wingspan, with a very distinct white bar across its hindwing, copper-brown and black scales. It was beautiful.

It was also a *Charaxes brutus*.

I was certain.

I stood up and grinned at Jack, who was standing with the others just a few metres away on the other side of the creek. Charlie looked at me, then at him and asked, "What does that look mean?"

Jack laughed. "Well, Lawson only smiles like that for two reasons: me or butterflies."

"He found it?" Travis asked excitedly. "It's the African one?"

I nodded. "I found it." Then I amended. "Well, I'm almost certain. But I'll need to send the photos for verification. Get samples and take some specimen, if I can." I looked at Jack. "Would you mind getting the bag of spoilt fruit from the back of the four-wheel drive?"

"I'll grab it," Travis said, already turning and jogging back the way we'd come.

Jack opened the research tubs and took out specimen jars. He leapt the small creek easily and helped me collect egg casings and an empty chrysalis. Travis came back and set the bag down, as I instructed. "Rip it open and let the fruit spread out like a banquet."

Twenty minutes later, while Jack and I were still busy documenting what we'd collected, Charlie called out, "Uh, guys?"

I looked over to him to find all three men facing the bag of ruined fruit. Like vultures to a carcase, the White-barred Emperor had come. There were over a dozen, maybe more. Fast and fluttering, they flew seemingly without purpose, skipping on the air, but were zoning in on the fruit. I could see why Travis first thought they were small birds.

I grabbed the camera and splashed into the water, quickly snapping as many photographs as I could, zooming in for every minute detail. Jack slowly edged in, and without disturbing them, he picked up half a browned peach and smeared the juice and softened flesh on his hand. Then he just stood there with his hand outstretched and waited.

It didn't take long. One butterfly flittered over to him, settling on his finger. Jack's grin widened as the butterfly began drinking from his skin with its proboscis. "This never gets old," he said with a look of wonder.

And I would never tire of seeing him like that. Smiling at the awe of the simplest of things.

I laughed from behind my camera, taking photo after photo.

By this time, an entire kaleidoscope had arrived for the fruit. "Are all butterflies this fast?" Charlie asked, looking up at the sky.

"No, these are one of the fastest butterflies in the world," I explained.

"You sound pretty confident that it's the African butterfly," Travis said.

I lowered my camera and faced him. "There are many things in this world I am wrong about. Butterflies aren't one of them."

Greg's grin grew wider. "So, it is a rare species? Does

this mean we can tell the government to shove their pipe where the sun don't shine?"

"There is a process. A lengthy one, I'm sure," I added. "But the sooner I can gather enough evidence, the better."

"What else do we need to do?" Charlie asked. "Aren't some photos enough?"

"I'll send the photos to the National Lepidopterist Society, and I can contact Piers at the Cairns Butterfly Conservatory, and even my old boss, Professor Asterly in Melbourne. I know people who carry weight—"

Jack laughed. "Uh, excuse me, *Doctor* Gale."

"Brighton-Gale," I corrected. It was a kneejerk response.

"Doctor Brighton-Gale," Jack amended. He turned to Charlie, Travis, and Greg. "Don't let his modesty fool you. Lawson here is internationally acclaimed at what he does. If anyone in this country, if not the world, carries weight in lepidoptery, it's him."

I ignored his compliment. "We still need to respect the process. There are boxes that need to be ticked, the appropriate channels—We need to do this correctly so we don't trip over red tape that would impede us further."

"So, what do we need to do?" Charlie asked again.

"Photographic and video evidence is one thing, but a specimen sample would be best."

"A sample?" Jack asked quietly. He brought his hand in front of his face to look at the butterfly on his hand. "As in a dead sample?"

Jack's frown at the thought of killing one of these butterflies made my heart squeeze. I shook my head. "Only as a last resort."

Jack smiled, and Travis clapped his hands together. "Well, Doctor, tell us what evidence we need to get to make this happen."

CHAPTER SEVEN
CHARLIE

You know, for a nerdy butterfly guy, a doctor of all butterfly things, he sure could give some orders. "I'll need to document findings for as far as this creek runs. Photos, egg casings, caterpillars, leaf samples, and please, look for any specimen of butterfly that might already be dead."

"It's getting late," Trav said, looking up at the sky. "We got about two hours of daylight left."

I nodded. "Right, then. We'll head north up to as far as these shrubs things are and see what we can find."

"Butterflies aren't nocturnal," Lawson added. "They'll be roosting soon."

"Then we better get going," Trav said.

"You guys right to set up camp? Or you need us to give you a hand?" I asked them.

"Nah, it's fine," Jack said with a smile, putting the lids back on the research tubs. "I'll walk back to the cars with you guys. That way I can get our camp set up while Lawson finishes up down here."

"I should get going back too," Greg said. "What's the plan of attack for tomorrow, then?"

I scrubbed my hand over my face. "If Trav and me drive as far north as this creek runs, take photos and samples, camp there tonight, then do the same on our way back south every so often in the mornin' and Jack and Lawson do the same heading upstream, then we should cover twice the ground, right?"

"Sounds perfect," Lawson said. "I'll send these photographs off tonight, and hopefully by morning we should hear back." Then he turned to Greg. "If these butterflies are determined to be the White-barred Emperor, further field study will be required. Will you have an issue with allowing researchers and ecology specialists on your property?"

"If it stops a massive pipeline runnin' up the guts of my farm, I don't care who has to come out here."

Lawson nodded. "Very good. I've not had any personal experience with how such matters of ecological findings impact governmental infrastructure such as pipelines, though I've read similar cases. There will be reports, environmental studies, flora and fauna impact statements... the list is long."

"And?" Trav asked. "What are you saying?"

"That even if the pipeline is stopped tomorrow, this won't end quickly. These findings and reports can take years to unfold. I'd imagine you'll be on a first-name basis with the Queensland Department of Environmental Sciences and a dozen other ecology specialists in no time."

Greg stared at him. "But in five, ten, fifty years from now, I'll have butterflies on my farm and not a pipeline, right?"

Lawson gave him a smile. "I'd like to hope so."

Greg smiled. "I can live with that."

We left Lawson to watch the butterflies while we all

walked back to our vehicles. I made sure Jack had half the food Ma had given us, half the water, a radio, and a swag. He was already collectin' firewood before we left, and I knew they were competent in the outdoors. So, we said goodbye to Greg, then Trav and I were in the Cruiser and heading north.

We followed the creek as far as we could. Those weird-lookin' shrubs were there, but the ridge had become deeper and it'd take some climbin' down. I was grateful we'd taken the more difficult end of the creek, though. I mighta been okay with Jack and Lawson camping out here, but I was more confident in my and Trav's ability to handle the terrain.

I grabbed Trav's phone for the camera and some of the specimen jars, that looked like the ones the doc made me pee in, and headed for the edge of the bank. "Be careful," Trav said, as he pulled the swag out of the back of the Cruiser, threw it on the ground, and unrolled it.

Careful of my footing, I climbed down the rocky ledge to the creek. The water was deeper here, and as a whole, it wasn't too unlike our lagoon. And that gave me an idea. But first, the butterflies... And there were butterflies here. Not as many, but enough. So I took a bunch of photos of them on the leaves, and because Lawson wasn't there, I shook the branch a little to make the butterflies fly, snapping pics as they did. Then I found some old cocoon things, a caterpillar or two, and as the first-prize trophy, along the rock face, I found a dead butterfly.

Happy with my findings, I climbed back up the ledge and found Trav starting a campfire. I showed him everything I collected and put them in the back of the Cruiser. "Hey, the water looks good down there. Fancy an evenin' swim?"

Trav looked up at me, and a slow-spreadin' smile crept along his face. "I do believe you have bad intentions?"

I chuckled. "That would depend on your definition of bad." He sat down on the swag, and I pounced on him, straddlin' his hips and pushin' him till he was lying on his back. "You know the only thing I find better than a hot and sweaty Travis?"

Trav laughed and his blue eyes shone with somethin' that looked like a whole lotta fun. "A wet Travis?"

I kissed him hard. "Correct."

He grabbed the back of my head and brought me in for another kiss, liftin' his hips a little. "Or you could fuck me right now," he murmured in that give-me-goosebumps way he did. "Skinny dip later."

I crushed my mouth to his and settled my weight on him, my legs between his. He spread his knees wide and rolled his hips, his fingers dug into my scalp, and he bit my lip, making me moan.

But then the radio crackled to life, and I drew my lips away from Travis', half expectin' George's voice to boom through the speaker, checkin' in on us, but it wasn't George. It was Lawson.

"Charlie! Charlie, can you hear me? It's Jack. He's been bitten by a snake."

I WAS UP AND OFF TRAVIS IN A HEARTBEAT. TRAV THREW OUR GEAR into the back of the Cruiser while I kicked dirt on the campfire, and we were on our way back literally ten seconds after Lawson's call.

I drove faster than I'd ever driven.

Trav kept tryin' to talk to Lawson, but it was kinda hard

to hear him. All we knew was it was a bite to the hand. He'd been climbin' along some rock face above the creek and stuck his hand on a ledge when he felt a jab on his finger. He'd fallen back in shock but saw the snake. It had a black coloured head and was kinda yellow underneath.

Oh fuck.

Trav looked at me, frowned, and reached for my hand. I took it real quick and threaded our fingers. We both knew what kind of snake that was. And it wasn't good. Inland taipans were the world's deadliest snake.

Jack was conscious. And Lawson couldn't stop crying.

All I could do was squeeze Trav's hand because I knew—I knew in my heart—that if it were Trav layin' down bein' snake bit, I'd be a fucking mess too.

I pressed down on the accelerator, and Travis put a call into the Station. "Ma? Get George. Get him real quick. There's been an accident."

IT WAS ALMOST COMPLETELY DARK WHEN THEIR CAMPSITE CAME into view. The fire was out and I knew they'd still be up the creek. So I drove down a bit further and put the Cruiser down over the ridgeline. It was a bit of a shorter drop, but we still bounced in our seats, Trav needed to hold onto the dashboard, but we made it okay. I turned the Cruiser up the creek and floored it again until we saw Lawson kneelin' in the dirt, wavin' at us.

Jack was layin' in front of him, and we both raced over. I could see Lawson had correctly applied a bandage from his fingers to his armpit, and Jack was real still. I was almost scared to ask because it'd been a good forty minutes... Taipans could kill in less time than that.

Then Jack smiled. "Hey."

I dropped to my knees beside him, relief rushin' out with my breath. "Oh, Jesus. How're you feeling?"

Jack blinked real slow. "My hand hurts."

"Headache? Nausea? Dizziness?" Travis pressed.

"Nope."

Lawson sniffled. He was holding Jack's other hand, and I realised then that his eyes were red and he looked real pale. "He says he feels okay, but we're in the middle of nowhere. We're so far from help, it wouldn't matter anyway." His bottom lip trembled.

I put my hand on his shoulder. "I radioed for George. He's bringin' the chopper in now. Should be here any minute. He'll take him to hospital."

Tears fell down Lawson's cheeks, and he sobbed. "Thank you."

"Lawson," I said gently. "It sounds like an inland taipan, and I gotta tell ya, that's not good. But the fact he's not dead yet is a real good sign."

Lawson's teary gaze shot to mine. "What?"

"If it was a bite to kill, he'd already be dead or in so much pain he'd wish he was. The fact that he's okay tells me it was a dry bite. A warning bite. The snake was probably sleepin'. Jack still needs to get to a hospital, though, just to be sure. You did everything right. You kept him still. The bandage looks good."

Travis put his hand on Jack's chest. "You still feeling okay?"

Jack gave a small nod. "Yeah. More worried about Lawson."

Lawson laughed through his tears. "Usually it's me that needs saving." He put Jack's hand to his lips and kissed it, then cried some more.

"Can tell you what, though," Jack said soothingly, looking above our heads. "I've never seen a night sky look anything like this."

We all looked upwards. The Outback sky was putting on a show, that was for sure. And I guess with Jack being on his back looking up at it, it was hard not to marvel at her. She was a blanket of stars, of galaxies, that weren't nothing short of spectacular.

"Ya know," I said, figurin' he was trying to placate Lawson some. "I've seen thousands of night skies out here, and it still amazes me every time."

Jack smiled at Lawson, and Lawson leaned down and kissed him on the lips. "Trust you to be too busy to die because you're looking at the sky."

We all laughed in a relieved kinda way, and then we heard it. A far off helicopter getting closer until we saw the spotlight. "George can't land down here. We need to get Jack back to camp without moving him too much," I explained. "So, we're gonna lift you into the Cruiser then drive you out, okay?"

Jack nodded, so Trav and I both lifted him up, and Lawson quickly ran to open the door. We lifted him inside and Lawson scrambled in after him. I reversed the whole way down the creek until the bank was small enough for the Cruiser to make it up. The last thing I wanted to do was roll it and see us all end up in hospital. By the time we got out, George had the chopper down, the rotors slowin' to a stop, and he was out of the cockpit waitin' for us.

"I can walk to the helicopter," Jack said.

"No you won't," I said, puttin' an arm around him, helping him out of the seat. "You need to keep your heart rate down."

Trav and I carried Jack in more of a sitting-up position

to the helicopter. It was kinda awkward going, but we got him there. Lawson stood back, his eyes filled with water. "I can't go with him," he mumbled. The helicopter was only big enough for the pilot and one passenger.

"We'll follow you," I told George, knowing Lawson would hear.

George started the chopper and the rotors began to spin. I grabbed Lawson, but he shook off my hand and ran over to Jack, grabbed his face, and planted a kiss on his lips. Trav raced in and grabbed Lawson's arm, pullin' him back so George could get the chopper off the ground. Dust swirled and bit our faces and we had to shield our eyes, then by the time the air had settled around us, so had the darkness. And that too-loud silence.

Lawson just stood there. Not knowin' what else to say, I put my hand on his shoulder. "Come on. Let's get packed up and go."

Fresh tears fell down his cheeks, and he looked so utterly, horribly lost. But he nodded, and five minutes later, he had his research tubs squared away, Trav rolled up the swag, I collected the water and food, and we headed home.

I drove Lawson's Defender, knowin' his wits were far from with him, and Trav followed in the Cruiser.

Lawson was quiet a while, lookin' out at the darkness. "I'm sorry I lost it back there," he said, breakin' the silence.

"Nah, that's all right. If it were me, and Travis was lyin' there like that, I'da done more than lose my shit."

He nodded and went back to starin' out the window, and I had to wonder if he was crying some more. He gave himself some time before he spoke again. "You know, a few years back, I almost died from cane toad poisoning. We were in the tropical rainforest of North Queensland and it was pouring rain... Anyway, he carried me on his back, in the dark, and walked me to meet an ambulance. He must have carried me for a kilometre or more, through some slippery and rugged terrain." He swallowed hard. "He saved my life."

"And tonight you saved his."

The look on his face told me he didn't believe that. He surprised me by barking out a laugh. "There is a long-running joke in our families that I'm the one who constantly needs saving. They'll never believe me because he's always the strong one; there's nothing he can't do." He frowned, and his voice went real quiet. "I can't even think about what would happen if..."

"I'm sure he's okay," I said, though I had no real idea of knowin'. "Like I said, if it was a taipan and a full-venom bite, he wouldn't be sittin' up in a helicopter right now."

Lawson nodded, but it was a hollow acknowledgement. I didn't blame him none. Because if it was Trav in Jack's shoes right now, I wouldn't believe what anyone told me until I saw him with my own eyes. Lawson's mind must've been goin' down the same track as mine. "Where's George taking him?"

"Home first. He'll need to refuel. Then to Alice Hospital."

He nodded slowly. "I hope you don't think it rude of me to follow him tonight. When we get back to your house, I'll be leaving as soon as I'm packed. I don't mean to offend your hospitality—"

"I get it, Lawson. And I'm not offended. If it were Travis... well, I wouldn't be anywhere else either."

He gave me a bit of a smile. "Thank you."

I was just about to ask where this left the whole butterfly thing when the CB radio cracked to life. It was

George. "Hey Charlie," he said, his slow drawl a familiar welcome. "Everything okay?"

Instinctively, I checked my rear vision mirror to check on Trav's headlights not too far behind us. "Yeah. All good here. You refuelling?"

"Well, I was, but our patient here says he's well enough to stay."

"He what?" Lawson asked.

"Lawson," George drawled. "Thought you might want to speak some sense into him, son."

I handed the radio mouthpiece to Lawson, and his jaw set. "Jack? Have you lost your mind?"

There was a ruffling sound, a muffled voice, then Jack's voice came on the radio. "Lawson, I'm okay."

"Do you have a degree in neurotoxicology that I'm unaware of?"

Jack snorted. "No."

"Then why won't you go to hospital?"

There was silence so long that Lawson looked at the mouthpiece like it was a phone with a screen. "Because I won't go without you."

Lawson let the hand holding the radio mouthpiece fall into his lap and he put his thumb and forefinger into his eyes, I realised, to stem his tears. "How long until we get back to your house?" he asked me quietly.

"Hour and a half."

He spoke into the radio. "I'm ninety minutes away. And I'll drive you to the hospital myself."

"Lawson, I feel okay. My hand hurts and my arm aches, but I have no other symptoms."

"Then you'll have no problems in letting the good medical doctors of the local hospital assess you."

"See you soon, Lawson."

The radio clicked off, and Lawson smiled, clearly more relieved in hearing Jack's voice and that he was okay. "Stubborn man."

The drive was silent after that, which was just as well. Driving out here durin' the day was hard enough; driving at night was a whole new world of worry. There was no road, as such, but the track to Greg's place from mine was worn well enough that we could see it, but it took all my concentration. I kept an eye on Travis' headlights in my rear-vision mirror, makin' sure he wasn't too far behind us. I radioed him to tell him what was going on and how George was grounded for a bit—and just to hear his voice—and soon enough, the homestead came into view.

George met us out front, and I had a fair guess that wherever Jack was, Ma was keeping him company. Lawson rushed inside, and I followed him. Jack was on the sofa, and sure enough, Ma was on the recliner watchin' him like a hawk. Lawson quickly sat beside him, needin' to touch his face. With better lighting, the bandage wrapped tight around his arm looked worse than before, and he looked pale as hell. I heard Travis pull up outside, followed by his boots on the veranda steps. That screen door openin' had never sounded so good.

He was quick to slide his arm around my waist and plant his lips to my temple. "How's the patient?"

I gently tapped Travis' chest. "I'm gonna get the hospital on the phone. See what they reckon."

He hadn't taken his eyes off Jack. "Good idea."

Lawson stood up and looked right at me. "I'd appreciate it very much if you could tell them to expect us in about three hours. We're leaving."

"Lawson—" Jack started to protest, but Lawson spun to give him a look of fire and determination. I'm pretty sure

Travis used the same one on me, and there weren't no point in arguin' with it. Just no point at all.

Ma nodded wisely. "I'll help you pack, dear."

When they'd left the room, I grabbed the phone, and when I came back out, I found Trav'd sat down beside Jack. "You feelin' okay?" he asked him.

He nodded. "Yeah. But Lawson's right."

I had to agree. "Yes, he is."

Travis laughed. "One person in every couple always is."

I chuckled at that and Jack snorted, but his smile faded away. He looked right at Travis. "Thank you for having us out here. It's a beautiful place. Beautiful home, family."

Trav just gave him a knowin' smile. "I wouldn't trade it for the world."

I got through to the hospital, so I left Trav with Jack and went back out to the Cruiser while I explained down the phone what had happened and how they were on their way into emergency now. I had those samples Lawson wanted, and when I clicked off the phone call and collected all the specimen jars, Lawson came out with the first bag.

"Where's my car?" Lawson asked, looking completely baffled.

I almost laughed. "George's fuellin' it up for ya."

He put his bag on the veranda. "Oh. I hadn't even thought of that. You have your own fuel tanks here?"

"Have to." I handed him the specimen jars. "Got everything you asked for. And found a dead butterfly, so I grabbed it too."

"Thank you." He sighed, long and loud. "I will forward everything I have onto the appropriate experts first thing. I can imagine there'll be plenty of waiting time at the hospital."

I nodded slowly. "I truly do appreciate you comin' all

this way. And I'm sorry it ended like this. He'll be fine, I'm sure of it."

George drove their rental up to the house, and I opened up the back tailgate. Lawson put the specimen jars into one of his tubs, and I grabbed their bags. By the time I'd thrown them into the back, Travis appeared at the door with Jack. "I offered to carry him," Trav said, "but he declined."

Jack laughed, but he was clearly tired and walkin' like he'd rather not be upright. He held his bandaged arm out awkwardly, and he still didn't have much colour. He made it down the steps, and Lawson got him buckled into the front passenger seat. Lawson turned to us all. "Thank you again."

I waved him off. "Drive safe. Watch for roos."

"And emus," Travis added.

"And camels," George said.

Then Ma threw in, "And road trains."

Lawson's eyes widened with each one, and I'm pretty sure he mumbled something about never leaving Tasmania again, got in behind the wheel, and we watched them drive away.

The four of us stood in silence on the veranda, watching the red tail lights disappear down the driveway.

"Think he'll be all right?" Trav asked.

"Sure he will," George said. "If he ain't dead yet..."

We all nodded, but none of us made a move for inside.

"You boys want a cup of tea before bed?" Ma asked.

"Nah," I answered. "How was Milly tonight? Not too much trouble?"

"She's an angel," Ma said. Which was true, if angels were cute as they were stubborn and could swap out their halos for horns any time they wanted.

I sighed, still lookin' up at the stars. "The sky sure is pretty tonight."

The four of us stood there, all lookin' upwards. George hummed and put his arm around Ma's shoulder. "Always is."

Travis hung his arm around my neck and kissed the side of my head. "Always."

CHAPTER EIGHT
JACK

I WOKE UP IN HOSPITAL TO FIND A SLEEPING LAWSON IN A CHAIR beside the bed. It was daytime out the window, there were bandages up my forearm, and whatever drugs they'd given me took away the pain.

And sweet Jesus there had been pain.

I'd tried not to let on too much because I didn't want Lawson to worry any more than he already was. In the creek bed, when it first happened and he was strapping my arm, he was certain I was going to die. He was a fucking mess.

And maybe it was foolish of me to not get to the hospital sooner, but I just couldn't leave him. I didn't want to go without him, as much as I didn't want him out all those miles away without me. God, he was so upset in that creek bed...

I knew I had to do whatever it took to never put him through that again, but when we'd arrived at the hospital, the doctor had asked me to rate my pain from one to ten. I couldn't lie, so I'd said it was a nine. When he asked me to describe it, I said it was kinda like someone hit my hand with a sledgehammer, then poured acid over it while stabbing it with an ice pick.

He stared at me and asked what could possibly be added to make it a ten out of ten because that sounded as unbearable as it could get. My answer was simple. "If it had happened to my husband and I had to watch. That'd be a ten."

Lawson started to cry when I said that, but a nurse put her arm around him and they wheeled me away. They gave me something for the pain and it made me sleepy, but I do remember seeing my hand when they'd inspected the wound, and I remembered them taking me to a room for observation.

Which is where I woke up. I found myself just watching Lawson for a minute. He was sound asleep in one of those ungodly uncomfortable chairs, and I wished like hell he could climb up onto the bed with me.

Watching him wasn't too bad either, though. And as if he could feel my eyes on him, he stirred awake. "Jack," he said, sliding forward in his chair. He took my hand. "I was so worried. How are you feeling?"

"I feel good."

"They've given you pain relief."

"I'm hungry."

"Shall I go and find out what you can eat?"

"Yes, please."

He stood and planted a kiss on my forehead. "Won't be long."

I must have dozed off while I waited, because I woke up again to the sound of voices. Lawson, of course, and some other voices I recognised. Charlie and Travis, and Milly too.

"Hey," I said, trying to sit up.

Lawson fixed my bed so I was more upright, and Charlie gave me a huge grin. "Didn't mean to wake ya."

"No, it's fine. I must have dozed off again." I shook my head a little, trying to clear it, and Lawson took my good hand. "What time is it?"

"Ten," Charlie answered. "We just got here. Thought we'd come and see how you were."

"And Daddy said we can get me some ice cream," Milly piped up with. Her eyes were big and brown, and her red curls were gorgeous.

Travis grinned and scooped her up and sat her on his hip. "And Dada. Because Dada lurves ice cream," he said. Milly laughed then, and she clung to him. She was wearing a blue tutu, brown boots, and a Dallas football shirt. She really was equal parts her fathers' daughter.

Lawson was looking at them with a happy sadness I'd never seen on him before. It was a look that never quite went away the whole time Charlie, Travis, and Milly were there, even when he was explaining he'd heard back from the Australian Lepidoptery Society, who had confirmed from the photos and video evidence the butterfly was indeed the African White-barred Emperor.

The plant had been confirmed, also, from my request, and the Fauna Conservation of Queensland was extremely interested.

"I'd imagine I'll know more within forty-eight hours. As I explained to Greg, the stay on the pipeline might be immediate, pending reviews and reports, but the long-term process can take years."

"So, it's all good?" Charlie asked excitedly.

"Do you remember the bell frog that almost stopped the Sydney Olympics?" Lawson asked.

Charlie and Travis both shook their heads. "Nope."

Lawson explained, "The government was all set to develop a large area of disused land near the Olympic centre until they found a rare frog. There were ecological studies done to the nth degree, as you could very well imagine. But they won. A new location was found; the frog and its habitat remains."

"So if a little frog can stop the freakin' Olympics, then we stand a chance, right?" Charlie pressed on, clearly trying not to sound too hopeful.

Lawson nodded in a so-so manner and gave him a tired smile. "I certainly hope so. I'll let you know as soon as I hear so Greg can start the paperwork and legal proceedings. I'd hazard a guess there will be a lot of it."

"That's real good news," I said. "I'm glad it worked out."

"I'm sorry you're in here, though," Charlie added. "But it was real good to see you again, Jack. Maybe next time we can come down to Tassie?"

"Fly fishing?" Travis asked, his eyes almost as wide as his grin.

"Definitely," Lawson answered. "You're most welcome anytime. I don't think we'll be leaving for any more butterfly expeditions in a hurry."

I snorted. "Until you get asked."

"Maybe not even then," he said, and that sad smile was back. "I think I'll stay homebound for a while."

Charlie, Travis, and Milly stayed for just a few more minutes before the lure of ice cream became too much for Milly. With fond farewells, they left, and Lawson wheeled the table over. "You must be starving. You're allowed a light meal, so I got you a sandwich and some fruit, and juice and water."

He unwrapped everything for me because of my

bandaged hand, and I devoured it all. "Have you eaten?" I asked him around my last mouthful of food.

"Yes, earlier. I'll grab some lunch soon and get you something else as well."

He was still quiet, sad even. I held out my good hand and waited for him to take it. "Want to tell me what's wrong?"

"Only you almost dying."

"Pretty scary, huh?" I joked. "I remember when it was you in the hospital bed almost dying. Took ten years off me, so I know you've had a rough night. I'm sorry."

He squeezed my hand. "I wasn't joking about not leaving for any more expeditions. I'm done, honestly. There's enough work with my Tillman Copper, and I'm sure there's more academia I can contribute to—"

"Want to tell me what's really wrong?" I interrupted. I knew him. I *knew* him, and there was something he wasn't telling me.

He frowned and his eyes became glassy. "I don't think now is the right time to bring it up. When you're home and well, we can talk about it."

"Lawson, please just tell me. Something's bothering you, and I can't stand not knowing what it is."

"If I tell you, I don't want you to answer. Not yet. I want you to think it over for the time it deserves."

"Lawson," I urged.

His bottom lip began to quiver, and I worried I might not like what he was about to say.

"I want a child."

I blinked.

"I want what Charlie and Travis have. Their very own child. I never thought about it before now. It wasn't anything I ever considered... I didn't know I wanted it until

I saw them. They're a family. I want that with you. I don't know how to make it happen or if you even want that, but I do, Jack, I want that. I think we'd be pretty good fathers. Well, you would be. I started to picture it, you know, which wasn't helpful at all, because I could see you working on the gardens and a little boy in gumboots, just like you, trudging behind you, copying everything you do, and Jack, so help me God, I've never wanted anything more in my life."

I was stunned.

He frowned. "You don't have to say anything right now, and I told you this wasn't the best time or place, and I do realise I've just dropped a rather monumental bombshell, but if you'd just consider it. I was thinking adoption, if you agree, of course. Just give it time to get used to the idea, the possibility even."

"No."

His eyes shot to mine. Hurt and sorrow became instant tears. "You won't even think about it?"

"No. I don't need to think about it," I said, squeezing his hand and fighting a smile. "I think that's a bombshell I'd like to explore. Being a family with you."

His tears fell down his cheeks; but his whole face lit up. "You do?"

I nodded. "You're wrong about one thing, though. The little boy who's following me around the backyard would wear gumboots *and* a bow tie."

Lawson laughed, then got to his feet. He cupped my face and kissed me hard on the mouth. Then he wiped the tears from his cheeks, turned, and headed for the door. "We need to leave. We need to go home. Right now."

I laughed as he went in search of someone to discharge me, impatient as ever. I let my head fall back on the pillow and sighed to the empty room. If we thought our lives had changed when we met each other, when we married, that was nothing compared to how our lives were about to change. Did I want a family with Lawson? Did I want to become a dad like Charlie and Travis? You bet your life I did.

If imago was singular and imagines was two, I made a mental note to ask Lawson if there was an entomological term for imago times three.

EPILOGUE
CHARLIE ~ TWO YEARS LATER

I KICKED THE DUST OFF MY BOOTS ON THE VERANDA STEPS AND PUT my hat on the hook inside the door, just like always. I found Milly, Nugget, and Trav on the couch. She was readin' them a book, and they all looked up at me and smiled. Yep. All of 'em.

"Can I get you two a drink or somethin'?"

"Juice please, Dada," Milly answered.

Travis held up two fingers. "Two, please."

I wandered into the kitchen and found Ma at the sink. I grabbed two glasses and a plastic My Little Pony tumbler from the overhead cupboard and gave Ma a kiss on the cheek. "Need a hand with anything?"

"No, love. Nara's just grabbing me some veggies from the garden."

I grabbed the juice, poured the three drinks, and put the bottle back in the fridge. "Trav's having a lesson on *Green Eggs and Ham*. I better go save him."

Ma smiled contentedly. "Oh, I popped the mail on your desk."

"Thanks," I said, leavin' her to it. "I'll grab it." After I'd handed the drinks out and put mine beside the sofa, I collected the mail to open and sort through while Milly did her reading. I almost sat on Nugget, then had to wrestle with him so he didn't eat the mail. There were bills and statements and the usual crap, but the letter on the bottom was handwritten. The envelope was thick, quality stuff, as was the paper inside it.

It was an invitation with a photo on it. And I knew who it was from before I even read it. Because the photo was of a little boy, maybe a year old, cute as freakin' hell with his little fancy suspenders, long-sleeve shirt, and a bow tie. There could be only one couple I knew who'd dress their kid in a bow tie.

Charlie, Travis, & Milly
You're invited to celebrate the first birthday of Brennan Brighton-Gale.

"Trav?" I said with a smile.

"Yeah?"

I held up the invitation. "About that trip to Tasmania...?"

Trav's whole face lit up, then he melted. "Oh, I'm so glad it came through for them."

We knew from Jack and Lawson's last trip to Greg's farm that they were in the middle of the adoption process. They'd told us it was their time here, seein' me, Trav, and Milly, made them realise bein' a family was a possibility. Which apparently had now become a reality.

"He's wearing a bow tie." I gave Trav a smile, then looked back at the photo. Brennan had real chubby cheeks, dark brown eyes, and the cheekiest grin. "He's a real cute kid."

Trav gave me a look that made my heart beat itself all outta rhythm. "We should go. To Tasmania for the party. For them."

"We should." I tickled Milly. "Wanna go on a plane trip?"

She nodded excitedly. "Yes! Can Nugget come?"

I shook my head. "No."

She pouted and Nugget stared at me with his little mouth open like he couldn't believe it. I tried not to smile. "But there'll be butterflies. And we might find a Tasmanian devil."

Milly's eyes went wide. "Can I have one?" Even Nugget bounced on her lap like he was all excited.

Travis and I both laughed, then answered resoundingly and in unison. "No!"

~ The End ~

imagoes

CHAPTER ONE
JACK

THE WIND WAS HOWLING OUTSIDE, SLEET WAS COMING DOWN IN A flurry of different angles, and I was grateful to be inside with a warm fire. Rosemary was asleep by the hearth and Brennan was on the couch, perched up with his lap table and a colouring book, his pencils in a perfectly organised row.

He was all of four years old now, with a better vocab than most adults. He wore little sweaters all the time and tidy pants, his hair combed to perfection, his manners as sweet as he was.

God, he was so much like his daddy.

Then, right on cue, Daddy came in through the back door, a burst of cold wind behind him. Closing the door, he let out a breath, unwound his scarf, and pulled off his beanie. He'd been mostly data collating in his butterfly house office. Given most butterflies were dormant in the winter, there wasn't much happening. But his work never stopped. "My word, it's abysmal out there," he mumbled, straightening his hair. He gave me a kiss on the cheek. "Dinner smells amazing."

"Beef stew with dumplings," I said, pulling the oven door down.

Lawson inhaled, his hand at my back. "I would marry you again if I could."

I chuckled and he went over to Brennan, sitting down beside him, put his arm around him and kissed the top of his head. "You finished work, Daddy?"

"I did. What are you working on there?"

"Colouring the sea turtle," Brennan replied. He took his work very seriously. "Did you save the butterflies today?"

Lawson smiled. "I sure did." Then he proceeded to point and explain the parts of the turtle's anatomy, and Brennan nodded, wide-eyed, soaking up every drop of information he could.

He was *so* much like his daddy.

They were just so cute, I could barely stand it. My heart was full, like it had been since the day I met Lawson, and then doubly so from the day we met Brennan. Our lives changed forever the day we officially became parents. We'd never been busier, more exhausted, sleep-deprived, and stretched thin between work and home. But we'd never been happier.

Lawson's butterfly research had been elevated to a whole other level, and while he was internationally acclaimed and famous within the lepidoptery world, he never let it go to his head. He never once made his work more important than mine or more important than our family. It wasn't even that he was humble about it. He just had no idea of his own brilliance. Don't get me wrong, he knew he was intelligent and good at what he did, but he never could see what all the fuss was about.

It was something I loved about him.

"Are we ready for dinner?" I asked.

Lawson smiled at me. "Absolutely. Brennan and I shall set the table."

Brennan neatly put his pencil in its place, closed the colouring book, then put his table tray squarely on the coffee table before he helped with the placemats and cutlery. It was like watching two Lawsons: one big, one small.

I put the casserole dish on the stovetop and walked over to them, taking Lawson's face in my hands and kissing him soundly on the lips, then placed a gentle kiss on the top of Brennan's head.

"What was that for?" Lawson asked, smiling but perplexed.

"You're both so cute, I couldn't help it."

Brennan giggled as he took his seat. "Dadda, you're silly."

So I tickle-kissed him again while he laughed and squirmed. Lawson plated up dinner and I poured everyone a glass of water, and like we did every night, we sat down for dinner. Lawson asked me about my day and we talked about the hazard-reduction plans I was implementing, given it was winter. Brennan had been at pre-school, so he had much to tell us about his day—and how, with a slightly sardonic rise of his cute little eyebrows, he was now allowed to use *safety* scissors—and Lawson told us of the data collation he'd been working on for the Australian Lepidopterist Society on the conservation of the purple copper butterfly: a rare butterfly in New South Wales that he'd been assisting on.

Talking about our day was our nightly ritual and one of my most favourite things in the world.

When we were packing up after dinner, my phone rang.

"Jack Brighton-Gale speaking."

"Hello Jack, this is Connor Tallis from Franklin-Gordon National Park. We've met a few times at State Park seminars."

I racked my brain . . . Connor, tall blond guy from the southwestern part of Tasmania. My national park was northeast, almost opposite corners of the state. But I remembered him. "Yes, mate. How's winter down your way?"

"Biting."

I chuckled. "I bet it is. What can I do for you?"

"Well, this is going to sound a bit odd. But I was hoping I could have a word with your husband, Lawson Brighton-Gale."

"Doctor Lawson Brighton-Gale," I corrected automatically.

Lawson smirked at that, but I had his attention.

"May I ask what this is in relation to?"

"Yeah sure," he replied. "We had some campers through last week and they'd done some abseiling and found their way into a cave formation in the cliffs there. I was talking to them when they got back, and one of them happened to mention something they found fascinating. There were butterflies and cocoon casings stuck to the roof of the cave."

I shot Lawson a look and he left the sink and walked over to me.

"Anyway," Connor went on. "Me and one of my guys went up and had a look. It's not an easy climb and it involves abseiling . . . but I found what they were talking about. I took photos and some of the old casings from the cave floor, and I found one dead butterfly. I brought it all back to document, you know, as we do." I nodded, though he couldn't see. It was procedure to document all fauna findings. "But I looked online and couldn't find anything even close. I was hoping your butterfly guy might be able to help."

I got that excited feeling in my belly. "I'll just put him on."

I handed my phone to Lawson. "Connor Tallis from Franklin-Gordon National Park. Found a butterfly."

Lawson made a face but took the phone. "Doctor Lawson Brighton-Gale speaking."

I left him to it and put Brennan in the bath and got him ready for bed. Lawson was still speaking to Connor and there was talk of photographs, and I could tell from the length of the conversation that Lawson was intrigued.

When I brought Rosemary in from her bedtime bathroom break, Lawson was off the phone but now staring intently at his laptop screen.

"What was it?" I asked. "Some never-seen-before discovery?" Which I said as a joke . . .

He looked up at me with wide-eyed excitement and that smile he reserved just for me and butterflies. And then he nodded. "Yes, Jack. I think it is."

He turned the laptop around so I could see, and there was a photograph of a small butterfly. The image wasn't great, but I could see it was pink with a band of black along the outer hindwings. "It's pink," I said. "I don't think I've ever heard you talk of a pink butterfly."

Lawson's excitement was contagious. "Because, technically, there is no such thing."

"Really?"

He shook his head. "Slight variations of purple and light refractions give the appearance of pink, but no."

I nodded toward the screen. "Could this be light refractions?"

"Possibly. The photo isn't great. But where they found the specimen is most interesting."

"How so?"

"In the end of a cave with no light. And these specimens are in the imago stage. In winter. Connor swore he saw them just two days ago." Lawson shook his head in wonder. "Jack, that's not right."

I grinned at him. A new butterfly. Well, another new butterfly. This was what dreams were made of. "Well, doctor, I do believe we just might need to go check it out."

"Are you sure your sister and mum don't mind?" Lawson asked me for the tenth time. We were loading gear into the back of the four-wheel drive while my sister Poppy and my mother stood on the porch with Brennan.

"Lawson, my love," I said, trying to be patient. "I hadn't even finished asking if they could please come and look after him and they were already in the car on their way here. Mum left so fast she had to call my dad and tell him he was on his own for four days. That's how excited she was."

Lawson almost smiled, but it ended with a sigh. "I just don't like leaving him."

"I know. I don't either. But it's just four days. He has pre-school for two of those and Poppy has plans for one art-and-craft day and one biscuit-baking day. They will be more than fine. Plus, Rosemary's here. She'll watch over him."

He finally managed a smile at that. "Okay."

With a final round of hugs and goodbyes, we gave them a wave and made our way down the drive. It'd be a decent four-hour drive, given the drizzly weather. Lawson hadn't been too keen to go, but given he was more than certain this was a new species of butterfly, his love for the species won out over his dread of hiking and, God-forbid, abseiling.

But me? I couldn't wait.

Not just the hike and abseiling and seeing the Franklin-Gordon National Park again, but also for four days with Lawson.

Sure, we'd have Connor and two of his team with us. But this was the first time Lawson and I had been away together without Brennan in four years.

And yes, while I would miss our son terribly, he was in very capable hands and I was absolutely down for some one-on-one daddy time. Plus, hiking and butterflies are what we do.

Lawson was quiet for a while, his hands in his lap, and he did that fingertip-squeezing thing he tended to do when he was nervous. When he began to pat down his hair, I knew he was starting to freak out.

I reached over and took his hand, keeping it on his thigh. "Lawson, baby, what's wrong?"

He blinked and his face twitched a little and he huffed out a few breaths while he was trying to get his thoughts in order. "I hate that you know me so well."

I snorted. "No you don't."

He scowled and rolled his eyes. "This expedition, while very exciting, also involves a considerable hike through difficult terrain and abseiling down a sheer rock cliff face. Not to mention the river systems. They call them the Wild Rivers for a reason." He swallowed hard. "I don't need to remind you of the incidents thus far in our expedition career, do I? The bushfire where we both almost got incinerated, the cane-toad-toxicity incident where I almost died, the inland-taipan incident where you almost died, and the ankle incident in the Snowy Mountains." He shook his head. "I would offer to stay at base camp and allow you to go on my behalf, because I trust you to follow proper collation procedure, but the idea of you going by yourself makes me feel ill. Then if we both go, I fear if something should happen to both of us, leaving Brennan without either of his fathers, I just can't—"

"Whoa, okay," I said, squeezing his hand. His anxiety was much higher than I'd first realised. "Lawson, my love. Nothing bad is going to happen. I promise."

"Please do not promise the outcome of things for which you have no control."

Well, that was fair enough. You'd think I'd be used to how literal his brain was. "Okay. Your fears are understandable and justified. Sorry I tried to downplay them. The Franklin-Gordon National Park is as wild as it gets. But Lawson, this could very well be the find of your career."

"The Tillman Copper is the find of my career."

"*Another* find of your career," I amended. "Along with the African White-barred Emperor found in the Northern Territory *and* the conservation work you've done for the Ulysses in Queensland *and* the Purple Copper in New South Wales."

He huffed but said nothing.

"From the photographs and details Connor sent you, you're certain this could be a new species," I continued. "That's really big, Lawson. It's important you do this. What I can promise you is that we'll be prepared, we'll be safe, and this will be an incredible experience."

He sighed and conceded with a nod, though he relaxed a bit if the release of pressure on my hand was anything to go by.

"I just worry, that's all."

"I know you do. It's what makes you a wonderful dad."

His eyes met mine and his face softened. "You're a wonderful dad too."

I lifted his hand to my lips and kissed his knuckles. "Now why don't you go over the details and tell me everything you're thinking about this butterfly."

If there was one thing that could take his mind off any potential dangers or worries, it was the finer details of his work. And truthfully, I could listen to him talk about barometric pressure, the biotic factors, and the non-floral factors and how the fact they were located in a cave made this quite remarkable, but it raised a slew of negative-variable questions, which Lawson spoke about—at length—for the better part of an hour.

"To surmise, it's all ecological theories until I can see it and study it for myself . . ." He trailed away with a smile. "You know, the way you can manipulate me is as embarrassing as it is endearing."

I barked out a laugh. "I don't manipulate anything. I simply know how your very brilliant mind works. And sometimes that means to de-escalate a meltdown, you simply need to follow protocol. Once you see something as just procedural steps and routine, you're fine."

He stared at me for a long moment, then blinked. "De-escalate a meltdown?"

Oh, shit.

"Not a *melt*down, as such. More of a stress-fest, or if you need a few moments to collect your thoughts and take a breath, that's all." I cleared my throat. "Remember when I was endearing just a few seconds ago? That was nice."

He tried to glare at me but a smile won out. "You're still

endearing. Though meltdown and stress-fest are two words I'd prefer not to hear again, thank you all the same."

I laughed and kissed his hand again. "And you've abseiled before. It's not like we have to do white-water rafting to get there."

Lawson pursed his lips and glared out the windscreen. "If anyone mentions white-water rafting, even in jest, you will see a meltdown. And it will measure on the Richter scale. Just so you know."

I stifled another laugh. "Duly noted, thank you, doctor."

CHAPTER TWO
LAWSON

I DIDN'T KNOW WHAT TO EXPECT WHEN WE MET CONNOR. JACK had said he was a tall man, thirty-one-or-two years old, pleasant enough the few times he'd met him. They had spoken a handful of times over the years at their national park meeting and seminars, though Jack admitted to not knowing him well.

And Jack was right.

He was tall and pleasant . . . enough. He also had sandy coloured hair, a roguish smile, and a striking face. I'd have placed him on a beach with a surfboard before I likened him to inland rainforests and wild river systems kind of guy.

We met them in a car park at one of the many national park's hiking trails off the Lyell Highway. Connor was out of his vehicle as soon as we pulled up, huge smiles and strong handshakes, and my immediate reaction was to take a step back. He gave off loud cowboy extrovert vibes that were enough to make any introvert want to run and hide.

"G'day, Jack," he said brightly, shaking his hand. "And you must be Doctor Brighton-Gale."

Well, he'd learned that quickly after Jack had corrected him on the phone, and now I had to correct him again, which was incredibly awkward. "Lawson's fine. Nice to meet you."

Two young off-siders had stepped out of the car, waiting to be introduced. They were mid-twenties, maybe. "This is Vince and Amy," Connor said. "They'll be coming along on the trip. Apart from being really good rangers, they can help us carry stuff."

Nice. Nothing like being called a pack mule in front of your peers.

I made a mental note to ask Jack what his parameters were when saying someone is "nice enough" and exactly what was the *enough* a qualifier of?

After some uncomfortable small talk about the weather, Connor waved to his park-issued vehicle. It was a big Cruiser, seven-seats, lots of storage. "We can load all your gear into the back," Connor said. "We can take one vehicle in on the fire trail, and it'll cut a good ten kilometres off our hike."

Well . . . well, maybe Connor wasn't so bad after all.

"This front is coming in by nightfall," Amy said, gesturing to the already-grey sky. "We need to be over the first bluff and have camp set up before dark or . . ."

"Or what?" I asked.

"Snow makes the ridge impassable."

Snow. Excellent.

Vince pulled out a map and he drew his finger along the path we'd be taking, from where we stood to where we'd drive to, then the hike. He showed us where we'd camp tonight and where we'd be hiking tomorrow morning to the cave site. It was an intense climb, a popular track with experienced hikers. Not in winter, obviously, because most hikers weren't idiots. At any other time of year, there'd be cars parked and people about, but not in weather as dismal as this. He then proceeded to explain the abseiling requirements.

Connor's team was entrusted to bring the abseiling equipment for all of us to minimise our carrying burden, and the way he and Vince checked off their gear list out loud did make me feel better about their competence. They took this seriously, and I was pleased about that.

The cave itself was two thirds of the way up a rock cliff face. It was easier to hike to the top and abseil down than it was to rock climb. The plan was to spend the night in the cave, then abseil all the way down to the bottom to complete the trip. The cliff had three tiers of ledges and there were anchors drilled into each section, making the descent three shorter drops instead of one longer one. I felt better about that.

I had done some abseiling before, at Jack's insistence. At first, I'd been horrified at the suggestion, but after he'd explained the science behind it—physics and force versus mass and gravity—I understood it and had no issue in taking that first step over the edge.

Since then, we'd done it quite a few times. It was exhilarating and, dare I say it, fun.

Connor pointed his finger guns at me. "Now you did say you've abseiled before, right?"

I looked at his still-gun fingers, then at his face, wondering why on earth he thought that was a good idea. "Yes."

Jack chuckled beside me. "Come on, let's get our gear and get moving."

It was just after eleven o'clock, and the grey clouds were already low, the wind was cold, and everything was damp already. And there was a likelihood of snow, in which we were supposed to camp out.

Jack popped the boot of our park-issued four-wheel drive, which wasn't anywhere near as big as Connor's, and I glanced back at where Connor, Vince, and Amy were moving gear around.

"I thought you said Connor was nice enough," I whispered.

Jack grinned and stuffed his beanie into his coat pocket. "Got your beanie?"

I held it up to show him before stuffing it into my pocket, then I pulled my bags closer. "I cannot think of one scenario where finger guns are an appropriate form of communication."

Jack laughed at that and heaved his backpack strap over his shoulder. "Which is the bag with your lab gear in it?"

I patted the bag I was holding. "He probably does white-water rafting."

Jack looked at me then. "Who?"

"Mr Finger Guns." I slung my backpack over my shoulder. "I may not be adept at reading social cues like you, but I'm not naïve enough to know that he thinks I'm a book nerd who won't last five minutes out here."

Jack stopped pulling the tent bag over. "Why do you care what he thinks?"

"Because he's your colleague." Which I thought would be obvious. "Usually when we go on expeditions, we meet . . . people like me and my colleagues. People who know me, or know of me, and what to expect. But these are your people. I want to make a good impression for you."

Jack glanced over at the others and made a face. "Well, I'm gonna let you in a little secret, dear husband. I don't give one fuck what they think of me. I could not care less. I care what *you* think of me. All I expect from them is professionalism, their local expertise and knowledge, *and* that they respect you as a lepidopterist. Don't get me wrong, I'm grateful he called and notified you of the butterflies. But if he, or any of them, say one word to you that isn't appropriate, I will set them straight."

"I can remind people of their manners," I reminded him. "I'm very capable."

Jack snorted. "Oh, believe me, I know. But I'm pretty sure Connor wouldn't understand the big words you use, and I didn't bring a thesaurus or the crayons to explain it to him."

That made me smile. "Not even Brennan uses crayons anymore."

Laughing, Jack handed my last bag to me, closed the boot, and locked the car. We loaded everything into the Cruiser, Jack and I climbed into the back with Amy, and we set off down the fire trail.

WHEN CONNOR SAID THE DRIVE WOULD CUT TEN KILOMETRES OFF the trip, I was grateful, yes. But the trail we were driving on was no more a road than it was a billygoat track. It was all rough ups and sharp downs and bumps and belly-swooping jolts.

I now understood why Connor got a bigger four-wheel drive than Jack. This was hardcore off-roading, though I didn't dare complain or even squeak, even though I wanted to several times.

It was foggy, misty, wet, and incredibly cold. The forest had closed in on all sides, the track barely recognisable in front of us. But Vince and Amy kept conversation with Jack, asking him about the regeneration progress after the bush-fires and, of course, Jack could talk about his work, his park, all day long. I spent the trip trying to read over the information I had on the cave we were heading to and the photographs Connor had taken of the specimens he'd collected. I couldn't see much detail, granted, but it was enough to keep me looking. There were photos of the cave that defied belief, and I couldn't wait to see it for myself.

And soon enough, the track was too rough for me to read anything, and after an eternity of off-roading hell, it ended. Though the spot Connor had declared was the end of the road looked no different to the path we'd just driven, if I was being honest. But I could hear a river now, rushing and loud, and the sounds of the forest came to life.

We sorted our bags, fitted our backpacks, attached our helmets to said backpacks, and ensured everything was secure and even-weighted. Knowing getting to this location was difficult, I hadn't even brought most of my gear. I was bringing only the basics, given we had to carry our camping things as well.

When we were ready to set off, Connor declared the direction and said we'd find the hiking trail about forty metres through the thicket, and sure enough, we did.

I feared we'd be hiking through rainforest without a path, but the track was well-walked and the footing easier than I'd expected. We walked single file, Connor at the lead, then Jack, then me, then Amy and Vince. Every so often, without stopping, Connor would call out, "How's my team?"

And without fail, Vince and Amy would reply with some variation of "Good, boss" or "All square, boss," and I liked that.

Perhaps I needed to reassess my initial impression of

Connor. Though the finger guns would live in infamy of awful.

We kept a good pace and made good time. We stopped an hour in for a drink and energy bar break, finding some quartzite boulders to sit on. It was a semi-cleared area and I got the impression it was a popular hiking stop.

"We start the ascent from here on in," Connor explained. It had been a steady incline for the last hour, but apparently now we were about to climb. "Everyone feeling okay?"

He looked at everyone, but his gaze finished on me. "Yes, perfectly fine, thank you," I replied. If he was expecting me to complain or cry for wanting to return home, he would be sorely disappointed. I slipped on my backpack, then picked up Jack's and helped him into it.

"You guys have obviously done this before?" Amy asked.

Jack gave her his charming grin. "Once or twice."

"I didn't know butterfly research was so . . . hands-on," she added.

I knew she meant no offence, but still. Did she think a butterfly's natural habitat was a research lab? "Lawson's been all over the country in his career," Jack said. There was no malice in his voice, just stating a fact. "And actually, I've learned more about ecology and environmental impacts by traipsing all through the wilderness with him. It's really fascinating."

Amy smiled. "I bet it is. And you've saved how many species from the brink of extinction?"

"Oh, um," I replied. "Well, I didn't save them single-handedly—"

Jack laughed. "Yes, he did. His modesty belies the truth."

"A lot of my time is spent in my research lab," I said,

ignoring Jack's boasting. "But to observe a specimen in their natural habitat is very important. There is a direct correlation between the species' health and the habitat in which we find them."

"And you built your own butterfly house?" Vince joined in. "I read about it when Connor said you were coming here."

I gave a nod. "Yes. Jack built it for me. It's amazing."

"Will you take some of these species back to your butterfly house?" Amy asked.

"That depends on a few factors, and I won't know until I see them," I replied. I rather liked that Vince and Amy were excited about this expedition. "Should we keep moving?"

"Yep," Connor said, and we began on the path again.

Up and up the path went. He wasn't kidding when he said the ascent started. It didn't seem to ever stop. But onward we went, never complaining, never stopping. Rocks and tree roots made a natural staircase for the most part, and my thighs and lungs were starting to burn. But we trod carefully and Connor asked every so often how his team was travelling.

Then the trees and forest suddenly thinned out, and we simply appeared to climb out of the forest and into shrubland that hunkered down from the wind. The entire side of the mountain was low brush and grasses and sheets of ancient quartzite we had to clamber up.

The wind was biting now and it was hard to tell if it was sleeting or biting rain. I couldn't see how high up we were as we were fully immersed in mist, or cloud, for all I knew. I had my beanie and gloves on and was thankful for the weatherproof outerwear that Jack insisted we buy for our Snowy Mountains trip a few years ago.

And we trudged onward and upward further still. Until we stopped again at a wall of craggy rock that provided a bit of a windbreak. And, pridefully, I was pleased to see I wasn't the only one out of breath.

We all were.

"We're almost there," Connor said, his cheeks flushed. "We cross the bluff, then we set up camp for the night."

Everyone nodded and sipped their waters and gluco-gels. It was three o'clock, and it'd be dark by five. Jack gave me a look with a smile that asked me if I was okay without saying a word. I gave a slight nod and he returned the gesture. I took my phone from my thigh pocket and began taking photographs of the flora interspersed between the grey rock formations that now dominated this landscape. Trying to record much else was futile with the mist.

"I wish you could see the view," Connor said, nodding out into the grey cloud that surrounded us. "It's amazing. Fingers crossed the cloud's lifted by tomorrow. You can see near all the way to the west coast."

I took barometric readings and could only shake my head. "And the photographs you sent me were taken this week?"

Connor gave half a shrug and nod. "Sure. Is that unusual?"

I wanted to laugh at that, but it wasn't his fault he didn't know. "Extremely. Butterflies are dormant during winter. Especially at this elevation, given the rainforest below us would typically be an ideal habitat. I'm yet to see inside the cave, obviously. But these readings," I held up the barometer. "To say it's unusual to find a colony of active butterflies in these conditions would be an understatement."

Jack's smile was breathtaking. "This is exciting."

I nodded, smiling right back at him. "It could be, yes. Very."

Amy clapped her hands together, the exhilaration tangible. "Then let's keep moving."

Getting to the bluff itself was steep. We basically had to use narrow-formed footholds while climbing up the rocks, sometimes heaving ourselves up. Connor had called them natural steps, but I had to wonder which giant he was referring to.

By the time I'd pulled myself up the last step, I was fast approaching done. Everyone was puffing and panting, so thankfully it wasn't just me. But I was glad the top of the bluff was relatively flat, though the wind was a hundred ice needles into my face. The mist was dense now, so I could barely see a few metres in any direction. The patches of grass and rock were slippery, and while it was tempting to hunker down and run to get out of the wind, treading slow and sure was safer.

A twisted ankle or broken leg up here was a helicopter ride out, and no helicopter was landing in this weather.

We crossed the bluff and made our way down a rocky escarpment and found ourselves on a grassy area that was blocked from the wind by a rock face. Connor took off his backpack and grinned at us. "We set up here tonight."

"Oh my word, that's so much better," I said as I shrugged out of my backpack.

Jack did the same and put his hand on my arm. His cheeks were pink and he was puffing out steam. "Remind you of anything?"

I chuckled. "I was only just thinking about how an ankle or leg injury would be a disaster up here."

"Don't jinx us," Vince said, dropping his backside onto the ground. He was puffing hard.

"I wouldn't be piggybacking you down this mountain," Jack said, taking a sip of water. "The Snowy Mountains incident was . . . character building." Then, much to my dismay, he explained for the others. "Lawson twisted his ankle on an expedition on Kosciuszko."

"On the bright side," I said, aiming for funny, "at least there are no cane toads or inland taipans here."

Jack laughed. "There are tiger snakes in these parts."

"Oh good."

"But they're all be hibernating right now," Amy said.

"I've heard that before," I mumbled.

Jack chuckled. "Inland taipan bites are not recommended."

I shook my head. "Neither is cane toad toxin."

The three of them stared at us, wide-eyed. "Are you two cursed or something?" Connor asked.

I snorted. "Not at all. We've been on dozens of expeditions together. Our near-fatal incident rate is well below ten per cent."

"Oh good," Vince deadpanned. "Ten per cent."

Jack laughed. "What good is almost dying if not to remind us we're alive?"

Amy smiled at that. "I love that you two go on these adventures together. It is honestly relationship goals."

I sipped my water and wiped my mouth. "It has its perks," I said. "Like when my husband says he'll put the tent up and start dinner while I go over my notes."

Jack laughed again. "Or when your husband does his share and stops being lazy."

I sighed and tried not to smile. Jack unclipped the rolled-up tent and threw it near my feet. "It was worth a try."

We were fast running out of daylight, so we all did our

tents first. They each had those single pop-up tents, which made sense. But Jack and I had a two-man style. Well, it fit two men . . . if they didn't mind getting cosy with each other, which luckily we didn't. We rolled out our sleeping bags, which I promptly unzipped and rezipped up as one larger sleeping bag for two men who didn't mind getting cosy with each other.

Jack smiled and waggled his eyebrow at me. "Don't get any ideas, Mr Brighton-Gale," I whispered. We were in our tent and it wasn't as though they could see us or hear us. "We'll be warmer if we share a sleeping bag. I'm far too tired and sore for anything else."

He chuckled, that throaty and warm sound I loved so much. "To be honest, Mr Brighton-Gale, I'm more excited just to camp out with you. We should do this more often."

"Camping, yes. Hiking, maybe not."

"It wasn't an easy one, was it?"

I shook my head and spoke to ensure the others would definitely not hear. "Not that I'd ever admit it to them, but I was very glad to stop tonight."

Jack kissed me quickly. "Same. And Lawson, don't feel like you're not on par with them, because you are. You hiked and climbed like a pro today."

"We still have the abseiling tomorrow to get through."

"And we'll nail it." Jack was so sure of it, and I wished for his confidence. "Don't worry about that right now, and think about the butterflies you're going to see tomorrow. I'll make us some dinner."

CHAPTER THREE

JACK

AFTER DINNER, EVERYONE WAS EAGER FOR SLEEP. IT HAD BEEN A long day: a pretty gruelling hike after a four-hour car drive. Connor had run through a few safety specs for where we were camping. "If you get up for a midnight pee, don't go too far. We're fairly secure here, but if you wander off too far in the dark, there's a helluva drop. Hope no one sleep-walks." Then he stopped and stared. "No, seriously, does anyone here sleepwalk?"

Vince and Amy both laughed and said no, and of course Lawson and I would be fine. There was no way I was letting Lawson wander off by himself in the dark when we were camped on the side of a mountain.

But we all bid each other a good night, said we would see each other at six o'clock. I doubted there'd be any need for alarms . . . I had to wonder how much sleep we'd be getting.

Lawson and I zipped up the tent, took our boots off, and climbed into our sleeping bag. It was freezing cold. All of 2ºC and a wind chill factor of -9ºC. The ground was cold but Lawson snuggled himself right into me, and I wrapped him up tight and sighed.

"I wonder what Brennan's doing," he murmured.

"He'd be reading a book with Grandma. Already bathed and in his jarmies, he'd have had his dinner, and I think Aunty Poppy will be making hot chocolates right about now."

He sighed. "I miss him."

"Me too." I held him a little bit tighter. "But I love being here with you too."

"Same." He stretched, then groaned. "My legs hurt."

I chuckled. "Mine too."

"Can't wait to see these butterflies tomorrow. They better still be there."

I rubbed his back and kissed the side of his head. "I'm sure they will be. After all, they're waiting for you to find them."

He let out a happy sigh and he drifted off to sleep. I tried to fight the weight of my eyelids, the ache in my legs and my back, but the day beat me. With Lawson safe and warm in my arms, I drifted off to sleep.

The howling wind woke me up around midnight, pulling at the tent and trying to fling us off the mountain. Then all of a sudden the wind was gone, replaced by a gentle pattering sound on the roof of the tent. It took me a moment to realise what it was.

It was snowing.

I smiled into the darkness and pulled Lawson against me. He mumbled something that sounded mostly like my name, but he never woke.

I hoped the snow didn't impede the final leg of our trip. Inclement weather would often close walking tracks in national parks, but we weren't the public. We weren't some public liability risk. We were national park employees on a work-related trip. We did this kind of thing all the time.

Plus, Lawson would be devastated to come this far and not be able to take the final step.

Knowing only time would tell if this expedition was over, I closed my eyes and hoped for a few more hours of sleep before we found out.

THE SOUND OF A ZIPPER WOKE ME UP, FOLLOWED BY THE TRUDGE of footsteps as one of the other three got up, presumably to go pee.

"What time is it?" Lawson mumbled.

I lifted my hand and peered at my watch in the dark. The sky was beginning to lighten but only barely. "Five thirty," I replied. I tried to stretch out a bit to test my muscles. "I'm not as sore as I thought I'd be."

"Hmm." He stretched his legs and rolled his shoulders. "Same." He sat up and scrubbed his hands over his face and let out a bit of a groan. "Though my back says hello."

I chuckled, but then I remembered last night. "I think it snowed during the night."

Lawson sat still for a second until it seemed he remembered what that could mean for our expedition, and then he was climbing out of the sleeping bad. "Come on. Let's take a look at the damage."

The damage was a light dusting of fine white snow and clumps of build-up driven by the wind around tufts of grass and rocks. It was a cold -4ºC on the thermometer, but the wind was, at the moment, thankfully, gone.

The mist was absent too, leaving behind an amazing view. Behind us, to the northeast, was a valley of forest and, further out, farmland, as far as the eye could see. The sun was just beginning to make its mark on the horizon with a light show of blues and pinks and yellows across the entire valley, and honestly, it was one hell of an impressive view to wake up to.

I stood there, not quite believing how pretty it was. "Wow."

"It's gorgeous, isn't it?" Amy said, walking back into camp. It must have been her we'd heard earlier.

"What do we make of the snow?" Lawson asked. "Enough to call a stop to our trip?"

She looked around at the snow and made a face. "Honestly, hard to tell. We'll wait until Connor makes a decision and how long we can put it off. We might just have to hold leaving off for an hour or so, but I'm just guessing."

Within a few minutes, both Connor and Vince were up and out of their tents. Connor wasn't happy about the snow, or maybe disappointed was more the case. But after breakfast, it was decided that Connor, Vince, and I would walk on and scout out the area. If it was too dangerous, there'd be no abseiling, and that was a decision I respected.

How long we'd wait it out for, though, would be the true test of patience for Lawson.

Leaving Amy and Lawson to pack everything up—and hopefully keep him busy and distracted enough—Connor, Vince, and I climbed up the rockface and trod our way to the edge of the cliff. There were a few clumps of snow but not as much as I thought there would be.

The view was . . . oh my god, it was beautiful. Connor had been right. We could almost see the west coast from the top. The hike, the difficulty, the aching muscles were worth it for the view alone. It almost looked like something from a movie. Obviously an extinct volcano, the rocky edges formed a somewhat-circular basin which was now a lake and rainforest.

I took out my phone and snapped some photos. "Wow."

Connor grinned. "Nice, huh?"

"Stunning."

"Never gets old," Vince said.

"What's your assessment?" Connor asked him.

Vince looked around, scraping his boots on the rock, and he peered down over the edge. Then he went to one point of the rock we stood on and scraped away clumps of snow to reveal a row of u-bolts drilled into the rock. He inspected them thoroughly. "Anchors look good. There's no surface ice, it's just powdery, and the sun'll make short work of that." He stood up and met Connor's gaze. "I think we're good to go."

I grinned. "That's gonna make someone very happy."

Vince's smile matched mine. "Do you reckon they've finished packing everything up yet, or should we give them a few minutes?"

Connor snorted and shook his head. "Get your arse back down there and help."

He laughed and began the walk back to camp, and Connor rolled his eyes. "Kids, huh? If he wasn't an expert climber..."

"I heard that," Vince called out without turning around.

I chuckled as we made our way back, and Lawson had the tent put away and was staring at Vince. Then when he saw me, he rushed over. "Well, what's the verdict? Vince wouldn't say."

"I wasn't giving the news," Vince said, trying not to smile.

Lawson was bordering on panic, and I could see the

disappointment creeping into his eyes. Until I smiled. "Get ready to find your butterflies. We are a go."

Lawson beamed, then shot Vince a foul look. "You made me worry."

Vince laughed. "Let's finish here and run through our safety specs and descent details, yeah?"

I rubbed Lawson's back. "You wait till you see the view."

"Amy, have we got a weather update?" Connor asked.

Amy read directly from her device screen. "Light southerly, three knots, tops. Temps today to reach twelve degrees, clear skies."

"And tomorrow?"

"Storms expected to roll in around noon. We'll need to be down the mountain by the time that hits."

Connor looked directly at Lawson. "You have all of today and tonight to collect whatever you need, but we're abseiling out of there tomorrow morning after breakfast. No questions."

Lawson gave him a nod. "Understood."

Vince had pulled out a large folded map of the cliff face with black lines drawn down it, and he proceeded to tell us how this would happen.

The mouth of the cave, eighteen metres down, had an excellent landing ledge.

Connor would descend first, then Lawson, then me, then all our gear, then Amy, and Vince would watch anchor and be the last to come down. Tonight would be spent inside the cave, and tomorrow morning we'd take the same order down to the two ledges as we made our way down to the bottom.

This wasn't a difficult abseil. All abseiling was dangerous, granted, but in the warmer months, people made this descent every other week. It was listed as intermediate. The lack of wind was good and there were no overhangs. Vince had done much harder as a child, he'd boasted. But still . . . all abseiling was dangerous.

When we got everything packed away and made our way up to the top, the rising sun made the view even better. "How are you feeling?" I asked Lawson quietly.

He knew I wasn't questioning the decision to do this or his ability. I was simply asking if he was in the right mind-set. Yes, he was excited and eager to get down into that cave, but one wrong move and this could all end very badly. "Good, and you?"

"I'm good. This is going to be great."

He gave me a hard nod, his gaze focused and serious. "I'm ready."

CHAPTER FOUR
LAWSON

Watching Connor step over the edge put my stomach through the wringer. Vince, albeit young, was very good at what he did. If I'd thought him to be frivolous and rambunctious—and I could admit that I had—then I was wrong.

He'd been rock climbing and abseiling since he could walk, apparently. And admittedly, I felt much better knowing he was in charge of the ropes and anchor.

I'd discerned that Vince was the wild one, Amy was the science one, and Connor was the older brother who kept everything in line. Together, the three of them made a pretty good team.

When Connor was safely down and it was my turn, Vince and Jack helped me into the harness and triple-checked everything. But when it came time to step backwards over the edge, my feet were literally on the precipice, Jack stood too close to me. Worry etched his features, and he looked a little pale.

"Please move back," I told him.

Jack blinked. "I'm two metres from the edge. I have a safety harness."

"Jack, I'm not joking," I said, firmer this time. "Please step back from the edge."

Vince tried not to smile, Amy just grinned away, but Jack refused to step back. "Be careful. Watch your footing," he said.

"I've done this before, you'll remember."

"Lawson." Jack's tone was sharp. "Focus and concentrate."

"Mm," Amy said. "Maybe it's not relationship goals to do this with your partner."

I pursed my lips and stepped out backwards, meeting Jack's eyes. "See you down there. Don't be late."

He smiled then, and step by slow-and-steady step, I descended. I daren't look out at the vastness of open air behind me, and I certainly didn't look down. I kept my breathing even, concentrated on where my feet and hands were at all times, keeping each movement steady. I was relieved and surprised when Connor's voice got closer, and then he was directing me down to the ledge and then beside me and holding me steady.

I unhooked myself free, with adrenaline-shaking hands and knees, and quickly made my way into the mouth of the cave. With terra firma under my feet, I could breathe a bit easier.

But I'd breathe a whole lot easier when Jack was with me.

Connor talked him through it, like he did with me, and as soon as his legs appeared, I was ready to grab him until he had two feet on the ledge. We got him out of the rigging, and I pulled him in for a hug.

"You okay?" he asked, his arms wrapped tight around me.

"Better now," I replied.

He kissed the side of my head. "It's as easy as stepping off a mountain."

I laughed then, just as Connor said, "Here's the first of the gear."

We unhooked the bags and I set them down to one side, out of the way. I could see enough of the front of the cave. The mouth itself was perhaps four metres tall by three metres wide, but inside it opened up like a room. But without lighting, I couldn't see much more than jagged rock walls and dirt for a floor.

More gear came down next and I put it to one side. I found my bag and pulled out a lamp, switching it on, amazed at what it revealed.

We seemed to be in a first chamber, some ten-metres wide by ten- or twelve-metres long. The ceiling was uneven and jagged rock probably five-metres high. And it was, for all intents and purposes, empty.

There was a fissure in the rock wall toward the back of the chamber, like a narrow doorway. I would imagine that led to the other two parts of the cave, and that was where I needed to go—I told myself to be patient. The last of the gear came down, then Amy followed, and Jack and Connor helped get her down. She looked as relieved as I felt, and I patted her shoulder when she came over.

"Solid rock never felt so good," I said.

She grinned. "God, yes." Then she looked around. "Oh wow."

"Amazing, yes?" I shone the torch toward the fissure. "There's a doorway through there, to the other two chambers, I would think."

She nodded and already had her barometer reader out. "This is so cool."

It was warmer inside the cave, and if it was warmer for us, that meant it would be warmer for other creatures too. Namely butterflies, but also . . . "Uh, will there be snakes in here?"

Jack and Connor were helping Vince plant his feet on the ledge, so my question fell to Amy. "Uh, I don't think so," she replied. "I mean, I can't guarantee there won't be. But the rainforest below is warmer, and that's where the birds' eggs, frogs, and rats are. I can't imagine there's be much for a snake to eat up here."

Sounded reasonable, and we could hope.

Vince came in, holding his ropes and gear, grinning. "Starting without me?"

"Thank you," I answered. "Your expertise in rappelling is most appreciated."

He grinned some more, as though what I'd said was funny. "No worries. You handled it like a pro."

"Made easier by your confidence and assurance," I added, the compliment most deserving in my opinion. But Vince cast me an odd look as though I was making fun of him.

Jack chuckled and clapped Vince on the shoulder. "You did good." Then he turned back to the entrance. "Look at that view."

The mouth of the cave now framed the most spectacular landscape picture nature could probably provide. And truth be told, I could appreciate it more from here than I did at the very top. It felt like we were on top of the world.

"And there are just the three chambers?" I asked.

"Yep." Connor nodded toward the end of the cave.

"There's no secret passages or channels, just three large rooms, much like this one. The third one is a bit smaller."

"And are there other caves in this mountain range?"

"Uh, yes. Several. None this high up though," Connor replied. He gestured to the rock wall. "This is quartzite and limestone, some seven-hundred-million years old. Last time that volcano probably erupted would have taken out some dinosaurs, but it left some remarkable formations."

I nodded, my interest piqued. If the cave played a part in the required ecosystem for this butterfly, we could have several locations to inspect. I turned toward the fissure at the end of the first chamber. "Well . . . shall we?"

"Hell yes," Jack said. "Let's just look first, worry about the scientific stuff second."

I rolled my eyes, not even mad. His excitement about finding butterflies made my heart so happy. I lifted my torch. "Okay then, let's go. Now the butterflies were in the third chamber, right?"

Amy nodded. "Yep."

So I walked first, Jack close behind me, and we passed through the split in the rockface into the second chamber. It was so dark, and my torch lit a halo of light around us, but I'd hate to think of being in here without it.

The second chamber was roughly the same size as the first, though it sloped downward at the end of the long room. The ceiling was rougher and darker though, and . . . did it just move?

"Um," I whispered, staring up.

Then, like something out of a nightmare, the entire ceiling rushed toward us—and toward the only escape—in a swarm of screeching bats.

Jack grabbed hold of me with a sharp intake of breath;

Amy let out a startled scream. Or maybe it was Connor. I couldn't tell. Not that I could blame them . . .

"Bats," I breathed, shaking off the residual heebie-jeebies.

Amy still had her hands over her head, ducking down low, and Connor looked three shades of white. Vince just chuckled. "Southern forest bat," he said.

I held the light up again and there were still a few bats clinging to the ceiling that seemed content to stay, and I was happy to leave them.

This chamber definitely sloped downward and the crevice-like opening at the far end seemed to go down deeper still. The temperature dropped the further in we went and we scanned the craggy floor for snakes and thankfully found none. It was probably too cold for them. Though there were a few bugs and scurrying whispers, the cave floor was mostly critter-free. The critters hanging from the ceiling were fine . . . as long as they stayed on the ceiling.

The entrance into the third chamber was narrow and long, downward-sloping and cold, and a little slippery. But soon enough the passage opened up into a very dark and dank room. We scanned the floor area first for any potential danger. There were sharp rock formations, some of the walls were jagged, some were smooth, but it was thankfully minus snakes.

Then I scanned up to the ceiling.

I'd seen photos, but what I saw took my breath away.

An entire kaleidoscope of butterflies hung from the ceiling. A pink kaleidoscope.

There in the dark of a remote cave, halfway up a cliff face, was an entire colony of butterflies I'd never seen before.

Pink.

In the dark. In winter.

It was mind-boggling.

I put my hand to my mouth and blinked back tears. I glanced to Jack to find him staring upward with a huge grin, and when he felt my eyes on him, he turned to me. "Lawson..."

I nodded, not trusting my voice to speak.

"So, Doc," Connor said. "Whaddya think? Is it a new species?"

I swallowed hard and tried to settle my nerves, my excitement. "I'll need to examine and study..." I trailed off. He didn't know, nor care, about the process. "But, yes. I do believe we might be looking at a new species."

The three of them all grinned, excited and probably relieved. There had been a good chance that we'd have come all this way for nothing.

But Jack's smile was something else. There was so much love, pride, and happiness there. He put his hand to my shoulder and pulled me in for a hug. He was all warmth and sweat, and being in his arms was my one true happy place. But this wasn't really the time for that.

"Uh, Jack," I mumbled. "You're squashing the light."

"Oh, sorry." He pushed me back to arms-length. "Okay, so let's get started. We need a grid set up, torch in every corner. Do not step on any casings or ... actually, just stick to the walls as close as you can. Don't walk underneath them, no direct light on them, no loud noises—"

"Uh, Jack. Thanks, but I can handle this," I said. Well, I would have had it, but now it was too late. I turned to the other three. "Okay, well, what Jack said is fine."

And so the real work began.

I took a myriad of readings, images, footage, and some

fallen, expired casings and already-dead specimens from the cave floor.

Vince and Connor eventually left us to it, choosing to spend their time in the first chamber, which was probably for the best. Where we were was an enclosed space and I'd eliminated most of the floor space, so room was limited. But Amy stayed, thrilled at every turn. Most would find the work boring and tedious, but she loved the data collation. She monitored humidity, temperatures, and she was fastidious in her work. Everything was neat and precise, and I was duly impressed.

"What kind of lichen is that?" she asked.

The ceiling had a rivulet of water, filtered by a few hundred thousand tonnes of rock that fed a patch of moss-like lichen that clung to the ceiling like a carpet.

"It looks like a pink or purple lichen," Jack said frowning. "We're going to need a sample of that."

I turned to him. "What do you mean a pink or purple lichen? Usually you speak in botanical names."

He smirked and shrugged. "I'm not familiar with it."

"You're not . . ." I blinked, trying to piece his words together. "You're never not familiar with a plant type."

He pointed upward. "That resembles something like the *Cryptohecia rubrocinta* or the *Arthoniaceae*, which is a lichenised type of fungus." Then he looked at me. "But neither of those should be here. Not in a cave, not at these temperatures, and not in Australia. I mean, we have some lichens that are close, but not like that."

I blinked again and felt a little light-headed, if I was being honest. "A new species?"

"I can't say. Not until we've taken samples for analysis." He looked back up at the ceiling. "Could it explain the colour of the butterflies?"

"You think there's a dietary pigmentation transference?"

Jack shrugged. "Honestly, I have no clue."

I thought about that for a moment. "It would make sense. Similar to a flamingo, per se. I don't like the chances of a coincidence. Pink lichen produces pink butterflies." It was all so much to think about. Two new species found together?

Then Amy, who had been quiet all through this, said, "What are the odds of the lichen changing colour because of *its* diet?" She looked at each of us in turn. "Flamingos are pink because of the carotenoids in shrimp, right? Like you said. But in the plant world, it's like the hydrangea. Too much aluminium in the soil, you have blue flowers. If you want to turn them pink, add lime." She then looked up to the ceiling of the cave. "Not much of a stretch to presume that water trickle runs through limestone. Perhaps this lichen is similar to the hydrangea?"

I grinned at her. "Deductive reasoning. I like it."

"I like it too," Jack said. "We'll know more when we can get it analysed."

"And to find butterflies in winter is not common?" Amy asked as she took more readings. "I know Connor said it was odd."

"Caterpillars usually spend colder months as eggs or larvae, even pupa," I explained. "They have an internal thermometer, of sorts, called diapause. It's found all through nature, including mammals. It tells them when to hibernate or migrate in winter and when to mate for spring. Butterflies will usually migrate. Overwintering will see a decline in egg production . . ." I stopped myself from going on and on about it. "To answer your question, finding butterflies in the imago phase, which is active sexual maturity in this case, at these temperatures and in complete darkness, is rare. Possibly unique." I added another dead specimen to my collection. "Normally, butterflies prefer temperatures above ten or twelve degrees to fly and function. What temperature do we have now?"

Amy read off her screen. "It's five-point-three degrees."

"And being wet and cold usually kills butterflies," Jack added. "The lichen provides a food source and a water source but acts as a sponge for them. So they can drink without getting wet."

"Even lichen as a primary food source is rare," I pointed out. "Caterpillars and moths can live on lichen, and there is one type of butterfly in Sri Lanka I'm aware of which prefers it. And to be honest, this butterfly shares some behavioural characteristics of the moth. But the lichen food source is an odd symbiotic relationship. Lichens accumulate large concentrations of secondary metabolites, like aromatic phenolic compounds, such as atranorin and usnic acid." I glanced over at Jack. "It must deter the bats from eating them." I shook my head in wonder. "How remarkable."

"Can I ask a really obvious question?" Amy asked. "You'll probably think I'm stupid."

"No I won't," I replied. No question in the quest for education was stupid.

She made a face. "What's the difference between a moth and butterfly? I mean, except the fact that moths are usually brown and butterflies are all kinds of colours. And that we see butterflies during the day but see moths at night."

I smiled. "You almost answered your own question. There is a colour differential. Butterflies typically have more colouring. Butterflies are diurnal, moths are nocturnal. But there are other differences. The way they fold their wings in a resting position is probably the most obvious, but also the antennae are different and the frenulum."

She blinked. "I'm sorry, the what?"

Jack laughed. "Not that kind. This is a different kind. In insects."

I caught on to what she meant. "Oh." Dear God, I hoped she couldn't see the flame of my cheeks. "Heavens no. Uh, moths have a wing-coupling for flight that butterflies do not have. Also, the butterfly pupa is made from hardened protein; the moth pupa is spun from silk. The casings here in this cave are not silk."

I held up the dead specimen in my jar, inspecting it as best I could with the poor light. "But these eyes are . . ."

Jack walked over to me. "They're what?"

I took a deep breath and exhaled slowly, not really believing it myself. "I want to get a better look in my lab, but I might have a theory."

"You noticed something," he prompted.

"I can't say with any certainty yet, and I may be jumping to conclusions."

"What is it?"

"Ask me how I know this species has never been documented before."

"Christ, Lawson, just say it."

I smiled at him. "This species is almost certainly a butterfly. The thorax, the scaling, the wings, antennae are all butterfly. But the eyes . . ."

"The eyes are what?"

"This species has superposition eyes. Butterflies do not have superposition eyes, they have apposition eyes. Moths have superposition eyes because they're nocturnal; the eye reflects light differently."

Jack's brow quirked upward. "And you've never heard of a butterfly with the eyes of a moth."

I grinned. "Never."

"So is this a new species of butterfly?" Amy asked. "Or a whole new species?"

I chewed on my lip and looked again to the specimen in my jar, trying not to smile. "I can't say with certainty."

"Holy shit," Jack said. "It is. It's a whole new *specimen*. Because if you've never heard of it, it doesn't exist."

"Well, it may have existed a long time ago," I interjected, trying not to sound too hopeful. "Perhaps it was lost a few hundred years ago and we've only just *re*discovered it. I'll need to do a lot of research. And there is much we don't know. Do they spend their entire lifecycles inside this cave? Do they see daylight at all? What is their lifecycle? Have they simply evolved over thousands of years to adapt to the dark? Many troglofaunal species do this."

"Troglofaunal?" Amy repeated.

"Cave-dwelling animals."

"Well," Jack said regardless of my information dump. "It's exciting nonetheless."

"It is," I agreed. "I think we can leave them be for the time being. I don't want the light to upset them any more than we need to. Let's pack up and go out to the others."

I had no idea what the time was, given the inside of the cave was impervious to day or night.

"Though I would like to try one thing," I added after we'd packed up our gear and were just about to walk out. I took one live specimen, held it very carefully, and we made our way back out through the chambers toward the daylight.

Then, standing in the middle of the first chamber, with daylight still streaming in, I opened the jar. The butterfly crawled up out of the plastic specimen container, tasting the air with its proboscis. I wanted to see if it was drawn to the daylight, but it took off, flittering through the air toward the back of the cave, through the fissure, and disappeared back into the darkness.

All I could do was shake my head. "Remarkable."

CHAPTER FIVE
JACK

THIS WAS GROUND-BREAKING STUFF. AND I'D SEEN LAWSON discover new butterflies before. I'd seen his face, his smile, the light of wonder in his eyes.

But this wasn't just a new butterfly.

This was a new species. A butterfly-moth cross. A sub-species? A new lepidopteran classification? A new species entirely?

And to see Lawson discover this, to be part of the team that discovered this, was an extraordinary thing.

He got the same look in his eyes when he watched Brennan. When Brennan took his first step, said "daddy" for the first time.

That was the look Lawson got when he realised he was seeing something utterly wondrous.

It did things to my heart I wasn't quite prepared for.

"Pretty special, huh?" Amy asked me quietly. We were taking soil samples from the second chamber, and Lawson was spending time with the butterflies, recording their behaviour patterns.

I realised I was smiling at Amy like a crazy man. "It's pretty special, yeah."

"You're very lucky," she whispered, "to get to work with your husband."

There was something wistful, or wishful, about how she said that. I tried to piece it together. I nodded toward the first chamber. "Do you . . . are you and Vince or Connor . . . ?"

She looked aghast. "Oh, no!"

"Oh, sorry. I just wondered if you meant . . . you've mentioned relationship goals a few times, and I thought . . ."

She chewed on the inside of her lip for a second. "My partner," she whispered. "Works for a Tassie Devil conservation group. To work with her every day would be . . . amazing."

To work with *her* . . .

Oh.

She'd just divulged something incredibly personal to me, and I wasn't quite sure what to do with it. She swallowed hard. "It's just that I see you and your husband doing this . . ."

I reached over and gave Amy's arm a squeeze. "Don't let anyone tell you no or that you can't."

She nodded quickly, relieved and a little emotional. "One day we might get to make it happen."

I finished writing on the label of a sample of bat droppings. "You know, it takes a special kind of tenacity to make it happen. And that guy in there," I said, pointing my pen toward the third chamber where Lawson was. "He's the brave one out of us two. He never gives up, and years ago, he told his boss at the university how it was going to happen and how he was in charge and how he would be moving to Tasmania to pursue the butterfly he found. His thesis was also basically an open letter to the butterfly association to tell them they were a bunch of idiots." I chuckled at that. "Which was before I even knew him. But he was right. Add in the fact that he's a genius, it's kinda hard to argue with anything he says because he's right almost all of the time. But he's stubborn and he knows what he wants, and he wanted to involve me with his work, and it's been incredible. Not just to be part of it and to experience it myself, but to see *him* experience it."

God, I was off-track.

"So, Amy," I added. "If you want to work with your girl, you find a way and you make it happen. Be the tenacious one. Don't let the boys-club attitude dictate anything."

She smiled and tucked a strand of hair behind her ear. "Sounds like a dream."

"You know," I said. "Lawson saved two devil joeys from certain death. He almost died doing it, by the way. And then I almost died hauling his arse out of there. But . . ." I was getting off-track again. "We have a listed colony of devils in my park, up north. If your partner wanted to apply through my office to come and observe them, I'm sure I could make that happen. And it is protocol to have someone from the national park assist them, which you could also apply for, through my office. Because if someone from my office can't attend, then I'm sure someone from a different national park, such as yourself, could step in."

Her smile became a grin. "Are you serious?"

I chuckled. "Absolutely." I packed away my gear. "You've proved yourself here. I know you're capable, and I know Lawson's impressed with your work."

"He is?"

"Sure he is."

"How do you know?"

"Because he hasn't asked you *not* to touch anything. If he didn't think you were capable, he'd have told you to sit with the others and not touch anything. In fact, he's trusted you with *his* work, and he doesn't trust anyone who isn't great at their job. And I'll let you in on a little secret," I whispered. "He's not impressed by many people."

I could see the blush on her cheeks, even in the darkened cave. She smiled at me. "I'm very honoured."

I looked up at the bats. "How about we get out of here. I don't want to get peed on."

"Good idea."

We took all our samples and gear back into the first chamber and packed it all away; then I was about to go check on Lawson, but he walked out holding his laptop. He propped it up on one of the bags and opened the screen. "The night vision camera is all set up," he explained. "I'd rather not disturb them any more than we have. Hopefully they'll settle down now and return to normal behaviour, and hopefully the night camera will return some good footage."

"That'll record all night?" Connor asked.

Lawson gave a nod. "I'd like to get one set up on a more permanent basis, but that's something we can discuss later. If this proves to be what I think it might."

"And you think it's a new species?" Vince repeated. "Not just a new species of butterfly."

Lawson smiled. "It's a strong possibility. And I'm afraid of what that might mean for your national park, your team, and how busy this might get for you. This is going to create quite the buzz."

"So we can expect to make this trip quite a bit," Connor deduced.

Lawson shrugged. "Well, Vince perhaps."

Connor blinked back his surprise. "Oh."

Lawson made a face. "Given his rappelling expertise." Then he looked to me and made another face. "Not for any other reason."

All I could do was laugh because the idea of Lawson wanting to spend time with Vince by choice was just funny. "I think we'll be back a fair bit." I looked to everyone in turn, still smiling. "How about we think about dinner?"

LAWSON KEPT AN EYE ON HIS LAPTOP SCREEN, AND HE TOOK ONE last temperature recording, but soon enough it was late enough and cold enough to crawl into bed.

We still set up our tents inside the first chamber of the cave. They gave an added layer of insulation for warmth, and they gave me and Lawson some privacy.

Once the door was zipped, we brushed our teeth the best we could, pulled off our boots, and climbed into our double sleeping bag. It had been a pretty incredible day, and I had to wonder how much sleep Lawson would be getting tonight. I was one hundred per cent certain he'd be up every hour looking at that night vision screen, watching, tracking, and reporting on the butterflies.

"I'm cold," he mumbled, snuggling into me.

I pulled him closer and rubbed his back. "Is that better?"

He snuggled in some more. "No. Still cold."

For a brief moment, I wondered if he was beginning to feel unwell, but then he ran his hand down to my hip and gripped the waistband of my pants. "Still cold," he said again, pulling me closer. "Would be a lot warmer with your body weight on mine."

I chuckled but obliged. I would always oblige him. It took a bit of manoeuvring, all while trying to be quiet, and Lawson opened his legs as wide as the sleeping bag would allow.

Right, then.

"Lawson," I murmured. "There are others close by. They might hear."

"Hear what?" he whispered. It was dark, but with our noses touching, I could see his eyes. "I wouldn't be so bold as to suggest anything that might make noise, Jack. But you could kiss me. You could kiss me for hours."

I ghosted a kiss over his lips. "Promise you'll be quiet?"

He smiled, victorious and daring. "Can you?"

I kissed him then, like I owned him, like he was mine to do with whatever I wanted. I slid my arms underneath him and held him, devouring his mouth and sucking on his tongue. I could feel it in his body when he surrendered to it. He relaxed and welcomed it, and he groaned low in his throat.

I pulled back abruptly. "Quiet, or I'll stop."

It took his eyes a second to focus, and then he shook his head. "More."

Mmm, this Lawson was my favourite. The uninhibited, lost-to-the-pleasure Lawson who had no idea how sexy he was.

If we were home, I'd have him undressed and be buried inside him right now. And god, how I wanted to be.

But we weren't at home.

So I took a second to cool it, despite how hard we both were, and I just enjoyed it for what it was. We weren't going to get off, there would be no mind-blowing orgasm. We could just enjoy a make-out session instead.

We hadn't just made-out in so long. Since Brennan came into our lives, basically. Our daddy time was spent getting from point a to z in the most efficient ways possible. Which was fine. It's what most new parents did. But now we had some time to enjoy all those letters in after the a without getting to the z.

There was such intimacy in just kissing, in holding each other, in nuzzling necks, and more kissing. Soft kissing, deep kissing, tender and hard, tasting and biting, with no intention of taking it further.

It was fun and sensual, and my god, it felt so good just to reconnect with him like this.

"I love you," I murmured into his ear.

He put his hands to my face and pushed me back so I could see him. He was smiling, kiss-swollen lips and a spark in his eyes. "I love you," he mouthed before bringing our mouths back together.

CHAPTER SIX
LAWSON

I COULD KISS JACK FOREVER. OR MORE TO THE POINT, I COULD have him kiss me forever. There was something to be said about the way he took charge, how he used his strength and his body to remind me that he was mine.

That I was his.

I would have loved for him to have owned me right then and there, in that tent in the cave. But it was neither the place nor the time for *that* level of sexual intimacy. Despite how badly I wanted it.

But having him kiss me like that, to have his weight on me, to have his hands and mouth on me like that, was just as good.

It all simmered down to gentle and tender, sleepy kisses. Jack was warmth and safety, and I almost fell asleep with him on top of me. But eventually he rolled us onto our sides, wrapped me up in his arms, and fell asleep.

I wanted to check on the butterflies, but I wanted this more.

And God only knew how long those butterflies had

inhabited that cave. A decade? A hundred years? A thousand?

I only had my husband like this for one night.

It wasn't a contest.

So wrapped up in his arms, in his love, I closed my eyes and drifted off to sleep.

I AWOKE BEFORE FIVE, AND PEELING MYSELF AWAY FROM JACK, I pulled on my boots, coat, and beanie and checked the butterflies on my laptop. They were active, which was utterly confounding to me. Though it shouldn't have been. This butterfly was not exactly nocturnal—it was active during the day making it diurnal. The difference being the cave was pitch black. It thrived in perpetual night, during daylight hours. I knew I'd be researching the variable factors of lepidoptery between night and day, and a species that thrived in the absence of light.

This tiny little creature was about to upend everything we thought we knew about the species.

Everything about its existence, its behaviour—everything that defined it as a butterfly—was different.

It was incredibly exciting.

And I knew this trip to this cave would be the first of a lot in our future. I dreaded being absent from Jack and Brennan for any length of time though. I had no qualms with Jack joining me, his work permitting, of course. But there was no way Brennan could do this. Even considering bringing him on the hike and then abseiling was out of the question.

No, it would mean time away from both of them. And that wasn't something I looked forward to at all.

Or leaving my butterflies in my butterfly house. Or my other research, or my whole life back in Scottsdale, for that matter.

Perhaps I could assign this find to someone else. After my initial report, of course. And after our findings were substantiated and confirmed, of course. I would still have a lot of work to do . . .

"What are you frowning for?" Jack's warm hand rubbed my back.

"Oh. You startled me. I didn't hear you."

"You were miles away," he said gently. "I asked you if something was wrong with the butterflies."

I looked at the screen in front of me. "Oh, no. They're fine. Great, actually. Active at night." The others were still asleep. I didn't want to wake them, so I kept my voice low. "Well, what night is for us. I don't know if the cave eliminates the diurnal and nocturnal barriers, though I can only assume the change in barometric pressure of a night time would play a part. The bats have all mostly returned to roost."

"So why the frown?"

He looked so handsome with his three-day growth. I ran my thumb across it. "I like this," I mumbled.

"Lawson." He used that tone that told me he wasn't interested in vacillation.

"I was just thinking about how much time this will draw me from you and Brennan," I admitted quietly. "And I don't know how much I'm prepared for that. Or even if I'm prepared to do that, at all."

"Lawson, this find is huge. As if all the other work you've done isn't enough to define your career but, my love, this discovery is career-defining."

"I don't care for accolades, Jack. I never have." Then I

shrugged. "Well, except perhaps for the Tillman Copper because my old university professor thought me maladroit."

"This is a lot of big words before—" He checked his watch. "Before 5:00 am, and my first cup of tea. But that tells me you're serious and quite possibly over-thinking things."

"I care for the survival of the species, Jack. That is my number one priority. Facts, research, conservation, longevity. It doesn't matter whose name goes on it. I know my value in this work."

Jack sighed patiently, even smiled a little. "And that's one of the many reasons I love you. But don't make any decisions now. We'll get all the information we can back to the lab, and take it one step at a time." He put his hand to my cheek. "Don't worry about me and Brennan. Our little home on our little farm isn't going anywhere, and if you need to spend time away, we'll be just fine. Don't underestimate how important your work is."

"Don't underestimate how much I don't want to leave. That little house on that little farm is where I belong. With you and our son. Don't underestimate how important that is to me."

"What are you saying, Lawson?"

"I think I might hand this one off. After the initial report, which is still a few months away anyway. I can give a couple of months," I replied. "But I'm busy enough. I can consult and help if they need, but this could turn into years of work and I'm not prepared to miss that much of us. The idea of being away from Brennan for too long makes me feel . . . Is iniquitous the right word?"

The corner of his lip curled upward. "Honestly, I wouldn't know."

I put my hand to my forehead. "Perhaps bereft is more accurate."

He pulled me in for a side-hug and he kissed my temple. "Whatever you decide, you have my full support."

I closed my eyes and allowed myself to lean into him for a brief moment. It dawned on me then that I'd not once doubted his support. He was my absolute rock. "I'm so lucky to have you."

He planted another kiss to the side of my head and rubbed my back. "You only say that because it's my turn to pack up our gear."

I leaned my head on his shoulder. "True."

Jack gave me a playful tap on the backside. "You go pack up your camera and gear in the third chamber." He handed me his torch, then nodded out to the cave entrance where the sky was beginning to lighten. "The sun's about to rise, we've got weather rolling in, and we need to get down this mountain."

I gave a nod and switched the torch on, picked up my backpack, and took it with me into the third chamber. I was careful on my walk through by myself; I'd rather risk running a few minutes late than another sprained ankle or wrist should I fall. But I made my way through to the third chamber without incident. The butterflies all reacted to my entrance, or to the torch, I should say.

There was a ripple of wings across the kaleidoscope. A wave of pink and mauve, almost like they were saying goodbye. "I will be back," I told them softly. "I just want to say that even if I hand this research over, I promise whomever I deem satisfactory will be respectful and non-invasive. We will only return to observe and learn. You have my word."

They didn't answer, of course, though I did receive a few waves in response.

Smiling, I began packing up my gear, making sure it was all fine and stowed in my bag correctly. And with a final glance upward at this absolute marvel of nature, I let them be and made my way back out to the first chamber.

"I had it," Vince was saying. He had his neatly sorted rappelling gear spread out over the cavern floor, his hand was pulling at his hair, his face somewhat pale in the early morning light. "Of course I had it. We used it to get down here."

"Could you have left it up at the bluff?" Amy asked.

Vince shrugged before scrubbing his hand over his face. "No. I mean . . . maybe. I have never left any gear behind. Ever. I'm fastidious. It is ingrained in me, like breathing." He picked up his ropes, clearly looking for something.

Oh, dear.

"What have we misplaced?" I asked, slowly putting my backpack down. I was fairly certain I didn't want to know . . .

Jack gave me a tight smile. "A descender?" he said, sounding unsure about it himself.

Vince let an exasperated sound. "It's a fall arrester. Safety gear. It's a buckle, of sorts, that acts as a brake if you need one. There are two of them, buckled together."

Oh.

"Oh."

"I had it," he said again. "They've got to be here somewhere."

"Can you rig up something instead?" Connor suggested. "I've heard you talk about rigging gear up all the time."

Vince deflated. "I guess. I can make a carabiner brake. It's not my preferred kind, but it's better than nothing." He reached out and picked up a few carabiners, which were a metal buckles that climbers used all the time. Vince had quite a few of them. Then he took one neat bundle of ropes and mumbled to himself, "I'll just need to work out some load bearing and force, rope tensions . . ."

Amy, somewhat stricken, looked at Connor. Connor was staring at Vince. Vince was staring at the ropes in his hand. Jack smiled at me.

"Um, maybe I could help with that," I suggested.

The three of them then stared at me. "Well, it's just physics. When Jack first insisted I go abseiling with him, I was . . . well, horrified. But once I applied physics and worked out a few equations, it's really rather simple."

"Simple?" Connor blinked at me.

"Well, yes." I cleared my throat. "Given we'll need to allow for variances in height and therefore centre of gravity and the angle of the climber's legs in relation to the cliff face, for the sake of this exercise, we can apply the equation to Jack. Factor in his weight of, say eighty-five kilograms and his height of 1.9 metres, and we can assume he has a centre of gravity approximately 1.1 metres from his feet. It would be fair to assume he rappels down the cliff with his body raised thirty degrees above the horizontal. Give or take. If he held the rope approximately 1.4 metres from his feet—" I indicated this position and height using my hands. "—which is fair, given his height, it would make a twenty-degree angle with the cliff face. Give or take. And then we want to find the minimum static coefficient of friction that his feet on the cliff need to have, which will produce the least amount of tension on the rope. We know the force of gravity is vertical, the force of the legs being at thirty degrees multiplied by cosine—"

"Ah, Vince," Amy said, interrupting me mid-explanation. She was holding up a large metal buckle with several lever-type parts. "Is this what you were looking for?"

"Oh my god, yes!" He scrambled to his feet and rushed over to her. "Where was it?"

"Under your tent bag."

"Holy shit." He took the device and held it to his chest. "Thank you."

"Do you think you should maybe not have clipped them together?" Connor asked. "So you could lose one and not both?"

"I didn't think." Vince shook his head, clearly mad at himself. "I just packed everything up together to save space. It was stupid."

"So I can finish explaining the equation if you'd like?" I offered.

Vince grimaced. "Another time, perhaps."

"The answer is approximately 280 newtons," I finished. "Just so you know. Your makeshift braking device would have been more than adequate."

Vince smiled eventually. Connor blinked at me again as though I'd spoken a different language. Amy gave me an approving nod, and Jack . . . well, Jack grinned right at me. "Genius is, genius does."

I ignored the heat in my cheeks. "So, we're ready to leave then?"

Vince was busy sorting out his ropes and harnesses. "Am now."

CHAPTER SEVEN
JACK

THE CLIMB DOWN THE MOUNTAIN WASN'T AS HARROWING AS I thought it might be. There were two more decent ledges on the way down, each equipped with rigging bolts for abseiling. It was slow, but it was safe. Vince and Connor were very good at it and put safety over everything.

Lawson, on the other hand, was more worried about his samples and equipment.

I wasn't sure what to make of his announcement to me that he was considering passing this find off to someone else. I was surprised, but maybe I shouldn't have been. Hearing him say he wanted to be home with us more made my heart so damn happy, but I knew his decision to stand down as lead lepidopterist might change.

If he thought for one second the person he'd hand it to wasn't capable, he simply wouldn't hand it over.

If he did decide to stay on board with it, I knew it was going to take up a lot of Lawson's time and focus. And I knew in all likelihood we'd be making this trip a lot in the next few months and possibly exploring other caves in the region. And it was going to be ruling our lives for some time to come.

But I couldn't even be mad about it.

Lawson was rightly excited about this new butterfly, but you know what? I was too.

This was his life's work, and I was a part of his life—butterflies had become such a central part of our lives together—so it was only natural for me to be almost excited as him.

Once we made it down to ground level, with no injuries or damage to any of Lawson's research samples, after we all took a few minutes to use the rainforest "bathroom" in private, we made the hike back to Connor's four-wheel drive and made the rough and bumpy trip through the forest back to where we'd left our SUV.

As great as the trip had been, and as grateful as I was to Connor, Vince, and Amy, I was very relieved to see our car. We unloaded all our gear out of Connor's vehicle into ours, said our rounds of thanks and goodbyes and promises to be in touch—we'd no doubt be seeing them again real soon—and we were on our way home.

It was going to be about a four-hour drive home, and we'd only been in the car for about twenty seconds before Lawson turned in his seat to face me. "Oh my god, Jack," he blurted out like he was suddenly overwhelmed. "There is so much work to do!"

And he talked and talked and talked non-stop about every detail. The butterfly, the remarkable differences, the similarities, the diet, the relationship to the dark, to the lichen, to the bats. He was certain the bats played some part. As did the temperature, the air pressure, the elevation. Maybe other caves in the area had some too. We'd have to explore all of them. There were so many questions.

"I have one question," I asked. He'd taken a much-needed breath, his palm pressed to his forehead. I thought it might be my only chance to get a word in.

"What's that?"

"What are you going to call it?"

Lawson blinked, stared at me, then out the windscreen, then back at me. "I don't know," he whispered. "You name it."

"No, I will not."

"Yes, you can."

"Okay, call it the Lawson."

"Don't be ridiculous."

"Why is that ridiculous?"

"Because it's egotistical and self-serving."

I snorted. "Then you name it."

He sighed, his conversation derailed. "I would need to consider a great deal of factors."

I took his hand and kissed his knuckles, smiling at how much calmer he was now. At least he was breathing normally. "Are you still considering handing it over to someone else?"

He chewed on his bottom lip and stared out the windscreen for a bit, then nodded. "I think so. Once the prelims are done and the groundwork is established. There's still a lot of work in that, but by then the weather will have warmed up and my work at home will be in full swing. I'll have enough to worry about. Plus, I meant what I said. I don't want to be traipsing all over anymore, Jack. I want to be home with you and Brennan."

I kissed his knuckles again. "I love you."

He smiled at me, clearly tired but happy. "And that makes me one very lucky, very happy man. I love you too, Jack."

He scrolled on his phone for a while, sent some emails off to Piers in Queensland, asking him to come at his earliest convenience, then went back to scrolling. He was quiet, reading, researching, double-checking, and we were soon pulling into our driveway. The clouds were low and dark, the weather had turned miserable, but there had never been a prettier sight to me.

Brennan ran out onto the porch, his coat, boots, and beanie on, his grin wide. "Daddas!"

Lawson was out of the car and had him in a big hug before I'd even opened my door. I walked over and collected them both in a big bear hug and said hello to my mum and sister over the top of Lawson's head.

"Did you save the butterflies?" Brennan asked, his brown eyes wide with innocent wonder.

Lawson tweaked his little chubby cheek. "We sure did."

The cold wind snapped around us. "How about we get all of Daddy's gear into his butterfly house, then make hot chocolates and we can tell you all about it?"

We all carried bags, and Brennan carried one with the utmost importance. His daddy's work made him a super-hero according to Brennan, and that was the sweetest thing ever. Raising our son to understand ecology and conservation like he understood colours, shapes, letters, and numbers was never a question. Between my work at the national park and Lawson's butterflies, Brennan was always going to be aware of the world around him.

But then we sat at the dining table, hot chocolates all 'round, and told Mum and Poppy all about the butterfly. Brennan sat on my lap, listening to every word.

Lawson's phone rang and Piers' name appeared on the screen. He flashed me a smile before excusing himself to answer the call.

Mum watched Lawson disappear down the hall. "Life's about to get a whole lot busier," she mused.

"A whole lot better," I corrected gently. I gave Brennan a squeeze. "Daddy's a superhero, isn't he?"

Brennan nodded. "He saves butterflies every day."

Smiling, I kissed the side of his head. "He sure does."

Three Months Later

"I FINISHED IT," LAWSON SAID NERVOUSLY AS HE HANDED ME A copy of his submission to the Australian Lepidopterist Society. His work on the new butterfly had created interest from all over the world. Piers had spent some time here helping him, mostly spending time in Lawson's butterfly house. He wasn't up for the hike or the abseiling, which was understandable.

Lawson and I had made that trek more than a few times in the last three months. We never did find any other specimens in any other caves in the area, but the size and health of the colony led Lawson to believe they might be found in other caves in colder parts of Australia and even New Zealand.

They were out there, just waiting to be found. They just happened to be hiding in places no one would have ever expected to find butterflies. They had taken everything ever known about butterflies and turned it on its head.

Other butterfly enthusiasts were now actively searching their local caves in hopes of finding them. This new species, a remarkable find, had set the Lepidoptera world abuzz, but even further afield, the whole insect and even reptile world had taken note. This was a cold-blooded animal that never saw the sun. It preferred and thrived in absolute darkness in the colder months. Sure, the cave was protected and had a steady climate all year round, but that climate was cold, and this was an exciting find.

Even the lichenology and mycology world was abuzz. The pink lichen turned out to be known in the *Cryptothecia rubrocincta* family, but not in caves and not at these temperatures. It was basically a fungus living off the water source, and the algae and cyanobacteria deterred the bats from eating both the lichen and the butterfly, and the bats protected the butterflies from other predators.

It was such a remarkable symbiosis.

And the butterfly was also, still to this point, nameless.

I'd suggested something to do with the cold or winter. Even something to do with the colour. It was pink, after all. And pink in the animal kingdom was rare.

"But they're not pink," Lawson had argued. "There has been much debate regarding this, as you know."

"Uh, I don't know everything about butterflies like you do, but I know what the colour pink is," I'd replied.

To which Lawson gave me a condensed rundown on structural colourisation. The butterfly was technically purple but appeared pink due to iridescence. They looked pink to me, but I wasn't about to argue the point with Lawson.

Anyway, the newfound butterfly was still nameless. Until now. If he'd finished his submission, which meant he'd given it a name.

I took the folder he'd handed me. He raked his fingers through his hair, patting it down, blinked quickly a few times, and licked his lips. I stood up. "Lawson, my love. What are you nervous about?"

"I'm not nervous," he lied. Then he frowned at the folder. "I'm not nervous, but if you'd care to read the first page, that would be most appreciated. Put me out of my misery, at least. And if you don't like it or would rather it be called something else, I will understand, but I am of the opinion—"

"Hey," I murmured soothingly. I put my palm to his cheek. "Don't be anxious about it."

Then his expression became one of annoyance. "Would you just please look at it?"

I opened the folder, and under a photograph of the butterfly in question was its name.

The Brighton-Gale Butterfly.

I read the name again and looked at Lawson. He'd put our name on it.

He'd named it after us.

"Lawson . . ."

"If you don't like it—"

"Are you kidding?" I was a little teary, not gonna lie. "I love it. I'm honoured. I'm flattered, and I don't know what to say, to be honest. I'm speechless . . . But you named it after us?"

He nodded. "For you and Brennan." He swallowed hard. "Not for me. I have no need for such things. But for you, because I love you and your support makes my work possible. I couldn't do this without you. You've never questioned the importance of what I do, and I want you to know how much I appreciate that." He blinked back tears. "And for our son. A legacy for him, so in a few hundred years his name will still be remembered."

Sliding the folder onto the table, I took Lawson's face in

my hands and kissed him. "I'm so honoured. Thank you. I never expected this. I'm . . . *so honoured*. My heart is so full right now. And I don't think you need to worry about Brennan's legacy. I'm pretty sure he's gonna be saving butterflies when he grows up. You two will be working side by side for a long time."

Lawson gave a teary laugh. "You think so?"

"I know so. And I wouldn't have it any other way."

He hugged me, his face buried in my neck. He nuzzled me for half a second before stopping. "Brennan's asleep, yes?"

I chuckled. "He sure is."

He pulled back and met my gaze. "I've been so busy and it feels like forever since we . . . since you . . ."

I kissed him softly. "Want me to remedy that, Doctor Brighton-Gale?"

"Immediately." He took my hand and led me to our room, closing the door quietly behind us and snicking the lock shut. His eyes were full of fire and love. "Immediately and for as many times as you're able."

I pulled his sweater over his head and pushed him onto the bed. Crawling up his body, I left a trail of butterfly kisses over his skin. His quiet laugh became a moan. "Jack, I'm not a patient man."

I laughed and, like I always had—and like I always would—gave him everything he wanted.

~ The End

SPECIAL MENTION TO JULIE BOZZA

I'd like to offer a heartfelt thanks to Julie Bozza. For offering her support, feedback, and input for Imago.

Readers, if you enjoyed Imago, please do yourself a favour and pick up Julie's Butterfly Hunter. You won't be disappointed.

Nicholas and Dave are gorgeous.

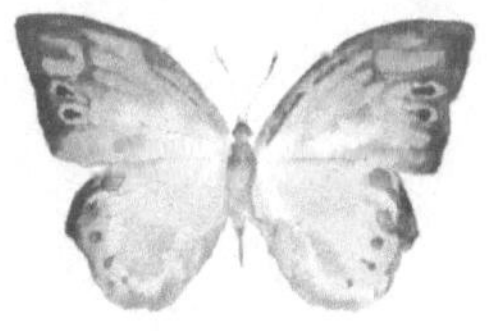

GLOSSARY FOR AUSTRALIAN TERMS

- Esky: a portable cooler
- Pub: (short for Public House) A hotel, primary function is a drinking establishment and meals.
- Bowlo: (short for bowling club) A community sports centre for lawn bowls.
- Kitchen bench: kitchen counter.
- 2iC: A person who is 2nd in command/charge.
- Ute: (short for utility) Trayback utility
- Rouse: (rhymes with house) To scold

ABOUT THE AUTHOR

N.R. Walker is an Australian author, who loves her genre of gay romance. She loves writing and spends far too much time doing it, but wouldn't have it any other way.

She is many things: a mother, a wife, a sister, a writer. She has pretty, pretty boys who live in her head, who don't let her sleep at night unless she gives them life with words.

She likes it when they do dirty, dirty things... but likes it even more when they fall in love.

She used to think having people in her head talking to her was weird, until one day she happened across other writers who told her it was normal.

She's been writing ever since...

ALSO BY N.R. WALKER

Blind Faith

Through These Eyes (Blind Faith #2)

Blindside: Mark's Story (Blind Faith #3)

Ten in the Bin

Gay Sex Club Stories 1

Gay Sex Club Stories 2

Point of No Return – Turning Point #1

Breaking Point – Turning Point #2

Starting Point – Turning Point #3

Element of Retrofit – Thomas Elkin Series #1

Clarity of Lines – Thomas Elkin Series #2

Sense of Place – Thomas Elkin Series #3

Taxes and TARDIS

Three's Company

Red Dirt Heart

Red Dirt Heart 2

Red Dirt Heart 3

Red Dirt Heart 4

Red Dirt Christmas

Cronin's Key

Cronin's Key II

Cronin's Key III

Cronin's Key IV - Kennard's Story

Exchange of Hearts

The Spencer Cohen Series, Book One

The Spencer Cohen Series, Book Two

The Spencer Cohen Series, Book Three

The Spencer Cohen Series, Yanni's Story

Blood & Milk

The Weight Of It All

A Very Henry Christmas (The Weight of It All 1.5)

Perfect Catch

Switched

Imago

Imagines

Imagoes

Red Dirt Heart Imago

On Davis Row

Finders Keepers

Evolved

Galaxies and Oceans

Private Charter

Nova Praetorian

A Soldier's Wish

Upside Down

The Hate You Drink

Sir

Tallowwood

Reindeer Games

The Dichotomy of Angels

Throwing Hearts

Pieces of You - Missing Pieces #1

Pieces of Me - Missing Pieces #2

Pieces of Us - Missing Pieces #3

Lacuna

Tic-Tac-Mistletoe

Bossy

Code Red

Dearest Milton James

Dearest Malachi Keogh

Christmas Wish List

Code Blue

Davo

The Kite